510

# THE GENTLEMAN

# FROM CHICAGO

"Poisoning," says the author, "is a particularly English method of murder," a fact which held true especially in the last century. This is the story, eight-tenths fictitious, of an exceptionally repellent murderer (his method was usually strychnine), Thomas Neill Cream, M.D., 1850–1892. He was born in Glasgow, educated mainly in Canada, practiced medicine (and other things) in Chicago, killed extensively and horribly and for pleasure (his victims were very often prostitutes), mostly in London, and was hanged in Newgate prison while the assembled crowd cheered.

He learned about poison in Montreal from a man named Ramsbottom, and his first victim was a drunken old man named Ursus. A Kitty Hutchinson followed soon thereafter, and that was just the beginning.

There was little about Thomas Neill Cream that was not strange, and *The Gentleman from Chicago*, which records his bizarre career, is a tour de force, a chilling re-creation of a weird part of quite recent history.

JOHN CASHMAN

# THE GENTLEMAN FROM CHICAGO

*Being an Account of the Doings of*
*Thomas Neill Cream, M.D. (M'Gill),*
*1850–1892*

HARPER & ROW, PUBLISHERS
*New York   Evanston   San Francisco*
*London*

A JOAN KAHN–HARPER NOVEL OF TERROR

FIRST EDITION

*Designed by Dorothy Schmiderer*

Library of Congress Cataloging in Publication Data

Cashman, John.
  The Gentleman from Chicago.
  "A Joan Kahn-Harper novel of terror."
  1.  Cream, Thomas Neill, 1850–1892—Fiction.
I.  Title.
PZ4.C3412Ge3  [PS3553.A7936]    813'.5'4    73–4145
ISBN 0–06–010663–8

St. Saviour's Hospital
Beckenham
Kent
9th January, 1893

1758394

To: Professor Gustav Fallenberg, Ph.D., M.P.M. (Vienna)

My dear Professor,
    Herewith the papers in the "Neill" case.
    I imagine that you have now had opportunity to study the reports of the coroner's inquest and The Times as to the doings of Thomas Neill (Cream). I, in turn, have attempted to assemble Neill's own account of himself. Strangely, the doctor has written of his life in the manner of a novelette—as if describing the activities of a character of fiction. I say "strangely" without the least surprise on my part, however; there was little about the man that was not "strange," and he delighted in his peculiar ways. You will observe a careful selection of chapter headings; those are his and not mine. You will see a breakdown of actual chapters into parts; once again, I have followed his original manuscript. And never have I interfered with his punctuation or unusual figures of speech. I accordingly present the ghastly work of Thomas Neill unadorned and without tamper.
    Neill scribbled furiously day and night, forever demanding a fresh stock of pencils of the authorities. The latter—happy to keep their charge quiet—obliged, and only the final insanity mars a complete revelation. At this stage, I choose to forgo observation upon both Neill and his writings. Instead, I have added a commentary, which I respectfully suggest you ignore until you have read Neill's recital.
    Much of what he has to say is distasteful and slanderous to the extreme. For example, Neill has seen fit to libel Her Majesty, my queen; for what purpose, I know not. I do most sincerely beg that you dismiss these vile aspersions from your mind. I must

v

*further ask that you do not cause to be published within this realm what has been written, lest I find myself open to professional censure and, possibly, an action for criminal libel. I rely upon your discretion, Herr Professor, as I rely upon your inspired conclusions with regard to Thomas Neill. But—lest you accuse me once more of hiding truth under what you call "the mantle of British hypocrisy"—pay heed to this: Neill was obsessed with the thought of a "John Brown." Twice do we find a person of that name within his writings. And Thomas Neill hated the famous and celebrated with a passion most malign. Show Thomas Neill two men of fame bearing the same name, and Thomas Neill would seek to tear each of them asunder. Such was his character. Medicine was his profession, and poison was his interest. Murder was his trade, and cruelty was his lust.*

*With such sharp words do I leave you with the nightmare of his life.*

*I am*
*very truly yours, Professor,*
*Vernon Radcliffe Cogswell, M.D., F.R.C.P.*

## PART ONE

*1850–1876*

*Being an account of
Thomas Neill's childhood
and early life*

# AT DR. COGSWELL'S REQUEST . . .

## I

I have been asked to set down on paper my own account of matters. The good doctor claims to be a student of a new science —"Criminology"—and he prays in aid the fanciful names of certain Continental gentlemen. In my view, the notions of these people are suspect and young Cogswell is just humbugging. They simply wish to disguise what they fail to understand; if they cannot justify a man or his occupations, they invent some clever label and pigeonhole him away. I say Cogswell would be better minded to sell this narrative to the gutter press and make a nickel or two. He can footnote his own pretentious opinions if he wishes—add a lick of "science." Young Cogswell, with his scrawny neck and tweedy suits, has less claim to medical knowledge than a Hottentot bone-thrower.

Minding you, he's an enthusiastic shaver. He must have hoodwinked quite a few people getting in here to see me at all.

So I'll oblige him—I'll tell what he wants to know, and I'll tell him the truth. Reckon he'll believe about half. . . .

He'll believe such parts of my story as fit in with conclusions he's already drawn. The rest he'll shrug off as the ramblings of a sick man. They won't make sense to him—and nobody chooses to believe something he can't understand.

Maybe he'll rewrite this manuscript—add a bit of polish. I

deem it right to make apologia for my style. I write as a traveled man, and I've picked up some of the darndest turns of phrase. Your old colonies across the water tend to brutalize finer expression of the language.

I'll start at the beginning and get as far as I can under the circumstances. My timepiece says past seven right now, but the fuel is good and the lamp wick burns quite steady. Maybe I'll make some passage tonight.


## II


I was born in Glasgow City, May 27, mid-century. Of that place I have little to remember except the cold.

My father was about twenty-seven when I was born—some kind of shipyard clerk, working hard for little money. Honest and God-fearing even in his youth, his two sources of education lay in a volume on accounting and the Bible. He carried a Bible all his life—like some men carry a six-gun.

My mother was an Elder, of course. Her folk came from further south—from the countryside. I guess she hated the city, with its fogs and dirt. Maybe she was responsible for our big step west.

I've mentioned cold, so I'll say a bit more. There are types of cold. There's the cold of Ontario or the Midwest—sharp and cutting, so you hurt as you breathe, likely as not to kill you if you're not prepared. But that's a dry cold, something you can face with pleasure in suitable garments. Then there's the cold of Glasgow—chill and damp, an evil cold that makes you sweat and throw off steam, a cold that envelops you like a shroud. So I think I can remember the cold. Slow-burn coal and peat in a tiny grate—me lying on a rush carpet. Or walking to church, holding my mother's hand, stepping a pace or so behind my father. Certain visions come to mind—white faces over black broadcloth walking brown streets. No hands in sight. Yes, and I had a doll, made of wood. I think I called it Hamish.

My father later informed me that he'd headed west for my

*4*

sake. I doubt that; he headed west for his own sense of pride and the silver dollar.

I know that my mother's family objected to the plan. Scottish folk tended to go south, or to go to sea under bad masters and get themselves drowned. Only "bad 'uns" went to the Americas. Engineering folk and railroaders went to Canada. Clerks like Willie Cream did not. If you earned your respectability in Glasgow, you stayed there. That was the view of the Elder tribe.

But this was back in '55, and my father just over thirty. He saw his chances. He had a trade to carry with him—ships and accounts. At the close of the rainbow was that bag of silver dollars. And my mother was on his side.

"Mary mine," he must have said, "I'll no have ye kin interfering!" I can imagine his whiskers bristling (they were red then) and his big chest heaving. Maybe I clapped him from my crib.

Reliable memory starts in my case with the journey out from Liverpool. We set sail in a fine three-master with family accommodation—not in one of those sieve ships reserved for the hopeless sons of Ireland. Twice a day I was exercised on the decks by my father—clean decks, holystoned as white as whalebone, with neat coils of rope at the sides. The seas must have been calm. I can't recall any storms. My mother was poorly, however. She was with child and stayed in her cabin. I guess my father thought it was seasickness. Anyway, I spent my time in his company, which was first rate. For supper I'd be given cocoa and shortcake biscuit. I had a ripping trip.

I remember our arrival at Quebec City pretty well, with all the dockers screaming at one another in the French tongue.

We put up at a hotel near the waterfront, a tall building with shutters on the windows. It was springtime with a lot of snow about. I was allowed out into the garden most afternoons.

My father had no trouble getting work. Carsons signed him up at a good wage. They were about the biggest lumber and shipbuilding outfit in town; my father always held the Carson brothers in high esteem.

The French population tended to occupy the commercial parts of the city, so when my father eventually bought a house he made sure his immediate neighbors were of Scots or English origin. This meant we moved to the outskirts of town. Most people did this—they'd suffer minor inconvenience to get away from the French. Maybe the French were pleased to see the back of them as well.

My father had savings with him when we arrived—not much, minding you, but they helped with the purchase of our first house. We moved in during the fall, and my mother gave birth to twins one month later. Now I had two brothers, Eric and Anselm. Anselm was born with a crippled foot. I nicknamed him Lame Duck throughout our boyhood.

We lived in Rue de Montcalm for two years, during which time my mother had another son and a daughter, Gervaise and Emily. I had five years on my brothers and little time for them. My father was my real friend and companion, and by the time I was seven I could quote the Old Testament like a professional God-botherer. My father liked me for this—it's safe to say I became the apple of his eye. And that was my plan, of course. He was the family lawmaker. His word alone was of consequence. Common sense told me to keep him sweet as possible; in that way I'd always be able to pick up the best cookies.

My mother was a quiet woman, born to produce children and housekeep. She had little influence over me, nor did she attempt to exert any. She cuddled and pampered the younger children, wove tapestry, and sighed a lot. I don't think she was ambitious for my father—she didn't need to be.

Carsons prospered and so did my father. Each year his position and salary grew. At first I went to the general Protestant school, but soon my father found he could afford to send me to St. George's Private School for Boys. Naturally, this was also Church of England. No doubt my father would have preferred it to be of the Scottish Church. But at least it wasn't Papist. The Roman Church was a powerful influence over the French citizens of Quebec. My father saw this as a Jesuit plot. To him, with his fierce pride in Kirk, Queen, and Covenant, Popery smacked of the devil and treasonous activities. Now I realize that his fears were well justified.

I had inherited from my father a capacity for hard work and

a natural superiority over my fellows. I excelled both at my lessons and in sport. I was artistic and musical. I developed a powerful physique and a hearty manner. My popularity and authority were immense. My teachers recognized in me something exceptional, while the other pupils feared and respected me. From Monday to Friday I labored at my studies during the day, and pursued my hobbies vigorously in the evenings—botany and chemical experiments. On Saturdays I'd devote my time to manly sports—shooting, football, and skating in the winter months. On Sunday I'd sing in the choir—I had a fine and lusty voice.

I had few friends—in fact, I can't recall any particular friendship. I guess many were jealous of my prowess at things, and I did not take disagreement kindly. Indeed, I had a terrible temper when roused. My overall popularity discouraged individuals from attempting to secure my friendship. They would have been accused of currying favor by the others. No, my popularity was of the kind that made the whole class cheer, or stand in silent awe whenever I performed some feat.

Not that I minded the lack of any boon companion. I had my father and the small-bore rifle he gave me on my twelfth birthday. Together we'd hunt the woods outside the city, he with his Bible, reading extracts and explaining the teachings of John Knox, me with my gun. My mother bought me a dog—a spaniel, a smelly beast without intelligence and no good in the field. I was relieved when the ridiculous brute died, after licking up rat poison some careless fellow had left around. My father permitted me to dissect the body in the woodshed. I can recall delving among the gore and intestines hoping to find some visible sign of the creature's death. All I got for my childish pains were bloodstained shirt cuffs.

I think that it was about this time that our family split into two distinct camps: my father and I, my mother and my four brothers and three sisters. My father had become manager at Carsons with a hundred and fifty men to boss about. But he had his eye on even better things. He wanted to set up a business of his own. We'd lived in the same house and kept expenses down, so I reckon my father had saved a fair degree. Anyway, the risk of leaving Carson security bothered him not a trifle. But it did trouble my mother, and that is how the split began. A simple woman, she organized her brood about her, forgetting their tender years. I considered with care what my role should be, and later events proved my decision to be the right one. I pretended to side with Mama and became a spy in her camp, reporting back to my father all the nonsense she told us young 'uns. My mother could never have constituted a serious threat to my father's fancies and, indeed, she soon capitulated; but my father showed me his gratitude and had less interest in the remainder of his offspring. My first reward was at Christmas— a new gun and a makeshift chemistry set. Many was the pound of powder I made for my gun with that set. I experimented until the grain and charge was perfect. My efforts also incurred my father's approval; powder was expensive in those days.

Far from being hurt by my father's decision, the Carson brothers presented him with a silver coffee pot and advised him as to premises available at the docks. Yet it was eighteen months before my father finally left Carsons. Bad times hit the trade for a short spell, and he worked on to help the company. All this I remember very well. I had just turned fifteen, still a pupil at St. George's and doing well. Then something happened which had a profound effect upon my life. I have potted the history of my childhood because my memory is unreliable until about this time. If I have wearied you, Cogswell, I crave indulgence. Perhaps you attach great importance to the early development of the child? Perhaps you claim that it is during this period that the man is made, for good or bad? I beg to disagree. My childhood was normal up until the age of fourteen and a half years. Exciting, yes—but normal. But it was this incident to which I shall now refer that changed the nature of things. Within the blink of an eyelid, I grew up.

# THE REVEREND MELVIN SOLLOWAY

## I

The principal of St. George's was the Reverend Melvin Solloway. A tall, frowsy-haired man sporting magnificent whiskers, he had become my idol and mentor for some months past during 1865. He was a fine skater—I can still see him now, gliding over the ice, frock coat hitched up, his hands clasped firmly behind his back. In December of the preceding year I had the distinction of being junior champion iceman of entire Quebec. It brought credit to my school and endeared me to the Reverend. He took to seeking out my company a great deal, and come springtime I saw him as a great man. His claim to fame lay in the fact he'd once supped with John Brown shortly before the buffoonery at Harpers Ferry. During the madness that gripped the United States afterward, the Reverend became an oracle. Now, of course, I appreciate that this man's interest in the fate of darkies was little more than a futile grasp at a rope that might pull him out of a swamp of insignificance. As in the case of John Brown. But at the time, all his jawing misled a considerable number of people into believing he was some kind of saint. And believe me, sir, the Reverend Solloway was no saint. . . .

During the summer of our acquaintance he'd lecture me on matters other than the Civil War ("the War of Christian Charity," he called it). He lectured me on many evils, talking about them as if the pleasure they gave outweighed the Hellfire they promised. "See that hill over there," once he said, his face enraptured. "The sight of that hill alone, dear Thomas, might instill a terrible temptation." So I looked at the hill, trying to understand.

"The shape, boy, the shape! Don't ye see? It has the smooth round firmness of a young woman's naked breast!"

He pronounced the word "naked" as "nekkid" so that it stuck in the mind.

Moreover, he ingratiated himself upon my family. He impressed my father, which is not surprising, although my mother remained curiously abrupt. The Reverend would invite himself over for tea, praising my mother's flapjacks and scones, holding her limp hand whenever he could, calling her a "daughter of Christ." My father would get him to read from the Bible, and I used to marvel at his histrionics, each phrase or sentence pouring slowly from his broad lips like blackjack molasses.

Approving of the Reverend, my father clearly saw me as his disciple. He encouraged me to visit the holy man for Scripture lessons. The Reverend must have been nigh on fifty, but he had a way of talking that came down to the young—lowered itself to their level. Fact is, he was trying to pull me up to his own—he was preparing me.

One evening, late August, we were in his study. Books ran round the walls and a small harmonium occupied one corner. The Reverend and I sat opposite sides to his desk. He'd been reading from the Good Book when he snapped it shut. He looked at me, and his eyes were kind of fierce.

"Do you play with your gender?" It was almost a snarl.

"Nossir," says I.

He grunted, then: "D'ye think about it, then?"

"Nossir!"

"D'ye think about the fair sex from time to time, I daresay!"

It wasn't a question, not even an accusation. It was a statement of fact, and I remained silent.

"Such thoughts are evil, Cream," the Reverend went on. "The fire of bodily lust must be quenched. By prayer, d'ye understand? By prayer!" We both fell to our knees. The Reverend mouthed feverishly, and then took me by the wrist.

"Harken to me, boy," he said, pulling me up. "Woman is here to torment the flesh. Woman's form has been molded by the Prince of Darkness. Within the smoothness lies the serpent!" His eyes opened wide and bemused me. "And you must learn of the truth of carnal torment before it is too late." He stepped back, releasing my arm. "Drop your britches, Cream. . . ."

I hesitated, but he grew impatient and I obliged.

"And your undergarment," he insisted.

Modesty slowed my fingers, but again I obeyed.

The Reverend studied me without moving. I confess that I blushed.

"Make yerself decent, Cream," said the Reverend after a while, and he resumed his seat behind the desk as I buttoned up.

"Within the loins of a well-formed man," the Reverend said, "lies the kernel of his possible destruction. Come here, Cream. . . ." His voice was kindly. "Tonight I shall extend to you a rare privilege . . . tonight I shall reveal to you things that might spare you untold misery. D'ye follow?"

I shook my head, but I was excited.

"I'll put it to you plain, then. D'ye know what a bordello is, boy?"

"Some kind of boardinghouse, sir. . . ."

"Aye, that it can be. But it can—upon extra payment—provide more than a steak and a bed. And d'ye know what it is that it provides, boy?"

"Nossir."

"Come, come, boy, don't ye play the moosehead with me. I think ye know right well!"

"Bad women, sir . . ." I ventured.

The Reverend closed his eyes for a moment.

"Aye, ye can't live ye life in Quebec for long without the knowing of that fact." And he got to his feet, a desperate look on his face. "And here's the nub of what I've been a-saying: At the age of only near sixteen ye know about the loose whores that inhabit this City of Satan. No, don't ye look ashamed—it's no fault of ye own! Yet my mind is disturbed by your knowledge. Without your telling, I can understand the dreams you must have suffered. The bloom of youth brings a cruel temptation.

The Flesh"—he shook his fist—"desires while the Soul suffers! Only sight of the Devil at his works can bring ye understanding!"

The violence of his speech alarmed me, but my excitement grew. "So tonight I propose to teach ye—tonight I make ye a man!" The anger died as he added: "D'ye want to learn to save yerself, Thomas?"

I nodded. What else could I do?

"And if I help you—if I show you, young Thomas Cream"—the Reverend's hand was upon my shoulder and I observed it to be shaking—"will ye promise me something?"

"Yessir."

"Promise me ye'll pray, boy. Pray hard!"


## II


Now, for your information, Dr. Cogswell, a word or two about the waterfront of Quebec City, 1865. "Old French" we called the sheds and houses; "Old French" we named the eating places; "Old Hob" I'd call the night life. . . .

Whalers with a thirst and too much money; loggers wanting to try their strength at fisticuffs; poxed-up deck-hands, from Lascar to Eskimos, without a cent to bury them. Frenchie floozies and their shiv-carrying "husbands," too bad for New Orleans or the Cayenne settlements. Blackamoors from God knows where, sick with bad liquor and incanting in the gutters, shivering with a cold they didn't believe existed. Chinee men —less than Frisco, but there just the same—selling young girls for the first night, trading dope doctored so bad it could kill a man in a minute. Portuguese, dagoed with nigger blood, anxious to sail south on any ship, prepared to sell their bodies to any sex to get passage.

Dr. Cogswell, your bristle coat would stand up straight were you to even smell the place.

Reverend Solloway took me down in a hired buggy. We didn't talk too much, though he patted my knee from time to time. I guess he thought I needed reassuring.

Once he took out his watch and read the time, mumbling, "Not to be too late" and something about my father. But we'd arrived by then, the driver pulling the horses into a slow walk and the Reverend reaching for his purse.

The Reverend paid the man five dollars—a lot of money. Makes sense now, though. The old blackguard didn't want tale-telling, did he?

And we went into this two-floor house of grit-gray stone and a wooden roof. It was past dark, and the cobbles shone from a light more than fifty feet away—the only light in the narrow street. I recall also that the house had red shutters which were closed.

I can't say who opened up for us—it was pretty dark. But the Reverend led me into a murky hallway with baby pine trees scattered here and there, as if pretending to be palms. A belay pin hung on a bit of thong in one corner.

We didn't have to wait too long before some curtains brushed aside and a woman came in. Thin as a bean shaft, with red-brown hair styled high on her head, she slipped on a smile. Her face shone devious cunning in the extreme—arched painted eyebrows over black inquisitive eyes, thin nose and lips, deep hollows in her cheeks. The face of a starved and painted prairie dog.

She spoke in French, and it was clear that the Reverend was no stranger to her. He answered her in the same tongue, which surprised me somewhat—I scarce had imagined that the Reverend spoke French. Then they were laughing and looking at me, forcing me to admire the pictures on a wall. And what pictures they happened to be. Scenes of naked flesh entwined. The matters they concerned held me riveted, and when a voice spoke next to my ear I jumped a little. It was the Reverend, and his aspect was solemn.

"This lady will attend to you," he said. "I shall not be far away. Have no fears, dear boy." And so he was gone—leaving me alone with the clever Prairie Dog.

Now, for me to describe in any detail what this pernicious woman and a colleague forced upon me would, I have decided, be both revolting for you to read, dear Doctor, and unseemly for me to record. I therefore propose only to outline the events

*13*

that followed, confident that you will shudder at the thought of so young a lad thus foully treated.

The Prairie Dog—or "Madame," for such was she—led me off into a small chamber beyond lace hangings. There, on a couch, one of her subordinates lay stretched out in an abandoned fashion, her state of dress immodest in the extreme. With black hair cascading about her shoulders, this young vixen wore a quilted gown untied and open to the navel.

"This is M'selle Georgiana," the madame introduced me, crossing over to converse in low tones with this dark she-devil. The pair of them tittered, clearly at my poor innocent expense. I suppose I lowered my eyes and changed the position of my stance in my embarrassment. "M'selle Georgiana will be your tutor and examiner, schoolboy," the madame said to me, translating what she had said immediately to the other so that their laughter might continue.

I believe that these were the last words spoken for some time. The recumbent figure on the settee fairly leaped at me, coiling her arms about my neck, her face close to mine, her perfume enveloping me like a mist. I retreated a fraction, but she followed, pushing her lower half into mine with circular and thrusting movements. Her hands sought my collar, fairly tearing the studs through the linen. She had my jacket off and my shirt open wide in an instant, all the while gyrating with an impish look in her sloe eyes. With my trousers at half-hitch, I seized that garment, but her will and determination were beyond the tolerance of a hapless boy. In a state of near-nakedness I was dragged to her couch, forced on my back while further clothing was stripped from my trembling body. Madame was there still, make no mistake. She remained to one side, her lips slightly parted at the sight of my discomfiture. And M'selle Georgiana knew her trade, tormenting me as she divested herself in a savage way, commenting upon each aspect of her ripe form as she did so. She made me touch her, she made me lick her—oblivious to that great look of woe that must have possessed my eyes. She spread herself upon me, smothering me with her fleshiness. She sought out parts of me with her fingers in a vile and disgusting manner, so that I felt that I would swoon.

Then she crooked up my head, arching my naked back in a way that caused pain. Sliding her body astride mine, she then committed me to a nauseating and wicked trick, suffocating me until I wept, besmirching all honor I had ever felt toward my fellow man. Cackled laughter filled the room—I presume from the attendant madame, come close on hand to fully enjoy this base spectacle. But when she pushed me back and her own rancid lips sought me in similar fashion, something within my finer nature came to my rescue. Flinging this writhing wildcat to one side, I was upon my feet, shouting and reaching for my clothing. Hands stretched out to restrain me—soft words from Madame as well as snatching fingers from that other abominable. But I had become resolved upon my purpose, and flung the two of them angrily to one side. One tried to halt me physically. I struck out with the strength of a big fellow, and felt my fist sink in as it connected with soft fatty flesh. A shriek and a curse—but nothing further was done to hamper me as I pulled on my clothing. Tears of fear and outrage blinded me as I fled that awful room.

I was in a narrow passage, groping in the half-light, stumbling over knick-knack furnishings. Potted ferns and plants brushed against me like groping hands as I sped down the corridor. A light under a far door caught my attention, and I made toward it as if beyond lay salvation. Fearing it might be locked, I spun the handle and threw myself against the frame. But the door was not fixed tight in any manner of means, so that I lurched into the room at furious speed. And the scene that met my eyes is one that I shall scarce forget. . . .

The room was lit by candles—candelabra in every corner and perched upon divers cupboards and chests. A lighting of shadow and flickering brilliance such as a visitor might behold in any Roman chapel.

But instead of altar, the premises was dominated by an outsize bed, massive and four-posted, a hideous oaken monster occupying near one third of the room. And beside it stood this woman, curiously attired in the habit and cowl of a monk—the white and black of the Cistercian order.

She turned to face me as I blundered to a stop. I saw then that her habit was open at the front and that beneath it she was naked save for a rosary about her neck. I saw also that in her right hand she carried a thin switch of birch branch.

As she turned, another figure revealed itself. A larger form, bending as if in prayer over the white linen of the bed. The figure of a man with head bowed. And from him came anxious sobs, as if he was unaware of my recent intrusion.

The woman spoke to me, but my attention was otherwise engaged. The man at the bed had moved slightly, and I was struck by his attire. He was wearing the frock and surplice of a choirboy, complete with Elizabethan ruffle. Although he moved his head, his back and lower body remained as before. I saw that a large hole was cut into the seat of his frock, so that his posterior—bare—jutted through; and the latter was heavily marked, clearly by the scourge held in the woman's hand.

She repeated her question with impatience, attracting the man's attention so that he spun round and faced me. My bowels contracted upon recognition—it was the Reverend Solloway.

Maybe my face was in shadow, perhaps my expression disguised my features, for the Reverend didn't realize it was me for a moment or so—just peering at me like a parboiled crawdad. But once the truth dawned upon him, his reactions were swift and terrifying. In a second my throat lay in his hands and I was being shaken. His curses embarrassed the cloth of his calling and were hugely expressive. Twice he slapped my face, his facial contortions suggesting he was a man possessed. Then he flung me to the floor. He reached to snatch the birch from his woman's hand, and I feared a thrashing. But she protested and drew back—for the first and last time I was to be grateful to one of her sex. She calmed the Reverend with quiet bickering words, and at last he relaxed. I picked myself up, endeavoring to appear nonchalant, brushing myself down, humping my coat into better fit about my shoulders. This concern for my clothing had a strange effect upon the Reverend. Suddenly he was laughing and pointing at me.

"Lucifer pawn my scrotum!" he cried, a sight too hysterically for my liking. "The young ass reminds me of Cap'n Brown, I say! Off to the gallows astride his own coffin went he, and all he fussed about was his confounded cloak!"

He stepped forward as quickly as I moved back.

"No, no, boy! There's naught to be afeared! Why, I'll wager the crypt silver that you've seen some pastimes this night." He turned to his woman. "I left him with the bag of bones to learn a trick or so!"

She giggled and eyed me slyly, so I retreated yet again.

"I say don't be afraid, boy!" the Reverend repeated. "Come now—we've both had our pastings. Let's be on our way." He slipped behind a small screen and hummed a tune.

His woman watched me as we waited. I watched the switch in her hand. We exchanged no words, and presently the Reverend reappeared, his cloak buttoned up to hide his bands. Taking me by the arm, just above the elbow, he marched me from the room and along the corridor. His pace was quick, and soon we came to the entrance hall with those frivolous pictures. Nobody seemed to be about, and the Reverend appeared to know the way. Velvet curtains were brushed aside, a door opened, and we were in the street.

The Reverend looked about us. Lights were dim. Sounds of raucous laughter came from a long way off. The grip on my arm tightened again, and I was propelled toward a dark mass in the gloom. A carriage, and we climbed in, the Reverend behind me.

He spoke not a word to the driver, but we were away with a clip-clop as soon as the carriage gate was slammed. The Reverend leaned back into the upholstery, and spoke.

"There'll be things you'll want explaining, that's for sure."

I said nothing.

"You've been in an evil place tonight, make no mistake." Once more he felt my thigh. "A snuggery for the Devil and all his tricks. But you've learned, have you not?"

I wasn't sure if it was a question until he jabbed me in the ribs. "Yessir."

"Yes, you've learned, I'd say. Dirty hands sought to torment you? Base suggestions whispered in your ears provoked your passions?" His fingers dug into me so that I wriggled. "Yes—all this I know! Once I was like you, wilted by thoughts of carnal embrace. That is why I have shown to you, Thomas, the destructive temptations the Almighty permits Lucifer to inflict upon us. In His wisdom, of course. . . ."

He muttered on for a while. I took note of the street along which we passed. Rue Champlain . . . A brightly lit establishment on our right, the Strop and Block—a name I was to remember.

He was watching me. The muttering had come to an end.

"So you're wondering what *I* was doing in such a place," says he, and he took his hand away from my leg. "Well, I'll tell you, boy—even if I lay bare a cry from my tortured soul." I looked at his face; a great despair had become exposed. "I go there," he went on, "because the flesh of young women has tormented me since long ago. I go there because I refuse to satisfy my desires. I go there, as you have seen with your own innocent eyes, to have the evil in me scourged from my body. I go there but to be *purged* and, if the Almighty sees fit to show my humblest of spirits mercy, to save myself from the fires of Hell itself."

I was amazed.

"D'ye understand me, Thomas?"

"Yessir!"

"And not a word to your dear parents," he added. "D'ye understand me, boy!"

"Yessir," said I once more. My throat was yet tender in the extreme.

# CRIMPS AND TIMBER-STOWERS

## I

Of my visit to Champlain Street, it's fair to say I made no mention to either of my parents. Nor did the Reverend Solloway ever refer to the subject again. Fact is, he began to lose interest in my company altogether. I took it that he chose to shun me because I'd failed to prove myself a worthwhile candidate for the sharing of his "interests." I was to reckon out the true reason a few years later—I'd caught the Reverend with his britches down, and the good man didn't take too kindly to my knowledge.

Now, my curiosity had been greatly aroused. You will appreciate that I'd hitherto led a sheltered life on the fashionable outskirts of town. The hills and forests beyond I'd grown to know quite well. But of the Quebec waterfront I knew nothing. Oh, I knew it was ten miles long and a rough place to be avoided, but that's about all. I don't believe my father ever described it to me—though his work must have taken him away from the office and down to the water from time to time. Pretty soon I was just about itching to find out a bit more.

So I took to visiting the city on Saturday afternoons. I'd leave the house with my gun and game bag to make out I was heading for the woods. But I'd stash away these camouflages in a convenient bush once I was out of sight, sneak back past the house, and jog into town.

19

I was timorous at the beginning, venturing no farther than the borders of sailortown, hanging about street corners, scoffing the hot jacket potatoes sold there, just watching the world go past. This went on for several months. Nobody paid me any attention, although I must have been better dressed than the average urchin of my age in those parts. This made me bolder, and by the time my sixteenth birthday had been and gone, I had walked the length of Champlain Street. I can still recall the names of various establishments which flourished in those days —Hucks', the Lazy Logger, La Ronde . . .

Down on the waterfront I'd perch myself high on top of one of the lumber stacks and take in the scene—the big ships bound for Liverpool, sailors with clay pipes being hollered at by blue-coated skippers and mates, and the timber-stowers. The last were a breed by themselves; drunken, brawling French-Canadians or Irish, they did the toughest work of all, loading the cargoes of lumber. "Was you ever in Quebec—a-launchin' timber on the decks?" goes the song, but you'd never guess what lies behind those words until you've seen a gang of timber-stowers in action. They'd work from sun-up right through the day, and then by bonfire when dark came down, sweating and puffing as they jostled the mighty trunks aboard, their mouths crammed full of plug tobacco and foul language. I took to watching them every Saturday, until I became familiar to them, so that I might get the occasional nod or wink. I was never asked to account for myself.

One of the stowers was a brute called Wideawake Larrigan, a man in his forties, hairy and filthy, with teeth as black and thin as lead in a pencil. I began to admire him more than most when I witnessed his fighting prowess. It happened like this: the stowers' gang boss tended to upset the men with his shrill tones, scampering among them, getting in everybody's way. One hot afternoon the boss man got in Wideawake Larrigan's path and caused him to drop a large section of timber upon his foot. Larrigan made certain observations about the boss man's manner of birth, whereupon the boss man ordered that he be docked a day's pay. Larrigan was hopping about in some pain as it was, but this was too much for him, and he bum's-rushed the boss man down thirty feet of quay and into the St. Lawrence. We all decided the boss to be a dead man, swept away and drowned, or crushed between the ships. But somebody pulled the fellow out, much pacified by the cold sousing he'd received, and Larrigan became my hero.

That evening I tried to follow him home, but he turned and fetched me a clip across the ear, telling me to be off. Next Saturday I used cunning, lurking in the shadows, out of sight, to see where he went. He turned left off Champlain Street, down some steps and along a narrow passage until he reached a small courtyard. In the corner, light flooded out from under a door. He rapped three times and went in.

For a while I hung about outside, uncertain what to do. I listened at the door and heard sounds of laughter—men's laughter, so it probably wasn't a whorehouse. Cockfighting? Ratting?

Youth and good sense being ill-wed companions, I lifted the latch on the door and crept in. It was a tavern, pure and simple —half a dozen plain wooden tables and chairs, sawdust strewn about the floor, a strong smell of beer and rye.

Only two of the tables were occupied. They had been drawn together, and four men sat in discussion. Larrigan was seated at the head, facing my direction. His chair was tilted back upon its legs, and when he saw me it crashed forward.

"The Devil have it . . . !" and he was on his feet and at me in a jiffy. Held firmly by the collar, I blurted a series of explanations for my sudden appearance, none of which did anything to lessen the anger in the other's face. What I didn't know, of course, was that I had trespassed upon a crimpers' conference, and that Larrigan and his colleagues took me for a spy. Dragged to the center of the room, I was knocked to the ground and given a couple of savage kicks.

"Search the little swine," said somebody, and my pockets were turned inside out.

"Who is he, Wideawake?"

"Hangs about the stacks," Larrigan mumbled, examining my possessions. "Tried to follow me once before. . . . Hello, then, what's this here?" He held up my pocketbook. My name and address were engraved upon the morocco. "Thomas N. Cream, 32 Rue de Montcalm," Larrigan read.

"Fancy part of town," another said.

"I daresay." Larrigan stepped over to me, and his boot lashed out into my side. "Who are you, boy?"

"Cream, sir. And that's my . . ."

Another kick in the ribs.

"What's your interest here, boy?"

"I followed you, sir."

"And that's plain to all. But why, boy, why . . . ?"

"I saw you fight that foreman." Pure luck made me say what I did. Larrigan looked surprised for a moment. Then he laughed, showing his pink gums through his black beard. He was an unpleasant sight and sound.

"God's blood, you did!" Larrigan roared. He helped me to my feet, one arm about my shoulder. This I took to be a change of attitude on his part, a sign of friendship, so I made noises and smiled.

"Crafty little liar!" he added, and struck me a blow that split my upper lip to the nose.

I reeled back, just keeping my balance, standing there on rocking legs while the claret ran down my shirt front.

Now, my temper is short, as I have already mentioned, and this I held to be sharp practice on Larrigan's part. So I retaliated.

With bloody face and un-Christian words, I flung myself at the fellow. I caught him a mite unawares, as he'd turned to laugh at my discomfiture with his colleagues. Being of good weight for my age, I bore him to the floor. I certainly had the element of surprise on my side, for Larrigan offered little resistance at first, and I punched, clawed, and butted at his doltish countenance. But the blackguard didn't lie still for long, and soon I found myself riding a Calgary roan. One mighty heave and he had me off him. I scuttled my distance, expecting a terrible beating to follow. Larrigan's bulk made him slow to get up. I saw my chance for a last attempt to put him down again, and I aimed a desperate kick at his groin. My foot connected well, and Larrigan folded in the middle, yelling hard. His friends at the tables had done nothing to help him, and, to my utter amazement, they now cheered. I backed in among them, my eyes still on Larrigan as he recovered himself. His face was white and his breath came in short gasps. Then he smiled a wicked smile and reached to the waistband behind his back. When his hand returned, I saw he'd drawn a shiv and I squeaked with terror. But the others came to my rescue.

"No!" one of them—called Curtiz—barked at Larrigan.

Larrigan glared at him. "And why not? The dirty little . . ."

"Because he beat you fair," Curtiz said.

"He beat me foul!"

"Maybe—but still he beat you. D'ya want the world to know you were hobbled by a boy?"

This had an effect on Larrigan, but I didn't feel safe until he'd sheathed his dirk. Shock now got the upper hand on me, and I began to shake and snivel.

"Wipe your face," Curtiz said, and tossed a filthy bandana at me. "Now tell us your business—or I will let Wideawake please himself with you."

I repeated what I'd begun to say before, and this time the men listened.

"You're a strange one," Larrigan muttered when I'd finished.

"And you'll land yourself in mischief," Curtiz said.

A clock on the wall showed me it was time to take my leave, and I said so. Maybe they didn't catch my words, for my lip had thickened and affected my pronunciation. The men just continued to talk among themselves, ignoring me as I stood at their side.

"I'd best be going," I insisted two or three times.

"Not yet," Curtiz said. He began to quiz me about my father, and I gave him straight answers. Perhaps they all thought me crazed, but at least I was now considered harmless, for after a while Curtiz told me I could go. Larrigan still watched me with suspicion as I went to the door, and I was glad to find myself outside in that small courtyard once again.

I ran most of the way home as if pursued by a pack of hound dogs, only pausing when safely in the residential part of town. I then straightened up my clothing. My exertions had caused my lip to start bleeding again, and I tried to stanch it with Curtiz's handkerchief. This I eventually threw over a fence. Only when I reached the front gate to home did it dawn upon me that I was without my pocketbook.

## II

I have always enjoyed a versatile kind of imagination, and the account I gave to my father to cover my absence and battered appearance was accepted without question. In the dark of the forest, it is only too easy to slip down a rocky slope. While my mother's tender hands bathed my face and my father stood attentively by, I talked all this humbug and thought of other things: Would I be able to retrieve my purse? Should I dare to encroach upon the lives of Wideawake Larrigan and Curtiz again?

Yes, I decided, and as soon as possible.

And so did I—on the next Saturday. I slipped away to hunt, amid congratulations for courage from my father and sad words of fear for my safety from my mother. I slipped away as the intrepid hunter, injured but determined, fearless of the forests.

I reached the waterfront in the early afternoon, and gained a convenient pile of lumber. In due course, both Larrigan and Curtiz, together with one other from the liquor establishment, made their arrival.

I expected to be ignored by these ruffians, if not, indeed, ordered to leave the docks. But this was not to be, and well flattered was I by my reception.

All three of them approached me with wicked smiles. I let myself down from my perch with a polite "Good day." Before I could say any more, Larrigan handed me my pocketbook.

"Check it, if you want," Curtiz said.

I didn't, and I guess I looked confused, because they laughed and Larrigan pushed me in a friendly fashion. So I grinned and became accepted—a rabbit to amuse the pack of wolverines.

In any event, my weekly appearance at the water became a positive fixture. "Young Thomas" was I henceforth—firstly to these three alone, but soon to all the stowers. And within six months I'd become a kind of mascot, encouraged to screech at them in their own language from my timber stack like a pet monkey: "That man's idling!" "Too much women, too much

wine!" "Good old McQuirk, scared stiff of work!" And I felt as
fine as Old King Cole, and I reckon the men knew it and this
made them happy.

They were the scum of the earth, of course—I think I knew
that even then. Dangerous scoundrels who'd slit your throat for
a dime. I suppose my position was as precarious as that of a frog
on a railway track with his hopper broke. But I didn't care.

Want of time forces me to skip details, but this much you will
appreciate: I was leading a double life. All week I did my school-
ing, working and playing hard. Reverend Solloway had little to
say to me, and me nought to him. And I told my fellow pupils
nothing about my Saturday adventures. My parents suspected
me not at all, Mother being given over to the care of my brothers and sisters, and my father just showing his usual blind faith
in me.

Meanwhile, I was getting acquainted with the true Quebec.
I got to know most things about the waterfront, and I don't
believe the men bothered to hide much from me. Of course I
wasn't invited to attend their "social" gatherings, nor was I
included in their schemes. But soon enough I learned about the
side occupation of Messrs. Curtiz and Larrigan. They were
"crimpers." Between them they ran that small dosshouse of our
first acquaintance. Curtiz was the caretaker. Their job was to
encourage some poor deep-water Johnny into resting up there.
Then they'd ply him with strong liquor and put him at his ease
in the arms of a local m'selle. If that didn't work, they'd simply
blackjack him. But whatever tactics they might be forced to
use, one thing was for sure: next morning simple Jack would
wake up at sea with a thick head and a dose of pox. A crimper's
job was to provide sailor flesh for ships that needed it, and he
was well rewarded for his services. In San Francisco they call
this the "shanghai."

Pretty soon I got to know that Curtiz and Larrigan were a
powerful influence on the running of things in the port. To an
outsider they were just a couple of stowers, but among their
own kind they were some punkins. And they were to oblige me
and my father (although *he* never was to know) in a manner of
which the consequences were immeasurable—and which I
shall now relate.

25

# BELAYING-PIN PERSUASION

## I

My father, being anxious to set up a business of his own, had given Carsons due notice some while ago—as a matter of honor.

But the lumber trade was a restrictive practice, and a good concern not easy to come by—either you bought out an established firm or else you started your own with a considerable outlay of capital. Getting into the timber line wasn't like opening up a store. You needed dollars whichever the way you chose.

And my father was not a rich man. Sure, Carsons paid him a fair wage, and I think they even offered him a helping hand. But they spoke in the terms of a few hundred dollars—not of the two or three thousand required. Such a fortune lay beyond my father's grasp, and he began to despair.

Since he treated me on equal terms by the time I was near seventeen, my father told me all of this in the most saddening manner. What was he to do? He was asking me a question he guessed I could not readily answer. He outlined the highfalutin plans he'd made for me and my brothers, should his ambitions become realized. Canada was a country bound to boom, prosperity lay within the reach of all, American ambitions to swallow us up had been successfully foiled, and a bundle of notes and a sack of coin blocked my father from assisting our fair land in its natural growth. A couple of thousand dollars . . .

One time I asked him what exactly he'd do if ever such finance came his way—asked him for details concerning his plans. And he made quite plain what he wanted. It seemed that one of the older companies had been forced upon hard times. Shipping troubles and a poor selection of pine over the last year threatened to lay them low. The staff employed by this company, established in '51 as Dinwiddie & Co., lacked loyalty for one easy reason: the boys had no confidence in the founder and top dog himself, old Alfred Dinwiddie. For Alfred persisted in the running of affairs, ignoring better advice and pursuing his principles in the most arrogant of fashions. And he was nigh on seventy-three, drank too much, and had no sons. Everyone else he distrusted.

I nursed this information in my mind for a few weeks, and then one day casually mentioned Alfred Dinwiddie's concern to Larrigan and Curtiz. I recall that we were standing by the prow of a ship watching the loading of a massive tree section at the time.

Curtiz seemed to know about the old man.

"I hear he's short on payment of his boys," he said.

"My father wouldn't be like that," says I.

Curtiz continued to watch the chaining and hoisting of the log in silence for a while.

"I'll be making a few inquiries, then," he said at last.

They approached me again on the following Saturday—Larrigan, Curtiz, and a few more whose names I've now forgotten.

"We think we can do something," Curtiz said.

"Persuade Dinwiddie to sell?"

Larrigan shook his head. "The old bully wouldn't be after listening to the likes of us. . . ."

"How will you do it, then?"

Curtiz laughed. "Ye want him busted, don't you? All right, so we'll bust him."

And that's how it was. Naturally, I knew nothing of the tactics these men would employ. I guessed they might be fairly uncouth. But that, after all, was not my concern—the method interested me not in the slightest.

"I'm sure you'll be rewarded," I said to Curtiz. "I'll see to that."

"And we'll be expectin' it, young Thomas," he replied.


## II


In recent years the United States has solved the difficulty of striking employees in the most robust of manners. Managers hire the services of what are termed strike-breakers—men of the criminal classes who terrorize the others back to the grindstone. Kill off the leaders and the lesser mortals soon fall into line.

But Quebec, in the '60s and '70s, had no such solution—and I doubt the ability of any man to terrorize a timber-stower.

In the case of Alfred Dinwiddie, the boys moved swiftly. They began by sabotage, pure and simple, and they made each act of sabotage dangerous to the employees. Fires broke out among the lumber stacks and pitch caldrons, holding chains were loosened, and a man lost his life. Pretty soon Dinwiddie's men got plenty scared and work slowed down. Then the work tickets and wage packets disappeared, and the men began to grouse a fair deal. Rumors were spread around, hitching the blame to Dinwiddie's coattails, and two men who voiced opinions to the contrary were tarred and feathered. If old Dinwiddie's position had been unstable at the start, now it was most precarious.

This went on week after week, and the news drifted even to the outskirts of town. My father talked of little else, having not the faintest idea that it was all being arranged for his benefit. I reckon I listened to him with a surprised look on my face. Of course, I knew much more about matters than most—I was fed details each weekend by those in charge of operations. I began to feel pretty important.

Good fortune had it that the strike itself broke out on a Saturday morning when I was down on the waterfront, so I was able to witness the best part of it.

Hollering started at Dinwiddie's yards shortly after eleven, and black smoke was coming from the principal buildings. Tools were downed, and we left the front for a better view—although I kept myself hid in an inconspicuous manner for obvious reasons.

And what a sight met our eyes! Somebody had fired Dinwiddie's offices, and several woodpiles were burning. Dinwiddie's men had split into two groups, the larger being the strikers, the smaller consisting of his boss men and the odd renegade. And they had finished just slanging each other—weapons had been seized: belaying pins, axes, lengths of chain. The larger crowd advanced across the yard, forcing the boss men to retreat. Once backs were up against the fencing, the blows fell fast and furious. The boss men, being outnumbered, came off the worst and began to panic. Somebody produced a scatter gun and both barrels were discharged directly into the surging mass. But the ensuing screams didn't check the strikers, they appeared to incense, and I saw several men laid low by the sharp edge of axes.

The man with the shotgun had reloaded, and clambered up a smoldering timber stack for better aim. He was plain to see, kneeling down, his gun at the shoulder. He fired once, and I saw the blast cut a man down. Then, apparently from nowhere, a harpoon streaked through the air. I know not whether you've ever tried to throw a harpoon—if you have, you'll know the weight and difficulty. Whoever threw this one must have been a veritable Hercules to throw it upward with such force and accuracy. It took the fellow with the gun full in the breastbone, the barbed blade smashing through until it stood a foot beyond his back. I heard later that they were obliged to cut off the head to pull the shaft out of his body.

This was the first time I'd encountered death, and I can't say that I was particularly shocked or upset. Intrigued, but not alarmed. Again, I cannot agree that I was in any way responsible for the demise of this man. He was little more than an animal, and butchered by one of his kind. If they had not indulged in murder when and where they did, they would have done so later, in some dosshouse brawl.

It seems that four men at least were dead by now, and Alfred

Dinwiddie had been summoned. It occurred to nobody for to call up the city constabulary.

The fighting abated when old Dinwiddie arrived in his buggy. A strange scene as the iron-headed skinflint was helped down and handed his sticks. He peered about him with rheumy eyes, his expression stupid and bewildered. One of his boss men was busy outlining the recent fracas, but the old man was scarcely listening. He could see the bodies now, hear the moans of the injured, and smell the smell of disaster. The boss man appeared to be urging him to speak to the men, pulling at the old man's arm, leading him toward a slight rise in the ground to serve as a platform. Dinwiddie walked with a dream-like quality, and turned to face the men when he reached the spot.

The first stone was thrown by Larrigan—I saw him chuck it— and it knocked off the old man's stovepipe. The rest came in a hail, and the old man and his boss man fled, hiding behind the buggy. But the boss man was possessed of courage—I'll grant him that—for he stood up and shouted for all to stop and listen to their employer. I felt some relief when he was struck down from behind and dragged off. Hands were laid on old Dinwiddie, and it crossed my mind that we might have a necktie party on our hands. But the hands simply bundled him head first into his buggy and whipped up the horses. And away he went, thin old legs waving about, followed by yells of good-natured abuse.

Matters now got out of hand, the affray turning into a riot. Liquor arrived, and the bottles were distributed. I reckoned the police must be called down soon—if they had the spunk to come. So it was time for me to take my leave as quietly as I'd come.

When I left, the looting and burning that was to sweep the waterfront for fifteen hours had only just begun.

Eighty-five thousand dollars' worth of damage was done, and twenty-two men got themselves killed. Most of all, old Alfred Dinwiddie—to quote my friend Curtiz—got himself "busted."

# III

The authorities closed down Dinwiddie & Co., having discovered Dinwiddie's men to be at the root of the disturbance. The lumber society decided that his nit-picking ways had encouraged the disaster, so they fined him two thousand dollars and ordered that his name be removed from the register of their association. The old man was left with a pile of charred timber, no men to work for him, and a bad name. One month later his body was retrieved from the St. Lawrence, and a verdict of suicide was returned at the coroner's 'quest.

My father moved with a pace that infuriated me—as if he was personally mourning the old man. Indeed, he said something about "the clay having time to settle over the coffin."

As I have mentioned, Dinwiddie had no sons, so we were not to be hampered by troublesome heirs. And the Royal Bank executed his estate, only too willing for my father to make them a fair offer. I guess there was some quibbling, but not much, considering the ruin left by the strike and the company's loss of good name. In the end, my father bought the business for twelve hundred dollars—a sum he was able to raise from the Royal Bank itself, fortified by a guarantee from the Carson brothers.

This was the beginning of a new era. Our family situation could only improve. We were not prosperous yet, but good fortune lay like a small star on the horizon. And I had been instrumental in the creation of that star.

I didn't forget Wideawake Larrigan and Curtiz, minding you. Between us we engineered it so that Curtiz became my father's boss man at the yards. It was kind of pleasing to pretend I'd never made the acquaintance of Mr. Isiah Curtiz when my father first introduced us.

Larrigan? He stayed a timber-stower by his own choosing. I guess he was loath to quit his crimping activities for a regular job. To do so would have constituted a considerable fall in income.

Naturally, my weekend visits to the quayside came to an abrupt finish. Maybe I was sorry at first—I don't recall. But in a while I took an interest in other things, and I have always been adaptable.

Moreover, I was pretty busy. This was my final year at St. George's, and terminal exams loomed ahead, in the fall. My father stressed the importance of my succeeding; my brothers tended to be both stupid and idle, and they lacked my inborn enterprise.

"I canna die until I see ye in my shoes, Tommy!" my father said to me more than once.

So I worked to the limit—part to please him, but mostly to please myself. Mathematics and the sciences being my forte, my father saw me as a potential engineer or shipbuilder. Yet I believe that even then I wanted to be something bigger than just a glorified carpenter.

# JACK PINE AND EASTERN HEMLOCK

## I

I left St. George's as planned, in the fall of '68, having obtained honors in all my examinations and marks of distinction in several. My father was well pleased with me, and decided that a vacation of at least six weeks should be my just reward.

He offered me passage to Nova Scotia for some fishing and hunting, should it take my fancy. But I elected to remain in the Province of Quebec, hiring the services of experienced French or Indian guides to take me exploring nearby terrain. My brother Eric accompanied me on several of these expeditions at my father's request—I guess he figured that time spent by the boy in my company would help build his character. As it turned out, I found Eric a useless and boorish companion, forever asking damn-fool questions and getting in my way. I think I should have preferred Anselm, but this could not be—Lame Duck's foot caused pain and hobbled him. Maybe it was this very disability that gave Anselm the sense of irony I found so amusing.

I tracked and shot over a period of about a month, journeying as far north as Lake St. John and the River Saguenay. Pretty wild territory in those days. While I was away, my parents moved to a larger house not far from the last one.

When I returned the move had been completed, and you can imagine my joy to find that a special outhouse had been constructed wherein I could hide myself away to conduct my scientific inquiries.

For I had become a young man possessed—the world of biology, chemistry, and anatomy held me in the grip of fascination. And my father's increased fortune enabled him to purchase equipment which tended to be expensive in Canada. I soon found that a successful dissection or chemical experiment gave me a satisfaction matched only by the stalk and execution of one of the larger prey to be found in the forests.

Winter came and my six weeks were over. For a while no one paid me much heed. My father was busy in the city, and my mother preoccupied with the new house and what she termed her " little ones." So I just drifted awhile longer—cramming my head with scientific facts, skating when I took the notion. But by Christmas my father was insisting that I accompany him several times during the week, so that I might observe the yards in operation and be introduced to various company men of my father's acquaintance.

"The sooner ye be a-learning what's what, t'better," he told me, and it was arranged that I join the firm of De Merait & Sons with the advent of the new year.

Now, I'm not proposing to say much about the next couple of years because I spent this period—as in the case of Joliet—in a kind of limbo. Trade was not for me. I found my fellow apprentices a nerveless crew, wasting their youth in the most futile of ways—examining ledgers, counting load sheets, checking documents for errors their masters seldom made. I guess some men are born to be clerks, and can only develop the kind of mentality to suit such an occupation. I also believe that promotion has little effect upon this kind of person—he still remains a clerk, whatever his position, whatever his profits. Slip into the clerk's rut and there you stay. Minding you, I was an apprentice, not a clerk. But as an apprentice I was obliged to associate with the lesser mortals of De Merait, sharing a small desk in their office, listening to their ridiculous small-talk. And I guess they resented me, too, for pretty soon I had shown the managers my worth and intelligence, whereupon the pittance I earned was trebled and I was given certain specific duties. I set out to make myself popular with the management even though I'll own this lowered me in the esteem of my fellows. I had no choice—it was the only way of escape from the humdrum world of the clerks' office.

In less than a year my progress was reported to my father, and my apprenticeship came to a halt. It was considered that I had learned all there was to know in ten months instead of the customary eighteen. It was decided that I should start working with my father without further ado, a satisfactory state of affairs as far as I was concerned. I have never taken kindly to working for others—I have always been my own master—but working with my father was preferable to being a minion of De Merait & Sons.

Recognizing my natural talents, my father allowed me time off to keep up my study of the sciences. And I spent so much of my free time pursuing this hobby that I believe my mother despaired of me. She, of course, wished me to socialize with the better class of my parents' friends and neighbors. "Be neighborly," she'd say. "Be neighborly!" I was nearly twenty-two, and a pretty handsome young brute at that. So she organized parties and picnics, inviting the daughters of those families she considered suitable. Some of the gals were damned fine to gaze upon at that, and I was possessed of that easy charm young ladies find so irresistible. I became a first-rate dancer—an exponent of the polka and the waltz—and I would invariably be invited to sing at the social gatherings I attended, for I was blessed with a rich baritone voice. Life should have been dandy.

But it wasn't. Something was amiss. I felt inhibited, unable to behave in a normal manner. I couldn't indulge in serious courtship because all the parents were nosey-parkers who plotted and gossiped and spied. And the girls themselves were more titters than tits—if you get what I mean; if you put a hand anywhere unusual, they'd begin to squawk like wild fowl. I reckon scarce a fraction of them knew the facts of life before they married, and then they learned the hard way, ridden sore by some brute of a husband liquored up for the wedding night.

All those picnics, too—by God, how they used to stick in my craw! A whole party of us draped about the banks of the river like a collection of well-dressed seals, curly-brimmed bowlers crammed down until your head ached, listening to some soft-faced squirt plunking on a banjo and singing some song that wouldn't offend a nun. I recall that on one such occasion I could stand it no longer. Our songster, a funny little lad with a lot of money and no brains, treated us to the entire repertoire of the nigger-loving songs of Stephen Foster. Then I was asked if I knew any plantation ballads. I said I didn't, but that I did know of a shanty dealing with the plight of our poor suffering friends.

"Sing it for us!" went up the cry, and so I did.

"A Yankee ship came down the river—blow, boys, blow . . .
Her sails and riggin' shone like silver—blow, boys, blow . . .
And who d'you think was the skipper of her?
Why, Bully Hayes, that nigger-lover . . .
And what d'you think we had for dinner?
Why, nigger's nuts and a blackbird's liver . . ."

That's about as far as I got. Later I was obliged to deliver written notes of apology to everyone concerned.

Yet apart from that minor indiscretion, I conducted myself with great finesse. I imagine that the scheming mothers of many of the young ladies I met looked upon me as a potential son-in-law and a good prospect.

My father first became aware of my frustrations and unhappiness when he caught me drinking in secret—I kept a bottle in my scientific laboratory. Instead of showing contrition, I flew into a rage and cursed the dismal life I was being forced to lead. He was shocked, but I had the sense to make him feel at fault, pointing out that while he was doing his utmost to assist me in a worthwhile career he was really withholding me from greater possibilities.

"Of course I'm grateful, Father," I assured him, "but I must make the right choice now—and I am not choosing the commercial world."

"What's it you're after, then?"

I waved a hand in the direction of my equipment.

"Ye want to be a scientist?"

No such profession existed to my father, and I knew this to be the case.

"No—of course not. I wish to become a physician!"

For a long time my father made no comment. At last he said: "If that's what you want, I suppose that's what it is to be."

I could have embraced him, but he looked unsure, so I aimed at his social-climbing instead.

"It's a fine profession, and a well-respected one hereabouts, Father," says I. "Look at old Dr. Sinclair. People treat him like a lord! Gain the qualifications of a profession and you enter into a special class!"

Could be all of this influenced him, because my father gave the impression of being happier.

"Just supposing you don't like it?" he asked of me.

"Then I'll come back crawling after a job, won't I, Father?"

He laughed a bit, picking up the bottle I'd been indulging in.

"And how long have you been drinking this brand, boy?"

I confess that the label affixed was a cheap one. Larrigan's favorite.

"It's all right for half a dollar."

"That's true enough." Scots blood will out. "Have ye got a second glass? If so, we'll drink a peg—to the new Dr. Cream!"

And between us we finished what was left, while I rambled on about the good sense of my forthcoming adventure.

"Have ye any fast ideas in mind, son?"

"For this kind of thing," I replied, "you go to the top. I should select M'Gill."

"Is that so?"

"It's more expensive, but it's by far the best. Ask Doc Sinclair."

"But I thought he was at Edinburgh?"

"True. Call M'Gill the Edinburgh of Canada."

"But you say it's expensive?"

"Money for value, Father."

"Ye'll try for a scholarship?"

"I don't think that's possible."

"No? What an infernal shame—it's no just the fees, it's just that you've got the makings of a scholar."

*37*

Sometimes my father could be a lying skinflint.

And so it was to be M'Gill. Life immediately became more bearable, and I took up my duties at my father's office and my mother's social engagements with a renewed vigor. I pinched and teased the lassies until they adored me; I loaned my gun and experience in the field so that the local lads claimed me a good fellow; and borrowed my brothers and sisters to examine my medical knowledge with vigorous questioning.

I made application to M'Gill, armed with references from the Reverend Solloway and De Merait & Sons.

My letter of acceptance came on the 7th August, 1872—a morning of great happiness and satisfaction. Although I was certain that I had earned a place, my relief was extraordinary. It was a dull morn, the clouds swollen with summer rain, and yet I can still recall that superb moment.

I decided to celebrate, and looked for an outlet. A maid named Charity Van der Burgh was holding a party to which I had been invited. But her Dutch kin were dull and straitlaced —I could visualize endless turns on the floor with her porcine mother. No, I required greater stimulation, a prospect of excitement. I guess I ferreted in my mind for something simple. Nevertheless, one thought, one memory, lingered on. And in the end I capitulated. I'd pay another visit—alone this time— to the Rue Champlain. . . .


II


It had been close on seven years since my evening out in the company of Reverend Solloway. Much about the Rue Champlain had changed over those years. Buildings had been pulled down and others erected. I don't believe that the establishment we had visited still existed; at least, I was never able to find it.

But the Strop and Block carried on business as usual, with a reputation that exceeded other places of its kind. Wideawake Larrigan once told me that the Strop's name was known throughout the sailortowns of the world, although here I think he was exaggerating somewhat.

On the far side of the street from the Strop was a drinking dive without a formal name but called locally Sally's Tail, and to this bar I went first. I guess I needed a snort or six to prime me.

It was past eight when I went in, informally attired in a Hudson Bay sweater and checkered pants. The long bar was crowded with folk of near every nationality, which figured: six or seven tall ships had recently come in from New York and Savannah.

I chose myself an inconspicuous spot and purchased a jug of red-eye. I downed several glasses without much pause, listening to the jabbering all around me. Jabber's the word, too —pick a bar and fill it with seamen from Holland, America, Norway, France, and Germany, and you'll get the Tower of Babel.

Pretty soon I was feeling just fine, and elbowed my way out on unsteady feet. You will appreciate that this was my very first visit on my own to such a place as the Strop and Block and I was fair agitated.

I banged on the door, firmly but not too loudly. It was opened by a slit-eyed fellow who could have been Indian or Eskimo. Probably an Indian.

I didn't have to say anything regarding the nature of my visit. The Indian merely closed the door behind me and I followed him into a small salon—plush with silk curtains and velvet upholstery, and not unlike the one in Reverend Solloway's whorehouse. Two girls were sitting there, their faces heavily painted to hide true age or the presence of disease.

The Indian offered me either or both of them, and I declined. He then disappeared, leaving me with the two whores. One asked me if I wanted a drink. I said I did, and a bottle was produced from a cupboard with only one glass. The girls watched as I gulped down the cheap gin.

The Indian returned presently with a third girl. She was a great deal younger than the others—fifteen or sixteen, I guess —and fair-haired with gray eyes. Caucasian stock—which pleased me. I asked the Indian her name and he misunderstood or plain refused to give it. But he said she was experienced, which surprised me, having regard to her tender years. She would cost me seven dollars—a sum which took the bottle of gin into account.

I agreed, and the Indian beckoned me to follow him. I did so, with the girl trailing along behind. I assumed a nonchalant air, as if well accustomed to this procedure.

We climbed some stairs and entered a room—no larger than a closet, and dominated by a brass-framed bed. The Indian held out his brown hand for payment, and I handed over the seven dollars, too nervous to quibble. The Indian counted the coin with difficulty, gave me a sly look, and then left us.

The fair-haired girl stood by the side of the bed, observing me. I supposed that I was expected to do something constructive, but I wished she would make the first move. She didn't, so I poured out a stiffish gin and handed her the glass. She drank it up in one, and I poured her another, which was consumed in like manner. She wanted more, and I obliged her. In the end, I handed her the bottle.

While she drank, I took the opportunity of examining the room and locking the door. My overriding fear was that I was likely to be taken for my pocketbook. I could imagine the slit-eyed Indian creeping up on me from behind and cracking my skull. Better to be locked up in this dungeon with the judie rather than that. . . .

I looked at the girl again. She was halfway through the bottle. She pulled a face every time she took a peg, as if she didn't like strong liquor. It should have crossed my mind that it was unusual for a judie to indulge rather than to encourage me to do so, but I guess I was too green.

The room was stuffy, and I took off my Hudson. The girl interpreted this action in another way, and put down the bottle and her glass.

First she removed her shoes, then her stockings and her dress. She was thin in her undergarments—tiny little bird-boned arms and legs. She paused to watch me pull off my trousers, so that I felt shy and awkward and stumbled a bit. She giggled—the gin—and turned her back, inviting me to loosen off her bodice. I had a try, but the laces were all tangled up, forcing me to rip them apart in my clumsiness. She didn't take kindly to this, and rounded on me. I murmured my apologies and stepped back, hoping that she'd complete the task. But she cursed in French and took to the gin once more. She bent over to fill her glass so that her upper garments came away. I grew excited—and a mite impatient having to stand there and watch her guzzle. I touched her shoulder, but she shrugged my hand away. I wished to fondle her hair, but the thought of another scolding restrained me.

Only when the bottle was dry did the girl pay me any heed. But even then she simply lay back on the mattress and looked up at me with a bored expression. She placed her hands behind her head, oblivious to the fact she was naked to the waist. I observed, with some distaste, that her armpits were hairy in the extreme. Black hair that didn't fit her head. She laughed at me a bit, and I realized that I must look a ridiculous sight in my combinations. I started to undo the buttons, but she reached up and pulled me down on top of her. Her lips were ice cold and she stank like a distillery, but I didn't care too much—by now I was desperate.

Decency forbids me to describe what followed, but let me say that I did not find my first experience particularly enjoyable.

When I had finished indulging myself, I made to get up and away from the girl. But she clung about my neck, babbling stupidly. Her manner and her eyes made it clear to me that she was very drunk, and I again endeavored to release myself from her grasp. A slight wrestling match ensued, the motion of which I assume triggered off what followed. In any event, I was still being held close with my face only inches from her own when she vomited. I believe that this was the most revolting experience it has ever been my misfortune to suffer, for she fairly showered me with her puke. I broke free and in so doing gripped her savagely by the throat. A combination of this pressure together with what filth still remained in her wind passages darn near choked her unto death, and I stood back in alarm as she spluttered and gasped with her head over the edge of the bed. For a long while—or it seemed to be so—she did not appear to improve, but then her breathing became more natural and I was able to relax a fraction. Her face was ghastly white

—no doubt the blood had been temporarily cut off from the brain. I took advantage of her state of semi-unconsciousness to pull my clothes on. Then I quietly unlocked the door and stole out and down the stairs. I was fearful lest I run into someone—the Indian in particular—for I must have looked a dreadful sight.

But I didn't, and eventually found the salon and the front door. This was bolted but not locked—to my relief—and so I escaped out into the night.

I shall never forget my walk home—I dared not take a cab. I was certain that passers-by were peering at me all the way. The odor of the woman's vomit hung upon me. And the puke was everywhere—in my hair, on my face, and rapidly chilling in the evening air about my undergarments. I felt like a leper, and wanted to retch myself.

Yet I completed my journey back to my home and up to my rooms without mishap. I stripped and washed myself all over, and hid my polluted clothing in a sack for disposal in the morning. And all the while I cursed myself for a fool and a wretch. I had wasted myself upon a drunken harlot and paid the just penalty. From that day to this I have felt a deep concern and an absolute revulsion toward women who imbibe. For myself, they can sink to no lower depths.

Before I slept, I knelt at my bedside and prayed to the Creator that I had not become tainted with some foul disease.

# URSUS HORRIBILIS

## I

For days I dwelt upon my experience with the vomiting blonde; the smell and sense of uncleanliness haunted me like a phantom. At last, so distressed did I become that I vowed on a course of action. If this is what had been my unhappy lot, what fate might lie in store for other stupid young visitors to the Rue Champlain?

Some "course of action." But what could I do? Were I to hire the services of Wideawake Larrigan and others, I doubted their proper cooperation. I was certain that they'd laugh at me for a bounder. Besides, I'd not associated with any of that number for a considerable time.

So I determined that my tongue should be my weapon. I'm an articulate man—always have been—so I resolved to lash the object of my furies with acid words.

Of all the newspapers in circulation at this time, the Protestant *Tabernacle* was deemed the most sincere and moralistic. Other news sheets, particularly those of Papist editorship, tended to be callous and indifferent. The *Tabernacle* I chose without hesitation.

My article, accepted without refinement, was headed: "Street of Sin." Let me say, sir, that I spared not the reader. I uttered a savage indictment of the Rue Champlain, of its whores and savages and places of unsavory passions. Naturally, I can't now put down on paper exactly what I wrote. I kept a copy of my published work for some years, but in the end it became so tattered and frayed that I was forced to cast the epistle aside. I do recall that I named the Strop and Block and pointed out to the more innocent of readers that this name alone was one commonly employed by the baser class of sailor to describe the act of intimate relations. I guess I also spun a tale or two for good measure, masking my own recent misfortune as something suffered by a close and hitherto goodly friend fallen to temptation. I further reminded readers that most of the more notorious properties stretching along this den of iniquity had long been of an acreage owned by the Roman Church. While I never chose to suggest that clerics of the Vatican aided and abetted the misconduct which took place during every hour of the day and night, or that they openly obtained revenue for their gilded churches in such a manner, I made it plain that a sensible man would have his suspicions. Here there was an element of truth, of course. I believe that it is quite accepted now that the cruel evils of syphilis stem solely from association with the Mediterranean kind, and that the fathers of the Popish creed actively encourage sins of the flesh so that their flock must unravel their past misdeeds in the confessional —and so be open to blackmail.

All this, and more, I wrote. I signed my name as "Felix McIntosh" lest embarrassment follow my family.

I'm not sure whether my father read the publication. Certainly he made no mention of it to myself or in my presence. Yet I remain confident that, had he read it, he would have approved of the content most mightily.

Honor being satisfied, I next set about the preparation for my great opportunity ahead.

M'Gill, I realized, would cost my father a fairish sum of money. I must not fail, and from the outset I determined not to do so.

M'Gill has since been described to me as brash—mainly by those educated at the teaching hospitals of London, or by the stuff-shirts of Oxford and Cambridge. But of what they have to say, I shout out: "Pooh!" The majority of these gentlemen appear to have been bequeathed cash rather than good sense. Their arrogance cannot set my teeth to grind because their opinions are ill-qualified and the manner of expressing them, raucous.

I signed the register on the 12th November that year, having spent six days in the city of Montreal in order to find my bearings. Montreal was new to me—as French as Quebec, and not, therefore, wholly to my satisfaction.

College proved to be a heartily constructed building with sufficient amenities. My mother had fondly kissed me farewell when I left Quebec, sure in her mind that I was embarking upon a period of acute hardship—as a starved student adrift and neglected in some alien township.

Happily, she was very wrong. Within two hours I had secured a small letting close to the college, owned by a Mrs. Somerset, whose mincemeats I ate with gusto. My rooms themselves were cosy and well furnished, and at this little nest I bided my time until graduation.

Upon my first lecture I found chance to study my fellow students. All hailed from families as respectable as my own, and most of them were as dull as ditchwater. It therefore took little time for me to establish my personality and become wholly accepted as a leader. To be frank, I had nature's grace upon my side, for I was tall and massively built, bristling red hair and mustaches and a jutting jaw adding to my formidable aspect.

Moreover, I struck out upon the seas of learning with ease. My private study of medicine and associate sciences leaped to the fore in an instant. My tutor, Edward Ramsbottom (an able if ridiculous man), placed me in the upper section of our class immediately, choosing me as an example whenever a practical problem was in issue or the more stylish essay required public reading.

I think it was Edward Ramsbottom who introduced me to the power of poisons.

Life trickled on—slowly, repetitive, but not without reward. I shunned the social life for a term and more, a courteous reminder to some that there was hard work to be done. Examinations placed me second out of sixty-three. First place went to Arnold Gold—a clever fellow, like so many of his race, who later became a knight in a most distinguished Dominion post.

Vacation, and a return to Quebec. Happy times—hunting by day, and interesting study during the evenings. I formed the suspicion that many students did little or nothing in the way of work while released from the confines of M'Gill. Here, then, was my best opportunity to snatch an edge on them.

I guess I exceeded what was expected of me. Ramsbottom soon began to treat me as some kind of djin—the pupil who possessed the quick solution to his more awkward style of question. As in the case of the Reverend Solloway, this man gradually sucked me into his confidence. He was a chemist—a good one—and after class dismissal he'd invite me to bide awhile in his company. Together we'd perform simple experiments, breaking down and testing a drug until we appreciated powers therein in a hundred manner of ways.

For example—if my memory serves me true . . .

Take opium. Greek for "juice," and sneaked out of the quietly blooming poppy with a Turkish smile. Take a mouse and give him a drop—not too fierce. Now, opium nudges the spine somewhat, and if you indulge our cheese-eating friend with about 0.01 mg. his defecating system becomes a mite wrangled. Up goes his tail like a flag, and there it stays until either he dies or feels his normal smelly self.

Or take strychnine, and take a frog with his spinal cord exposed. Slip a fraction onto the spine—paint it onto both the motor and sensory sides. Then step back and watch the frog's reactions. He will go rigid, with his hoppers stretched out behind as if the next lily pad was two hundred miles to go.

In next to no time, pharmacology and myself merged into a close friendship. I set about learning from Ramsbottom like I'd never learned before. I wanted to know everything and more. My notebooks became packed with information, and soon I had a fair library of manuscripts. These I learned—some by heart like a parakeet, others by practical application in the laboratory.

Now, it could be said that I devoted too much time to my studies over the next eleven months—I guess that would be

*46*

termed "fair comment." Certainly I was neglecting other activities suitable to a red-blooded youngster like myself. Not that I noticed any feeling of loneliness. No, sir—I was entirely preoccupied.

But in the summer of '73 I put my passion to one side. Our class held a competitive essay. An entry might write upon any subject of which he had knowledge, provided he be recommended by at least one of the tutors. Needless to say, I was oblivious even to the existence of such a competition. In fact, it was Ramsbottom himself who informed me one morning that he was of the opinion that I should make an entry, endorsed with his reference.

So I did. And my essay dealt solely with the subject of chloroform. It was not a writing of any great length—in fact, I think I completed it within the space of under an hour.

Time being what it is, I shall say no more than this: the treatise obtained for me first prize, and was published not only in the *M'Gill Journal of Medicine* but also within the pages of a Montreal circular used by medical practitioners.

I had become acknowledged an expert of my chosen field, and I decided to relax and enjoy myself for a spell.

Students, I find, tend to lead a split existence—one part of them intent upon impressing their fellows by the frantic downing of hard liquor, and the other part wildly in pursuit of adventures with ladies of the town. I mixed up pretty good.

My father's allowance, virtually untouched for a year, had accumulated. I was living off the dollars of a year before, so I found plenty to spend.

I bought myself a fine carriage and pair—leather and brass furnishings throughout, and a couple of grays. I ordered seven tailor-made suits of British cloth, and had myself measured for a recent Westley Richards double-barrel. My hunting clothes were those of a gentleman, and my evening wear varied constantly. At one time I owned no less than sixty-one cravats with matching pins.

During the week I slugged myself silly in the haunts of my compadres. My genial manner and good humor soon provided me with a host of friends.

47

On Saturday mornings I sported myself in the various parks, making the acquaintance of several young belles of good family. My charm and flattering ways impressed my glamorous friends, and I invariably found myself invited to meet their families of an evening.

Sunday—a day for self-criticism and reflection. So, after church, I took to the surrounding wilderness, my Westley Richards by my side, and an Indian guide hired at a dollar a month to the forefront.

## II

Grizzly Joe, they called him—the story being that he'd once dispatched a bear when armed only with a bowie knife.

Ursus Horribilis, I named him—for he was a bloated sharper of some forty years, with the personal hygiene of a gorilla. Never did he wash, oiling his yellow skin with the fat of animals instead. And animals long dead, was my suspicion.

He was a Cree, but made claim to both the Mohican and the Iroquois tribes—a positive lie based, no doubt, upon an ignorant knowledge of the works of that mountebank Fenimore Cooper.

I took not kindly to Ursus, but I must own that he was an excellent tracker. Keep the lout away from the flask he secreted in his buckskins, and he'd pursue *la chasse* all day with the utmost certainty. It's fair to say that this man made the gamekeepers and beaters of your own country look positively imbecilic.

Together we'd head for the country to the north, traveling as far as possible in a buggy, and thereafter relying upon the services of a pair of fly-blown mules. My successes with fowl and small furry prey were immediate and exhilarating. I soon chose to forsake my Saturday gallivanting in order to set out at break of day, pitching camp in the open before the weather became too intemperate.

But to camp with Ursus held certain disadvantages. Not only was the fellow a repulsive glutton, but he also prayed (or brayed) to various indistinct gods before lowering his shaggy head. Thereafter his snores were such as to numb the brain, and first light would find me red-eyed and dismal. Only the shooting made me continue to employ him.

Now, I had shot nothing larger than a middling deer, and my interest in smaller game began to pale. I wanted something grander—an elk or a moose, even a bear. But quarry of this kind was rare in the vicinity of Montreal. Civilization had driven the animals away. I despaired, and one day told Ursus of my disappointment. I recall that we were in the buggy at the time, driving home, with the skies packed up with a promise of snow.

Ursus laughed.

"No fretty, boss'm," he said. "Joe knows the ways to plucky hunting—dingdong place, no quittin'!"

I looked at his black eyes and anticipated a trick for extra cash.

"No quittin', boss," the rogue insisted. "Plenty branch-horn and old Ursy too!"

"Where?"

He waved a hand—two miles or two hundred—and then explained in his extraordinary way. We'd have to go to the Mountains of the Storms, twelve days' march and more. About seventy-five miles—to the north, beyond the parts we normally visited. No paths—only tracks known to Ursus. No people of any kind. And moose and elk seldom seen. But now the great cold was approaching, sometimes they came to this area from the west and northwest, for food or a winter refuge. Ursus knew where to find them.

He patted my gun. No good—a larger firecracker with a bullet would be required. Better to have two guns—one for himself (a clear invitation for me to provide him with a present).

I nearly shook off his suggestion. But I guess the promise, however remote, was too much for me. So we made plans instead.

That following week I obtained ten days' leave of absence from the authorities at M'Gill. I then purchased a Remington .58, old in style, but a great single-shot capable of reloading at fourteen to the minute by practiced hands. For Ursus I acquired a .66 Snider carbine and a dozen paper cartridges. Some of these were a mite peculiar, expelling a collection of ball-bearings rather than a single ball; I gathered that their design had in mind the quelling of riots among some of Her Majesty's far-flung colonies. Leastways, Ursus seemed happy, especially impressed by the Queen's emblem upon the lock-plate.

Ursus and I high-footed it on a Wednesday afternoon, abandoning the buggy after a short distance in favor of one mule. The weather was with us—just.


## III


The "Mountains of the Storms" weren't mountains at all, as it turned out, but simply hills stretching on without end. But the firs grew as thick as the hairs on the back of a dog, and there were rivers and lakes in abundance.

Moreover, Ursus showed confidence about the trail, trudging along as if this might be the terrain from which his kith and kin had hailed. In a couple of days he became less inclined to converse, so that it occurred to me that he might be ill. He took to muttering about "spirits" when I voiced my fears. I took it that his liquor supply had fallen short, hence the sulk, but later I came to associate his spirits with the odd twisted tree or outcrop of rock, and I figured it out: we'd hit upon holy ground. Six hundred square miles of territory the Indians regarded as some kind of church.

We came to a place called Split Rock. No rock, split or otherwise, caught my attention, but Ursus insisted that here was our destination.

We camped in a clearing, close upon a stream. It was after three in the afternoon, the ground was soggy, and the wind cut a man to the quick. I fancied a night here not at all.

Again Ursus insisted. At twilight, he said, we'd have our chance. Bear.

I was not convinced that bear might roam these parts at all, and said so; maybe one of the Indian spirits made his appearance in the guise of Ursus Horribilis?

Not so, I was told—and he took me down to the stream bed and pointed out a collection of indistinct footprints. I still considered his notions damn-fool. . . .

No fire was lit, and we loaded up at four. A mist was rising even as the darkness began to fall. Pine forests enjoy an eerie silence. Strange shadows are flung out by the branches. A time for illusions. And in half an hour the visibility was very poor indeed.

Ursus and I sat side by side, our rifles nestling the same trunk of tree. Indians make no noise, squatting or moving, so I didn't realize that he'd left me until he'd gone. And it was the strange crunching sound that made me turn to find out that he'd disappeared.

The crunching sound. A brushing of the undergrowth, a rustling of the lower branches of the pines. Then a savage grunting. Deep-throated snorting. Deer? Not that kind of noise. River hog? Not in this region. Bear . . . !

When he came into view, I fair painted the inside of my pants for pleasure. He wasn't very big—about two-forty pounds. But he was Old Man Ursus, black-coated and as ugly as the Devil.

Crash and smash, huff and chomp, and on he came—straight toward me. Thirty feet, twenty-five, twenty . . . then he stopped.

He began to sit back on his rear legs and sniff the air. Through the swirling mist I could spot his shiny nose. He'd got my pong, I daresay, and was worried. I scooped up my gun, my right hand sliding along the top of the breech to thumb back the hammer. No hammer! Imagine my panic in that second as I examined my gun. I found the hammer, of course, but it lay upon the right-hand side. I'd got the Snider.

Something of my predicament must have conveyed a message to the bear, for he fell upon all fours again and lolloped over to my hidey-hole.

Every hunter must know the feel of his gun. I did not recognize a single line of the contraption I was holding. But waste a single moment and I knew I'd be discovered and decapitated.

My shot took the bear in the belly—when he was virtually upon me. So close was the beast that I can say that the Snider's tongue of flame scorched his fur.

I suspect that the impact stood him stock still, if it failed to knock him backward. I don't know—for I was gone in a flash, tearing through the trees like a man deranged. The sound of another blast roared out, but I did not check my stride until a thickish limb smacked me across the forehead and downed me. For a space I just lay still and quivered.

A most terrible hollering then ensued, and I had pictures of my guide being flayed alive by four-inch claws. The cries were scarce human, but I took it that an Indian does not die in mankind's usual fashion. These must be calls upon his spirits. I hugged the ground closely in my fear. But at least I was relatively safe for a while, and Ursus' death throes made interesting listening. Then a second boom of gunfire, and all was still. Strange . . . perhaps a second round had been triggered off by fluke. Stay still, a voice advised me, stay still. . . .

A kick in the leg brought me to my feet once I realized the foot was human. And when I saw Ursus standing before me, I was certain he had become reincarnated.

"Plenty mistakens made," the fool said. And his look was of the kind that held me to blame.

"What happened?" A feeble question on my part.

"He gone."

"Dead?"

Ursus shook his head. "But we looky when time over."

"You hit him?" A nod. "Then we both nicked him. . . ."

"Yep—but 'nick' not so plenty. We make him cross-ways. You belly shoot. No so good. No quittin'."

I pointed out that he'd taken my Remington and left me with his cannon, but he shrugged the matter aside.

"Ursus catch running beary—can't say when, can't say who. Ball smack and uff, but no tellin'. But boss'm shot belly-bango. Bad." He looked a trifle sad. "Hurt Ursy plenty, boss."

With a wave of the hand, my gamy friend led me back to the clearing. His quiet contempt for me I found infuriating. A matter borne in mind shortly, as you might imagine.

While he pitched camp and lit a large fire, I did the rounds to establish recent events. By my tree I retrieved the Snider. I clipped open the breech, expecting the spent case to jump out.

Not a bit of it—I was finally obliged to use the ramrod cleaner to push out the paper through the muzzle. What kind of a weapon was this?

During my search of the clearing I examined the blood spoors. They were plentiful, and in one I discovered a small length of intestine. Blown out of the beast by my shot, I decided. And my medical experience told me that this must be part of the lower gut. If so, some stomach pains for our horrible friend out there in the woods. . . .

Beans and badly burned steak. That's how we dined—for I had little or no time to assume the responsibility. I left my share, but Ursus gorged clean his pewter plate with gusto, and then scraped off my remnants noisily.

He sought not the guidance of his gods that night, his simple mind being more concerned as to the reloading failures of the Snider. Finally, he abandoned the problem, and I watched him as he waxed his face with hideous ointment and slipped into his usual disagreeable slumber. One day, I vowed, I'd teach this ape a lesson. . . .

The misty atmosphere had developed into a dense fog, and the cold very soon became an agony. I draped my sheepskin about my shoulders, stirred the fire, and smoked a cigar. Clearly, one or the other of us was obliged to remain awake and keep watch, and since Ursus had retired without so much as a by-your-leave, I held that position. I vowed I'd wake the wretched Indian in none too gentle a fashion when his turn came. . . .

I'd not been sitting for more than forty minutes before the surrounding area was split by the most fearful wails and groans, as if the very devils had come to claim us. I snatched up my Remington and peered into the gloom with terror.

It was the bear, of course—hiding in some lair and nursing his frightful wounds. Pain had come to him with the passing of time, a searing pain which he could neither lessen nor understand. I relaxed again—the bear would not be concerned about our presence even if he knew where to find us. The bear would not be capable of exercise of any kind in his condition.

Now, sir, it may be that you have been wondering about just

why I have related the events of this incident in such detail. I now propose to tell you, although I reckon that your city-slicker mind will appreciate very little the import of what I have to say.

Some say that the pleasure of a hunter lies in the tracking. Very few admit that it lies in the killing. Badger an honest man, and he might concede the both. But one thing no huntsman will be prepared to say is that he gained any kind of satisfaction by wounding his quarry: on the contrary, he will raise his hands and beat his brow as if he'd been responsible for the breaking of a cardinal rule.

And, of course, he'd be a damned liar.

He'd be humbugging because even a badly placed shot constitutes a score. The very fact that his bullet has penetrated the hide of his chosen prey means that, while he hasn't got a bull, he's punctured the innards. Imbibe an honest sportsman and he might come close to admitting this fact.

Yet he'll still deny a true satisfaction—he'll plead an aching conscience as hard as he can.

And again he'd be a damned liar.

Now I'll tell you for why: a man with a good rifle becomes a superman—his to kill or not to kill, from the very outset. Watch a man holding a gun. I'll declare that you see him grip it in his hands as if the organ of his manhood.

Give him a gun and he'll shoot at anything, any time, anywhere. He has been mentally captivated by the iron and wood he holds in his sweaty palms.

He then sees his prey, ups the barrel, and shoots. During one small moment he becomes controlled by his firearm. He cannot resist—his brain is unwilling or unable to resist. Common sense and obvious perils are brushed aside.

If he kills outright, well and good—the extra feather to sport in his cap. If he maims, well and good—until his mind deciphers the possible comments of his fellows. Bleat like a fool and accuse yourself, say the rules of conduct. If you slip into this routine, you're safe: friends will stay friends and slap you on the back, buy you a drink or ten, and sing "Yankee Doodle Dandy" when they take you home.

Utter humbug, says I. . . .

For I am an honest man, whatever ill-wishers say. And I now say this: the cries of that bear that night gave me some satisfaction. I'd faced the beast with inadequate arms, shot him full of holes, and sent him to his bed squawking like a well-thrashed urchin. His misery had been executed by my hands; in every way I was the author of his misfortunes. And now he yelled— and his yowling gave me pleasure. I had seen his blood splattered about the ground and found a section of his insides; I was aware that my roundshot racked his body during every breathing instant. His cries and animal moans now filled my ears to corroborate this fact. And come the morning he would either be dead or would be killed by me.

I fair challenge any hunter to deny the satisfaction I was feeling. Say nay, and I declare the unbeliever a crooked miscreant and self-deceiver. For my interest and sense of accomplishment were massive. A finger on the trigger possesses a man of enormous power. The savage bleats of wounded quarry show him that he has made use of that power.

And I formally defy those true of heart and spirit to deny this!

I woke Ursus after three hours, pulling him from his reeking bed by his hair. Thereafter, until dawn, I slept quite sound, lulled into repose by echoes of our injured friend nearby.

Come the morn, we set out to find the bear—which was not difficult, having regard to the obvious spoor at our disposal.

I placed four .58 shots in his head, and Ursus had the sense to follow me up with solid ball. The bear thrashed and jerked a short while and then lay still, whereupon we skinned him.

Ursus suggested a further trek in search of moose, but I felt satisfied and we headed off for home.


IV


A Montreal taxidermist did what he could, but, alas, the facial fur and skull of the bear had been badly shattered. Only the body skin was worthy of exhibition.

My fellow students expressed their envy and congratulations

55

in no uncertain terms. I doubt whether a single one of them had gunned down anything finer than a buck, so my recent adventure soon became a talking point. Eventually, I wrote an article for our news sheet describing in detail what had happened.

As for Ursus? Well, I let him keep the Snider—with a secret hope that perhaps the proofing was unsound. And I continued to employ his services, determined that we might venture out unto the Mountains of the Storms yet again once the elements became less inclement.

For now the snow had come—light and stinging at first, driven on by high winds; later, heavy and smothering in endless downfall.

Lakes and rivers froze hard, and I found happiness in a return to skating. My prowess had not deserted me since leaving Quebec, and I was able to hold a casual audience spellbound by my antics. Jumping five barrels laid out on their sides was one of my especial feats.

But the early nights forced me to spend much of my time at study again. Naturally, I returned to pharmacology and Edward Ramsbottom. Furthermore, I made the acquaintance of a certain Zachary McDougal, a city practitioner who had received his formal education in London and Edinburgh, and was thus a member of various important colleges. I guess this man had forgotten more than I was ever to learn in my entire lifetime. I determined that one day I might attend the places at which he'd acquired his skill.

My social life I did not permit to fall into abeyance—not at all. I constantly attended parties and dinners arranged by the more cultivated strata of city society. Some men are born bad talkers and poor listeners, and this I declare is a terrible shortcoming—I pity them. I am an interesting talker and an interested listener—a boon in the case of human intercourse. When a personage, male or female, talks to me I am able to engulf them with a fascinated stare they find most flattering.

At this period of my life, maybe some of this was a genuine reflex on my part. Yet I do believe that my eyes were of considerable moment.

My eyes—light gray, as you are aware—had been troubling me for a while. The constant poring over tiny-printed texts in poor light and squinting down the odd gun barrel may well have started the damage. I needed to rub them a fair deal, to avoid cigar smoke, to bathe them in the morning with a light solution of strychnine. I became worried. I visited an eye specialist and told him of my fears. But he either failed to recognize any positive symptom or else eschewed total worship of the dollar coin, for he sent me away and told me not to study in bed. All through that winter I ignored the warning of fierce headaches.

An early spring, for once. Blue skies, a lessening in the night freeze, and warmer breezes. Christmas in Quebec had been hard—only work and news of my father's continued prosperity carried me through. My mother and the remainder of her brood interested me not in the slightest—even Lame Duck had lost his appetite for irony. The boys on the waterfront and the Rue Champlain? I don't think the thought occurred to me.

Montreal again—and the two cold months followed by the promise of that spring. And a promise kept; no chill interrupted the massive thaw. By the close of March I'd ferreted out old Ursus, drunk and dirty in the Fort dosshouse.

Would he come? You bet he would! But his tariff had doubled with an extra creak or so in his joints. He'd come—but not until six weeks had passed. I argued, but he said the mules couldn't stand it.

So I reverted to my studies and socializing for a time. The latter occupation was proving fair irritating: nice young gals, I daresay, but every one of them with the heart and mind of a longtime spinster. The trollops of the town bore some grudge against the student population which they reflected in their price. No amount of sassiness on my part appeared to relax this attitude. By the month of May I was of a decidedly mean disposition.


V


Could be that I'd forgotten about Ursus' natural habits—and they were of the kind a man would choose to shutter his mind

57

from further consideration of. But I was reminded soon enough.

My fat phony hadn't changed in any way—indeed, he'd become a mite worse. He now carried his rank odors like a cross, even in fresh air and from a distance if you fell windward. To be near him and share the warmth of a fire put a stop to eating —a full stop.

Sleeping near this man—nose- or earshot—belabored even an exhausted brain. The snores and groans and snufflings rent the air and stilled even the beasts. The hides and skins under which he slept were no less than an unwashed relic of the year before. They stunk—worse still, they stunk of him.

And he'd lost several teeth and equipped his rubber lips with dentures from another face. Clackety-clack they'd go—else they'd fall out, smothered in half-chewed food. Then he'd grin with bony gums, blow his nose with his fingers, and push back his teeth, dirt and all. I became fair sickened.

He still had his flask, of course. He'd guzzle some kind of mixture—slug gin and lamp fuel, I guess. Gone were the days of straight red-eye. So he got drunk as a fiddler's bitch most nights, lurching about, falling over, and yelling out half-breed songs in Old French.

Throughout May and into June I tolerated Ursus as usual. But whereas his behavior had once been a matter of no more than pungent irritation, I now began to feel a hatred for the man. He was also getting a trifle long on mouth, answering me back without any show of respect, and maybe this had something to do with it.

So I resolved to educate him as to the folly of his ways, and dreamed up a little plan.

In the last week of July we made preparation for an eight-day hike into the interior. Ursus reckoned a moose or two might be in the area—something to do with their feeding habits.

Ursus still had his Snider, and I traded in my Remington for a Winchester repeater (a weapon I was to hate the sight of during my time in Joliet). The rifle was low-caliber but reliable.

On the Sunday morn we packed the mule and trailed it behind my buggy for as far as the ruts in the road allowed; thereafter we tramped off in a direction slightly different from that

"Bit sharp?" I asked.

"Pharrr . . . !" was his answer. But no more, so I checked my pocket watch and set back to absorb the proceedings.

A rise in blood pressure? In a matter of moments Ursus was decidedly flushed—a pinky hue under his yellow skin.

Soon he began to sweat, tearing at his scarf while the perspiration gleamed on his face.

An enhancement of the eyesight? This I could not tell. He looked here, there, and everywhere, but I can't swear that the stars above revealed any great secrets to him.

Restlessness? Yes, that had started very quickly—a shuffling of the feet and juddering of the arms and shoulders. Quite involuntary.

I examined my timepiece. Still safe . . . of course it was safe! The real reaction had yet to start.

And so it did, even as I looked up from my clock. Incredible! Ursus was in a rigid position, jerking back his shoulders, while his legs were stretched out before him in unnatural fashion. He relaxed slightly, bent down, and rubbed his left thigh. He might as well have placed that unsuspecting hand in a rattler's hole, for he lurched back with his upper body, uttering a dreadful crowing sound. For many seconds he retained this posture, eyes and veins bolting from his head, gasping for breath as if some terrible weight now crushed his chest. Then he relaxed again —exhausted, gurgling but producing no vomit.

I consulted my clock. One more tantrum only.

The third convulsion came after a longer period of time than I'd truly expected. Yet when it began, I knew that I was obliged to react speedily.

He huffed and panted with a face suddenly scarlet with exertion before the moment. Then the forest silence was split asunder with a cry the likes of which I've never heard before or since—a desperate sound—an echo on this planet of Hellfire torment—the sound of utter and absolute agony. . . .

Ursus fell right over the logs on which he rested, his whole frame snapped back in the manner of an army jackknife. It was as if his spine had melted within him, so complete was the arch he completed.

And his face, as this happened, also belonged only to the

tortured caves of Satan. The blubber lips were parted in savage grimace, as if to challenge anything less than the torments suffered by their owner. A smile only to be expected from some fearsome creature of mythology. The smile I'd read of—the "risus sardonicus."

The smile itself, together with two or three more severe convulsions, promised death, so I leaped to my feet and set about the antidote with speed.

Would it work? I had good reason to suspect that it might. "Suspect" and "might"—bad words to place upon the administration of strychnine. God damn it, I swore, surely my dose had been small enough? But I suffered a degree of apprehension: suppose I'd laced the drink too hard?

Ether—a complete relaxation within the patient. More ether —an endeavor to lay him quiet so that the convulsions might not occur again and so kill him by respiratory failure or exhaustion. . . .

It was a fair fight to subdue the fellow, to hold back his head while he sniffed in the fumes. His jerking threatened me. But at last my beastly Indian relaxed a mite and eventually lay still.

Nevertheless, it was some while before I dared pump out the contents of his stomach.


# VI


Having nearly taken the life of Ursus Horribilis, I was able to save it by a very narrow margin. One-sixteenth of a grain had proved somewhat high; I realized that as little as half a grain of Nux Vomica might prove fatal, whereas anything approaching a full grain was certain to kill.

So a lesson had been learned by both myself and my guide. Certainly he had benefited from his unpleasant experience. If, as they say, the guillotine is a sure cure for a headache, then a dose of strychnine works wonders for the sin of gluttony.

I nursed Ursus for two days, so weak did he feign to become —at least, I reckon he was shamming much of the time home.

I blamed the food for his misfortunes, and he accepted my explanation; I guess he'd forgotten about the little bottle he'd drunk from. Anyway, it was interesting to note his sudden indifference and suspicion as far as food was concerned. I practically had to force him to partake of a plate of beans. By the time our little hunting trip came to a close, I declare he'd slimmed down by twenty pounds or more.

And that, sir, is the tale of Ursus Horribilis. . . .

# ROMANCE AND SARSAPARILLA

## I

The summer of '74 was a joyous time for me. A host of social engagements caused me to be entertained by some of the great names of Montreal, while I repaid such hospitality by organizing a series of pretty fancy picnics, personally driving the more handsome of my guests in my splendid carriage and pair.

But imagine not that I played truant from my academics. No indeed—not only had I published a further paper on chloroform, but I also delivered a highly praised lecture on opiates to staff and colleagues. By this time my lodgings at Mansfield Street contained a valuable collection of notebooks, etc., covering my research, and I saw fit to insure the same against loss with the Commercial Union Company for the sum of one thousand dollars. A wise move, as events were to have it. . . .

Summer went and winter came again. I spent a happy Christmas in the bosom of my family at Quebec. My father and myself formed a mutual-admiration society for two. Canny investment had brought him massive dividends that year, and he was a rich man. As for me? Well, I took home letters of high approbation from my tutors, and my father had me read aloud the text of my recent lecture. A Yuletide photographic canvas exists, showing my family in its entirety, with yours truly seated at the piano, my father standing beside, his hand upon my broad young shoulder. I further recall that in a moment of great

64

generosity I presented my youngest brother, Fletcher, with the skin of the bear so close to my heart. I must own that I am a sentimental man during the season of good will and brotherly love.

And so we enter into the year of 1875—short and of little event as far as I was concerned. Serious study claimed priority, for this was my last full year before I faced my qualifying examinations. Not that a freezing of my social life concerned me one trifle. Oh, I was pursued endlessly for my company, while the cadgers of the college slunk about my door, hoping to enjoy my own brand of effervescent hospitality. But I determined to be serious during '75—there was to be no shilly-shallying.

The year passed, and it's not for me to weary you with my trials and tribulations during this period, for I must describe in some detail the year that followed. But let me impress upon you the diligent manner in which I labored at my studies. And 1876 brought me just reward—it was not just a case of Lady Luck dealing me a good hand. . . .


## II


Her name was Elizabeth Brooks, and our paths first crossed in February. I had cause to visit Mr. Onegin, who ran the best bookshop in Montreal, and Mistress Brooks was browsing among the shelves. Her trim and pretty appearance caught my attention immediately—moreover, her fine style of dress made it clear that she was of good heritage, so my curiosity was aroused. I reckoned I knew all the ladies worthy of acquaintance in the city, yet her face was new to me. Who could she be?

Since she was having difficulty in finding what she wanted, I took advantage of this situation.

"Thomas Cream at your service, ma'am—can I be of any assistance?" I made a low bow and raised my beaver.

"Yes—I am in search of Miss Stowe's *Uncle Tom.*"

Her manner was curt but her voice musical—and not Canadian.

"A volume of very little merit, ma'am," I said.

She snapped an angry look at me. "I cain't say that's for you to be opining, in your position, young man!"

She'd taken me for the bookseller. I felt somewhat vexed that my clothing and mien should have caused this impression.

"And what position is that, mamselle?" I asked with a small smile.

"Why . . ." But it dawned upon her then that she'd made a mistake, and further words failed her. She hung her head, very abashed and contrite.

"Thomas Cream." I laughed. "Student of medicine, and never once a counter jumper."

"Well, I do declare . . . I feel most ill at ease. . . ."

"No need to. We shall make amends in the following fashion: first, I shall find you your *Uncle Tom;* secondly, I shall invite you to drink a cup of coffee with me at Mme. Requin's—an invitation you dare not refuse, ma'am."

She hesitated, but my charm won her over as I chatted easily while searching out her book.

Over our beverages, within the Parisian atmosphere of Mme. Requin's, she told me something of herself, and vice versa. She came from Waterloo—a hundred miles and more from Quebec —where her father ran the principal hotel. Her family hailed from Indiana, which I guess accounted for the strange pronunciation of a word or two when she spoke. I find that the American accent overpowers the Canadian—for that reason I have long been taken for an American born and bred.

"And you will receive your diploma shortly?" she asked of me when I'd outlined my career to date.

I shrugged my shoulders modestly. "So I pray to Our Creator."

"You are a religious man?" She sounded excited.

"I am of Christian upbringing and have faith, yes."

"The Protestant faith?"

"Yes, of course."

I think she was relieved by that answer, as well she might be within this haunt of Popery.

"My father sets much store upon the Christian way of life," she said. "He is a good man."

"He sounds the kind of man I would feel very much privileged to meet," says I, and her blue eyes shone with happiness. Then she went shy.

"I'm sorry," she said. "I must appear too forward. We've only just met."

I raised a hand and cut her short.

"No, no! It is I who have been presumptuous, Miss Brooks, and I beg forgiveness. It is the joy of meeting a young lady of your gentility that causes my tongue to run away in my head. I feel as if we have known each other for years. . . ." I stirred my coffee in a mournful fashion.

"Good sir," my companion said, "you have done nothing to offend me. Please believe me in this! Indeed, I have found our introduction not only of the most proper kind, but refreshing in the extreme."

"Then I may see you again?" I cried.

I knew she'd be hard put to turn me down.

"At the church where you worship?" I suggested, to help her out.

"Yes." Her reply was breathy. I had set the scene without difficulty.

All well and good, I thought, as I watched her depart on the midday train. Or was it? Hell's bells—she and hers lived some distance! Was I seriously going to put myself out by traveling so far on account of Miss Elizabeth Brooks? I doubted it. . . .

Yet on the following Saturday I journeyed to Waterloo, stopping over at the New Brunswick Hotel. I was minded to put up at Mr. Brooks' establishment, the Albion, but decided instead to bide my time till the morrow lest I appeared over-eager.

Waterloo was a half-mule town—dirt tracks running criss and cross ways and shabby houses. An attempt to improve appearances presented itself in an ornate town hall, the church, and two hotels—one mine, one Brooks'. But the place was still a slithering, squelching boghole.

The New Brunswick suited me just dandy—a large room, a tub if required, and an annex off the bar where eats were available at a fair price. With nothing else to do, I took a bath, liquored myself up into a good frame of mind, made a few discreet inquiries about the Brooks family, and retired early.

The Episcopalian Church of the Redeemer was packed next

morning. I chose an unobtrusive spot to stand at the back, and watched as the hotelier and his brood filed in. Brood? A bad choice of word, for Flora Elizabeth and a wizened old hag of a wife constituted the sum total. They took their places in a reserved side pew so that I faced them throughout the service and had a chance for study.

Elizabeth was surely the prettiest little creature yet modeled by the Devil's hands. The sweetness of her features became accentuated while at prayer, and that perfect heart-shaped face captured my heart (and a mite more), framed as it was in a fur-lined cape. My long trip here had not been wasted. . . .

As I say, her mother offered the appearance of a harmless witch—tiny and shriveled, wispy gray hair poking out from beneath her bonnet.

Not so Mr. Brooks himself. Tall and upright in a dark frock coat, he scowled straight ahead, his beard jutting out aggressively—a fine beard to boot, flecked with white and red, with an occasional streak as black as Lackawanna coal.

Army man when south of the border—so my hotel reception clerk had told me. A man who spoke to few, and then only in a whisper. A man with a past he didn't choose to discuss with the citizens of Waterloo. But a man with a crock of gold under his pillow. He'd purchased most of the town and outlying farms with silver dollars and little fuss. Once in a while he'd be called upon by the preacher to address the congregation, and most times he refused. I now wondered if such a request might be made of him today. It was, and I had the benefit of a rare performance . . .

"Colonel Brooks—to say a few words," the preacher told us between hymns. Up gets Brooks, picking his way over to beneath the pulpit with a care nurtured by acute rheumatism and wounds, but never by age.

Colonel? Yes—I understood. Brooks had been responsible for the renovation of this church, and the preacher was his lapdog. He had earned the prefix of Colonel.

A hush in the assembled many—their "master" was about to call the tune.

I'd expected a booming voice, not the whisper promised by

the receptionist. But a whispering sound—autocratic—I heard.

"Pastor Williams has asked me to address you," hissed the colonel, "but it is not my intention to preach a sermon, good people. Instead, let me just raise a thought for you to turn over in your minds until the next Sabbath. And it is upon the subject of duty that I speak to you—duty to yourselves and duty to Our Lord. . . ."

He stopped and lowered his head for a moment, and various sycophantic heads in the congregation followed suit.

"Was a time when duty stretched me upon a rack of misery," went on the colonel. "Was a time when my duty obliged me to fight my own brothers—to maim and butcher men whose lives and homes I might have cherished, to devastate with cannon soft valleys I might have been brung up in, to pursue and slaughter hapless boys crying for their mothers. Was a time when I had to do such things because my brothers followed a different flag and rigged themselves out in gray. . . ."

A terrible look of torment crossed the colonel's face. My, oh my—had this man got a conscience about something!

"Yes, good people. I savaged a fair and pleasant land because it was my duty to do so. Had I failed in that duty, then I would most surely have failed myself. And then, one day—" his pause was clever—"one fine and sun-blessed day the blast of war was stilled. And so I came north—to this great country, to you dear folk. Duty had been my religion, and I had done my duty. And now I urge you, fair Canadians, citizens of Waterloo, to hear my cry, a cry enlightened by Heavenly beams. And my cry is this: let religion be your duty, just as duty had once been my religion!"

Stirring stuff indeed. I watched the parch-throated old fool return to his pew, his expression still torn with anguish, and decided that either he was a fraud and a damn fine actor or he was off his head. But the adoring looks given to him from young Elizabeth warned me to be very careful never to criticize the ramblings of her strange papa.

I introduced myself formally to the Brooks family on the porch after the service, and I complimented the colonel upon his moving oratory. The grace of my manner caused me to be well received, although I had the feeling that the colonel was summing me up pretty careful. Anyway, I was invited to dine at the hotel in their company, and the colonel expressed regret that I was staying at the New Brunswick. Elizabeth, of course, was thrilled at the sight of me.

The Albion I had already observed to be a fine building from the outside, and the interior certainly didn't disappoint me either. Good French furnishings, imported carpets, and silver and best crystal on the tables. Why was this man running an establishment of such a kind in a place like Waterloo?

I poked a number of searching questions at the colonel over dinner. Mellowed by several goblets of wine, he began to talk. Yes, he was a veteran of the Civil War fiasco, a brevet major and honorary colonel of the Ninth Indiana. Reverend Solloway had caused me to be well informed upon the subject of the conflict, and now I pleased the colonel with my knowledge of Snodgrass Hill and Chickamauga.

"Snodgrass Hill," the colonel said, pulling aside his cravat to show me a round indented scar near the windpipe. (Hence his speech?) "I can still hear the Rebs yelling now."

Why had he left America for these parts?

"For peace of mind, young man. For my peace of mind."

But he'd been on the winning side?

"No side won, young man. Both sides lost."

Had he ever been back?

"Not.in more'n ten years."

I expressed my own desire to visit America.

"Then go to Chicago, young man. Mighty fine city."

I told him that I understood Chicago to be infested with anarchists.

"Don't you go believing everything you read in the papers, boy. Pretty soon those so-called anarchists will find themselves run out of town by the decent folk, and that'll be an end to them."

And so we talked on, sweet Elizabeth very happy that her father and suitor found each other good company. Mrs. Brooks seldom spoke to anyone, as if it were not her position to indulge in conversation, and nobody troubled her in consequence.

That, sir—in a nutshell—is how I first met with my future

wife, and how our courtship began. I took to visiting Waterloo a great deal, although I was grateful when Elizabeth paid the odd visit to Montreal, staying with a married cousin on her mother's side of the family. I took care not to allow our friendship to make interference with my studies, and she in turn appreciated this need for discipline. What she failed to understand was my more natural need. I guess she'd never met up with a virile young thoroughbred such as myself before, because she wished for no more than to stroll arm in arm and discuss topics of religion. A peck on the cheek she didn't resist, but my first attempt to kiss her resulted in woeful tears and the necessity of our kneeling down on the spot to pray for forgiveness. Very delicate, you may think. I daresay—but not exactly to my satisfaction. Moreover, my reminder that she would soon meet my family in Quebec and that our engagement might be announced come summer impressed her not one bit. Only the sacred state of matrimony allowed for such behavior, and even then we were not to over-indulge, lest passions be permitted to develop into lust and so let Satan govern our bodies. Fine chatter for me in my frame of mind!

February, and the examinations came all too soon. But I was prepared. Some of the restlessness my association with Elizabeth had brought me dissolved as I labored at the papers. It now struck me that I had been ill-advised to indulge in this frustrating love match, because the examinations were a trifle harder than expected; clearly, my concentration must have suffered over the past month. I would have done better without thoughts of Elizabeth badgering me day and night. Now I was paying the price. . . .

Yet I passed out with distinction, obtaining the highest marks for biology and chemistry, as well as for practical therapeutics. My concern had been unjustified—although the thought lingered on that higher honors might have been mine if my mind had been less disturbed. On the last day of March I received my diploma of M.D. from the Dean of Faculty, whose address to us assembled graduates upon the evils of medical malpractice was as verbose and stuffy a dissertation as I have ever heard (Attorney Russell's recent effort being a possible exception).

For the next week or so, myself and other qualified colleagues celebrated in the taverns of the town, spending freely. Being of a generous nature and having more money than the majority of my fellows, I did a fair amount of treating, with the result that by the time our heads and livers could take no more of this frolicking my savings were exhausted. I was due to visit my family in the immediate future, so my lack of funds was of no consequence, but I realized that my father—being a thrifty man —might take a dim view of so much spent in the entertainment of a coterie of cadgers. I contemplated approaching Colonel Brooks for a temporary loan on the basis that I was soon to become his son-in-law, but disliked the idea of his becoming my benefactor. Then one evening I hit upon what I thought might be a simple solution.

First removing my more important memoranda and those articles of special attraction to me, I saturated my rooms in Mansfield Street with kerosene and fired the premises. I made out a claim for the full thousand dollars next day, and presented it to the Commercial Union head office. Call this crookery if you must, but I acted without the slightest twinge of self-recrimination; after all, companies such as this make their living by tricking others into parting with cash on the off chance that something might happen to lives or property. It's right and proper that insurance swizzlers be made to pay out from time to time. Not that the Commercial were over-ready with their wallet either; indeed, they sent round a smooth-tongued minion to check out my lodgings, a crawler who had the ill-sense to suggest that the fire might not have been an accident, and who had to be sent packing with a well-aimed kick. May I add that it took me six weeks of constant quibbling to get just three-fifty dollars out of the company. So I went home short of cash in any event, and confessed my indebtedness to my father in a light-hearted fashion. I don't think he cared a jot.

Of my association with Miss Brooks, I was less revealing. My father's delight in me as a doctor of medicine led to his having pretty highfalutin ideas with regard to my future. I was to become the greatest surgeon this side of the Atlantic; I was destined to be as great an authority on the subject of therapeutics as Sydney Ringer. He was humbugging himself, of course, but his enthusiasm was infectious.

"Ye'll be completing yer research at Edinburgh, I'll wager," says he.

"I haven't given it much thought," says I.

"Well, get alive to it now, laddie. I'm no short of the shekels these days, so I'll guarantee yer don't starve."

So you understand why I neglected to mention my impending marriage.

Marriage! The true significance of the word gradually became apparent. Marriage is a mighty fine idea when you're just a student; the event always lies just around the corner, a pitfall never to be reached for just as long as you stay a student. But now I was a fully fledged doctor, a man able to earn a good living at once in a country short of qualified practitioners. In a short time I had ceased to be an ineligible young tearaway and had become an extremely eligible bachelor toward whom lots of fine young ladies would care to let fall a glove. The more I thought about it, the less inclined to surrender my freedom I became. . . .

But still there remained sweet Flora Elizabeth Brooks, with her auburn hair and creamy skin, neat as a bristle brush in her crinolines; was she simply going to be by-passed? Not so, I decided.

I called upon the Brooks home upon my return from Quebec, and we celebrated my recent success with a small party at the hotel.

"Mighty fine accomplishment, boy," the colonel whistled at me, and innumerable toasts were drunk.

Dear Elizabeth looked like an angel, of course—thrilled to bits by everything.

"We shall have to find a nice home, Thomas dear," she cried, and I was forced to agree for the sake of peace.

"You'll be setting up in Montreal?" asked her father.

I said that this was likely.

"A nice little house—a garden with fruit trees and flowers," persisted my fiancee.

"Find a place pleasing to my child, Thomas, and I'll make it a wedding present," added her Yankee father.

Sure as Hell, the walls were closing in upon me. . . .

## III

Elizabeth came to stay with her cousin throughout the month of August. She came for a number of reasons, but I guess the true one was this: I'd done nothing about finding her a "purty little house." Her heart was set on an autumnal marriage, and time was running out—maybe she even suspected that some of my ardor had cooled, but I can't be sure about that.

In any event, she parked herself with her cousin and I was obliged to abandon some research I was doing at the college in order to be at her beck and call.

We lunched and dined together most days, chaperoned by the cousin and her husband as if we were a couple of kids. Well, I suppose Elizabeth was an innocent at that—nineteen years old and mollycoddled since birth. Why I was dad-blamed stupid enough to seduce her one hot evening I can scarce explain, sir. . . . But here's how it happened. . . .

Being something of a chorister, I had long been a member of the M'Gill songsters' association, and my services had been retained by popular request even after graduation. Come summer, it was the association's practice to hold open-air concerts in one or another of the principal parks.

One evening we were due to sing our repertoire of hymns and assorted airs of religious strain, and it occurred to me that my Elizabeth might enjoy the occasion.

"Oh, what a treat!" she exclaimed, her eyes wide with delight. "I shall feel so proud of you!"

So I secured a good seat for her, and it was agreed that she come with her watchdogs. But all was not well with these sentinels of chastity—the cousin's husband had been feeling poorly throughout the day. Two hours before the concert was due to commence, he asked me for my professional opinion. I suspected over-indulgence on his part, but I masked my conclusions with a mumbo-jumbo observation and gave him a savage dose of bromo. The performance had scarce begun before the

74

fellow took himself off like a rocket, with his wife in tow, and they departed home in a carriage I had arranged to be on hand. The singing came eventually to an end, and I had Elizabeth to myself.

We wined and dined at Fouche's, a popular establishment in those days. When I say we "wined," I mean that I was able to persuade Elizabeth to break her strict rule about the Demon and swallow half a glass of Moselle. Yet even a measure so small as this caused her to become quite tipsy, and she chattered away delightfully. Indeed, in this way I was made party to her great family secret, the knowledge of which may well have actually saved my life in due course. . . .

You see, she told me how it was her father came to leave Indiana.

"Dear Papa's heart was never in the war, Thomas. I mean it was never with the Union. He felt a traitor, and when it was all over, there were some cruel people who called him a traitor—and said other terrible things."

"How so?" I asks, very understanding.

"He was a Democrat, and a member of the Knights."

"What knights?"

"The Knights of the Golden Circle, Thomas. The Knights were for slavery, they supported the Confederate cause. When Father was commissioned, he had to leave the Knights. Later his friends called him a traitor."

"He did what he knew it was his duty to do," I said. "But what were the 'other terrible things' you mentioned?"

"They also accused him of misusing organization funds—he had been the Knights' treasurer. It was a base and wicked lie!"

Aha, I thinks, so that's the reason for the ten-year exile and his solid bank account!

"People sometimes do tell wicked lies, my sweet," I assured her. "Did your dear father tell you about this himself?"

"Never! Mama told me—and swore me to secrecy, as I now swear you, Thomas, my heart. . . ."

"And your secret is safe with me."

So the "colonel" was an outlawed trickster; the thought intrigued and pleased me.

"Is that why he'll never return to Indiana?" I asked.

She nodded. "Mother says the Knights were influential people, and memories are still long about the war."

"But now your life is in Canada," I said, and pressed her hand in mine.

"I pray in thanksgiving for that, Thomas!"

"And tonight we shall pray together," I added firmly. "We shall pray in thanksgiving for all manner of things—and especially for our own future, dear sweet Elizabeth!"

And she drank from my glass while we listened to a plaintive chanson played on a squeeze-box.

I had envisaged some difficulty getting Elizabeth to visit my lodgings, and I'd anticipated the demand for a carriage to whisk her away to her cousin's as soon as we left the restaurant. But she fell in with my suggestion that we go for a drive in the park, and canoodled away quite merrily in the back as the pony trit-trotted round and round. When I instructed the cabby with my address, Elizabeth made no comment.

At my rooms, I showed her evidence of the recent fire and the scorched remnants of my manuscripts.

"So much effort senselessly gone—how great must be your sadness, Thomas."

I shrugged bravely, and presented her with a glass of sarsaparilla. This, I confess, I had doctored with Number Two gin. Not too much, mind. I didn't want her drunk.

"One discovery not even the fires of misfortune could destroy," I said, still on the subject of my manuscripts. I gave her a very serious look. "A drug, Elizabeth—a drug from ancient Cathay. A drug they call the Seeds of Heaven. A name well chosen, for this drug opens both the mind and the soul, giving to the taker a vision of the infinite—perhaps even of God Himself. . . ."

She began to speak, but I held up my hand, peering at her intently over flickering candles.

"It is said that the holy men of mysterious Tibet take this drug before prayer. It enables them to concentrate their minds—to pin-point thoughts until nothing can distract them from their communication with their deities. Their minds become all-powerful, their bodies nothing more than a shell.

76

*"I* have experienced this drug, Elizabeth. *I* have felt the divine communication of these holy monks. . . ."

Elizabeth showed little unease, even though she must have known what I was suggesting. Her glass of sarsaparilla was nearly empty, and sufficient time had elapsed for the Number Two to soften her up.

"For this reason I have brought you here, my treasure," I went on. "So that the prayer we promised ourselves tonight might be a true call upon the Almighty. Together we shall take this opiate."

"You're sure it's not sinful to have it?" she asked. Her voice was barely audible.

"No—no! It is a fine thing for us to do. I am positive that I would never have been allowed access to this secret, were it an evil thing!"

Well-chosen words on my part, for Elizabeth took the preparation of opium I had mixed without a murmur. For myself, watered-down milk looked very much the same.

A languid drowsiness and sense of well-being quickly settled over Elizabeth. For five or six minutes we knelt together, side by side, and said our little prayer. As soon as Elizabeth began to ramble incoherently I picked her up and laid her upon the settle. Lowering the lamp wick slightly and blowing out the candles, I then read to her from the Scriptures. Her breathing became very shallow. I touched her forehead—slightly moist. I bent over and studied her eyes—she was well under the influence. I then stripped her and myself and set to it.

# ULMAS FULVA AND A TRANTER

## I

Now, don't you go looking upon me as some dirty-minded miscreant devoid of all human compassion; that, sir, would be an injustice. When I initiated Elizabeth into the joys of carnal intimacy, I knew what I was about. I expected a bit of blubbing from her when she'd the time to recover. But at the same time I had the answers to every question she might ask of me—sweet answers, devilish in their flattery.

What I didn't expect is what I got. The simplest loon around might have been surprised. I surely was—I was so confounded I could scarce believe it!

She put it all down to "the most wonderful dream I've ever had, Thomas dear!" She mumbled and purred about a feeling of "utter relaxation" and "bodily well-being"—she mumbled and purred about it until I was pretty damned distracted. And all of this at seven o'clock in the morning.

Of course, I'd made her ready and dressed to face the day—no mess from our tête-à-tête was to be found anywhere. But her naïveté foxed me till I was cold all over: how could any girl not realize—not feel—that something was amiss? Surely there must be a physical peculiarity, surely the most wee of brains must register something?

Nothing. Her mind was as clean as the pan of a gold-rusher. And who, in the name of Glory, was I to disillusion her?

I returned her unto the care of her cousin, explaining that she'd taken ill and slept on a couch in safety. Her cousin was too disturbed about the health of her husband and the washing of sheets to bother either of us with questions. I was asked to examine the husband again, and I did so. The fellow's concern about himself irked me somewhat, so that I became overcome with a feeling of mischief rather than pity, and I prescribed another hearty dose of bromo. This I insisted he gulp down in my presence, and later I was amused to learn that the meddler soiled the family bed considerably.

If you don't like a dog, make him dirty and enjoy his mortification. . . .

But a biter oft gets bit and I got bitten.

Throughout the hot months I saw a fair deal of Elizabeth. I guess I secretly hoped for another chance to oblige her with the favors of Tibetan prayer medicine. I can't recall—I got the feeling that she became a little somber within a week or so.

Somber indeed did she become on 15th August—not a day I'll likely forget. She caused to be delivered a note asking me to meet her, alone, at Mme. Requin's.

I think the tone of this note was demanding; certainly the tenor made me suspicious. And I was dumfounded when she told me what she did.

She was with child—my child—and her voice merely strangled the hysteria she was feeling. Gone was her naïveté and blind faith in Tibetan dreams. In a matter of ten or twelve days the truth had dawned upon her. Her monthly functions had ceased—*ipso facto*, her belly was bearing an unwanted secret. Not even dear sweet stupid Elizabeth believed that hers was an immaculate conception. . . .

"What are we to do, Thomas?" And she twisted her purse in her hands.

I guess I hemmed and hawed awhile, as jumpy as a stump-tailed bull in fly time.

"You have deceived me, Thomas," she cried, tears of anguish filling her blue-green pools of delight.

"Soon we'll be married," I murmured.

"But what will Pa say?"

79

"Pa need know nothing."

"How shall we explain away a well-formed babe after seven months!"

How indeed? A "well-formed" child, to boot. I had no doubts as to the shape and structure of the cursed brat. I had no doubt that the seeds of my loins were as pernicious as those of the poppy which had landed me so high and dry. . . .

A thought crossed my mind, returned, and caught hold.

"Foul snake that I am," I said from the heart.

"No!" she exclaimed at the sight of my expression. "Both of us have sinned, Thomas. You are but the frail image of Adam —I have been temptress Eve. My body has been the serpint!"

I can recall those poetic words in detail.

"Between us," I said, "we have besmirched what was to have been beautiful. But what of the child you bear? Do we allow the cruel world to chortle at its origin? To mock at it throughout its life? To flourish the stain of illegitimacy in our babe's face?"

Elizabeth lowered her head. A tear fell upon the saucer of the cup before her.

"So we have no option, my love," I continued. "We must spare this little creature from such misery. We have no choice. . . . No, no! Don't look so! We shall send that tiny soul to Heaven, where Almighty arms will stretch out to it with love and understanding. The sin is with us—preserve us from visiting the sin upon the little child! Hear me, Elizabeth, I beg of you. This is the only way. The loss of the infant you carry will punish us forevermore, make no mistake. But we must be strong and do what must. . . ."

She was staring at me in horror, but there was no vim in her expression.

"Sometimes, to do as we must do is not sinful," I explained. "Sometimes it amounts to an expiation of ourselves."

And I argued on awhile, assuring her that this was not the case of our saving personal embarrassment, but a necessity on behalf of the unborn. We had *no* alternative.

Since both of our interests were at stake, I was endowed with a certain persuasiveness, and I won Elizabeth over. Back came her original trust in me—both as an oracle and as a man versed in the mysteries of medicine.

No pain, I assured her, no pain at all. A simple operation performed by the tender hands of the one who loved her. But she was not to breathe a word, not even to Cousin Sarah. She was not even to think about what lay ahead. Buck up and be cheerful.

I dabbed at her eyes with my own handkerchief, and she gave me a forlorn smile.

Slippery elm? I wondered. . . .

## II

I was very much afraid that Elizabeth's agreement with my decision might become affected by any great lapse of time, so I resolved to act quickly.

It would surely be unsafe to operate in my rooms, or even at the home of a friend. Somewhere quiet was required— some place where we shouldn't be disturbed by a nosey-parker.

I then remembered a small cabin once used as a base by Ursus and myself on the occasional hunting trip. A ramshackle hut and only roofed in parts. But secluded—in some woods, about fifteen miles out of town.

Come Saturday morning, I made things ready and called for Elizabeth in my buggy. In order to scotch any queries on the part of the cousin, I explained that Elizabeth and I had been asked to join a boating picnic given by friends. I had stashed a wicker hamper in the buggy as a precaution, and the cousin and her husband were satisfied.

On the way to the woods I told Elizabeth the true purpose of our little trip, and babbled away unconcernedly to boost her confidence. "May God forgive us," she said once. Otherwise, she was quite resigned.

Upon reaching the woods, I unhitched the carriage and trundled it into some bushes, out of sight. The horse I led off a couple of hundred yards and tied to a tree with a rope long enough for mooching space.

I then led Elizabeth up to the cabin, one hand holding hers, the other carrying the hamper and my box of tricks. She tended to stumble—a bit wobbly in the knees, I guess.

The cabin had now become little more than three overgrown planking walls—no roof at all—and I was obliged to clear the undergrowth for a decent space within. All around, the big trees swished and groaned, stirred by a gentle wind.

I kept up my small-talk as I emptied the contents of the hamper out onto the ground. There was food for me and a bottle of sarsaparilla "cocktail" for Elizabeth. I offered Elizabeth nothing to eat because I wanted her stomach to be empty while she imbibed, and I insisted that she drink the entire contents of the bottle. She complained about the taste, but did as I bade her. I don't think she noticed the juniper juice in the "cocktail"—but there were other things in the sarsaparilla which must have been unpalatable. Oils of pennyroyal and turpentine.

She became dizzy and drowsy after a time, so I laid her back on a rug, cooing over her like a dove, one hand on my folder of instruments.

Then, sir, I performed the first surgical operation of my medical career. . . .

Afterward Elizabeth rested propped up against a tree while I set about cleaning up the mess. She was very pale—which I attributed to shock, blood loss, and a slight case of hangover. I confess that I had no idea just how ill she was, but pranced about singing a cheerful little ditty.

"Thomas dear," she called out to me, "I feel lowly. You're sure all is well with me?"

I bounded across and kissed her twice. I pulled a flask of brandy from my jerkin and made her swallow a mouthful. She was sick as a dog, and I came to the conclusion that the sooner she was back home in bed, so much the better. It was past four, anyway.

She slept at my side throughout the trip back. She must have been enduring a peculiar selection of dreams, for her face screwed itself into fearsome knots from time to time and she called out pitifully. I lashed the horse with the reins to make haste, and covered the last part of the journey at a brisk trot.

"What's the matter with Liza?" inquired her cousin as I carried her in. She always had called her by that ridiculous name, the stupid meddling she-male.

"Crayfish," said I, and barged her out of the way. "She'll be all right!"

I was allowed to bear Elizabeth upstairs and lay her on her bed. Then I was summarily dismissed, while the cousin stroked Elizabeth's wrist to the tune of senseless cajolements.

Downstairs, I took rotgut with the he-male while he intoned against the eating of shellfish generally.

Ten minutes later I left—happy to leave.

I decided to get myself well and truly drunk and lose myself among the riffraff of Montreal. I further decided to ladle out another uncomfortable dose to the cousin's he-man as soon as good opportunity arose. Perhaps I'd find a suitable comeback for the she-male too. . . .


III


Since I kept well away from Elizabeth for the next couple of days, I had no idea of what excitement took place. I figured that she'd be resting up for a few days and then be as right as rain. I'll own that Colonel Brooks' sudden appearance in Montreal took me by surprise.

I was having a quiet drink in my own company at the Ottawa Hotel when in he came, looking like thunder. It was after nine and the bar was virtually empty, but the colonel gripped me by the sleeve and hurried me into the privacy of an anteroom, muttering savagely in that whispery voice of his all the while. . . .

"What's the matter, Colonel?" I asked as the other slammed the door.

" 'What's the matter?' " he mimicked, his face an inch from mine. " 'What's the matter?' Why, you sniveling scheming seducer of an innocent babe!" And he fetched me an almighty wallop across the side of the head.

"Elizabeth . . . ," I ventured, extracting myself from the potted palm in which the colonel's blow had landed me.

"Aye, Elizabeth—may Satan black your soul for what you've done!" And he came at me again, busting me on the nose with a straight left.

"Hold on—hold on!" I cried, pushing the fellow off. I was tempted to strike back, but thought better of it. "What of Elizabeth? What reason do you have for this conduct, Colonel?"

"My daughter damn near died last night, you cur!"

"What? How? What is this?"

"Don't play the half-wit with me, boy. I know what you did to her—and just why you did it. Her cousin Easy brought her home the day before—we heard your lying tale about the crayfish—we called in our own doc—said it was septicemia—said her dear sweet darling little body had been interfered with —said she was lucky to be alive. He only just saved her, at that. . . ."

"Now, wait a minute, Colonel!"

"And don't you go denying it, you blackguard." And the colonel drew a heavy revolver from inside his coat. There was murder in his eyes, and I swallowed hard.

Up came the gun until he held it level with my throat. It was a peculiar type of weapon—double-triggered, the lower trigger for cocking back the hammer, the upper for letting it fall—and it was cap and ball, of a kind twenty years out of date. The colonel obviously took note of my unhappy fascination.

"Don't you go laughing at this, boy," he snarled. "Last man who lipped my Tranter's dead!" And he operated the lower trigger.

I guess I thought I was done for, and I spoke without thinking. "Before or after you skedaddled with the money, Colonel?"

He looked surprised and didn't shoot.

"Yes, I know all about it," I went on, half expecting to be blown apart. "The Knights of the Golden something—eh, Colonel? Just itching to get their hands on you, aren't they?"

"Who told you?" Some of the anger had gone from his voice.

"Elizabeth. And I took the precaution of lodging this information in writing with a city attorney." A lie, of course, but a wise move, don't you think?

"I ought to kill you," the colonel hissed.

"Not worth the powder and ball, Colonel. Your secret's safe with me."

"You've violated my daughter—you came close to murdering her—and now you blackmail me. You're an evil man, Cream. You deserve to die."

"I understand your feelings, Colonel. But now I'll walk out of here and out of your lives for good."

The pistol came up to my face.

"The hell you will, you swine! You'll marry Elizabeth or I swear you're a dead man!"

I couldn't believe my ears. Grief had driven the fellow mad.

"Marry her? I can't marry her!"

My protest was met with a stinging slap, and the muzzle of the revolver was being shaken under my nose.

"You've got no choice, Cream!"

True enough—and the colonel's genuine desire to use his gun put an end to further argument.

Colonel Brooks insisted that we share the same room in the hotel overnight, in case I did a flit, and we journeyed to Waterloo next day by rail. Never once did he let me out of his sight —not even when nature called. I was his prisoner, a captive with a guard just itching to shoot me down should I attempt to escape.

At the Brooks establishment in Waterloo I asked to see Elizabeth, and my request was refused.

"Next time you set eyes on my daughter you'll be man and wife or dead," the colonel told me.

And so it came to pass that on the 11th September, 1876, I married Flora Elizabeth Brooks—a quiet ceremony (bride's immediate family only) held in the back parlor of the Albion Hotel at eight o'clock in the evening. I don't think a single toast or congratulation followed.

Formalities completed, Elizabeth retired once more to her bed, and we spoke not a word to each other, let alone exchange the usual wedding kiss.

Colonel Brooks ushered me into his study, and I stood before his desk like a schoolboy while he took a seat behind. He unlocked a drawer and took out a cashbox.

"I'm proposing to pay you one hundred dollars," he said, counting out that amount. "So's you can put one hundred miles between yourself and my daughter. Make it only ninety-nine miles, I'll load up again and kill you."

"What of Elizabeth?" I asked him.

"She stays here—with Mrs. Brooks and me. I can only pray that time will heal some of the wound you've inflicted upon her."

"But she's now my wife. . . ."

"A wife you'll never see again, young man."

"Then why force me to marry her?"

"That was your duty—something a scum-sucker like yourself would never understand, I'll wager."

He handed me the money. I was dismissed.

Next day I left Waterloo for Montreal. I had reason to believe that the colonel's threats were not idle, so I settled my affairs in that city, stopped over for only one night, and then took the Quebec train. I had in mind my father's desire for me to study abroad. My folk knew nothing of the Brookses and I saw no good reason to enlighten them. I believe I did feel a yen to confess all to my father at one stage—to play the prodigal son—but I decided against it. I'd kept myself to myself in the past, wiser to continue doing so.

Leastways I'd come out of this little episode with my skin intact and a hundred dollars richer. I'd also learned one lesson —that, as Mr. Bierce puts it, there can be no betting on the discreet reticence of any woman whose silence you have not secured with a meat ax. . . .

PART TWO

*1876–1881*

*Being an account of
Thomas Neill's further
experiences in the British Isles,
Canada, and the United States
of America*

# JOHN BROWN'S COUNTRY

## I

I sailed for Liverpool, with two trunks and my diploma, on the good ship *Ariadne,* a rough passage with boorish fellow passengers.

Liverpool—like any other sailortown; the Bramley Moore Dock flooded with judies intent upon robbing every jack ashore.

The British countryside viewed from a carriage window—flat and green, the smoke of northern cities creating colorful clouds in the sky.

London itself—immense wealth and squalor side by side; more people pounding the streets than I'd ever seen before. Some of the buildings looked so old they'd likely crumble into dust if you shut a door too fierce.

I took a room at Peabody's Hotel, close up on the Houses of Parliament, and spent ten days seeing the sights. I was Mr. Twain's "innocent abroad"—a colonial with a twangy accent. I guess a lot of people thought upon me as some kind of savage.

But I was a qualified savage, and had no difficulty in enrolling for a course of lectures and further instruction at St. Thomas' Hospital in Lambeth. I showed the authorities proof of my diploma and became entitled to the prefix of Doctor. However, they insisted that I should not attempt to practice in any capacity (in case I deprived their own meddling medicos of a groat or two?).

First impressions stick in the mind, and my impressions of London Town were no exception. Wide streets and dandy houses presented a façade behind which lurked a dirt and despair I found terrifying. March across handsome Westminster Bridge and keep heading south, or turn off to the east side. The well-proportioned boulevards soon peter out into something else—a warren of evil-smelling alleys without light or sanitation, and peopled by a troglodytic population, an illiterate scum of the earth. . . . Ever seen a man scraping up dog excrement to sell to the tanners for a livelihood? Ever seen a man kill a sewer rat with his teeth to earn a penny or two from the admiring crowd? Ever been given a discount by a prostitute on account of the fact it's her twelfth birthday?

But I enjoyed the music halls from the outset—gilded palaces, amusing turns, and good opportunity for me to impress the fawning toadies of the clerking class. And the women were as brazen as can be. . . .

Now, I'm not proposing to deal in detail with my two years in this hub of the universe. Little of interest occurred.

St. Thomas' holds its head high in reputation, but I was not particularly impressed. My fellow post-graduates struck me as a moneyed collection of snooty know-alls, and I soon dismissed my lecturer as a lackluster nonentity. When I repeated my famed essay on the therapeutic usages of chloroform, the authorities rejected its publication without reason. I guess the nay-sayers in charge considered my views "dangerously advanced."

My leisure hours I occupied between the music halls and acting as an obstetric clerk. "Clerk"—that was my official title, and one I cared for not one bit.

I moved from Peabody's into lodgings in the Lambeth Palace Road—hard on the hospital, still near the west side of London. Mrs. Shaw's—fifteen shillings a week (I could afford it) and a good breakfast.

Was I homesick? I reckon so. I missed the open country, the forests and the lakes. Most of all, I missed the hunting.

I tried to join a shoot enjoyed by some of the medical students —fowl only, of course. But the lah-di-dahs involved didn't take kindly to the application of a peasant-stock colonial. They said otherwise, but I knew the truth of the situation.

So I threw myself into study and private research.

A year passed, and I sat the primary examination in anatomy and physiology required for membership of the British "Royal" College of Surgeons. And I failed. . . .

I failed because I was unprepared to conform to the antiquated and asinine dogma thrust upon the medical profession at British teaching hospitals. I had views of my own, and lacked not the courage to express them. I was failed by the authorities because my pricking of their sacred cows nettled them; there is no other explanation.

However, I was young enough to be vexed. How dared these muttonheads disregard my years of careful analysis with such contempt? I decided to react. I penned a scathing and vitriolic letter to *The Times.* And I spoke in plain language.

My letter was never published—naturally. What I had to say had to be suppressed instantly! Fair comment's only acceptable where it happens to coincide with the opinions of those who rule the roost.

Now, one of my fellow students, a hook-nosed knave called Samuelson, had the temerity to make fun of my unfortunate position. I'd told him of this communication with the newspaper—and I'd told him in confidence. When the passage of time made it clear that I was not to be published at all, Samuelson informed the class of everything. His tone was mocking, and I determined to see him punished. Opportunity came in due course, and his hands suffered a terrible burning with acid after my cunning arrangement of certain laboratory equipment. Samuelson—a Christ-crucifier, as you might imagine—never knew it was I who was responsible, although I longed to tell him.

Life grew intolerable during the summer of that year, and on the 1st of September I received a cruel letter from Colonel Brooks; Elizabeth had died on the 12th of the month previous. Brooks said she'd died of consumption and a broken heart; he said that he held me to blame, and that my name had been on his daughter's lips at the end. He further admonished me for never having written to Elizabeth, saying that she had paled away and died feeling unloved and unwanted. Damnable hypocrite, that man! Who was it that banished me from his house under pain of death? How came it that I was supposed to send lover's letters to a bride I had been forbidden ever to see again?

Troubled by the fact that Brooks knew my London address, I resolved to quit the city immediately. Within a fortnight I had made the necessary arrangements for to study at the Scottish capital of Edinburgh.

## II

Edinburgh—home of shortbread and body-snatching.

Princes Street—the texture and hue of the stone reminded me of something far off. Probably of a Glasgow seen through infant eyes.

I boarded in with an elderly couple, spun a tale about my Scotch ancestry, and became an intellectual demi-god to be waited on hand and foot. The father of the house, a devout Presbyter who placed his Queen upon a plateau equivalent to a Roman with his Madonna, suffered a host of stomach ills. I prescribed, and I earned his undying gratitude. His adored monarch has long been my particular *bête noire*—a fat bad-tempered dwarf devoid of both intellect and humanity, with the arms and charm of a sourpuss storekeeper's woman. It's said that she hasn't been the same since deprived of her tumblings with So Good Albert—can you not imagine the Royal gasping in the grip of that whey-faced charlatan? I'll bet she was a tigress!

Of course, the Royals and their loathsome brood have for some years carried out a private invasion of Scotland. Up until recently the Grande Dame's been sanctifying the heather with that slavish fornicator Brown—I'll lay you evens that she was doing it when Alby Boy was still around, safely out of sight, plugging deer, his kilt chafing his skinny legs. Kilt! Show me a Prussian in a kilt, and I'll show you a humbug. The nitwit deserved to be cuckolded.

For myself, Scotland was close to home. Voices I heard might have been my father's; faces belonged to my mother; the hills and the sporting were of Canada. So great did a sense of association become that I several times considered remaining to run the full syllabus at the university and desert all over the water.

The womenfolk of Edinburgh took me by surprise. I'd expected a shivering pack of scarecrows, homespuns pulled around them from top to toe. Not a bit of it. They were sweet and jolly ladies, big-boned and rascally with the eye. But that's where their devilment ended—fumble with their frillies and you'd be smartly repaid about the ears.

On April 13th I obtained the double status of membership of both the Royal College of Physicians, and of Surgeons and Surgery. No real effort required—which tends to justify my comments upon London, does it not? And I was awarded an alpha in darn near every subject.

To stay or not to stay? I could be happy in Edinburgh, and I had the private means to assist me toward establishment. Yet there still remained the professional blockade. I was of Canada. The faculty doubters would make life difficult. But perhaps it was the vision of the Royal Witch occupying herself at Balmoral that really drove me away. . . .

# MISADVENTURE IN A PRIVY

## I

Upon my return to Quebec, my father met me at the gang-plank, and we fell about each other's necks like a pair of drunks around a lamppost.

"I've been a-prayin' nightly for yer return, Thomas," says he. "Now tell me all your news—be telling me how it was in Scotland."

I described my overseas experiences in some detail as we walked to a waiting trap and journeyed home to my father's house.

"Those southerners always were an arrogant kind," my father said when I'd finished telling him of my times in London.

"I was inclined to settle in Edinburgh," I said.

"No, Thomas. Yer did aright in returnin'; it's in the Americas you'll make yer fortune. Canada needs sons like yerself!"

With this feeling of belonging, I took a short vacation and stayed at my parents' home for six weeks. A most enjoyable time it was! Several parties were organized to celebrate my homecoming; my father's position in the city was now one of established respectability, and I was afforded the opportunity to meet several gentlemen of the utmost importance in the province.

My brothers and sisters were plainly fascinated by me, following me around like courteous dogs and hanging upon every utterance I made. I guess I was kind of a mystery to them—the elder brother, well traveled and versed in the affairs of the world. And I'll own that I appreciated their respect.

You could say that this would have been an opportune moment for to inform my father of the disastrous relationship I'd suffered with regard to Elizabeth Brooks and her kin. If I had done so, I've no doubt that Father would have forgiven all; if I'd done so, I'd have been able to paint my own version of how things were two years previous. But I didn't—a lack of perception I was to later regret.

Brooks and his vile letter being on my mind, I resolved to make contact with him again. I dared not write him, however, lest he take up badgering my family. I would have to visit the whiskery rascal in person—less like a dog returning to its vomit than a fool playing chance with a six-shooter.

I made the trip one weekend. I'd used hunting as a pretext for being absent from home before, and I used it again.

Waterloo was less dismal than I recalled, and some effort had been made to turn the main thoroughfare into a proper street.

The Albion Hotel, on the other hand, had a rundown decayed look about it. Had the Brookses struck upon hard times? I wondered. Had the vengeance for the colonel's past misdeeds caught him up at last?

When I went in, Brooks was behind the bar, serving customers himself—a bad sign. At first, I scarce recognized the man. He'd parched away, gone yellow in the face, like an orange left out in the sun. Apart from the fact he might be packing a gun, I reckoned I could handle him.

I made my way into the smoke room, checked that it was empty, and then sent a skivvy to fetch the hotelier in.

I decided to be blunt and to the point. I had a derringer in my coat pocket, just in case.

"I'm back," I said as Brooks stepped into the room.

I was sitting in a grandad chair, and didn't rise.

For a moment the colonel just gaped at me; next he began to cough and sputter. So great was his obvious rage that I feared he might burst a blood vessel.

"I got your letter, Colonel," I went on. "Can't say I like it much. But I'll put it down to your grief over Elizabeth. . . ."

"Hell to you!" roared the colonel, coming closer.

"Hold on—hold on, there!" I returned with equal volume, and cocked my pistol in its secret place. "Elizabeth's dead and gone, and we're *all* saddened at the thought. But I can't stay away from here forever, can I, sir? Struck me as plain duty to offer you my condolences in person."

"Duty! You don't know duty from . . ."

"Hold hard, I say! You spend your life preaching about duty —you say a man must be dutiful, come what may. Well, I'm doing my duty—and braving the consequences!" I decided I'd shoot him if he attacked me.

"Did you show duty toward Elizabeth?"

"I married her, sir."

"Only at gunpoint!"

"I still married her."

"Then to desert her!"

"Only for a while and upon your orders. Meantime she died. Now I've returned."

Brooks thought for a bit. I guess he was puzzled.

"Just why did you return?" he asked at length, suspicious.

"This is my country."

"No. Why did you return *here*—to Waterloo—to this house?"

"To see you, sir."

"And risk a bullet in the brain?"

"I considered that to be my duty."

"Don't say 'duty' again, for I know that's a lie. What's the real motive, Cream?" He was getting angry again.

"I was your daughter's husband," I said quietly.

"And her downfall—her assassin!"

"I was your daughter's husband, sir," I repeated, "and as such I believe I have certain rights, sir."

"Rights? You have no *rights!* A black soul, that's all you have!"

"Rights in respect of our marriage contract, and with regard to my late wife's property, sir." I made it as matter-of-fact as can be, like a dollar-a-minute lawyer.

Brooks recoiled as if hit by both barrels of my derringer; I've never seen a man so confused and shocked. I reckon my words shortened his life by ten days.

"To be exact," I said, "I want one thousand dollars from you, sir, and Elizabeth's jewel case."

I gave him time to recover his composure.

"You must be crazy," he said, shaking his head.

"No court of law would judge me so," I retorted.

"Court? What court? What are you talking about?"

"Courts of law decide contractual and matrimonial matters— or so I understand."

"But there is no marriage contract. . . ."

"You gave me money following my marriage to Elizabeth. I should say that such action supported my claim—an agreement between us is implied. And Elizabeth possessed valuable jewels, that I do know. As her husband, I now lay claim to those jewels."

"I shall see you in Hell first!"

"No, sir. You shall see me in the district courthouse, where details of your own affairs, past and present, shall be made public. No doubt to the interest of the citizens of this town. And no doubt news will reach Indiana."

"You blackmail me!"

Pure rage revived in the colonel some of his old spirit. I pulled out my derringer—pretty but lethal.

"Control yourself, Colonel," I entreated.

"You haven't got the spunk!" he snarled.

"I'll fire if necessary. But I'd rather see you ruined in the courts."

Could be that a combination of my reappearance into the man's life, coupled with my threats to his livelihood, proved too much for him to bear; for the puff went out of him, and he seated himself in a chair nearby, crumpled and broken.

"Rather the money and the jewel case any time, Colonel," I said after a moment's quiet. And I knew I'd won.

Colonel Brooks, late of the Ninth Indiana and first-rate fraudster, paid me two hundred dollars in cash and Elizabeth's morocco trinket box. I sold some of the jewels quite well. Others I retained, including a garnet brooch I fancied as a tie pin for

97

myself. I had no other reason for keeping these articles, minding you. I am impatient with the sentimental motives for retaining the baubles of the deceased.


## II


Having satisfied a two-year-old spite, I next set about finding an up-and-coming town in which to establish myself in practice. The almighty dollar bill being the great persuader, I abandoned the larger communities of Quebec, Montreal, and Toronto. I wanted a boomtown where medical men were too scarce to suffer from the competition of others already established. I was the vampire bat itching to sink my fangs into the fattest and most succulent flank available.

So I took my leave of my family, and headed southbound to London, Ontario, not far from the U.S. border.

Hosteling myself a few days, I finally secured premises in Dundas Street. Rooms to live in, and a comfortable annex big enough for surgery conversion. A stone-block building called Hiscock's.

Collecting patients was another matter—or so it seemed, for not a one crossed the surgery threshold for three weeks and more. I knew I'd have to advertise my services or else go bust. How to attract the attention of the populace? I could scarce hang around the doorway ensnaring folks in like a faro-bank lookout. So I placed a notice in the local newspaper, presenting the whole caboodle: Thomas N. Cream, M.D., etc., graduate of both sides of the Atlantic, and specialist in every manner of complaints including difficult childbirths.

There were a number of Irish in the community—frontier skippers from Buffalo and Milwaukee. The Paddy breeds like a gopher, tends to attract diseases, and hoards any money he doesn't spend on drink. Next to no time, I was administering to quite a few, and my successful dealing with one particular caesarian made front-page news. From then on, it was plain sailing.

During the next six months I made the acquaintance of a

certain dry-stock merchant by the name of Reinhard Rex Schroeder. He'd settled nearby in the town of Scathroy, building his own house on the banks of the River Thames (a darn sight cleaner than the cesspool by that name in England). Schroeder ran a couple of stores in London, doing pretty well, and I guess he was well appointed in the township.

I met with Schroeder through a sick relation; the latter was grateful for my services, voiced my name about, and saw I was fit to join the upper strata of London society. Hence my being introduced to wealthy cousin Reinhard Schroeder.

The Heiny hailed from the German province of Franconia—he'd made the big trip about eight years back; since then Franconia had been forgotten. He and I got on well. He was a helmet-head, and most helmet-heads are impressed by a profession like medicine. Quite right—after all, he was only a grocer. But he was a rich grocer with good contacts and a large family of toy straightbacks for me to look after. Schroeder was a man of forty who behaved like a kid with a hoop.

He introduced me to the "hobby" of gum, an occupation which has strengthened my jaw muscles over the years to the most prodigious degree, adding to a bone structure that'd do justice to a Mississippi alligator. He further introduced me to the pleasures of photography. Twenty years back, this was still a novelty. Plenty of Schroeder's pictures tended to be downright disgusting, although I must confess that I enjoyed the viewing.

Schroeder was two-timing his wife, you see—his wife, and the London definition of good behavior. Schroeder was a fornicator, and was able to pay for no end of pleasurable encounters with the baser class of womanhood. His was an endless quest in search of the young and nubile—the younger and more click-jointed the better. Not for himself, necessarily—sometimes he hired the services of a wildblood, just to photograph the entanglement. And within the secrecy of his study, while Mrs. Schroeder plucked out minuets on the piano next door, the Herr of the House showed me his developed reminders. I was tickled as a bat hitting a buzz saw.

One fine afternoon in May I was summoned to his offices in

town. I took it that one of the toy soldiers was ailing, and even brought along my bag. Not a bit of it. There was trouble, all right, but not of such a kind.

". . . and she swears she'll sue," Schroeder said when he'd finished explaining. "My money she will have, *hein?*"

One of prominent citizen's playthings was expecting his baby, *hein?*

Her name was Kitty Hutchinson, she was seventeen, worked in his second store, and what could I do about it, *hein?*

"Buy her off and away," I suggested.

Schroeder offered me a ball of gum. "Not to work. She will guts of mine for garters have, and I've know it!"

"Does she want to have the child?"

"*Nein.* She wants the dollar exemption; so is it that she wants!"

I waited, knowing perfectly well what he'd say next.

"Can you help me, Tom? Can you help *her?* You know I shall ungrateful never be!"

"It's a criminal offense," I said. I was thinking about Elizabeth.

"Complete immunity—I promise to you complete immunity!"

"One thousand dollars," I said.

"One thousand it is—the penny, every one of them!"

I hadn't expected him to agree so readily.

"She must visit me after hours," I said. "I must examine her. I can promise nothing, you understand."

"Naturally."

"How far has she held it?"

"How far? Oh, yes. I think for four months. .. .."

"Four months!"

"Is not good? I think not more."

"Not good at all." My expression closed the deal.

"Five thousand, perhaps?"

"Perhaps."

We rose from our chairs and rejoined Frau Schroeder, still tinkling at her piano. I recall that I sang "The Sailor's Grave" with great emotional feeling.

"We had no costly winding-sheet.
We laid two roundshot at his feet
And in his hammock, snug and sound,
A king-ly shroud, like marble-bound."


# III


Miss Hutchinson, a mere shrimp of a girl, presented herself at my surgery three days later. She looked angry rather than anxious, and took me to task from the outset.

"I want what's due me, you follow. I'll have no blithering about with me insides for nothing, you understand."

Her accent was mighty familiar—cockney, from that other London.

It was past ten, and my rooms were free from late-call malingerers. I led her into my salon and sat her down.

"A glass of gin?" I ventured.

"Don't mind if I do."

I measured her quite a peg. The rapidity of her drinking reminded me of the blonde of my "first experience." I refilled her glass.

"Suppose you get your fun this way," she said to me, gazing round the room. "Suppose you're one of those who snuffles about when a girl's under. . . ."

"Most certainly not!"

"Hold yourself to be a gentleman, I daresay. . . . Anyway, Rex is not to get away with it, d'you know. Not at all!"

Marvelous slut. With a heart as cold as snow. Her Rex might have been better advised.

"You'll appreciate that you're in a difficult condition," says I.

"How's that?"

"You're too far gone. It's bound to be a complicated maneuver."

She wrapped her hands around her treacherous midriff. "There's no danger, is there?"

I assured her to the contrary, in case she opted to keep the child and walked out.

"But anesthetics will be required," I told her. "And that way you'll feel nothing. It'll all be over in a jiffy."

I prepared the couch in my surgery with linen sheets that could be disposed of afterward. I then bade her undress, and drew up three powerful oil lamps on small tables at the foot, head and side of the couch. Placing my instrument case upon one of these tables, I left it closed, lest the sight of shining steel terrify the girl.

"Now lie down and relax," I said when all was ready.

I made my approach from behind the head of the couch so that Miss Hutchinson couldn't see the bottle and pad in my hand. Murmuring reassurances, I soaked the pad with the chloroform and leaned over to clamp it across her mouth and nose. Just as I did so, the girl looked up and into my eyes. Last-minute panic is not uncommon in circumstances such as these, although I can't say what it was that made the girl behave as she did. She let out a shriek and flung up her left hand. Her fingers caught the bottle of chloroform and knocked it from my grasp so that it fell upon her face; the stopper was out, and the entire contents spilled over and into her mouth. It was my turn to panic now, for I proceeded to ram the pad, sodden with more chloroform, down on her lower face. I knew as I did so that my actions would lead to dreadful excoriation—but I had to shut her up, and hoped that I might be able to repair some of the damage after I'd completed the operation.

But my hand turned out to hold the joker, for in two minutes she was dead.

I put her body in a privy to the rear of my premises, and left the empty chloroform bottle and the pad by her side. I took the precaution of dressing the girl, experiencing much trouble with the fastening of her bodice. I then hitched up my buggy and went to see Schroeder.

"She died," I told him quite simply when we were safely in his study.

*"Lieber Gott! Das geht ja nicht!"*

"She died, and we're both in it, friend."

"Not so! It was not of my doing. . . ." Schroeder looked plenty scared.

"You put her in the family way. You hired my services for money. We're both in it."

"I shall deny it!"

"And I shall swear it. I'll have no option. I'll be facing fifteen years and more."

Schroeder sat down behind his desk with a bump.

"What shall we do?" he pleaded.

"Stop fidgeting with that paperweight and listen," says I. "I shall find some story to satisfy the authorities. The girl was only a trashy vixen—no one's going to care that much about her anyway."

"My name—what about my good name? I shall be ruined for sure!"

"Keeping your name out of it is going to cost you ten thousand dollars. I already have five, now you must pay me the rest."

I reckoned he was worried enough to part with so great a sum. Catch a man at the right time and he'll give anything to save his neck.

I waved a hand in the direction of his safe. I knew he was flush —I'd seen the bundle from which he'd drawn my earlier fee.

Schroeder heaved himself up and crossed the room. He gave me a queer look as he passed my chair.

"I think you are not very much concerned of all of this," he said, twiddling the catch of the safe.

"Do as you're told and you needn't be concerned either," I replied.

Suddenly his hand fell away from the catch.

"No! I will not pay until I see with my own eyes—hear with my own ears—that all is well!"

I sensed that he meant what he said, and that further threats or argument on my part wouldn't be to any avail. I'd been holding his previous payment, a thick wad secured by a clasp bearing the names of Schroeder enterprises. I'd been hoping to double the bulk. Now I slid it back into my waistcoat with a weary sigh.

"Just as you wish. You take the risk. Let the consequences be upon your own head."

"I think not, Doctor," he returned. "I think we are like the Hydra: if one head is chopped off, the other is promised fate of the like." And he stood in front of me, hands on his hips, chin waggling away with suspicion.

"As you wish."

"And thus I wish."

And so I took my leave, not sure whether the storekeeper was plain damn-fool or quite clever after all.

IV

The body was discovered at noon next day, and two members of the town constabulary presented their cards to me at five. Questions were put by a bull-headed moron by the name of MacGuire. He was in charge, and it was like taking candy from a child.

Did I know her? And I was given her name and description.

I thought I did.

Would I care to view the body?

To be on the safe side, yes.

At the mortuary Miss Hutchinson's appearance took me aback. Her face was worse burned than I'd imagined possible. I knew a great deal about chloroform, but this was the first time I'd seen a fatal case.

Now did I recognize her?

"She had been enceinte. She came to me sadly distressed. She wanted for me to perform an illegal operation. I told her no. She became very excited, and threatened to take her life. I hadn't thought her serious. I'm sorry I didn't now." And I bowed my head in respect.

She had been examined by Dr. Shoemaker, town coroner. She had been found like this—a bottle of chloroform by her side. And a Dr. Jarvis did not regard her departure from this world as a case of suicide. What were my views?

"It's possible. I mean it's possible that she killed herself."

Dr. Jarvis was convinced to the contrary. People didn't do "it" this way. Dr. Jarvis had never encountered a suicide in this form during his thirty years' experience. What were my views?

I mulled the question over.

"I formed the opinion that this poor lost soul came from London, England—I've recently been there, you know?—and I do just recall that the pavement nymphs of that city were not only inclined toward self-destruction, but also used chloroform to satisfy their pathetic prayer-warranting needs."

Bull-head nodded. His assistant, a sharp-faced individual with greasy hair, asked the next question.

When she came to me, had not the girl mentioned the name of her illicit paramour?

I said I couldn't remember.

Try hard. She offered money for what she wanted done and what I had rightly refused to do?

I said that she had.

How much, then?

Two hundred—or thereabouts.

Did she produce the money? Try to recall every detail of that conversation.

No, she showed me nothing. I found her request distasteful to the listening. I'd done my best to shut it out of my mind the moment she'd gone.

Sharp-face was a natural ferret. He alarmed me. Best to get on his side, so I probed.

"The killing of the unborn is a crime worse than murder," I said. "I hail from deeply religious people, you understand. A man in my position chooses to ignore the mutterings of the Devil lest he become impaled upon Lucifer's trident."

Bull-head grumbled and shuffled his feet, but I'd struck up the right tune with Sharp-face.

He appreciated my position, he had great respect for the ethics of a Christian doctor. I'd behaved like a saint. But now his was the task—the duty—to root out the children of the ungodly. The wicked seducer of this innocent chambermaid ("chambermaid"?) had no right to the benefit of my silence. He was not my patient. He was not my friend. To shield such a monster would be to decry every principle of responsibility and rightful teaching. I must speak up!

"She made mention of a name of some importance hereabouts," I said.

No one was outside the law. I must speak his name.

"She was distressed—out of her normal sense. Why inflict such a slander? In her ramblings, she could . . . have been untruthful."

I must say the name, Sharp-face insisted.

What was I to do? When I thought of straightback Schroeder quarrying away at the smooth young flesh of supple girlhood, I suddenly decided to crush him like a boll weevil.

"She mentioned Rex Schroeder," was all I said, and the detectives left me in a flash.

The sergeant of police fairly bristled with importance in his smart uniform, stripes, and belt. He saw me next day in the morning. I'd planned to speak my mind as to the night before —to ask him how it came that two of his satellites had forsaken me without carriage in the mortuary to be able to step about their own business. I had intended to demand an apology.

But his first words drove such thoughts from my head.

"I'm minded to charge you with murder," said the sergeant quite gaily. "Don't look so—unfortunately, I can't. Unless you'd like to confess the whole of things to me right now . . . ?"

I drew myself up to my full height. Bull-head and Sharp-face were hanging about over on the far side of the room. Sharp-face was grinning, twisted style.

"You've spun lies since the day you came to this township," the sergeant went on. He was standing near his office window, more interested in the happenings of the street than myself. "You've set yourself up as a pretty loud noise. I've made inquiries, sent a few wires. I know that you're slick company under your father's roof. On account of his financial standing, I've no doubt. Monty Real speaks of you as a flash womanizing bloodsucker. Able doctor, yes. But warped and fancified. . . . "He tugged at the curtains with hairy hands. "But London wants no part of you. See? London wants you rod-riding out of here by" —he looked at his pocket watch —"by eight after dark."

I strode across to the mountebank, puce with rage.

"What's this! What's this!"

"Leave town by eight, else I'll book you as an undesirable."

"An undesirable! Why, you . . . Don't you know that I've

helped your thick-head morons? " I waved a hand in the direction of Bull-head and Sharp-face. "I've put them onto the true culprit in this matter! You've got a duty to act on information received, Sergeant."

"If I did my duty, *Doctor* Cream, I'd be putting you behind bars. But the adjourned inquest says I'm not to do so. Count yourself fortunate and get out of town as I say!"

"But what about Rex Schroeder?" I shouted.

"What about him?" He turned to Sharp-face and laughed. "You tell him, Constable!"

Sharp-face took a pace forward, grinning like a troublesome drunk. "Mr. Schroeder maintains you tried your hand at blackmailing him—threatened to tell lies and wreck his good name if he didn't pay you money. We reason that Mr. Schroeder's word's better'n yours."

My hand automatically went to my pocket, closing on Schroeder's wad of bills therein. I was about to pull the evidence forth and exhibit it to one and all when my fingers touched the clasp holding the notes together. Schroeder's clasp—with his company's brand upon it.

"Does that lying son of a whore suggest he paid me money?" I asked, hand still in my pocket.

"Of course not. He had sense enough to refuse you. Plain enough he had nothing to fear."

"Plain enough," echoed the sergeant.

So I had a choice. Produce the bills and the clasp—prove that Schroeder gave me black money? Or leave things alone?

Prove Schroeder a trickster, where did I stand? Maybe the sergeant and his mechanical minions would take the notion that I'd taken money to operate, or to kill the girl. . . . And the sergeant clearly wished to see my hide nailed.

Leave it, I decided, and leave town. Discretion before valor. Never mind Schroeder; most likely he'd be sweating blood right now, and for a few months to come, in case I yelled my head off. Let it go, this time.

"Well—Hell and God damn it!" I threw up my hands in a gesture of despair and resignation. "If you good people represent the authority of the community of London, I'll be doing myself a favor scraping as much shoe leather as possible. You're boneheads, the whole lot of you. Boneheads!"

The sergeant continued to smile. "Get and keep moving, Cream," he said. "And use no language of that kind between here and the station, else I'll book you as a vagrant!"

So I left the police office, and London.

I took the southbound run at seven ten, borne down only with the weight of my surgical bag, one tin trunk, Schroeder's dollar investment, and a keen brain.

So I left Her Majesty's "loyal" settlement of Canada, not to return for quite a while.

So I left the pea-brained institutions and prejudices of hypocrisy. And so I went over the border to the glittering gold mine of America—to Port Huron, Flint, Kalamazoo, and finally to the city of Chicago.

The injustice of London policemen beat like a drum in my head all the while, seeming to snap into line with the clickety-click of wheels over ties.

> Nine hundred miles from home,
> And I hate to hear that lonesome whistle blow.

Not at all. I was glad that it blew. I was for America—and I determined to exploit that country to best advantage.

# INYUN FUN

## I

Local bigwigs, being shy of inviting a Canadian national to earn an honest living, insisted that I "slip into the rut" and swear allegiance to their vulgar flag. Remarkable, don't you think, for a race incessantly jabbering on about "equality of man" and pioneer spirit? I guess I remain among the most unwilling adoptees of American brotherhood yet encountered.

Chicago—mecca of the beef barons from as far away as Texas. City slickers defrauding real drovers of their bounty; imported hussies used to convince the more cautious with filthy love-play and hammy chit-chat—bedspring prospectors, hearts as chill as clay, seducing the tall-hats away from their money belts.

Sickened, I determined to use this city of blood-suckers to the full, first renting accommodation overlooking Altgeld Park, and then setting up surgery at 434 West Madison Street—within walking distance. I proceeded to advertise myself freely, gathering up customers like bees around a pot of honey. The city was full of incapable quacks, so I guess my patients were relieved to be doctored at long last by a man with my high set of standards.

Sometimes a comment was passed as to the flavor of my accent (for in those days it was pronounced Canadian rather than American, as you might imagine). This struck me as mightily amusing—after all, most of those who chose to observe upon my accent hailed from faraway places; Chicago swarmed with Poles, Italians, Germans, and a curious and mongrel mixture whose avocations were uncertain. Stranger still were the Chinese—downtown, near LaSalle Street.

Now, I don't have to lecture an Englishman as to the sinister evils of a Chinese community; I have visited Limehouse on many occasions and have personally perceived the cancer of its "friends" to be found there.

The "Heathen Chinee" has wrapped his slimy tentacles about the circumference of this earth, from San Francisco to New York City to the settlement of Hong Kong. Some folk say "Let them be, for they do no harm." False thinking, I say! Chinese gangs—or "tongs"—may well prove to be the undoing of our civilization and culture. Red Dragon Tong is all the greater an evil because it is silent and cannot be seen. Chinese gangs must be crushed—or else! Mark my words!

Being something of a specialist, I became interested in the United Order of Opium "Fiends," nuzzling, like a serpent, in the bosom of Chicago. I have for many years been a taker of narcotics, and I reckon this habit—habit's the only word for it —began in the summer of '8o.

At first I ventured into the alleys of Chinatown out of curiosity. But one visit to a "joint" became repeated by more and more, until no thoughts other than that of a "lay-out" occupied my mind from the moment I closed the surgery. Very soon I became a paid-up member of the United Order; I was, as the Chinese have it, "inyun fun," compelled to smoke daily, driven onto morphia and laudanum at other times. Dearly do I now thank Our Lord that He fashioned me with a will of iron—for had He not done so, I daresay I'd have been another of those tortured miseries the devious Chinese campaign to create in their crusade to crush civilization and master the world.

It was during a "session" at the laundry shop run by a scallywag by the name of Yen Hock Herbert that I fell in with Black Bitch Sal—one of the few truly evil people I have ever met.

I recollect that it was toward the end of July, and I arrived at Yen Hock Herbert's shortly after ten in the evening.

"Who?" came a voice through the basement door in answer to my knock.

"*En she quay,*" says I, making the usual admission of intent, and I was let in.

A yellow face scrutinized me, and then I was led into a long low-ceilinged room. Extending the length on both sides was a platform raised two feet above the floor. Through the haze I could make out the shape of a small window set high in the wall. But this was shut, and the odor of narcotics was strong.

Yellow-face bade me lie between two prone figures on the right-hand bench. I lay on my side and watched as my "lay-out" was prepared—a small tin dish, the flattened knitting needle called a yen hock, a wet sponge, and a clamshell containing the tarry black opium.

Upon my first inhalation, I coughed less than usual, but I was still incapable of sleep. The itchiness, terrible thirst, and wild trembling came and finally went. Thereafter followed the comfortable dreaming, the wildest of fancies, all worldly troubles slipping from my mind. Six dollars' worth of Heaven.

I was just lying there, two or maybe three hours later, gazing at the glowing source of my pleasure, the pipe in my left hand, when I became conscious of a misty shape chying the opium in my bowl. Then a face looked into mine. The face was black and shiny with basalt eyes, and I first attributed this coloring to my strange imagination. But the initial effects of the drug were wearing thin by now, and I realized that the face was indeed that of a dark-skinned woman.

Heaving myself up on an elbow, I smiled at her, and she leaned forward to wipe the sweat from my mustaches.

A black woman, ugly as a crow, with gigantic flopping breasts beneath her shift.

"Enough," I said to her, for I reckoned my six dollars spent.

She stopped chying and put down the needle.

"Sleep more," she said. Her voice was both smooth and husky.

"No." And I swung a leg off the platform. She was watching me anxiously. Something was on her mind.

"What's the matter?" I asked.

"You're the 'Redhead Doc.'"

I knew Yen Hock Herbert called me that, and so I nodded.

"I'm Sal," the woman said.

"Charmed to make your acquaintance, I'm sure. . . ."

"I'm the Sal of La Folette."

"So?" I started to button on my collar.

"Maybe we can be of service to each other. Herbert thinks you're safe."

"Mighty obliged to Herbert."

"We'll talk, then?"

I had no idea of what she wished to discuss with me, but talk alone seldom harms anybody, so I agreed.

"Not here—not now," she said. "I be along to you in the morn."


## II


Black Bitch Sal—as I was soon to discover she was called—arrived at my surgery only seconds after I'd opened. I wasn't feeling in too good shape—heavy slumber after my visit to the opium den left me red-eyed, pale and sick to the stomach. At first I just stared at the woman, forgetting our appointment.

"I'll be obliged if we speak in your back parlor," said Sal. By her accent, I'd say she came from the South. For the sake of society, it'd been better had she stayed down there, picking cotton.

In my back room Black Bitch Sal came to the point; I'll never figure out how she trusted me so on first meeting.

"This town's full of pro's. Guess you've seen for yourself. Pro's need a particular kind of help from time to time, if you know what I mean. . . ."

"I'm not a pox doctor," says I.

"Not talkin' 'bout the Judas bug, honey. I'se talkin' 'bout fillies gettin' themselves babies."

"Oh!"

"Oh indeed. And they pay plenty for that kind of help. They

have to, mind—else the pimps punish 'em razor-style. They come my way desperate—so's I can shake 'em for ev'ry penny they's got."

"That's against the law," I commented.

"Takin' dope's agin the rules laid down fer doctors, I don't imagine!"

"Am I to take it that you're threatening me, Miss Sal?" Delicious irony.

"Not one bit, hon. Know better'n that. You've got the clock of a real bone-buster. Glad you have, at that—else I'd not be speaking my mind quite so free!"

We looked at each other, then both laughed.

"You want my expertise, I'll wager?"

"Damn right I do, honey," she snapped back. "Some of muh fillies leave the pup too long. Pups get kinda fond of the inside attachments; then they slow to budge; then things get awful complicated."

"I see."

"You bet you do. And you'll be seeing one hell of a lot of coin if you tag along!"

"You're a bad woman," I said.

"Peas in a pod we are."

"I've got my principles, you know. A code of conduct to follow. . . ."

"Codes and principles snap like git-fiddle strings when the dollar calls the tune. That's my experience, leastways. Experience also tells me that you're a liar."

The husky voice, the bamboozling charm. I couldn't be angry.

"Smile on. You're like that fellow Cassius, d'you know that? You've got that 'lean and hungry' way about you. Too much of it for a man your size."

"You're well read," I said, "for . . ."

"For a negra? Damn right I am. Once had to teach the cully-headed children of a negra-whoppin' bastard all 'bout Shakingspear. More'n twenty years back, that was!"

I added ten years—and now aged her at fifty.

"My congratulations!"

"You won't get me curtsyin' nowadays, honey. Make no mistake, I'se nothing for grave-men like yourself. Came here to ask no favors. Came here to ask you if you want to make a fine living. Do you?"

I threw back my head and watched the clock on the wall before answering.

"Well?" she insisted after a full minute ticked by.

"I'll have to consider the matter."

She shrugged her massive shoulders, adjusted the pin in her fruity hat, and picked up her muff.

"No need to show out the likes of me," she said. But I followed her out as far as the surgery door, where she turned.

"You think, then. Think good, and you'll be joining a mighty fine livelihood."

And she waddled off down Madison Street.

## III

Well, I joined her crooked enterprise, and performed a series of abortions. Whenever Black Bitch Sal came to the conclusion that her reeds and needles were unsafe, I stepped in—to provide what only the skill and know-how of a professional could attain. And I reckon I saved a life or two—that I spared a dozen young girls from the unsterilized torture of Black Bitch's weapons, or possibly from a watery grave in Lake Michigan.

But then came the complete catastrophe. . . .

The name of the girl was Julia Faulkner—a twenty-three-year-old slattern with a taste for good finery that verged on the kleptomaniac. Organized shoplifting was her trade. Come a busy time of the day, she and her associate, Mary Stack, systematically worked their way through the city stores. Miss Stack occupied the attendants with her fluent tongue while Miss Faulkner did a circuit of the counters, sweeping up trinkets, costly dresses, and sealskin sacques under her voluminous cloak.

Would she had stuck to petty thievery; but she didn't—for in the early part of August she fell in with a slaughterhouse worker and was soon with child.

Grapevine advice led her to contact Black Bitch Sal, who examined her at her own dwelling before bringing the girl along to me. I performed a thorough check on the girl, and took tests. Black Bitch Sal was right to seek my opinion. This was a complicated pregnancy and the girl had extremely high blood pressure.

I was against interfering—I deemed it best to leave the girl to her own devices. But Black Bitch Sal created a hullabaloo—the girl had been financed bountifully by the boy from the slaughterhouse (and these lads had money to spare, believe you me!). No, says I, and I stayed firm. Could be I had recollections of poor Elizabeth and the trollop in London. After all, chloroform would be required—and herein lay the danger. . . .

As it transpired, far better had I performed the operation instead of leaving Miss Faulkner to the mercies of the Black Bitch.

On the evening of the 26th August, I dined at the home of Dr. Marcus Aurelius Danziger, an important dignitary at the city faculty of medicine, and a highly respected citizen. Dr. Danziger I had met soon after setting up practice in The Madison. He'd sought me out, for I had availed myself of the facilities available at his hospital for scientific experiment. Dr. Danziger saw himself as something of an analytical chemist, and my great knowledge of pharmacology impressed him a great deal. Hence my invite of the 26th August.

On the evening of the 26th August, at approximately six thirty, Black Bitch Sal commenced her mischievous delving into the vitals of Miss Faulkner, and I took an apéritif with Dr. Danziger and his lady wife. At approximately eight o'clock Dr. Danziger, his wife, and their entertaining guest sat down to dinner and good conversation. And at about that time Miss Faulkner had become as dead as the fetus she bore.

Being downright perverse, Black Bitch Sal saw fit to deposit the savaged corpse of young Miss Faulkner upon my surgery premises. Whether she intended for me to dispose of the same in an acid solution or what, or whether she simply wished to fix me up tight with the legal authorities, I shall never know.

She made a dreadful mistake, of course. Not only was I with alibi—elsewhere with a noted physician—at the exact time of what she later alleged I'd done to Miss Faulkner, but also I was to find the corpse in the presence of that same illustrious gentleman. He'd driven me home himself for a glass of brandy and further discussion, and I had suggested the quiet atmosphere of the surgery.

Black Bitch Sal told a string of lies to investigating police officers, and they paid a call on me. I told them nothing. I was bland and outraged in turn. I denied all knowledge of a Negro woman with a livelihood culled from criminal abortion. The police officials, being as ignorant and mean as they are, concluded that I was a guilty man.

"You talk too little, Doc!" one empty-headed jay said to me. "You talk of yourself, of your fantastic medical accomplishments, and of your importance. But you don't talk sensible about the decedent—so you're under arrest."

Arrest, a short spell of unsavory confinement at headquarters, and trial.

Trial? Trial be hanged—as plenty are, under such procedure. My trial was a fizzle. I reserved my defense, and rejected the snapping jaws of the double-dealing lawyers who opened up their services in my case. I simply summonsed Dr. Marcus Aurelius Danziger and held his sweet wife in tow in the event she be needed. Naturally, the doctor gave his testimony in an air of startled indignation. The judge, being seven-eighths a crawler, joined in. . . .

I was discharged in half-time and five minutes; Black Bitch Sal notched up fifteen to twenty; and the police officers scratched their flat-top heads.

I lurked at the rear of the courtroom to witness sentence passed on Black Bitch Sal, resisting Dr. Danziger's attempt to whisk me off to lunch.

"Sally Bowman, you're a wicked woman and that's plain," said the judge, gray-faced with blood-red lips.

"And you're a dyin' man!" retorted Black Bitch Sal.

"No need for insulting behavior, woman. You've been convicted by the law, and I uphold the laws constituted in the state of Illinois!"

The judge looked rattled to me.

"Law's as may be, Mister Judge. You're still cheatin' your payroll. Better fer you to examine the Good Book than all these here legal epistles. I'll be purty gen'rous, and I'll give you one year to go at the mostest!"

The judge smacked down the mallet he held in his hand.

"Fifteen to twenty, woman!" says he. "You're asking for the 'mostest' yourself."

"I'll do the one of them, Mister!" cried out Black Bitch as hands gripped her upper arms. "I'll do just the one, mind! And by that time you'll be daid—you hear me, Mister Judge? You'll be *daid!*"

And they hauled her away.

(She was uncanny right, too: within nine months this particular letter of the law lay snug under the sod—brain tumor, so I heard.)

As I left the court, my attention was attracted by another back-seat spectator. Miss Stack—just a face? True . . . but a face I had seen once in the company of the Faulkner girl. I recalled their association. And now Miss Stack smiled upon me. Why so? I wondered—and why with the yawn of a friendly shark?

I sensed troubles ahead. . . .


IV


Troubles indeed.

Confound the wretched scamp! I'd scarce repaired to my surgery and opened the doors before this young vixen barged her way in. And her demands were fiercely put and to the point.

She knew all about me, so she claimed. Knew sufficient to ensure my incarceration—or "time"—for a period not less than that imposed on her friend Black Bitch Sal.

"I've got your listener, see?" she finished with triumph.

**117**

"My what?"

She shaped a description with her hands. She'd got hold of a stethoscope. One of mine, inadvertently left behind? Could be —at Black Bitch's apartments.

"So what d'you want? Money?"

"Sure do—but later. Right now I want some careful treatment. You got to fix me up good again. You understand, Dr. Slime?"

"What did you call me?"

"Slime—Dr. Slime. . . . That's how we call you around here, or didn't you know? You're missin' out on your reputation, Doc." She shrilled with mirth.

I reached across the desk and took hold of her little finger, bending it to breaking point.

"Mother of God!" she cried out, and shut up.

"What do you want of me?" I asked again.

She whimpered a bit and rubbed her finger, tears in her eyes.

"There was no need to do that!" she cried.

"There's no need for any kind of—misunderstanding," I assured her.

"But Judas be the True Savior, d'you do that sort of thing?"

"Your business here, woman!" And I groped toward her other hand. I didn't like Miss Stack. Not one bit.

The she-male readjusted her mask of fortitude and secreted both hands within her muff. Thus poised, she shrugged her thin shoulders, and said:

"I don't want to fetch for the po-lice, naturally. But—well, I've the proof that you've been indulgin' in the wholesale destruction of the unborn. Yes, wholesale. Sally told me, you know. And I've not the faintest reason to be doubtin' her word. If you follow. . . ."

I "followed" damn well; this tender colleen mixed nothing. "Po-lice"—what a wonderful pronunciation!

And so she contrived to pinch my purse in exchange for her silence. I studied her more closely, for the sake of memory (hence my uncanny recollection of the scene as now I write).

Orange hair, pale blue eyes, and the usual splattering of freckles designed by the Almighty to lower the charms of His savage Celtic creations. Bad-tempered and determined.

"What's worse with you than your itch for money?" I asked softly.

"Julia had her friends," was the answer.

The sneak-thief was suddenly bashful. I enjoyed it.

"Caught the pox, have you?"

"Johnny Fandango—he's the cause of a terrible misfortune befallen upon the both of us. . . ."

"Cowboy, or the imaginary man from the slaughter works?" I asked.

"Not so easy to prove. Yet Johnny's first on the list, I'd say."

"He made fine fools out of both of you, then."

"Maybe. The po-lice encried that was the case—but you don't trust the po-lice, do you? They'll lie to shore up the bibs and bobs of a bad investigation."

"All right. Forget the culprit. But tell me this—when was it? And what symptoms can you tell me of?"

She fell silent, so I swiveled on my chair and got up.

"Strip off—I'll take a look at you," I said, and put on an apron. She did as I commanded.

Miss Stack had syphilis, without a question of doubt. Yet her basic trouble lay further back in time than the investments of Johnny Fandango, or, indeed, the last seven years and more.

Miss Stack was riddled—way beyond second degree—and she stank like a skunk disturbed in springtime.

She made me queasy with her coarse face and reeking odor. And she had threatened to betray me—to cause me great troubles. She was the vilest of embarrassments, and so I resolved to kill her.

V

Now, a great deal of trash is said about the crime of murder —largely by those who write detection stories for the penny dreadfuls, and by those wholly unqualified in the subject. What of yourself, Dr. Cogswell? I've no doubt that you yourself will pen reams of balderdash about the present writer in due course. . . .

The elimination of Miss Mary Stack was an exercise as fascinating as it was simple, and as swift as it was essential.

Miss Stack had her venereal problems, and her concern for her bodily well-being instilled in her a trust toward myself and my potions that banned all thought of suspicion from her mind. She did as I suggested, and my suggestion killed her. Hence the simplicity of her end.

Since to murder her was so easy and she chose to rely upon me as her physician, I had now to decide the manner of her death. I guess it was her own misfortune that she displeased me so much, and in so doing reminded me of the wretched Indian "Ursus Horribilis." Had she not jogged my recollection in this way, perhaps I'd have been minded to terminate Miss Stack's earthly existence with a rapid poison, or even a scalpel drawn swiftly across the throat. Only her own unpleasantness induced me to use Nux Vomica. . . .

And fascinating—as I've mentioned—it was to do so.

I called upon Pyatt's Druggery, not far from my private apartments, for the necessary—and insisted that Mr. Frank Pyatt himself accommodate me. This unsmiling gentleman supplied me six separate prescriptive dosages, and signed his name in the ledger. Always ensure that a chemist adds his name to your own, else they'll spin a tale like a twist of candy if trouble blows its hot wind later.

Within the confines of my surgery, I combined the doses, resealing the lethal amount in an original paper flap supplied by Mr. Pyatt. From then on, I didn't shilly-shally, and I was with Miss Stack within the hour.

I had insisted that we use her own rooms for what had to be done. I said that no respectable doctor coped with her manner of infliction other than at dead of night, and elsewhere than in his own premises. This she accepted without question.

It was past twelve. No sounds from within her lodgings. No sounds from without—other than the sharp clicking of an occasional passing trap.

"Who's in?" I asked, busying myself with my bag.

"It's the Friday, isn't it? Nobody's here. They're all out— about their business."

Store-pickers and prostitutes. The house was as safe as can be.

"D'you want me to strip off, darlin'?" she asked.

"No."

"No? I'd have thought your pleasures lay in the undressin'.
. . . Well, you've got that 'culiar look about you now, or has no
one made the mention of it, then?"

"Not that I'm aware of."

Damnable little trollop. I daresay I looked my feelings, because:

"No hard feelings, you understand, Doctor? No hard feelings,
then. . . ."

I filled a glass from a water jug, poured in the crystals, and
added a slug of coarse brandy.

"Drink this," I said, and watched. "Drink all of it—right
down, do you hear?"

She did so, her grimace a mere fraction of what must follow.

"*Jee*sus, but it's bitter!" She shuddered.

"Drain the rest of what's left," I said.

Indifference to the unpleasant from a doctor convinces patients that they lie in good hands.

"What now?" she asked. "Is this the all of it?"

I nodded and sat myself down in an easy chair. Behind my
head lay draped a collection of used and unsavory slips and stays
which I pitched onto the floor before settling back.

"There's no need for you to be doing that, now!" screeched
Miss Stack.

She was a dying woman now.

"Lie down," I suggested.

"And why should I?"

She had become flushed under her painted mask, and her
eyes shone very bright. I'd say she looked more attractive then
than she had for many's the year.

I got up and locked the door.

"Lie down—you'll feel better," I said again from my chair.

"God save us, but I must open a window!" Miss Stack returned, rushing for the sill. Either the window was stuck or
screwed down, because she failed to slide it up. Most likely she
was too weak. The twitchings had commenced.

Stepping back from the window frame, Miss Stack slipped—

hovered—and crashed to the floor. I didn't bother to save her. I'd told her where to go. Her bed—her deathbed—was occupying a fair deal of space. She wouldn't have it, and her choice was her own. Now she could die on the bald floor carpet.

"God, I'm poorly!" she shrieked more than once. "Help me, Doctor! For pity's sake!"

And her heels began to rap a noisy tattoo. Noise—I didn't want noise—so I left my chair, picked her up, and slung her upon her reeking bedding.

"Water!" she called out.

I resumed my chair.

"Water! Savior, what's up with me! I'm sick to my heart, I just can't stand this!"

And so the convulsions took their grip. At the outset of the first I consulted my watch, holding the piece up in front of me so that I might study the subject and the timing of every spasm at the same instance.

Convulsion one—Miss Stack's hands fell upon and gripped the tall brass bedstead behind. She was perspiring heavily, and her legs jerked in a frantic way. Yet in a matter of moments her ordeal had passed.

"You've gotta help me!" she hollered. "Tell me what's wrong —please God, man! My back's a-breakin'!"

"Rest still," I think I said.

Convulsion two—it came suddenly, just after Miss Stack tried to brush back her hair. Incredible! She almost took herself off from the bed. Her back curved upward like an Arabian sword, her heels scratching along the bedspread as if desiring to find and seek refuge in the lower back. Every muscle in Miss Stack's neck and forearms stood out clearly defined. And on her face —risus sardonicus. The trauma passed, and I wondered if she was already dead.

Not a bit of it; her twitching was that of one still living, and she opened her eyes, cocked up her head, and stared at me.

"Please . . ." and something else I failed to catch, for her head fell back again.

Soon she commenced this fidgeting once more—involuntary, but as if a terrible being now possessed her muscular reactions.

This quivering increased all the time—over three to four minutes—and then, like a racehorse from the slips, sprang loose.

Convulsion three—an incredible feat of acrobatics and inhuman strength! Never in my life would I have believed possible what I now observed with my own eyes! Miss Stack was of average size and physique, and only inclined toward plumpness. Yet as the shock took her, as her lower back bent her spine once again, she actually pulled the hollow tubing of the bedhead down over her, bending the brass fittings as if they be made of wax. Her face had turned purple, and the spasm lasted longer than the others. So rigid and unyielding did her sinews and muscles become during these moments that she literally crushed the living breath out of herself.

Within a minute she had died, killed by a combination of asphyxia and pure exhaustion. Her body continued to twitch—like a dog in his dreams—but these movements had nothing to do with her brain. I checked her heart to make sure, and peered into her lifeless eyes. All the blood vessels of the latter had been ruptured, and they swam in a red froth.

Flicking a shawl over the girl's hideous countenance, I knelt at her side and bowed my head. A short prayer struck me as seemly. . . .

# THE DEMISE OF DANIEL STOTT

## I

The death of Mary Stack attracted not a jot of attention from the newspapermen. I gather she was provided with a pauper's grave and her departure was attributed to alcoholism. But her story was not to be free from any kind of epitaph.

I've made mention of Pyatt, the chemist from whom I purchased the necessary. Well, this fellow turned out to be a sniveling meddler. He paid me a visit about one week later, armed with his little book of drug prescriptions, and asking a lot of darn-fool questions.

For whom had the folders been intended, and what ailed this particular patient? He'd never satisfied an order of this kind before, and now he was worried lest the crystals fall into the wrong hands. He considered it my duty to inform him of everything.

"Patient-doctor privilege precludes me from saying," I told the man.

Not good enough, argued the little shopman. There were times when confidences must be broken in the interests of society. Of course he didn't want to consult the police authorities and ask their advice.

"You threaten me with the police?" I asked.

Not at all, not at all. He merely wished to satisfy himself—to have an explanation up his sleeve in the event of some mishap resulting from a misuse of what he'd prescribed. After all, he'd signed his name against the issue in the book.

I wondered how to answer him. I had a sneaky feeling that the druggist wouldn't be happy with a simple tale.

"I've worked hard for a good living, and I don't want no trouble," he said, and those words clinched what I'd just been thinking.

"I didn't want to have to tell you, Mr. Pyatt," I said quietly. "But I guess I'll have to. . . . You over-prescribed. Too much in each packet. Maybe you had other things on your mind when you made them up, I don't know. . . ."

"What happened?" The terror on the face was real.

"My patient died."

"Who? When? Impossible!"

"Miss Stack—on Friday last. She passed away pretty quick."

"I don't believe it!"

"That's the truth of it." I shrugged. "Naturally, nobody knows a thing about the matter. I had to arrange things carefully. Nobody's going to ascertain that it was your negligence that killed her."

"But I prepared the doses myself!"

"That's what I mean. But unless they dig up her body, no one'll be the wiser, will they?"

"My God! What am I to do?"

"Nothing. Just consider it your good fortune that I'm the doctor involved."

"Yes. . . ." He was rubbing his chin with his hand, tiny eyes darting about the room as if a peace officer lurked in every shadow. "People warned me about you, you know," he said quickly. "Told me not to do business with you, you know. Said you've got an unsavory reputation. That's why I came to find out what had happened." He was trembling.

"Well, now you know. And you don't want to go believing a lot of lies, either. I'm minded to speak of this matter to the authorities myself!"

"No, no—please don't. She's dead and buried, as you say. Let's leave it there. We can't help her now, can we?"

I began to pace about, looking as fierce as possible. "You've mentioned slanderous talk about me. I find this vexing. I must fight these libels."

Pyatt sighed with relief. "I didn't really believe what I heard," he said, lying little worm.

"I need money to prove my case," I added. "Litigation is expensive."

"You mean to sue?"

"If I can catch someone out, yes. And I surely aim to catch someone." I stepped up to Pyatt. "I've helped you, Mr. Pyatt," I said. "Now you help me. Five hundred dollars will do it. Two-fifty now, the rest when I catch myself a big fish."

The meaning behind my words was grasped by the worm immediately. He didn't even protest.

It was the commencement of a fairly lucrative association. Strange how muttonheaded fear can make a man who's got something to lose.

## II

Christmas came. I considered a trip home to Quebec, and later had cause to regret not having undertaken such a vacation.

The year of 1881—a cruel and unjust year in my life—began with heavy snowfalls, a freezing wind off the lake, and an emergency call to the home of Mr. Joseph Martin of 129 West Thirteenth Street. Had I paid my respects to my family as planned, never should I have made that fatal mission to the Martin household.

I'd known Martin for a few months previous. He was a furrier. He retailed for the Pollux Fur Store in the city, from which I purchased a fine coat in October. Martin fitted me up himself and, introduced, became my patient.

On the evening of January 3rd he sent round a messenger. Mrs. Martin had taken ill—would I get there as soon as possible? I hadn't met his wife before; had I done so, I reckon I would have told the messenger to go to Hades.

Mrs. Martin was all fat—one of those women who drape themselves about on settles throughout the day, eating sweet-meats and gossiping. Her body was a study in fat, a great mound of soft dripping no stay invented by man could stop from wob-bling. Her face was a picture of monstrosity—sharp weeny fea-tures buried in more fat, blubber lips painted crimson and mov-ing endlessly as she chirped her driveling observations.

Her January indisposition was little more than indigestion—over-indulgence throughout the Christmas festivities, I had no doubt. I prescribed and the ache eased in her great fat gut. My fee was twenty dollars. It was a high demand, I agree; but Martin had the cash in the bank, and I'd administered to his repulsive she-male.

Yet Martin must have been a Jew or something, because he just wouldn't pay. I sent him several fee notes during the month, but to no avail. Not a word did I hear for months and months.

Bad publicity had come my way as a direct result of the trial of Black Bitch Sal. My rightful acquittal did nothing to restore to me the many patients I lost upon my arrest. Frank Pyatt, of course, had informed me about the loose talk in circulation. I made determined efforts to establish the identity of these tongue-waggers, but vermin tend to scurry back into their hidey-holes when they appreciate the hawk is on his way. Frus-trated and dejected, I returned to the sweet embrace of narcot-ics at the den of Yen Hock Herbert.

I'd been disciplining myself since the inquiry into Black Bitch Sal, so the return to opium savaged me at first. A shirt-cuff bauble became a plate of gold, the reflected glint of the burner a mirror of visions, and recollections of Miss Mary Stack an eerie nightmare. Then my system absorbed without complaint, and I once again dreamed those soothing dreams of nothingness.

Summer came. My practice lay partly dormant, but I sub-sisted on a combination of cash: my personal savings, my allow-ance from Quebec, and the Pyatt contribution. This, however, couldn't go on—opium was expensive and had to be obtained. More dollars were required to satisfy my craving, and I knew full well the horrors ahead should I be shut off from my daily supply of narcotics.

If any man say that the habit of drug-taking does not lead to the commission of a dishonest act, I shall say you are advised by either a fool or a liar. I speak from practical experience, and I know what I'm talking about!

The happy slumbers at Yen Hock Herbert's caused me to perpetrate a serious fraud upon the populace. This I readily admit. What I was forced to do was, to my way of thinking, the most unforgivable of my various actions. You, sir, would doubt-less reject my confession, to screech about the abortions and assassinations I have also perpetrated. Humbug, sir—utter hum-bug! The inducement of a miscarriage requires a proper ap-plication of medical skill, and only an antiquated oath restricts good sense on the majority of occasions. Murder? Many killings are murder. What right have you to blast a man asunder in the name of war? What right has the state to deliberately end the life of a subject in the name of justice? Expediency—that cry will come out in both cases. Quite right—and expediency and good cause make the likes of myself destroy human life.

Fraud, on the other hand, is quite different. Governors and recent Presidents have obtained their positions solely upon a foundation of calculated fraud. And once in power, the deceit is continued. Were it not, soon would they be dispossessed of office. Yet I remain scandalized by all thought of fraud. . . .

The fraud I envisaged, the deceit I set in motion, was simple. Cures for epilepsy are scarce and chiefly bogus. So I devised a remote remedy guaranteed to check the lunatic frenzies, and advertised this nonsense in the Chicago *Tribune* (a paper which later sought to revenge itself upon me).

My nostrum—the ingredients of which sheer embarrassment precludes me from mentioning—picked up and sold. The sick are like voters—they'll swallow anything.

Early the following February, I was in my surgery filling tinted bottles with the rubbish I was now obliged to sell, when the door swept open. I didn't look up, but I knew my visitor was of the fairer sex by the block-heel sound of her shoes.

"May I speak with Dr. Cream?" asked a soft voice.

I raised my head, and there before me stood the most delightful lady I'd ever encountered. She had the face and complexion of an angel—free from paint—and her eyes were "veritable pools of delight."

"At your service, mamselle," says I, stepping round.

"Oh! So you're the doctor? You're not what I imagined." And she smiled beautifully.

"Well, I won't be asking what you expected," I said, "in case I don't like the answer."

She laughed—a musical sound. Hell's fire, here was one peach of a woman!

"I've come about your famous recommendation," she said, those blue-green eyes fixing me, turning me into a boneless fish.

"You don't look one bit sick to me, mamselle," I said. "No recommendation needed for you, I'd say. Just keep on living and give a lot of folk great happiness."

She gave a little curtsy, looking me up and down like a hussy.

"Don't tell me you suffer from epilepsy or St. Vitus?" I added.

"No."

"Just give the boys the trembles from time to time, eh?"

She blushed—but I could tell she liked me and my way of talking.

"It's not like that at all, sir."

"No? What a shame for the boys, then."

"I'm a married woman. And I'm here on account of my poor husband."

She surprised me.

"Is that so? And what ails the fortunate spouse of so perfect a flower?"

"Mr. Stott suffers dreadfully from the fits, Doctor. Has done so for most of his dear life."

"I see. May I ask the age of the good gentleman, Mrs. Stott?"

"Sixty-one last fall."

I put thirty years between husband and wife.

"Children?"

"No."

As I'd imagined. I began to note her answers in a pocket book.

"I'm sorry to be personal—but how long have you been married, Mrs. Stott?"

"Ten years—almost eleven."

Ten years married to a nerve-jangler old enough to be her father. No wonder she was free with the eyes—she was fair busting for what the old man couldn't give her.

"Where do you live, Mrs. Stott?"

"Garden Prairie—Boone County."

"You've come a long way to see me!"

"My husband's desperate, sir."

Not as desperate as his wife, I wagered.

"What does your husband do for a living, Mrs. Stott?"

"He's a station agent for the Northwestern." She hesitated and then went on: "I know it's humble work, sir—but we can pay for our needs."

"I'm sure you can!"

I knew what I wanted, and that she'd oblige. It had nothing to do with money.

I busied myself at the surgery counter for a while and let her watch me prepare a mixture.

"Give Mr. Stott this," I said, handing her the small opaque bottle. "He's to take a large spoonful morning and night."

"What is it?" she asked, examining the bottle. It had no label.

"Black magic."

"There's not much here. It won't last very long."

"That's twelve dollars' worth. Can you afford any more at the moment?"

"Twelve dollars! But your advertisement said only five."

"Your husband's case is special. I've been obliged to add further costly ingredients."

"Is this the treatment?"

"No. More will be required. When the bottle's finished, no doubt I'll see you again."

"And I'll pay another twelve dollars?"

"Well, we'll have to see about that. Could be—I'm no charity. But I reckon I might feel well disposed toward a fine lady like yourself—all depending. . . ."

"Depending on what, Dr. Cream?" A funny little smile on her face.

"We're both old enough to appreciate what I'm talking about, Mrs. Stott."

130

She treated me to that all-over examination again and then shook her head.

"You don't mince words, do you?"

"No. Would you rather that I did?"

"I guess not. I think I might grow to like you, Doctor. You an educated man and all." She gathered up her parasol, and I saw her to the door. "I'll call round Tuesday next—if that's convenient."

"I'll be here, Mrs. Stott. Meanwhile, keep a sharp eye on Mr. Stott's condition."

Her curious half-smile and she was gone.

Tuesday morning I received a telegraph to the effect that Mrs. Stott wished to meet me at the Wells Street rail depot in the city. I wondered about the chosen rendezvous, but, being as itchy as I was to resume acquaintance with this startling woman, fell along with her wishes. The telegraph mentioned that she was to be found at the hutment of a Mr. Nordstrand, at the end of terminus five.

I took a cab all the way, made inquiries, and took directions. Nordstrand's name was affixed to the shed door. It seemed he was a brakeman for the railroad. Hell—was I mixing with low-down company!

No matter, Mrs. Stott was waiting inside, and there was no sign of Brakeman Nordstrand.

"Who's lent us this palace?" I asked Mrs. Stott. The hut was filthy and smelly.

"Frank's a friend of my husband." She looked ill at ease.

"Why meet here?"

"I'm due to call at your offices at eleven with Daniel's cousin —my husband's second cousin. I'm due to meet her outside the Rush college."

"Who's this?"

"Mary Dunlap. She wants for me to consult Professor Haines at the medical institute concerning Daniel. I told her about you, but she still would like to meet you, Doctor."

"Call me Thomas."

"Call me Julia."

"All settled, Julia. Now—you and I walk out of this shack and pick up this cousin. I'll take you to the Rush. I won't come in —I've heard of Haines and I know he's got prejudice concerning Canadians, so I'll leave you with the old boffin, and then I'll treat you and Mary What's-it to lunch. How's that?"

Julia relaxed a bit. God knows what fears she'd had in any case. . . .

"You're a big man, Thomas Cream. I like big men. They're generous-natured."

Happy as a hog with his back scratched, we walked out.

I'll leave the rest of that day. Nothing of concern occurred— excepting the fact that this Brakeman Nordstrand and Mary Dunlap played their feeble roles in a later drama. So did Boffin Haines, nasty old miserable that he was.

During February my passions, greatly aroused, continued to remain unsatisfied. Julia Stott knew I had a free purse into which she could delve, and so she skinned me fine: hats and laces, bows and boots, chokers and fancy stuff of every kind. The milliners made a fortune. But her excuses and reasons for not delivering the goods agreed came fast and furious, and the more broke I became, the less inclined was I to swallow the apple. Meanwhile, Daniel Stott grew fat on my mixtures.

But I felt disinclined to remain the sailor to Julia's judie, and I accordingly planned an irreversible encounter.

I arranged it so that she came for medicine late at my surgery. I had ascertained that a breakdown on the Garden Prairie line had occurred, and informed Julia of this event while we indulged ourselves over a bottle of whiskey.

"How do I get home? Daniel will be awful worried."

"No home for you tonight. Daniel'll have to hop the sleepers if he wants to know how you are faring."

She sighed, and resistance collapsed all of a once.

"Where do I sleep, Doctor?"

"With me."

"You don't mince . . ."

"You've said that before. No, I don't!"

And a couch in my rear office—good for up to four hundred

pounds, claimed the makers—stood the test and justified the guarantee.

"You're a fine, fine man!" said Mrs. Julia Stott at conclusion.

"And you've undergone a birth of some difficulty," I said bitterly. She had told me that she had no children. Was there no end to the scheming lies of women?

## III

Angered by the lie of Julia Stott, I rendered myself unanswering to her calls and telegraphs for more than a week. But, flesh being as weak as it is, my dreaming moments and waking days plagued me with indelicate thoughts concerning this damsel. I was obsessed. I was besotted.

And so we met and continued to meet at the Wells Street depot, then to repair to the seclusion of either my surgery or my rooms. In satisfying her raging lust after so many years, I unleashed a panther. Once only had she splayed her body to a man —ten years back, when the feeble seeds of her hogger husband bore fruit to inflict upon the world a sickly child. Amy Stott— nine years old, with the brain of a guinea pig, a pasty-faced, flaxen-haired creature forever stuffing strip candy into her cruel little mouth. Once a week Julia brought to the city this revolting reminder of her springtime. Invited to play the part of uncle, I was obliged to saturate the puny adder with attention, jokes, and more candy. I formed the view that King Herod might have been a man after my own heart.

During the other visits of Julia Stott, ours was a tense arrangement. Frantic goings-on. Extreme and joint-twisting positions. One hot breath blown into another. The lion welded into the howling she-cat. March—April—May, on it went. . . .

And indeed I was the lion—my prowess and burly power enveloped Julia Stott, enshrined her within a cavern of carnal paradise. To this woman I was magnificent; the fiery hair on my head was receding only to reveal the nobility of my brow, and bad sight had endowed me with gimlet eyes. A series of extreme headaches instilled a violence into my passionate display that was quite animal.

"God save me!" was her frequent cry.

All should have been rosy, and was not. Still came the "treat" trips of the squeaking Amy, an event guaranteed to snip off any possibility of private session with her mother, and therefore plunge me into the depths of despair.

"Daniel says it's good for her," explained Julia.

Damn Daniel! Damn and blast his fawning child! The pair of them began to rile me sore. Did the father send the child to spy and then report? Did he envisage her as a chaperone to his own wife? Perhaps he knew his lot was done by reason of his debility, and that his woman had a suitor intent upon coaxing her away from his own senile embraces? Perhaps he planned to dissolve the marriage by divorce—to point the finger at myself and take me for every dollar I had? Very possible.

I began to feel threatened. I sometimes imagined a look in the daughter's eye that implied a cunning recognition of what was about. I suddenly realized that I must resolve this awkward state of affairs.

"Were you free, would you come to me?" I asked Julia. She was utterly spent. It was, I reasoned, a good psychological moment.

"You know that I would, Tittle Tom!" was her reply.

Good enough an answer.

"You appreciate that Daniel's life expectancy is short, m'dear?" I said two afternoons later. Again we were in bed at the time.

"I suppose so."

"Suddenly—very suddenly—he could pass away."

"Poor Daniel . . ."

"Yes. But is he insured?"

"Insured?"

"Yes, insured. You're a young woman, he's an old man— surely the company has given him life coverage?"

"He's never mentioned it. Is it important, then?"

"Of course. For your sake. I'm thinking only of you, my little sugar plum. But we must think of you, mustn't we . . . ?"

We slithered about and fondled for a while.

"I'll see to it. I'll need your signature," I added at some stage of the proceedings.

I engineered my plan with some degree of thought. Never having met Daniel Stott, and being disinclined to make his acquaintance at so late a stage, I proposed to remain a remote prescriber of medicines. However, I wanted the views of someone other than his wife to describe to me a typical fit this epileptic suffered. Hence I invited once again Mary Dunlap as my guest to luncheon. I made the appropriate impression upon the lady, and she commenced visiting my surgery for her private female complaint. From her I ascertained that Daniel Stott became subjected to violent seizures on a regular basis.

I further visited the home of Mrs. M'Clellan—a lady I'd known for times on and off—for she had recently lost her own spouse in circumstances pertaining to the condition of Daniel Stott. A fine and intelligent woman, Mrs. M'Clellan.

Being scary of using Frank Pyatt's establishment for the making up of any complicated dose, I next took to obliging the firm of Buck and Rayner's for customary requirements—making a point of showing myself to their prescription clerk.

The bow was strung. I had now only to notch the arrow.

IV

I waited until Friday, June 11th—last day in a week of three visits from Julia, and none in the company of the beastly offspring.

I had acquired certain proposal forms from the life-insurers, and was led to believe that the signing by the wife was sufficient to instantize a policy to the jig of fourteen thousand dollars. What lies these insurance sharks will tell for the smallest premium down!

Julia signed without question, and we dallied a spell on my

surgery couch. She was due to take the five-eight to Garden Prairie and I wanted for her to pay a call on Buck and Rayner's, so I held back my instincts on this occasion.

"No?" Julia complained.

"Would that we could, my little cotton bud," I replied, adjusting my cravat. "But you must away; and I'll prescribe more salts for poor Daniel. You must take my note round to the chemist's."

"But he's still got some left from Tuesday," came the interruption.

"I know, I know. But I shan't be seeing you until Wednesday next, so it's important we supply him a good mixture for to carry him through until then." I sounded urgent, and she didn't argue.

I dictated the prescription and gave to her a small package. When she finished writing, I checked her piece of paper.

"Make sure they put in the . . ." But there I left it. A better idea came into my head.

"Never mind, sweetness. You go round there now. Get what's written made up, and bring the mixture here. I want to inspect it, you know. I don't know much about this Buck and Rayner's outfit; better if I inspect their work personal."

Julia left.

She returned pretty soon, out of breath, and saying that Buck and Rayner's were not familiar with my custom. What nonsense!

But she had the medicine, a square bottle of brownish liquid. I took it from her and repaired into the small room at the back. Taking out the stopper, I had a good sniff. They had followed my instructions—a small dab proved to me that sugar and calomel were within. In all, I added over two grains of strychnine —a massive dosage on all accounts, but I felt no inclination to cause unnecessary distress to the poor man. I bore him no grudge—I'd never even met the fellow. Why should I add pain to his elimination?

"Here you are, honey-bee," I said when I returned to the front room and gave Julia the mixture. "See that he drinks it tonight."

136

I think she must have guessed something, for she studied the square bottle with unusual concentration.

"It's all right, isn't it?" she asked of me suddenly.

"But of course, my swallow. It will help make him sleep."

"I love him after a fashion, you know," Julia said wistfully.

"Like a mother loves her crippled child," I returned. This was no time for sentimentality.

"Perhaps. But he's a good man, Thomas. And he depends on me."

"So much, I daresay, that he'll never let you go."

"You wish him dead!"

"No—I wish only you, love of my life."

"Oh, Thomas!" and she flung herself at me.

"You've got a train to catch," I whispered more than once during our embracing.

"Promise me something, dear Thomas," Julia said, gathering up her bibs and bobs, ready to leave. "Promise me that you'll never hurt poor Daniel. You won't, I beg of you. . . . It would be like hurting a child. Just be patient!"

"Just so," says I. "Have no fear—never will your good husband suffer pain at my hands. And I'll swear to that, if you think me such a knave!"

Hurting a child? Greater justice might have I served had the awful Amy become the recipient of Daniel's "cocktail." Although in her case a lessening of the dose might well have been justified, just to hear the brat squawk awhile. . . .

I understood later that Daniel Stott died some twenty minutes following application of his medicine. Greatly disturbed, I tried to figure out what had gone amiss. I concluded that he must have taken much less than the entirety of the bottle. For all time the tardiness of his death has bewildered me.


V


The more I thought about the matter, the more convinced did I become that Messrs. Buck and Rayner had bungled dreadfully. Nux Vomica had always been an ingredient in my prescription for epilepsy, and this included dosages I had prepared for Daniel Stott. That being the case, the quantity of the poison within his body coupled with the minor grainage Buck and Rayner's were instructed to put in the final dose, together with my own secretly administered amount, should have laid the unfortunate Stott low within a single convulsion. Yet he survived more than a quarter of an hour. Buck and Rayner's must be responsible for this catastrophe.

It was, naturally enough, Julia Stott who informed me of what had occurred. And her tears were genuine as she described his last moments.

"Damn-fool chemists," I told her. "You must sue them for every penny."

"What was in that medicine, Thomas?" she cried.

"The hand of inexperience," says I. "Idiot of a prescription clerk, I've no doubt. We'll lash 'em in the law courts, dear girl. Mark my words!"

She looked uncertain. "Can we really do that?"

"Yes. Mop up your tears, woman. We can and we will. I'm not the one to let such carelessness pass unpaid."

Still she dithered. "I don't want trouble, Thomas!"

"Rubbish. We'll scare the wits out of them. You leave this to me!"

For I had decided upon a positive plan of action.

# BLACK WIDOW

## I

Armed with power of attorney from Julia Stott, I first wrote firmly to Messrs. Buck and Rayner, pointing out their negligence. That company saw fit to ignore my correspondence in a fashion ignorant enough to have been expected.

And so I made direct approach to the authorities. First I wrote and telegraphed Coroner Whitemen of Boone County. I insisted that the exhumation of my late patient Daniel Stott take place immediately, for I had good cause to suspicion the over-prescription of a lethal poison and held the druggist in question responsible.

Coroner Whitemen, being as lazy as any other servant of the public, remained silent. Many times did I send him communications, yet this latter-day dinosaur sat on his butt. . . .

I now had little option other than to inform the appropriate district attorney of my views, and I sent to him a complete report and history of my dealings with the deceased. Action at last! Two days later I received a confirmation that the cadaver had been disinterred, and the stomach removed for examination. I could foresee Messrs. Buck and Rayner presenting a considerable settlement in favor of Julia for matters to be hushed up.

Since I was now churning out letters, I decided to resume

contact with Joseph Martin. His owing me what he did—albeit only twenty dollars—had become a nagging affair; I was not proposing to let the smarmy little shyster off the hook, and I wrote him in the most straightforward manner.

He returned my letter, torn into pieces and without comment.

Add to this, Frank Gridley, my landlord, informed me that Mrs. Martin had been lately passing certain opinions concerning myself and my respectability as a doctor of medicine. Well, can you imagine my ire? That bloated witch daring to speak ill of anyone at all!

My next letter, composed under the influence of a mild narcotic, went to Mrs. Martin. Little did I dream that its content should lead to so much adversity. I merely stated that this she-devil and her creepy children were as syphilitic as the father of the house, and that they would all do well to shut their mouths and pay their debts before slandering others. I added that I was able to prove what I said about them.

I'll own that what I said was untrue—but there are times when the truth must be curved a mite in order to get things home to stupid people like the Martins. . . . And for this reason I sent yet another letter, warning Joseph Martin to keep a guard on the tongue of his damned vixen of a low wife.

Frank Gridley heard through a friend that the Martin household was all of a buzz as a result of receiving my communications, so I determined to finalize the issue with a spate of invective. On the Thursday I posted them three cards in all, from West Side station. I chose cards because they'd be open for the world to read before being destroyed by the recipients. I repeatedly warned Martin to shut his wife's foul mouth, and declared that I had been made aware of the fact Mr. Martin was no gentleman, but a scoundrel who had left a bastard child back in England, for which reason he'd been obliged to quit that country and inflict himself upon the good people of Chicago.

Of course, I signed all of this correspondence with either my name or initials—I had nothing to fear, was the thought; yet what a holocaust ensued! Glory be—next thing I knew was a visitation from the city police, asking questions, making accusations, and waving the letters under my nose like they were the conclusions of Professor Darwin. A fine from one to five hundred, they promised me, unless they managed a sentence of one to ten jail. Most excited and impertinent, although I explained to these gentlemen the nature of the unpaid debt and the rantings of Martin's she-male.

Two days later the peace officers brought me in on a warrant, like some criminal to the Criminal Courthouse, barely giving me chance to fix my bail.

Mary M'Clellan came down to the courtroom after delivery of a note I was obliged to scribble in haste. This good lady knew me for what I was—she was a confidante as well as a patient in the past. She also possessed a fair deal of loot in the bank, and stood me recognizance to the jig of over a thousand. Then they let me go—case pending.

They say troubles come by the sackload, and that's fair comment. I've made mention of the *Tribune*. Well, that journal took the notion to adopt a course of persecution in my case. Upon the selfsame day did some hack reporter inform the public of my embarrassment. "Dr. Cream," said this vicious article, as if my qualifications in themselves were suspect; and "in the toils again, with a prospect of being rewarded according to his just deserts" for the sending of "scurrilous postal cards." The paper made mention of my recent acquittal in the case of Black Bitch Sal as if the wrong party had gone to the pen. What right have these dirt-borers to say such things? What's more, they rounded off the lying passage by suggesting that hanging a man for what I'd done might be too good for the likes of me. I can't recall the exact words, but that was the import. . . .

Not too good. And worse round the corner.

Boone County lawmen had been seeing Julia Stott in the meantime, browbeating the sweet fool into a lot of talk. I can imagine the method of inquiry employed. In your own country, sir, the constabulary hop around and take notes—as if, scared to death, a suspect says something to self-incriminate. Not so in Illinois; the bulls out there make up their tiny minds in advance, shake and shout a person half to death, get or imagine what they require, and then clinch the lot with putrid lies in the courthouse.

They must have worked on poor Julia pretty good, because

the next thing I knew was this frantic telegraph. She was frightened and had told all to the authorities. That's all she said, but I guessed she'd shot them the full line about the medicine, and the taking of the same by her husband. I was in bad trouble—this I sensed at once—and I was in a state where they'll hang a man for looking unshaved. I had no option but to skip it back to Canada. . . .

## II

I took the ferry to Ontario and journeyed to Belle River near the township of Windsor, armed only with my medical bag and a scraping of dollars.

Belle River was not for princes: bums and dodgers wherever you looked, mud streets and shacks unfit for a dog.

But I had a refuge, and across the water lay more trouble than I reckoned able to cope with; I was "runaway"—Old Jim Crow with a white face.

I put up at the saloon, and thought about what I should do next. All roads led to Quebec and the security of my family. I'd move out in a day or two. Meanwhile, I'd stick to my room and stare at my woes through the bottom of a liquor glass.

Two short turnings of the clock proved to be my freedom. I'd never dreamed that a U.S. lawman could slip across the frontier with such ease—I was under the impression that I was safe within Britannia's cold embrace.

So when Sheriff Abraham Tennyson Ames presented himself in the doorway, stepped right up to me, and said: "You're a long way from home, Doc," I damn near fainted away.

"You must be mistaken," says I, rising from my bed.

"Not so."

"My name's Curtis."

"Your name's Thomas Neill Cream, and you're coming along with me."

"You've no rights—you're in the wrong country, friend!"

"State of Illinois is hand in glove with this province, Doc. But

I'll sit and drink with you until the formalities are over, if that's what you're wanting. . . ."

Sheriff Ames had this air about him. I gave him less than thirty years, looking into the wind-browned face, but he had this authority. He never stopped smiling, so that his teeth shone as bright and hard as his eyes.

"And I can get the jurisdiction making sure you don't leave this place, Doc," he finished.

He wasn't telling lies.

"How about it, Doc?"

"I don't want extradition," I said. Such news would be quickly relayed to Quebec.

Sheriff Ames made a little bow. "Most thankful to you, Doc. Saves me the paperwork."

I pulled on my coat and corked the bottle of whiskey.

"I'll have to pack up," I muttered.

"Sure. But before you do"—Ames came closer—"may I just relieve you of your Remington?"

"My what?"

"Information tells me you sport an over-and-under. Hate there to be an accident, Doc." The smile had faded.

I handed over my derringer.

"Best for both of us, Doc. Thank you!" The smile returned. "These toys sometimes go off. Can be nasty then—might spoil your whole day!"

He pulled up the barrels and extracted the cartridges.

"Fine. Go ahead and pack your grip, Doc."

I had no choice. Sheriff Ames' Colt six-shooter was plain to be seen.


III


The same train and the same steamer, followed by boxcar passage to Belvidere.

Boone County was new to me, and I looked out of a chink in

the buckboard as we passed through Garden Prairie, home of the *maison* Stott.

Sheriff Ames said virtually nothing throughout this ripping trip—just smiled and nodded whenever I addressed him.

"Where we going?" I asked at one stage.

"Jail."

That's how it was.

The train pulled into Belvidere after dark, and the car door was slid open from the outside. Two uniformed police helped us down, and I was relieved of my cases. Then one of them struck me in the mouth.

"What did he do that for?" I asked Sheriff Ames as we walked across the line and into the station.

"Could be he thinks you're a murdering sonofabitch, Doc. Don't know. Why don't you ask him? If he hits you again, my theory's proved right."

I fell silent, angered more by Ames' interminable smile than the blow.

They took me to the town jail and placed me in the first cell. Two bunks, small light from a top window, and a lot of bars.

They fed me a thin steak and cold beans on a tin plate one hour later, told me to shut my mouth, and thereafter left me to rot for the night.

In the morning I asked to see a lawyer. But the jailor was the local idiot and just sniggered and loaned me a Bible. Later he gave me pen and paper, and I wrote down the name of the attorneys I desired. He studied the paper upside down, screwed it into a ball, and stuffed it into his vest pocket.

For five days I read the Good Book provided, seeking solace. I despaired of my written message to the outside for help, and was thus greatly surprised when keys rattled in the lock and the Hon. Derek Munn came in.

"Dr. Cream?"

Stupid question—no one else was with me. Munn didn't take my proffered hand.

"Six hundred dollars," said Munn, peering into the cell bucket with strange interest.

"What for?"

"Name's Munn. Six hundred is the starter fee. If you've got it, we'll talk. If you haven't, I'll waste no more of our time. Got it? Good!" He perched himself on the opposite bunk, a large fleshy man about sixty, with years of hard living in his face. Silver hair covered his crown in a futile attempt to disguise baldness. I noted that his hands shook like a liquor merchant's, and that he had dirty fingernails.

"She's made a statement—she's going to see you hang to save her own neck," said Munn.

"Who?"

"The Stott woman—your paramour. She's top witness for the People. And you're standing on the trap ready to go. . . ."

"What's she said?"

"No idea. But Chase—I mean, Senator Fuller has informed me of her likely testimony."

"Fuller?"

"Senator Chase Fuller. One of the finest. A great and worthy man. A true son of the soil. One of my best friends—went to law school together. An upstanding figure of wisdom and finesse. That's old Chasey Fuller for you, that is!"

"What's he got to do with my difficulties?"

"A good deal—he's prosecuting you."

So it was that I became a fly in the political web. On the one side, I had sought the services of Derek Munn, a man I had the error to judge sound, a pursuer of lost causes (lost in the main due to his own ineptitude), a political fixer and legal charlatan —a man so possessed by his public image that it was rumored he avoided natural bodily functions in case he be reported human.

On the other side, I was to be pilloried by Chase Fuller and the Coon establishment. Chase Fuller I'll ignore—but the Coons were something different. Two brothers: Richard Coon, State's Attorney and puppet; Arthur Coon, creepy tag-along without brain or bowel.

So it was that my trial executives hailed from beyond the Dark Ages. . . .

145

# IV

Charlie Warren was sneaked into my cell one month later, and I suppose I was pleased to see him. At my trial Coon lied to say that Warren was with me from the start; Warren was a recruited spy, put in to bend my mouth much later.

Warren claimed proudly that he was a hotel sneak-thief, and, so desperate for companionship had I become, I believed the rascal. And such tales he spun me!

I told him something of myself and the injustices I now faced, but I chose my words with care lest the idiot jailor be lurking within the vicinity and be less of a cretin than he appeared. Never, never, never did I utter a word as to the relationship twixt Julia Stott and myself!

"Plead guilty to the second degree," ventured Munn during August. "The Stott woman's in jail, too—she'll fall in with a confession to suit you if you see sense, Doctor."

"Nonsense!"

"If you don't, she'll oblige the D.A. with a version to give you a lump in the throat. If you follow me . . ."

"I follow. But she's the one who gave her husband the stuff —and the mixture was made up by Buck and Rayner's. The two of them killed her husband. Not me, Mr. Munn—not me!"

"Damn the business," said Munn and withdrew.

He came again a week later, huffing with excitement. He insisted that the jailor remove Warren before speaking to me.

"Sign this," says he when the cell was cleared.

A thick manuscript, fourteen or fifteen pages and tied with a ribbon.

"What is it?"

"Just sign it. I'll tell you what it is in a moment."

I turned the vellum over in my hands. "Tell me first what it is."

146

"It's your confession, prepared by myself. Tears at the heart-strings. Any jury goes for the love of a good man for a woman, even if he has to kill her husband. Might save your neck, Doctor."

I flung the document down on the floor and kicked it across the cell.

"So much for that, Mr. Munn. No confessions."

The Hon. Derek Munn shrugged his shoulders.

"So be it," he said, and called for the jailor to let him out.

I'll tell you something, Cogswell. Never place yourself wholly in the hands of an attorney—never trust him an inch. Listen to what he has to say, but then digest it in your mind carefully. Lawyers are no more than trained liars, flim-flam triple-talkers who'll sell you down the river for sixpence. Place no credence in their trumpery. . . .

They kept me locked up in the Belvidere jail until the 20th September. Once I wrote an application for bail, but Charlie Warren said it wasn't worth the weight of the paper, and he was right.

Charlie Warren never seemed to come up for trial, and no lawyer attended upon him throughout the long weeks. I guess this should have made me suspicious, but I was too preoccupied with the assembling of my own witnesses, a list of whom I furnished to Derek Munn for interview. I analyzed the case for the People with some care. I concluded that no charge of willful murder could possibly endure. How could the People rely upon the testimony of Julia Stott, a witness they themselves held to be my accomplice, a person on the same murder rap as myself?

## V

Of course, the People took the precaution of indicting me first and separately from Julia Stott. As it transpired, they'd made a deal with her, Senator Fuller and his gaggle of assistants: if she spoke up against me in the manner they desired, no further proceedings were to lie against her. Lawyers' double-dealing once again.

Sheriff Ames escorted me to the Circuit Court on the morning of the 20th.

"Hello there, Bram!" called out the assembled crowd as we arrived. Bram Ames was clearly a very popular man, and he'd fixed his smile sweet and youthful for the occasion.

Derek Munn was sitting behind a small table on the left of the courtroom, and the table was bare. Derek Munn distinguished himself in the state by never employing the services of a law book.

An empty chair was placed on Munn's right hand. My handcuffs were removed, and I sat myself down.

Senator Fuller made a bold entry, followed by the Coons, and the prosecuting team was greeted by a cheer from the multitude.

"When's the hanging, Chase?" came a shout.

"After the trial, gentlemen!"

Such catcalls made me nervous.

Then somebody banged a table with a gavel, a door opened behind the bench, and in came the judge, robed in black like a gravedigger.

Judge C. Kellum was an old man—entirely too old. Judge Kellum had been trying criminal cases for nigh on forty years, which was about twenty years too long. Judge Kellum knew as little of the niceties of the law as Derek Munn, and he had all the prejudices of Fuller and the Coon brothers put together. Only in the shape of your own Hawkins have I faced so bigoted a tribunal.

Judge C. Kellum had a speech impediment and a left eye that watered almost continuously—an old saber wound, I understand. Throughout the finding of my jury—and that took Munn and Fuller five whole hours—Judge Kellum mopped his eye and made comments. He had in front of him a volume of legal tags and maxims, from which he quoted whenever he could. As a result, most of what he said during the sum of my trial was incomprehensible.

State's Attorney Coon opened the case for the People, and from the outset he told the jury that I had murdered Daniel

Stott as a means to be able to blackmail Buck and Rayner's—to blame the druggists for the death, suggest incompetence, and so obtain compensation. What nonsense!

Coon went on to submit that I and Julia Stott had indulged in an illicit relationship, and that he hoped to prove adultery. So Julia had spilled the beans in that respect. . . .

Derek Munn followed Coon to address the jurymen—a lengthy speech in flowery terms wherein he stated that we should prove that the wrong person was being tried for murder.

Who had he in mind? Surely not Julia . . . ? And there could be no suggestion that Buck and Rayner deliberately poisoned Daniel Stott.

Munn's jawing puzzled me.


## VI


The hearing was resumed at eight next morning, and the crowd was pretty excitable, expecting great things from the witnesses.

Judge Kellum was late arriving, and made his excuses in Latin. Derek Munn told me he was hung-over from the night before and showed me his tongue. Fuller and Coon regaled a Chicago *Tribune* correspondent with dirty stories and snide comments aimed at myself and Julia Stott.

Fuller examined three witnesses to the effect that Daniel Stott had been poisoned unto death by three 394-1000 grains of strychnine, of which two 622-1000 had been in the medicine prepared through Buck and Rayner's. I recall the amounts distinctly, because they were impossible. Coroner Whitemen exhibited my correspondence and told the jury about my other communications. He had no ax to grind, and told the truth. Not so Buck and Rayner's prescription clerk and James Rayner himself; both men claimed that I had never dealt with their company before—a blatant lie—and both men asserted that in their opinion I had threatened the company without lawful justification.

Sheriff Ames stepped forward to testify next, removing his hat and grinning while he took the oath.

"And you say the defendant was armed when you arrested him, Bram?"

"He surely was. Kept his gun in a handy place."

"Think he might use it, Sheriff?"

"Objection!" squawked Derek Munn from beside me. First time he'd spoken that day.

"Objection out of order and over-ruled," said Judge Kellum.

"Think he'd use it, Bram?" Fuller asked again.

"Surely did. Took it off him straightaway."

"Plainly a dangerous criminal," said Judge Kellum.

"So the People intend to prove," added Fuller.

"So the Defense will show otherwise," cried Derek Munn.

"You're out of order again, Mr. Munn," said Judge Kellum. "You must not interrupt during the examination of a witness."

When Julia Stott's name was called, such a hubbub arose from the spectators that Judge Kellum was obliged to pound the bench with his gavel.

"This is not a circus!" he lisped, handkerchief to his bad eye. "I must insist on order!"

"Order!" barked a court official, but it was some moments before the chatter died away.

I turned to watch Julia Stott walk up from the rear, craning my head to catch a glimpse of her through all the other bodies. She didn't come into view until she stepped onto the witness stand.

Recent time had ravaged her face, but she was neat and tidy in a green dress and matching hat with trimmings. She glanced at me as she took the Bible and compressed her lips. When she took the oath, I knew she was out to see me downed.

"You're admitting that you are an accessory after the fact to the murder of your husband, Daniel Stott. Is that not so, Mrs. Stott?" asked Coon.

She nodded.

"Let the witness speak out loud," Munn called out.

"The witness has made clear to the jury her answer to the question," said Judge Kellum. "Proceed."

"You're an accessory after the fact because you knew nothing of the killing decided in the mind of Dr. Cream until after that assassination took place, is that correct?"

"Yes." Her reply was barely audible.

"Your misdemeanor was doing nothing about the obvious—right?"

A nod. She was playing the sad and ashamed widow with great acting ability.

"But now you wish to make amends by telling the truth? Now you wish all God-fearing folk to know how you fell under the spell of this man and, so lured into the way of wickedness, want all to appreciate the consequences of temptation?"

"I do."

"And the portals of Heaven are seldom closed to the repentant, as we know. Now, Mrs. Stott, am I right in thinking you were first seduced by the defendant some six months back?"

"Yes."

"And that you began a sinful association with this man which endured until the death of your poor deceived husband?"

"Yes."

I nudged Derek Munn, and he left off holding his head in his hands to give me a baleful look.

"He can't get away with this line of questioning," I said.

"He sure can, with Judge Kellum presiding."

And so the State's Attorney was permitted to ask anything he chose and add his own comments without interruption. Coon just fed her the facts, and Julia Stott nodded or said yes.

"The defendant has been on criminal terms with yourself since you first saw him about his so-called nostrum?"

"Yes."

"You were never aware that this nostrum contained a poisonous substance?"

"Yes—I mean no."

"Of course you weren't—until it was too late. Now tell me this, Mrs. Stott: When you visited the doctor on June 11th, you obtained at his request a prescription from the distinguished firm of Buck and Rayner's? They filled it, and you took it back to the defendant?"

"Yes."

151

"And I think you saw him slip a little something else into it?"
"Yes."
"He did this furtively, at the back of his surgery, but you nevertheless saw his actions?"
"Yes."
"You returned home late that night, and later gave the medicine to your poor husband?"
"Yes."
"And he died in twenty minutes?"
She nodded.
"And in great agony?"
"Yes."
"Thank you, Mrs. Stott. I thank you on behalf of the citizens of Illinois for the courage of your testimony!"
Coon sat down and Munn rose to cross-examine.
"You've lied on your oath, Julia Stott. For the sake of your own soul, tell us now the truth!"
Kellum whacked the bench with his little hammer.
"What kind of a question is that, Mr. Munn?"
"I'll rephrase it, Your Honor. What I'm suggesting, Mrs. Stott, is that it was *you* who murdered your husband, that it is you who are now trying to fix the blame on Dr. Cream!"
Julia Stott gave a delicate smile and looked at the judge sorrowfully.
"You suggesting that Mrs. Stott's Lucrezia Borgia, Mr. Munn? Convince the jury of that fact, Mr. Munn, and I'll buy you a drink."
Roars of laughter followed.
"No more questions."
And Derek Munn sat down in a huff. I was trembling with rage.
"Who's this Grease Borgia?" Sheriff Ames asked from behind my right ear.

The black widow was followed by the offspring—diminutive Amy Stott, dressed up to kill in a white pinafore. The sight of her made me sick to my stomach. . . .

"Come and sit with me, Amy-girl." Judge Kellum beamed. "Come and keep an old man company!"

She dangled on his knee and he gave her some candy.

"Tell everybody what you told Mr. Fuller, Amy," Coon prompted.

Amy made a reply rendered impossible to understand by reason of her chewing.

"What was it Dr. Cream said to you about your mama, Amy?"

"Oh—he said he loved Mama and wanted her for his own and wanted to become my pa!"

"And I think you were present when your pa took nasty medicine and got sick?"

"Yes—he was awful sick."

"That's my girl," said Kellum, lowering her to the floor and pushing more candy into her sticky hand. "Off you go and play now."

Derek Munn was clearly barred from cross-examining the little wretch.

I'd not expected any of the next three witnesses called by the People. Mary M'Clellan, old and shaky, had been skillfully muddled by the prosecuting officers into saying that I'd been with her at her Warren Avenue address on the night of Daniel Stott's death. But that wasn't the end to it—no, sir—for Mary M'Clellan now claimed that I had been expecting news any minute of the death of Daniel Stott, and that I'd told her I knew the man to be poisoned. Fantastic!

"I'll give it to her, if you want," said Derek Munn when I'd explained what rubbish the old dame was talking. "But Kellum won't like it."

When Mary M'Clellan concluded her evidence, Munn slowly got to his feet.

"Your Honor," he began.

"What's this—what's this!" exclaimed the worthy judge. "Are you proposing to cross-examine this lady?"

"I am."

"Can't see why," and Kellum added something in Latin. "Anyway, you can keep your questions till the morning. It's after three and I've got a train to catch." He slapped down his gavel. "Court adjourned!"

No matter. I'd see Derek Munn in my cell that evening. I'd instruct him as to Mary M'Clellan—then he could pull her apart and expose the whole vicious conspiracy on the morrow. . . .

# OMNIA PRAESUMUNTER CONTRA
# SPOILIATOREM

## I

"Sign this." Derek Munn handed me a slip of paper. I looked at it—a banker's draft for six hundred and fifty dollars—and penned my name. "You'll be giving evidence yourself tomorrow," Munn added. He gathered up his coat as if to take his leave, and I sprang from my seat on the cell bunk.

"The M'Clellan woman . . ."

"Forget about her—I'll tell the jury she's too old to be believed."

"But Judge Kellum?"

"Put him out of your mind. By the time I get round to addressing the jury, he'll have forgotten what this case is all about. Fishing and retirement is all he thinks of these days!"

So much for my conference with my attorney.

The testimony of Mary M'Clellan went unchallenged—as did that of Frank Nordstrand, the Wells Street brakeman.

"I've seen the doc and Mrs. Stott plenty of times," says he. "Even loaned 'em my hut on occasion. Didn't know for what, naturally. If I'd known, wouldn't have done the lending— 'gainst company rules, see?"

But the final witness for the people it was who took my breath away: Charlie Warren. Up he pranced, looking important and manacled to a deputy sheriff.

"What the Devil!" I cried.

"Who's he?" asked Derek Munn.

"He's been my cellmate these past weeks!"

"What's he going to say, then?"

"How the Hell do I know!"

Charlie refused to swear on the Book. "It's against my religion, Judge. Been so since the day I was born."

"Witness excused," ordered Kellum. "Proceed."

"Charlie-boy," State's Attorney Coon began, "tell the jury what a bad lad you've been in your life."

"Sure will. I'm not ashamed to admit my shame, if you get me? I've been a thief and I've lechered after the sinful things of life. . . ."

"And now, Charlie?"

"Now? Now everything's changed. Now I'm truly repentant." Charlie Warren entwined his fingers and raised his eyes to the ceiling. "Now I've seen the wickedness of my ways. A great light has shone upon me. The wondrous love of that Great Shepherd in the sky has at last convinced me. Hallelujah, I say!"

"Well done, Charlie," Coon enthused.

"Proceed," Kellum said.

Coon approached the witness, patted him on the shoulder, and said: "You've been incarcerated with the doctor—sharing the same confinement. Has the doctor been saying things to you, Charlie?"

"He certainly has—dirty filthy things!"

Richard Coon pointed at me angrily. "What's he been saying, Charlie? Don't be afraid to tell us, now—we appreciate your embarrassment. . . ."

"Telling me 'bout his sleeping with a married woman—telling me 'bout the things they'd do to each other. I can't say what here, can I? There are ladies present!"

"So he confessed to you his illicit association, Charlie?"

"He did—and how he intended to have the woman to himself, come Hell or high water!"

" 'Acta exterior indecant interiora secreta,' " said Judge Kellum after consulting his book of tags.

Charlie Warren looked at him. "Don't think he said that, Judge."

"Did he tell you the name of this woman, Charlie?"

"Sure did, Mr. Coon. Said her name was Jemima Stott."

"Julia Stott," Coon corrected, and walked back to the Prosecution table.

"Your witness," he said to Derek Munn.

"No questions."

"But the man's a damn liar!" I yelled.

"Defendant will not interrupt due process, or I'll have him gagged," came the roar from the bench.

"That man's nothing but a hotel sneak-thief," I whispered to Munn.

"Well, he's sneaked on you this time," came the reply.

The People closed their case against me, and came my turn to present a version of events before the jurymen.

I gave my evidence slowly and concisely, masking all emotion; I wasn't prepared to snivel before these country flatlanders —I was a gentleman. Moreover, the People's arguments against me were ludicrous in the extreme.

I took the oath with due solemnity. Then Derek Munn sought to examine me in that roundabout method favored by lawyers, but I silenced him with a wave of the hand. I'd tell my story in my own fashion.

"Good people of Illinois," I said to the jury, "you have been humbugged by a series of crooked witnesses. Now you shall hear the truth!

"I am a physician qualified to practice the ancient art of medicine not only in the United States of America, but also in Canada and old Mother England herself. I am an honorable man—I defy anyone to say otherwise—and I have never been convicted of any criminal offense in my life. I am sober of habit and a scholar. Yet now I find myself unjustly accused of crime, and I am wounded to the quick.

"Mention has been made as to my sending scurrilous mail

through the Chicago post. This is so, and, indeed, I am at present on bail for this matter. . . ."

"And you skipped out!" one of the Coons chipped in.

"True—but I am innocent of that charge. And I intend to produce ten witnesses to prove that innocence. Then I shall sue the lying dogs who have brought this charge against me!"

"If the indictment's false, why skip out on your bail?" Judge Kellum asked me, his bad eye streaming.

"I'll own that I was foolish, sir."

" 'Omnia praesumunter contra spoiliatorem'—'all things are presumed against the wrongdoer'!" and he took to mopping his eye once more.

"Gentlemen . . ." I returned to the jury. "I knew Daniel Stott only as a patient. I doctored him about five or six months for epileptic fits. His was a terrible affliction, poor sad man, and I did what I could to ease the pain. In my nostrum I included minute doses of strychnine—the poison that killed him. Of course, I never put the strychnine in myself. I relied upon the druggist every time. And what has happened here must now be plain for all to see!

"Mrs. Stott has never been anything to me. To suggest that I have sported myself with this lady while her husband languished at home, a sick man, is a monstrous slander. I have never made love to Mrs. Stott, and never had a criminal connection with her. This I swear to you as a person of responsibility and truthfulness!

"I should have realized the nature of Mrs. Stott and acted a long time ago. It was way back last April when I first suspicioned this wildcat woman. She used to curse her marriage when she collected dear Daniel's nostrum. I recollect that more than once she said she wanted to 'fix him,' as she put it. She even asked me for strychnine. I just laughed at her—didn't take her seriously. It occurred to me that she might be two-timing Daniel with another man. But that was their business, and not mine. Never did I suspect that murder lay in her heart. I am a gentle Christian person, kind sirs; it is hard for me to recognize the evil in others.

"But murder, we know, *was* in her heart, and I became her

158

unwitting tool. On the evening of the 11th June, I gave Mrs. Stott a prescription for Daniel, and bade her take it round to Buck and Rayner's to be filled. In my prescription there was nothing to cause death. Yet from the effects of it Daniel died.

"Good people of Illinois, never did I handle the medicine after the preparation by the druggists! Never once did it come into my hands!

"Only later, when I was not informed of Daniel's death until after his body had been laid to rest under the cold ground, did I suspicion foul play. At first I blamed the druggists. I now wish to apologize to them for what I said. Then it occurred to me that Julia Stott had disposed of her husband—hence my telegraphs to the coroner of this good county. The brutally murdered body of the late Daniel Percival Stott was thus retrieved from the clay, and all my unhappy thoughts have become justified! And yet here *I* stand accused of the murder of that poor man!

"Fellow Americans! I ask only one thing of you—I ask for justice! Looking at your row of noble faces, I am confident that you will give me justice!"

Shaking with emotion, a-quiver with the power of my oratory, I feared not cross-examination by my prosecutors.

To my surprise, none came—and Derek Munn recalled me to the seat beside him.

"How did I do?" I asked of him after a while.

"I'm worried," says he, and began to call our witnesses.

His reply puzzled me to such an extent that I scarcely listened to the testimony of Mary Dunlap and the Gridleys. I do recall that Frank Gridley, my landlady's husband, looked smaller than ever. A natty midget, he upset Judge Kellum by his obvious desire to verify what he said by placing bets. In the end, Judge Kellum found him in contempt and imposed a fine of ten dollars.

"Mr. Gridley hasn't the means to pay, Your Honor," Derek Munn argued.

"In that case, tell Mr. Gridley I'll lay him two to one it's going to be one week's jail if he can't!"

Chuckles of delight ensued from the assembled sycophants.

# II

Speeches from the attorneys occupied the rest of that day and the whole of the next. Richard Coon was followed by the Hon. Arthur Coon, before Derek Munn spoke on my behalf. Munn's rhetoric did not impress me one bit—too apologetic. Most of his remarks and observations were addressed to Judge Kellum and Senator Fuller rather than to the jurymen, so I took the notion that my defender was after some political promotion (and right I was—Derek Munn did himself dandy in the field of politics over the years to come).

Senator Fuller closed for the People, taking the stand that both Julia Stott and myself were equally guilty of the crime of first-degree murder, that we'd conspired together from the outset. But the senator added a reservation which may well have saved my life: he opined to the jury that if I alone were guilty in their eyes of the murder of Daniel Stott, and if they had doubts with regard to the woman, then my crime was one of passion and it was open for them to convict me only of the felony in the second degree.

This view was adopted in toto by Judge Kellum—I use "in toto" because Judge Kellum repeated that expression endlessly. Kellum gave the jury twenty-one instructions on my behalf as against only fourteen for the People, but he made his own feelings damn plain.

"The Hon. Mr. Munn, for the defendant, warns you against blackening a man just because you've got suspicions. Mr. Munn says that a mere presumption's like an unshoed horse—won't get you far. Maybe, but the magisters long ago used to say: *'Violenta praesumptia aliquando est plena probatio,'* which, translated into good American, means: 'Violent presumption is often as good as proof'—and if you don't understand that, you may's well get back to your farming!"

And later . . .

"Dr. Cream's not one for hanging about when times get rough. Fact is, Dr. Cream took his leave of this state the moment law officers got interested in the cadaver of Dan'l Stott—lit out for Canada. And when Sheriff Ames shows him his poster, our *gentle* doctor's sporting a side-arm that's got nothing to do with the treatment of epilepsy. I've said it once, but here it is again: 'All things are presumed against the wrongdoer.' Why skip out on his bail? Why carry a gun?"

On September 23rd, following an overnight deliberation, my jury of prairie bumpkins found me guilty of second-degree murder and voted imprisonment for life.

This didn't surprise me—and I was indifferent to Derek Munn's plea for a fresh trial on the grounds of fresh evidence. Maybe I didn't care a hoot because this "fresh evidence" was a creation of the silly mind of Derek Munn—bound to fail, bound to earn Derek Munn extra dollars, bound to extend the issue for his self-glorification.

I'm not going to weary you, Cogswell, as to the fussing and fretting that went on throughout September and October. Just let me say that I had my rent paid by the state and continued to reside within the precincts of the Belvidere jailhouse. Charlie Warren had been removed, of course, to reap the reward for his perjury. I was alone but for the idiot turnkey, who continued to shamble his inspection of the cells—be they full or empty—on the strike of every hour.

"Heared you killed more'n a hundred men, Doc," he said to me once.

"A hundred and two, if you count my mother and father," I confided—and the dunderhead loped off, scratching his sloping skull.

Derek Munn strove with all his ineffectual might in respect of my retrial. "Certain overwhelming evidence" lay within our grasp—testimony of a kind guaranteed to obtain my pardon and apologies on behalf of the People of Illinois.

"Mr. and Mrs. Johns have sworn affidavits to the effect that they knew where you were on the Sunday, and therefore you couldn't have been telling Mary M'Clellan the things she said you did!"

"Mr. and Mrs. who?"

*161*

"John Johns! Of 436 West Madison. You know them, don't you?"

"Never heard of them, Colonel Munn."

(As in the case of my father-in-law, Derek Munn had peculiar addiction to the military prefix.)

"But you must have—and they'll swear on your behalf, you know. . . ."

What tremendous fibbery! Munn's closest approach toward truthfulness!

"If you please," I said, "by all means employ their doubtful services."

Munn rubbed his red hands. "Capital. Now for the second cause of appeal. . . . You remember that Judge Kellum instructed the jury that if they concluded you had lied to them about your association with Mrs. Stott, then they were at liberty to disregard the remainder of your evidence? You do remember that, Doctor?"

I recalled that Kellum had it in for me, that's all. How was I supposed to carry in my head every barb he had slung in my direction?

"He said, 'All things are to be presumed against the wrongdoer,' " I replied.

"Did he say that, too?"

"Several times."

"Then we'll have him on that point as well. You are exceeding well observant, Dr. Cream. I can already hear the key grinding in the lock of your liberty. Take heart, and I shall have done that which will accomplish all of this. . . ." He waved his arms furiously. "An inequitable deprivation of basic rights!"

And he walked out of my cell and out of my life—a highly successful bandit.


# III


At an adjourned session on 17th October the Circuit Court convened once more. Munn filed a written motion for his new trial on nine points, and each was rejected. Not surprising. Judge Kellum presided.

State's Attorney Richard Coon smashed the application for fresh evidence from the Johnses simply, and with an ability my own lawyer could only envy. The Johnses sought to impeach the testimony of witnesses long gone—surely, he argued, the Defense of myself should have produced the Johnses at a primary stage in front of the jury? Evidence of this kind was not sufficient in law to justify repeated trial. . . .

"Right all the way, Mr. Coon." Judge Kellum nodded. "The defendant had ample time to prepare his defense, and he had a fair and proper trial. I know—I presided. And let that be part of the record."

"But the Defense have only recently learned of this further evidence, Your Honor!" cried Derek Munn.

"Then the Defense have been misled by the defendant, Mr. Munn."

Kellum tapped the bench impatiently with his gavel, and hands jerked me to my feet.

"Thomas Neill Cream," Kellum said in his hoarse whisper, a silk cloth held to his Gorgon eye, "call yourself a fortunate man. Your jury have spared you your life. Another jury might be less magnanimous. You are surely fortunate in your jury's decision —a decision, I'll wager, mankind will perchance regret. But the law decrees that you shall live, and I therefore direct the manner in which you shall spend the remainder of your days: you shall be incarcerated within the penitentiary of Joliet, and you shall spend one day in every year in solitary confinement.

"Cream, you call yourself 'doctor.' Beelzebub has provided you with the learning to enact his fiendish desires. I judge you to be insane—I judge you to be insane because I am a charitable man and wish no man the chasm of Hellish flame. As a final word, I suggest you consider the words of Cicero: 'Whom the gods wish to destroy, they first make mad'!"

A click as the steel bracelets tightened round my wrists, and I was hauled away and out of that wooden courthouse. I moved as if upon a cushion of cloud, aware only of Judge Kellum's dreadful stare.

PART THREE

*1881–1891*

*Being an account of*
*Thomas Neill's imprisonment*
*at the Illinois State Penitentiary*
*of Joliet*

# NUMBER 4374

## I

Justice having been dispensed in the manner I have described, I was taken from the county jail to the penitentiary of Joliet by young Sheriff Ames on the morning of the 18th October. We journeyed by train, in the twenty-first car, and the manacles on my wrists chafed me sorely.

"Can you take them off?" I asked of Ames, as the train pulled out.

"Convicted men got no rights, Doc," he said sweetly.

"But you know I'm not a criminal. Sheriff. I wouldn't attempt escape."

"Jury convicted you, Doc. That makes you a criminal. Ain't two ways about it. Sorry—but the cuffs stay on."

He offered me a cheroot, which I declined. My urge was for something stronger.

"What's happened to Mrs. Stott?" I asked.

"In the county jail, waiting her trial, I guess."

"They'll never try her!" I exclaimed.

"Guess not. But they gotta pretend they're going to—they gotta keep up appearances, Doc."

I nodded. State's witness as she was, my conviction secured, now they'd spirit her out of sight and the public's mind.

"Do you call that fair, Sheriff?"

Ames sucked on his cigar, eyes closed, and considered my question. His eyes opened and he looked upon me.

"No fairer than anything else that happens every lousy goddamn day, Doc."

The train puffed into Joliet, a downtrodden outrider to the main city of Chicago, and shrieked to a halt.

Ames helped me down from the railroad car, and ground out the nub of his cigar on the track.

"We gotta wait here awhile, Doc," he said, peering about him. "Prison men aiming to collect you. Can't see anyone at the moment, so you can rest your bag a spell."

I had been permitted to bring along my medical equipment —everything except phials and bottles—and I lowered the valise.

"Ah!" Ames smiled. "This must be the reception committee, Doc!"

I followed his pointing arm. Three men were coming up the line, trudging along, heavily muffled in blue greatcoats, vast and ominous from this distance, peaked caps crammed down upon their heads.

The trio walked abreast, and stamped their feet in unison when they reached us: dreadful faces, cold and inspecting, regarding Ames and myself in the same light.

"Ames and Cream?" said the center brute.

"Cream." Bram Ames motioned a thumb at me, and handed over a slip of paper.

"Warden Passmore," said the center man, inspecting the paper. "Life for murder. Boone County. Thomas Neill. It figgers. . . ." Very slowly he extracted a pencil and scribbled something on the bottom of the paper, and returned the same to Sheriff Ames.

"He's all yours," Ames said.

"Sure is—until he's dead. Even then we'll keep what's left of him." Warden Passmore stepped over and snatched away my bag. "I'll have this. No booze, cigareets, or dirty pictures?"

I shook my head, and I'll swear he looked disappointed.

"Just as well," said one of his fellows. "This hotel provides only beans and hardtack. We provide a fine chance for reformed living." He was Irish—complete with monkey upper lip.

A train thundered in and stopped.

"Mine," Ames said. "You've got your prisoner, so I'll be gone."

Warden Passmore smacked his thigh, and I noticed for the first time that he and his retinue bore long clubs of a dark and highly polished wood.

"All right, Sheriff. See you sometime, then?"

"Guess so. 'Bye." And Sheriff Ames trundled off. A reasonable man, I believe, a final reminder of humanity. No love, clearly, was lost between this fellow and representatives of Joliet prison. Ames had fixed me once or twice during the charade they called a trial, yet I still preferred his lies and inaccuracies to the stolid cruelty of Warden Passmore.

"Right!" said Passmore to me. "Put wings on your heels, Cream."

My handcuffs had, of course, been removed—yet a twisting terror within my very vitals urged me along behind this man and his attendant band of thugeroos.

## II

I have described in some detail my initial reception into the clutches of Joliet penitentiary. I have done so because this was a time when my mind was most concentrated and a lingering memory was created which nothing will ever erase.

Yet for me to now recount every waking moment of my days of imprisonment is unthinkable. You will appreciate, sir, that the very nature of my present position prohibits such a venture, for the sands do run. Furthermore, my daily life within those high stone walls was humdrum and predictable. Nothing, in my experience, pleases the common felon or convict so much as to dwell upon his misfortunes, and wherever some naïve publisher encourages that type to recount his experiences, I find that the reader is in for a dreary time. I shall therefore be brief, confining myself to a short commentary on general matters, and particularize only when I feel what I have to say might be of interest. You, Dr. Cogswell, I am sure will accuse me of covering up; I promise you faithfully that this will not be the case. . . .

Of the first two years, only the first day springs to mind. Woken at five, I donned my issue of striped trousers and tunic. Since I was a new arrival, I had the comfort of solitary confinement. My clothing scratched the skin terribly. I had been roused by a banging on the bars, and I dressed in some hurry lest I commence my stay with a show of tardiness. Praise God no mirror adorned the rough walls of my cell! I can imagine that the sight of myself—a stickler for smart attire—might well have turned my mind.

The departure of Sheriff Ames, the escort of Warden Passmore and his gorillas, and the formalities of my entry into Joliet —all these things now seemed a thousand years behind. As I slowly circled my dingy cell, I tried to reconstruct. They had ordered me to bathe, and my ablutions had been supervised in case I carried lice or fleas. What temerity! They had dispossessed me of all my personal belongings—the tools of my trade, my jewelry, my watch with chain and fobs, even my eyeglass. Scrubbed and denuded of all natural personality, I had been whisked away into this dungeon. A coarse-woven blanket for my cover, I had sought and found the sleepy solace of a coward.

But I must check my anger; I realized that the crude authority who administered an establishment such as this required a cool and flattering tongue. I must coax and cajole these people into regarding me as something quite out of the ordinary—less of the normal criminal, more of the talented and respected gentleman forced to hotel in this place because of slight folly in his conduct.

Keys grated in the lock, and it was Warden Passmore.

"4374, you're to be on the field party today," said this horrible man. I saw that he still carried his bludgeon.

"No breakfast today," he went on, stepping further into the cell and pretending to inspect the area. "No midday meal neither if you don't bend your back. Show me your hands, 4374."

I did as he bade, and Passmore thumbed my palms.

"Soft as a girl's! They'll be red raw come sundown!" was his comment, and he laughed. It was a curious laugh, I think. A noise an actor might utter when playing the part of a warder. A false sound.

I smiled slightly, my head on one side in a woeful position.

"You find that funny, then?" snapped the warden.

"No. St. Joseph worked with his hands, so did his Son. Who am I to laugh?"

"You religious, then?"

"Naturally. And you?"

"Never believed a single sneakin' word of it!"

But I knew I had dented the "leatherin'" hide of the man. I gave him a pitying look.

"He never forgets the doubters," I said. "Look at Thomas— one of His favorite sons."

"Shovel Thomas into a pigpen!" muttered Passmore. Then he bucked up and added: "Round here, they call me Thistle-down . . . !"

This revelation he clearly hoped might blight my heart with terror. I smiled sadly once again.

"The prisoners will always insult you, Mr. Passmore. You must never let their words offend you. For they are no more than vicious scrapings from the lowest taverns, whereas *you* are a brave and loyal servant of America doing a difficult task in a cool and efficient manner."

"You're trying to be funny! I don't like . . . !"

"On the contrary, Mr. Passmore, I am in dead earnest. Believe me, sir, I have more sense than to joke with you."

Warden Passmore examined my face with suspicion, endeavoring to detect a flaw in my expression which might give me away. I returned his stare openly.

The warder grunted a couple of times, and then asked: "How come a man of your education gets himself holed up in the pen?"

"Some say I committed murder over a woman."

Passmore nodded. "That's right—I remember." His tiny

brain exercised itself for a time, and then he added: "Well, don't you worry yourself none, Dr. Cream. You and me's likely to get on just fine, unless I'm mistaken."

I bowed.

"We surely will, at that," said Passmore. "And I'll have you away from the field work pretty damn soon—don't you worry, now. A man's the right to be treated like a man for all of that, and I'm thinking you've got the ways of a first-classer."

"You're some punkins yourself, if I may say so," I rejoined, and Warden Passmore was smiling happily. He turned to the door, but stopped.

"You gotta work the fields today, understand? But I'll fix things dandy straightaway."

He slammed the door without relocking it and stared at me through the upper bars.

"And don't you go worryin' your head about nothing, Doc," he assured me. "Thistledown Passmore's got a way around most things hereabouts. Any trouble, you send for me. Understand?"

I nodded, with obvious gratitude.

"I'm obliged," says I. "Thank God for a good and kindly man!"

Warden Passmore's final glance satisfied me that he was completely won, and I reflected during the echoes of his retreating feet that I had scored famously. Within less than twenty-four hours, had I not recruited the services of an influential friend —an ally within this savage limbo?


III


The state of Illinois sported two penal establishments worthy of note—the southern penitentiary at Chester, and Joliet. A major fire having burned unto ruin a large portion of Chester, many inmates of that prison had been transferred to Joliet. Could be that their stay was intended as only a temporary measure, but somehow these outlaws of society lingered on over the next three years, crowding the premises like puppies in a barn. For this reason—and there were others—I was pretty glad not to have to mix with the greater mass.

172

I was obliged to work four days on the farm patch, from sun-up to sundown, and a grueling experience this proved to be! As you have been made aware, I am blessed with a stout physique. Nevertheless, I've got to own that two years' indulgence in the use of strong narcotics had run me down to a sorry condition. Pitching mud and rubble down the way at Stateville farm darn near stretched me out for the great come-uppance! Bones bruised, muscles wrenched, and blisters abounded; for forty-eight working hours I sweated away the mischiefs in my system, and paid and paid and paid!

Then it all stopped. No work roll-call—no requirement for me to report at exit nine and pick up a pick. I remember hanging about my cell—I was still in solitary—waiting like a jackass in my tunic. Time passed and nothing happened—not in the morning, not in the afternoon, not at all. And so it was on the fifth and sixth days. Warden Passmore?

I guess it was the warder, and maybe the warder decided I'd fret myself silly in solitary, because on the morn of the seventh day keys jangled in my door for something more than food. A black and hairy officer made his entrance. He went by the name of Machado—called himself a Portugee, although he was as half-breed as a 'breed can be. He told me I was wanted by the governor of the prison.

"Are you permitted to divulge the nature of my appointment?" I asked of him, adjusting the buttons on my tunic.

"I said you're wanted. Don't talk funny to me, boy!" and the 'breed's pockmarked face darkened.

"I apologize. I wasn't intending to be impertinent, I assure you."

"Best not," said Machado. "Last man who did round here don't no more. Mistook a man for a woman. Got himself killed real good. Funny talk's bad."

With this warning humming in my ears, I followed the quarter-wit out of the cell and down the passages leading to the governor's quarters.

Perhaps at this stage I should describe to you the over-all layout of the penitentiary.

The surrounding wall of the prison, more than twenty feet in height, formed a square. The front gate dominated the facing wall, and led into a large courtyard. Across this quad lay a second main gate, giving access to the cells and dungeons of the establishment. Three cell blocks formed the letter U, with accommodation for warders and guards adjoining. The governor's offices were situated at the end of Cell Block B, with a private gate and small yard to the front. At the corners of the four walls were perched turrets with guards armed with repeating rifles and those newfangled machine guns. (No doubt I shall have to sketch a small plan of Joliet at a later stage.)

*[Never found among the papers. V.R.C.]*

This minor digression aside, I now found myself face to face with the governor for the first time. An elderly man—a sad and crumpled face not unlike that of a bloodhound.

Warden Passmore stood behind the governor's chair as I was marched in, and something was whispered between the two as I came to attention.

"Life for two-degree homicide," Passmore said.

"Paramour's husband, I see," said the governor quietly. He was looking at my file.

"But there were extenuating circumstances, Governor," added Passmore.

The governor looked round and up at him. "No mention of that here, Charlie," said he, and tapped the folder in his hands.

"I've made a few inquiries," Passmore said. His voice and expression were final and brooked no nonsense. The governor caved visibly, and the hound-dog look returned.

"Just as you say, Charlie." Then the governor gave me the once-over and told me to relax.

He left his chair and walked past Passmore to the window and looked out. The sky was gray and foggy, but from where I was standing I could see the wall turret on the extreme right-hand side. One of the guards therein was polishing the brass barrels of a machine gun.

"So you're a proper doctor," said the governor at last, without turning.

"I am indeed, sir." My voice was a trifle shaky.

"Jail's a doggone waste for a man with your kind of know-how," said the governor.

I looked at Passmore, and he gave me a wink.

"I don't expect preferential treatment, sir," I said.

The governor nestled himself back into his chair. Held my file in his hands as if to weigh it, and then carefully put it down.

"Daresay," says he. "But strikes me as a doggone shame you can't be used by the state where you're needed. Farm work'll brown you up, all right—but it'll dull your brain."

"If I can be of service . . . ?" I saw my chance, and accordingly made my voice meek and hopeful.

The governor peered at me with a mite more concentration than before. His eyes, squinting as they were through pouchy flesh, reflected his character: weak enough for the likes of Passmore to manipulate.

"Maybe you doggone well can," he said. "Got a doc of our own, understand? Doc Brodie. Pretty fine doc, at that. But getting old—getting tired—getting too creaky to call round here 'less it's 'portant. You get me?"

"A man deserves rest in the evening of his life," I suggested.

"Could be—could be," muttered the governor in such a way that I concluded that he, too, was anxious for his own "rest."

"How can I help?" I asked—quite boldly.

"You can lend a hand to Doc Brodie," Passmore put in.

"Delighted, I'm sure!"

And so it was that I evaded the rigors and mindless existence of the ordinary convict. Dr. Brodie's tiredness proved to be more than just a question of old age. The man was a drunkard and a loafer; his face had become blued over the years by all the booze consumed.

Happily did I become his Number Two—and I kept him well supplied and fortified with rot-gut as a matter of self-interest: any improvement in the fellow's health or any sudden sobriety would inevitably threaten my position.

The pen authorities had provided the doctor with a small room for use as a surgery, and this little area became my retreat and haven for the next four and a half years.

Since the doctor seldom presented himself at the prison

before afternoon, I took over the responsibility of morning surgery for the convicted. And damn dull practice it was, after Canada and Chicago—a continuous lancing of boils, treatment for bedbugs, and patching up of injuries caused in fights. On the side, I brewed alcohol, which I sold to the prisoners at two cents a tot or in exchange for tobacco. Warden Passmore joined with me in this enterprise.

During the summer of '85, Dr. Brodie became very ill. I feared for his life, for his death would foreclose on my situation once a new physician was appointed. I nursed Doc Brodie through that August and September like an angel of mercy, and great was my relief when he recovered. But now the man was virtually useless, and I found myself taking all patients. In short, I needed help—and help came in the repellent form of Gustav Kindt. Burglar and "toolmaker," Gustav Isadore Kindt, alias French Gus, alias Frenchy, alias Gus Marechal, hailed from Alsace. A celebrated criminal and a skilled mechanic, French Gus (as I called him) manufactured housebreaking tools for thieves and robbers from Baton Rouge to Brooklyn, and he'd done time in Sing Sing, and Stillwater. While doing time, of course, his engineering talents were discouraged, and French Gus occupied himself by playing the professional spy and informer to the highest bidder. Indeed, he had the aspect of a devious scoundrel—beady eyes and the beard and mustaches sported by the late Maximilian of Mexico. French Gus. But he had his uses, and when he tendered his services to me, both Warden Passmore and myself concluded it a wise move to accept. Often does it pay to have the snake in your own camp where you can keep a good eye on him. . . .

I guess you're curious about Warden Passmore himself. Well, I'm afraid there is not much I can say. I never did learn the origins and history of that man. He kept himself to himself, as they say, and volunteered no information. A rough man and a bully—hated women, too. Why he interested himself in me? That's a mystery. Perhaps he saw me as a kind of good-luck symbol, as a talisman. Certainly we brought each other good fortune in the end.

But of Frank McCoy I'm able to say something. Frank—or

"Banjo" McCoy—was "top con" at Joliet, and hated by all. He'd made his fortune in quid tobacco, possessed himself of an army of bribed men, and now ruled the roost with a mixture of benevolence and terror. A huge man, twenty pounds heavier than myself, Banjo McCoy crushed all opposition ruthlessly. Even Warden Passmore was wary of the fellow. The eventual killing of this man gave to me the utmost satisfaction—gave me the thrill of my life! McCoy was doing a long stretch for armed robbery and manslaughter, but I reckon he hoped for some reduction of his sentence. His dying in jail hurt him almost as much as it amused me. But I'll come to that later. . . .

IV

Come the fall, French Gus had become my full-time assistant. I trusted him not with the preparation of medicines and dosages, and restricted his duties to bottle-washing and so forth. Sometimes I allowed him to help Warden Passmore and myself at the still.

Just before Christmastide I received my first communication from my father, and gladness filled my heart. I'd written him many times since my incarceration, and never did he reply. After a year or more I came to the conclusion that I had been forsaken, abandoned even by my own, in this, my greatest need for charity. In my letters I had reassured my father as to my complete innocence, and outlined in detail the terrible wrong done to me by the people of America. His failure to write me, I concluded, was positive proof that scandalmongers had filled his ears with poison, and that he had chosen to believe them rather than his own flesh and blood. For that reason I abandoned further attempts to contact him.

Now suddenly this letter from Buffalo! He had, he said, conducted exhaustive investigations into my case, and tried without success to contact Mrs. Stott. At first, he said, he had believed me to be a demon, and confessed that he'd rather have heard of me being hung than borne the shame of a son in prison.

But time, he said, had created doubts in his mind until he could stand them no longer, and for his own peace of mind he had made inquiries. Then it was, he said, that he discovered that the Stott woman had escaped without punishment. My own attorney, he said, had assured him of my guilt (what else would the likes of Derek Munn do in the event of losing a case?) but he was not satisfied. And he said that folk had advised him that I had been scapegoated because I was not American.

"My son," he finished the epistle, "I cannot say that you did not slay that man—God alone knows the truth of that, and God shall one day judge you accordingly. But I can say that if you did slay that man, then you were coerced by his woman into so doing, for no son of mine can be said to be the base murderer alleged. I shall never visit you. The sight of you in your present Valley of Despair would certainly kill an old man. But I shall go on to establish your guiltlessness for as long as I may live—my endeavors shall never diminish. I shall never desert you—and this I swear. Your continually praying father, William Cream."

So it was. No mention of my mother, brothers, or sisters. An old man's bleat for respectability. If his letter sought to comfort me, then it came too late. If it sought to pity me my condition, then let the paper light a bonfire. That was my reaction, and I did not reply.

In the month of March, 1886, Warden Passmore was promoted to chief warden, and the governor retired upon completion of his term in office. Chief Warden Passmore must have had a hand in the appointment of the new governor, of that I'm sure —for never in your life did you see such a fuzzy-brained nincompoop. One snap of the fingers from Passmore and his team, and the poor fellow would cringe and whine in an exercise of humility. The last governor tended to growl at some of Passmore's finer excesses, but the new laddie wagged his head or nodded in tune like a Dutch puppet. He was no more than forty, but I reckoned the job would stop him seeing sixty.

French Gus and I continued to run "the store," as the convicts called my surgery, and the profits poured in without change. Warden Passmore's elevated position now prevented him from being able to help manage the still in person, but he deputized some of his minions to take his place, and exacted certain dues from time to time. The man was famously corrupt.

Yet things commenced to go athwart come early summertime. . . . Illinois as a whole suffered a hard time during these months. No rain. Extremes in climate were the norm, but this was something different: not a drop of moisture for weeks on end, and no breeze—just the burning sun in a white brass sky.

Inside Joliet the atmosphere became as of lead, and men began to lose their minds. Alcohol doubled in demand, and I doubled the price of a slug. Sometimes the fierce liquor we made drove an imbiber mad and blind, and terrible brawls broke out. Farmworkers came back completely dehydrated—three died this way during July. Men confined in solitary for a minor infraction of the rules screamed the long nights through, and their calls became a real nightmare. The bars and steel fixtures acquired a heat by day never cooled at nightfall. Food—basic at the best—became foul, and our water, rationed to three mugs a day, became brackish. In short, Joliet became a hellhole.

And, like the subterranean mutters of a volcano, trouble lay just around the corner. I could sense it—French Gus could sense it—many of us could sense it; but neither Chief Warden Passmore nor the governor appeared to foresee what was likely to happen. Far from it—for did not the idiotic governor order a halt to outside working parties and confine all men to the prison proper? He most surely did. There were no limits to this jackass's foolishness.

I considered apprising Passmore of my misgivings. But who was I to butt in? Instead, I decided to hold my tongue and keep my eyes and ears well open. . . .

As you might well imagine, the one man to take good advantage of the situation was Banjo McCoy. A rabble-rouser by nature, here was his chance to exploit the misfortunes of his fellows in order to gratify a continuous desire to frustrate the authorities. He began by organizing chants among the men and the celebrated bar-rattling techniques so popular in U.S. jails. What urged him to take matters a step further I'll never follow, but the step he took was drastic enough to cost him his life. Generally, news within Joliet traveled like wildfire, bent and twisted during its passage until solid fact became no more than rumor or a pack of lies. McCoy's little plan must have been conceived in secrecy, and I'll wager men were told to mind their mouths or suffer the consequences if the plot was blown.

But notice of what was afoot reached the sly French Gus in next to no time, and one evening he told me. We were bottling alcohol at a late hour when all other convicts were abed in their cells, and French Gus turns to me and says:

"Could be all this moonshine's gonna go to waste, Doc."

"Why so?"

"Could be there's gonna be a ruckus pretty soon."

"How's that?"

"Could be all this heat's driving the boys sort of crazy. They don't take kindly to being locked in their cells so often."

I agreed with him.

"And it could be somebody's got something worked out as to how to rectify the situation, Doc."

"Is that so?" I was itching for him to come out with it, but decided to let him tell me what he knew in his own time. Never rush an informer.

"Sometimes happens that a governor gets himself put out of office if there's a lot of trouble with the cons, Doc."

"So I would imagine," says I.

"Could be some of the boys don't like our governor."

"A demonstration?" I said.

"Could be something a mite bigger—something like a 'break-out.'"

I stopped what I was doing and looked at him. He kept his sneaky brown eyes on his bottle, but his expression was serious.

"No one would be fool enough to try that!" I exclaimed, my mind on the machine-gun artillery in the watchtowers.

"Could be the man who's thought it out is pretty damn-fool, Doc," said French Gus.

There was no need for him to speak on; Banjo McCoy had

organized a jail-break. When was it to take place? I wondered.

"Today is Wednesday," I observed. "On Fridays the guards are four short."

French Gus gave a violent shake to the bottle he'd just corked, and lined it up with the rest upon the trestle table.

"I imagine they've taken that into consideration," I added.

"Reckon so, Doc," came the reply I wanted.

# SIX HUNDRED ROUNDS A MINUTE

## I

French Gus having disclosed this vital piece of information, I took it that he relied upon me to ensure that it reached the ears of the prison authorities. I told Warden Passmore Thursday morning when he did his inspections.

Warden Passmore advised me to mention the matter to no one, and promised that he'd arrange for my safety when the moment of the expected insurrection came. I did not divulge to him that French Gus was my informant.

An ominous silence reigned throughout the cell blocks during the next two days. I doubt if all the prisoners were fully aware of what was to take place, but most, I suspect, had a shrewd notion that the lords and masters within their community had something extraordinary planned. The guards and warders behaved quite normally, and I observed no increase of security.

Suppertime on Friday we assembled outside our respective cells to collect a ration of hash and water. The atmosphere was extremely tense, and I could see Banjo McCoy with some of his lieutenants gossiping quietly at the far end of the corridor. It was thirty minutes after seven o'clock, the air thick with the heat and the odor of bean-smudge and the perspiring multitude.

I ate in my cell, and swallowed with difficulty. When I returned my plate and mug to the push-table outside the cell door, I retained my spoon and secreted the same in my waistband and under my shirt. The spoon, when sharpened, was a favorite weapon among convicts. My spoon was blunt, but better than no weapon at all, having regard to the circumstances. . . .

Warden Passmore and three of his "bulls" suddenly filled the doorway.

"You're wanted in surgery, 4374," said Passmore, and I went with them. My departure was nothing untoward—often it was that I'd be called away like this to attend an injured man.

Warden Passmore spoke not a word until we reached the surgery.

"I'm going to lock you in, Doc," he said.

I pointed out to him that the office door had no lock.

Passmore shrugged. "I can't give you a gun, Doc," he said. "But I don't think you'll be bothered up here."

He was right. My surgery was situated well away from the walls, the gates, and the governor's quarters. It was hard to imagine any escaping body coming my way. I'd just sit tight until whatever occurred was over.

Set high in the wall of my surgery there was a narrow window, glassed but unbarred, of the kind to be found in European fortresses and castles. Dragging over the heavy trestle table, I set this under the aperture and clambered up. A good view of the right-hand wall, the governor's quarters, and of the central courtyard was to be had. I observed that the front right-hand watchtower of the prison contained no less than five men—as opposed to the usual two—and the turret bristled with armaments.

And I had not long to wait for the hullabaloo to begin. . . .

I was subsequently told that a duplicate key to the cells of C Block had been fashioned—no doubt with the aid of a wax image and the skills of a toolmaking inmate—and this instrument had been surreptitiously employed to release Banjo McCoy and his outlaws.

Once free—I was told—the ruffian band had beaten a trusty unconscious and proceeded up the main passages, slipping the

183

locks as they went. Eighty-nine criminals escaped their cells in this manner, most of them armed with shovels and hoes acquired from Stateville farm and introduced without notice into the prison.

The convicts moved in a mass from left to right within the premises—and their intentions had been anticipated by the authorities. Passmore and his bullies permitted the mutineers to reach the farthest block, Cell Block B, adjacent to the governor's quarters, and there it was that the mutineers met a barrage of gunfire.

It was this fusilade—the hollow boom of Winchester carbines —that stirred me from my dreams and made me leap up onto the table once again.

At first there was nothing to see, hard as I might squint into the yard below. The sky was orange with the setting sun, and great shadows flung their arms across the quad from the watchtower.

But I could hear shouting now—calls and cries interspersed with rifle fire. The tumult appeared to stem from the region of Cell Block B. As a matter of logic, I concluded that the escapers proposed to break their way out into the main yard, and from thence out of the main gate: a hazardous expedition befitting the lunatic mind of Banjo McCoy.

The wail of the steam sirens entreated the convicts to employ their better judgment, the awesome shrieking loud enough to call up the dead. But there is nothing short of hot lead to check the mad rush of an American jail-break, and I soon began to observe figures hugging the high walls of the main yard. Well could I appreciate their reluctance to venture farther out and so come into direct range of those in the watchtower. And it was, of course, Banjo McCoy who forced these men to abandon good sense and rush the far gate. To give the man his due, Banjo led the crowd himself, waving his arms like a berserker, a butcher's cleaver and a hoe held aloft.

The guards in the watchtower bided their time, waiting until the mob reached the center of the yard before they opened fire. Puffs of smoke advertised the operation of the machine guns before the firecracker sound reached my ears. Now, I'm in no way familiar with the technicalities of Mr. Nordenfeldt's lethal contraptions, but I'm given to understand that the watchtower housed two of these infernal machines, including a ten-barreled Gatling capable of firing nearly six hundred rounds of .45 caliber in a minute. In the first instance, the guns simply kicked up the ground a few yards ahead of the mutineers and stopped them in their tracks. Panic-stricken, the crowd began to rush hither and thither in the utmost confusion, and it was then that the deadly ball of the guns was concentrated upon the living targets. Never in my life have I seen such a shambles! For more than two minutes both machine guns exacted their toll, shooting indiscriminately into the writhing mass of fallen men below. Soon my view became obscured by the dust of the sandy yard, and a halo of blue smoke disguised the activities of the guards in the watchtower. But still the shooting continued—the blind killing the blind—while the screams and groans of the wounded endured until silenced by yet another hail of bullets.

This was butchery. A lesson was in the process of being taught. When at last the shooting stopped, I wondered what the toll would be. . . .

The slaughter stopped as suddenly as it had begun, and the silence that followed was more frightening than the noise of moments past. Smoke and dust began to settle and thin, until I could see the effects of Mr. Nordenfeldt's inventions. Bodies lay everywhere, and in the most contorted of positions—some, indeed, had limbs or heads missing from the trunk, and one fellow looked as if he'd been cut in two. From my point of vantage, and in the gathering gloom, the corpses and their life-blood stains began to merge into little dark patches, like rocks on a beach when viewed from the top of a cliff. A grim and fascinating business.

A sound at my rear jolted me from my musings. I jumped round quickly, the hairs on the back of my neck a-prickle. It was French Gus.

"*Lieber Gott!*" squawked the fellow. "They come to get me!"

I climbed down from my table, uncertain what to do.

"You must help me, Doc," French Gus said, grabbing hold of one of my arms. I let him jabber on while considering what he had to say. There was nowhere within the surgery to conceal a person. Moreover, if prisoners were out to kill the man, I wanted no part of it.

"Who's after you?" I said at last.

"Banjo! Banjo! He knows I told you. He look for me."

But McCoy had been one of those outside in the yard. I shook some sense into French Gus and pointed toward the window as I explained.

"He's dead, don't you understand?" I finished.

"Not hardly!" came this voice from the door.

We both turned, and French Gus sank to his knees in a partial faint at the sight of Banjo McCoy. And a grisly sight he was, too —face smudged black, clothing torn, one arm shot through and dislocated. But his good arm still bore the butcher's cleaver.

"Stand aside, sawbones," Banjo rasped, and I did as he bade, pulling my trousers free from French Gus's trembling fingers.

Banjo stepped forward and gripped Gus by the hair, pulling his head backward so as to expose the throat. Then with one mighty sweep of the cleaver he cut French Gus's throat to the neck bone. French Gus had time for only one short gurgling cry before he expired.

"Sneaky bastard," said Banjo after the execution, just standing there, saturated with the blood of his victim.

"He betrayed you?" I asked, feigning puzzlement as to the present situation.

"He did—but his sneakin' days are done, the dog!"

The man now seemed to cave in, as if utterly spent in both mind and body. The enormity of his failure was a crushing force —one that transfixed him to where he stood, limp and lifeless. Nevertheless, I stayed by the doorway until the warders poured in to seize him. The sight of his cleaver and French Gus's all but headless corpse occupied my mind most thoroughly during the wait. Even when Passmore and the others hauled him away, Banjo McCoy allowed himself to be relieved of his weapon without a struggle, and to be manhandled out of the room like a sack of oats. Of course, Banjo McCoy was as dead a man as the one he'd just slain—and well he knew it. . . .

The riot having been suppressed, the authorities naturally sought to mete out severe punishment to the ringleaders. The toll of those laid low by the machine guns amounted to some twenty-six men, and the lesson there was pretty plain to the small fry who'd survived. But in the cases of Banjo McCoy and two others guilty of murdering a warder, the ritual of a trial and public execution was called for. And so it was that McCoy, plus two, were afforded the semblance of legal trial in the District Court and sentenced to hang. I understood that McCoy's cleaver and the head of French Gus, transported in a leather bag, became exhibits alongside mine own sworn affidavit.

Hanging—or "necktie parties"—in the mid- and far-western states of America has now become something of a traditional institution; I guess the country is indebted to His Honor Judge Parker.

Popular opinion took the notion that no particular expertise was required in stringing a man up, and the usual practice was simply to tie one end of a rope around a fellow's neck, flip the cord over a crossbeam, and have five or six bullies hoist the offender aloft. This being the rule rather than the exception, I suppose Banjo McCoy, plus two, were indeed fortunate to find themselves dispatched at the hands of Mr. Rik van Bulger, executioner/preacher of Oklahoma.

It was my lot to assist Mr. van Bulger as medical orderly, and I was introduced to this gentleman by Warden Passmore the night before the hangings. Summoned to Passmore's office, the warder came to the point.

"This here's Mr. van Bulger—hangman. Happened to be around, so we've availed ourselves of the gentleman's services. Says he needs an assistant. Seeing how's you're a physician, thought you'd fit the job, Doc."

Van Bulger looked me over—none too friendly, I thought.

"But this man's a con," he said. His voice was shrill, and he had a way of cutting off his sentences. His mouth was curved and tight. He reminded me of a tortoise.

"That's as may be, Mr. van Bulger," says Passmore. "But he's a four-star prisoner. Fact is, he's the man who helped us bust the riot."

Van Bulger nodded. Bending down, he picked up an oblong bag and placed it upon Passmore's desk. "Ever attended upon a hangin', young man?" he asked, opening up the bag.

I said I hadn't.

"Well, it's a scientific art, contrary to what most folks believe, I can tell you now." He extracted a rope from the bag, one end already set in a noose. "This here's a hang-line, young man." He held it up. "Best Italian hemp a man can buy—imported, you see. Five strands, three-quarter inch, and a breaking weight of nigh on one ton. Had this rope two years come Christmas. Hanged more men on it than your ma's hung washing. The life of this here rope's eternal, see? Can't be broke. And looky here, young man." He directed my attention to a brass ring close to the knot of the noose. "This little addition's for the sake of humanity, see? The ring snaps the neck plenty quick. You gotta do it this way, see? You gotta be a humanition—a scientific humanition—in my line of business. My aim is to give a subject as little pain as possible." He looked very grave. Then he tucked the rope back into his bag, and pulled out two broad leather straps. "These here are for the pinionment, see? You gotta tuck a subject up nice and tight, see? One for the arms, and one for the legs. If you don't tuck 'em up tight, likely a subject'll get all overcome. One thing I can't abide is a sloppy subject yelling and fighting on the scaffold. Ain't seemly, see? Once took me five hours to see off a subject; down in Missouri it was—young lad of sixteen who'd took to rustlin'. Five whole hours, see?"

And he next drew out a white canvas bag to show me.

"Now, this here bag's got plenty of good purpose, young man. You slip it over a subject's head before you put on the rope. And you pull the bag good and tight, see? This stops a subject yelling, and if he bites off his tongue in his anxiety you'll never have to see it. Saw it once, I did, over in Kansas. Subject bit his tongue right off. . . ."

The lecture was over, and Van Bulger secured his box of tricks. "Still want to be of assistance, young man?"

I nodded.

"Right, Doc," Passmore said. "Mr. van Bulger now wishes to inspect tomorrow's 'subjects.' You'll be told when you're needed."

And so I withdrew.

Banjo McCoy plus two were ordained to die at dawn, and I was roused from my cell when it was still dark. I was taken to the main yard—scene of the recent slaughter—where I found a crude gallows already erected. Mr. van Bulger had been busy during the night.

Van Bulger was standing on the platform, and as I came up, there followed a resounding crash. Mr. van Bulger was in the process of testing his beloved Italian rope with a four-hundred-pound bag of cement.

"I've checked the subjects' weights," he called down to me. "The big one, McCoy, he goes at two-ten pounds. He'll be requiring a very short drop, see? No more'n two feet. Give him any more, like as not we'll take his head off. Saw that once, down in Carthage. Gave a big man a long drop, see? Head got took right off. . . ."

I mounted the steps to join him on the platform, and watched as he adjusted the rope's tie to the crossbeam of the gallows tree.

"What do you want me to do?" I asked when he'd finished.

"You? You gotta stay down under when I turn the subjects off, young man. Yes, that's what you do. Then, if things go bad, you can grab hold of a subject's legs and tug him out of his misery. Not that things are gonna go bad, see? Things are gonna be neat and tidy as can be. . . ."

"Do you want me to cut them down?" I asked.

"Cut? Nobody cuts this rope o' mine, young man!" He was truly outraged at the suggestion. "This here's Italian hemp— this here's the bestest bit o' hanging line you ever saw! See?"

"Yessir."

A representative detachment of convicts were brought out of the buildings and drawn up in three groups just before sunrise. These men were to constitute witnesses to the execution, and I observed that the majority of their number consisted of the worst criminal element from the prison. No doubt the authorities had it in mind to dissuade these men from a repetition of what had led the condemned to the gallows. And now we waited in silence for McCoy plus two to be brought forth. The sky had turned the palest shade of blue, and heralded yet another day of intolerable heat. At a few minutes after five, just as the red sun tipped the easterly walls of the penitentiary, a small door leading into the governor's quarters opened and a party of men came out. Two armed warders walked ahead of the three condemned, and four more marched behind. The governor, Warden Passmore, and the padre brought up the rear. When they came to the foot of the gallows steps, a halt was called. I found time to examine the countenances of the condemned. McCoy—huffed and humpy in a striped jacket made thick with the bandages that swathed his upper body. If he experienced terror, he didn't show it, and his face was frozen. Not so the other two—for their eyes bolted in a desperate fashion, and they shifted from foot to foot like a couple of polka dancers. I decided that Van Bulger would classify these as "bad subjects."

"Now hear me!" It was Van Bulger—the gallows platform had become his pulpit. "And hear this! You will go to your Maker as Christian soldiers. You will pluck up your courage, and you will pray. Like the good thief on the cross at Calvary, you will pray for His forgiveness. Though you have grieved Him sore, you pray that His arms of mercy be open wide to receive you into His Heavenly Kingdom." And his voice sank as he added in the lowest of octaves: "And I, for my part, will do my duty."

He began to sing a hymn, the tune and words of which I failed to catch, and McCoy was hustled up the steps by two warders.

Once he was on the platform, Van Bulger moved with speed, pinioning McCoy's arms and legs in a jiffy. Positioned over the trap, on came the white canvas hood. Still intoning the dirge he sang, Van Bulger secured the rope and drew it tight. I saw that the brass ring he carefully nestled just behind McCoy's left ear. All set—Van Bulger took a smart step back, and laid one hand on the wooden lever protruding from the floor of the platform.

"Unto the bountiful mercy of the Almighty I commend your spirit!" he shouted, and sprang the trap.

Down McCoy hurtled, to be checked with a suddenness that surprised me as much as it no doubt surprised McCoy. His neck broke with an audible crack—the sound such as is made when a raw carrot be snapped in half. His body swung no more than three feet away from me, and I wondered what to do, for my instructions had been vague. So I waited around until I became aware of Van Bulger's angry face peering over the platform rail and down at me.

"Unhitch, young man," he called. "And don't damage the rope, see?"

Lifting McCoy up so as to slacken the rope proved to be difficult enough, but easing the tie of the noose, so as to slip it over the masked head at the same time, was nigh on impossible. And no one came to my assistance, although my struggles must have been plain for all to see.

"Unhitch! Unhitch!" came the call again.

At last I succeeded and the rope came free. But under the weight of McCoy I toppled over, and the two of us lay in an untidy heap upon the ground.

"Pass me up the mask, young man," instructed Van Bulger.

I removed the hood from McCoy's head. His face was ghastly to behold—white tinged with mauve, deep abrasions about the neck. The ruptured eyes reminded me of the late Miss Stack.

"C'mon, young man, we can't keep folk hanging about!"

Perhaps it was the tardiness of the situation which caused one of the remaining condemned to lose his self-control. In any event, he broke the hold of his warders and tried to run off. But he was soon captured and returned, weeping, to the foot of the steps.

"I'll oblige him next," said Van Bulger. "Can't stand to see a subject suffer none. . . ."

And the wretched fellow was frog-marched up the steps and into position.

Once again Van Bulger intoned his hymn while he made things ready. "Unto the bountiful mercy of the Almighty I commend your spirit!" And down the felon came. As he came—just before the rope cut him short—I observed a furious movement of the canvas bag. I guess the man was calling out inside that bag for all his worth. But if he was, I for one didn't hear a sound until the final snap-bang of his end.

The third executionee held himself in a doughty manner. "Good boy—good boy!" I heard Van Bulger say from above, by way of compliment.

Sadly enough, this young bravo's final moments did not reward his good conduct. As the trap fell free, a misplacement of footing—I assume—caused the laddie to swing forward, so that the front of his body and face crashed hard into the edge of the aperture. A short cry was followed by the rasping sound of suffocation.

"Lay hold of his legs, young man!" came the call.

As if spellbound, I watched the lashing of the unfortunate's bound feet until another shout set me to my task.

I pulled and pulled, lifted and pulled and pulled again, until the kicking stopped. Bathed in perspiration, I crawled away and lay panting upon the sand. Cocking up my head, I took notice of a curious thing: so frantic were the efforts of this desperate creature to save his life that even in death did both his feet point downward and twitch in their futile attempt to find the ground.

"Unhitch—but don't remove the mask," came my instructions.

I got up and did as required. The laddie was lighter than either of his predecessors, and I experienced no trouble in setting him down. But the hood over his head had begun to seep blood, and the gods alone know what ruination of the features had been incurred by the blow on the framework suffered during the man's descent. I presume Van Bulger became acquainted with that aspect of the matter, and I have no doubt that the hanging of this man earned a place within his history of "difficult subjects."

# RECOURSE TO MR. PINKERTON'S
# REMARKABLE AGENCY

## I

Now I was in the happy position to receive a certain amount of helpful publicity in connection with my role in the quelling of the "Joliet Mutiny," as the attempted jail-break became known. Once again I feel that Warden Passmore had a hand in this; and of course when the chief warden of a prison says things favorable to one of the inmates, then the authorities take note. In short, Warden Passmore commended me to the Governor of Illinois, allowed me to be interviewed by the Chicago press, and henceforward I was singled out for preferential treatment. No longer did I dine with the other convicts or live in a common cell. I ate alone, exercised alone whenever I chose and without escort, and moved into newly decorated quarters close upon my surgery, where I continued to act as unofficial medical officer.

"Doc, an idea's crossed my mind," Passmore said to me once. "Could be that if you volunteered for a spell in the prison service, you'd get your sentence slashed. Just an idea, mind. But think about it."

Indeed I did consider his suggestion, and I was on the brink of requesting an interview with the governor when I received a letter from Quebec.

The epistle came from my mother—I do believe it was the only letter the good woman ever wrote me throughout my life. She said that my father was poorly and that she feared for his life. She said that he was now staying in Dansville, New York, on account of his health, and that soon she would be joining him there. She added that my father had never forsaken me—that his search for Julia Stott still continued after all these years. She said that she herself had never questioned my innocence, and many times had she desired to visit me in my confinement. She claimed that only the thought of her own terrible distress in seeing me caged like an animal held her back. Now she asked me to pray for an improvement in the condition of my "own dear Papa."

Utter humbug! I tore the letter into fragments in my fury. What base hypocrisy! I accepted the fact that my father was dying—that in itself justified the tone of her letter. The two old frauds now sought to salve their consciences. As in the case of my father's letter of yesteryear, the memory of how they had abandoned their eldest son in his greatest need now tormented my mother into corresponding. But she'd get no acknowledgment from me!

My father died on May 12th of '87, aged sixty-four years, and the news touched me not one bit. In a final gesture to make amends, the old man bequeathed to me in his will the sum of twenty thousand dollars. And for this I'll own I was grateful; such funds well appointed might assist me to obtain a commutation of my sentence. So you will see why it was that I held in abeyance my opportunity of enrolling in the Illinois prison service, as a final resort if all else failed.

The money left me by my father was held in the form of stocks and bonds by the Merchants' Bank of Canada, up in Montreal, and I was unable to lay my hands on a single penny piece of it.

But I duly informed Warden Passmore as to my inheritance, and made it clear that, should the chief warden help me in my cause, I would be generous. I think the sum of four thousand dollars was mentioned.

## II

Warden Passmore made noises calculated to reach the right quarters, but all agitations in favor of my release were met with failure. Perhaps if I'd had access to sufficient cash I'd have been able to bribe both the prison governor *and* the governor of the state, and so secured more suitable backing. As it was, three years passed and I was still in Joliet.

"This Stott woman," Passmore says to me. "If we can find her, so much the better, Doc."

I despaired of success with regard to her. For all I knew, she might now be dead, or playing the whore in some faraway place. Fact is, I was despairing quite a lot at this time. My eyesight, never good over the last twelve years and more, had taken a turn for the worse. Vision in my left eye was very poor, and headaches were frequent. Happily, I was in a position to obtain and find solace in drugs—morphine chiefly, and sometimes cocaine. Memories of Chinatown warned me of the possible consequences of what I was doing, and I was careful to keep my dosages small. Nevertheless, by the fall of '90 I knew I was addicted.

"Ever heard of Pinkerton's National Detective Agency, Doc?" Passmore asked me that December.

I said that I was aware of their existence, and that I understood the company tracked down train robbers on behalf of the railway magnates.

"They'll track down whoever you like, Doc—provided the money's right," Passmore informed me.

And so I wrote to Mr. Frank Murray, detective, with a request that he occupy himself in tracing the whereabouts of Mrs. Julia Stott, and I enclosed an open banker's order up to the sum of five hundred dollars. I gave the detective all the information about the woman I could, and offered a further five hundred dollars should a sensible affidavit be obtained from her. More than that I couldn't do. Now I could only wait.

Mr. Pinkerton's remarkable agency enjoys some renown in the United States, with offices in New York and Philadelphia as well as in Chicago. I never did get to meet Frank Murray, but his credentials were endorsed by George Bangs, the general superintendent of the organization. If Julia Stott was alive, I was assured, then Frank Murray would sniff her out.

But I guess Allan Pinkerton's agents were too much occupied in cases of grand larceny and kidnapping to concern themselves with my humbler expectations, for time continued to pass without news from Mr. Murray. Mind you, I set no store upon Mr. Bangs' promise of success. In my bones I knew Julia Stott to be dead.

So when I received from Warden Passmore the affidavit of a Mr. Edward Levy—claiming as it did that Levy had known me well in Chicago, and that he had met with Julia Stott two years back, when she had assured him, in confidence, as to my blameless role concerning the death of her husband—I knew that document to be a lie. Does the name Edward Levy now tinkle a bell in your ears, Cogswell? I'm sure it does. And let me add that this particular gentleman is no more than a professional witness and swearer of false affidavits for purposes of private gratification and financial reward. Under which mossy stone Warden Passmore found this perfidious sheeny I never did learn, but I was happy to part with my five hundred dollars in return for wicked lies he told.

I imagine that the second-hand nature of the yarn spun in the affidavit raised the eyebrows of the state law officers, but the document did the trick, and on 12th June (a date forever in my mind) Governor Fife commuted my sentence to a term of seventeen years. The authorities further recommended that I be allowed time off for good conduct—in particular for my assistance during the "Joliet Mutiny"—and on the last day of July, 1891, I was set free.

I reckon ten years' jail aged me before my time. I can recall examining myself in a mirror on my last morning in my cell room. I was still a handsome man, but my fine red hair had thinned away to leave me virtually bald. And I now wore spectacles all the time.

No matter. The heavy gates of Joliet were about to slam behind me, and I was at liberty to pay the world my cordial respects. . . .

PART FOUR

*1891–1892*

*Being an account of
Thomas Neill's activities
in London between 1st October, 1891,
and 13th November, 1892*

# EX *TEUTONIC*

## I

Upon my freedom, I made immediately for the city of Montreal to see about my affairs. Contrary to my expectations, I discovered that funds had been tied up by my father, and I was unable to realize my share of his estate immediately. The executors, however, gave me an advance sufficient enough to carry me through for the next few months. Naturally, I paid Warden Passmore as arranged, for let it be said that I am an honorable man. In the case of Edward Levy, I decided to forget my obligations—no honor is due to such scalawags. I believe that my failure to pay this man occasioned his perjury at a later date.

Medical practice? Well, I had been removed from the register of physicians able to work in Canada upon my conviction in Chicago, and I was uncertain as to my position in the United States. But even were I permitted to practice medicine in America, I had the sense to foresee the difficulties ahead; I would ever be a "convicted murderer" in the eyes of the stuffy majority. I reckoned it better to count my losses and quit the American continent altogether. . . .

I was in need of rest—I needed to build up my strength—and I considered myself due an exciting time in the fleshpots of some great city far away from bitter recollection. Edinburgh? The thought crossed my mind, but Edinburgh I felt to be too "proper" for the kind of holiday I craved. Paris? I spoke the language, of course, but I loved the Frenchies not at all. London? To London would I go, for all the squalor of the city.

I informed my father's executors of my intentions, and they agreed to finance me straightway on account of my health. But their suggestion that I make contact with my mother or brothers and sisters I waved aside. I owed them nothing—we were nothing to each other. My family was extinct.

And so I set sail for England late in September, arriving at Liverpool on the first day of October. My ship was the *Teutonic* and the passage calm—a good time for reflection and recovery.

Once ashore, I felt fit enough to indulge myself with various young ladies of that port, and ten years' celibacy was joyfully broken. But I couldn't linger forever in the company of strumpets, and after a few days I took a train to the capital.

I had been recommended a certain hotel in Fleet Street—Anderton's—and I booked in at this establishment under the name I chose to adopt in this country: Dr. Thomas Neill, M.D. The hotel was purely a stopgap measure, however, for I decided to remove myself unto suitable lodgings as soon as possible. Not unnaturally, I searched for rooms in that part of London I knew best—namely, in the area of Lambeth Palace Road, hard on Blackfriars and close to St. Thomas' Hospital. And I had no difficulty in finding accommodation—at a small house in Lambeth Road itself, owned by a Mrs. Sleaper and her daughter Emily. I chose the large front room on the second floor, and deposited most of my baggage by way of security.

That first evening, wet and windy, I resolved to spend time away from my dreary hotel and perhaps take myself to a music hall or some other cheerful place of entertainment. I strolled up Fleet Street to Ludgate Circus and found myself browsing in a small bookshop. Strange how it is that fate introduces me to people in bookshops—for I'd not been there more than five minutes when my attention became attracted by a young woman dressed in dark green chiffon. I could tell at once that she was a pavement nymph, although time had not yet started to savage her features; indeed, she was quite comely. . . .

Raising my hat a fraction, I asked the young woman if she

fancied a glass of wine, and she took up my offer immediately. We repaired to the Mermaid public house nearby and indulged in half a bottle of port. Her name was Elizabeth Masters, and she gave her age as twenty. She was, she said, a seamstress.

I gave her some chewing gum while we talked, and she was impressed by my American antecedents. I appreciated that Miss Masters desired a night on the town at my expense before she was prepared to tender her particular brand of services, but such was my influence over her that she consented to a brief adjournment to her rooms at Orient Buildings straightway. As I have said, she was comely—and I decided to see her again. In the meantime, I'd give her this night on the town.

"Let's go to Gatti's," she suggested, and I agreed.

The Adelaide Gallery Restaurant—or just Gatti's—turned out to be in the Strand, and we took a cab.

"How long are you over here in London, dearie?" she asked me during the journey.

"Alas, only a few weeks. I have a substantial claim to some property I must make. Then I return to New York."

And a gladsome time we had at Gatti's; the bright lights and cheap crystal reflected a certain vulgarity, but the band played a tuneful array of ditties and ballads and was much to my liking.

At the bar, Miss Masters introduced me to another young woman called (as well you know) Elizabeth May, who happened to occupy a room next to that of Miss Masters at Orient Buildings. She, too, was a woman of the streets, and looked that way.

Both damsels drank a fair deal, shifting from wines to hard liquor without a thought, until they became quite tipsy. Now, I have certain feelings with regard to women of this order imbibing—feelings I have expressed already—and I shall very soon say more upon the subject when I write of the plight of the lower orders of London life.

Much as I enjoyed the music at Gatti's, the noise made my head ache, and I begged my two companions that we might leave for some quieter place. Tipplers as they were, both Elizabeths chose the notorious King Lud public house at Ludgate Circus. Well, it was close by my hotel, and off we went.

By twelve midnight I longed for my bed and said so. Miss

Masters protested vigorously, and there was a bit of a scene. I suppose that, having tasted the pleasures I was able to provide, the young woman was justifiably loath to part from myself in this abrupt manner. She was drunk and therefore noisy, so I promised her I'd be in touch within a day or two, to quiet her tongue. Then a final nightcap, and we went our separate ways.

## II

You must now bear with me, sir, if I digress awhile, for I attach much importance to what I must say in respect of my activities over the first eight months following my arrival in London Town.

Second only to thè wandering Chinese as a force of corruption are the prostitutes of wealthy Caucasian communities. The crooked path trod by the Israelite is worthy only of contempt by comparison. And I do not make this observation lightly. . . .

Nevertheless, unlike the wicked smilers of Cathay, the harlots of this world are deserving of monumental pity, for they fall and swim in the gutter of their cruel existence by reason of fate, and not necessarily by reason of their own desires. As you know, I am skeptical with regard to your particular qualifications and motives, Cogswell, yet I assume you have had the grace to study the seamier side of London life? If you have not, then indeed you are a charlatan, a humbug, and my words are wasted upon you. But if you *have* forced yourself away from your comfortable chair and cosy fire to pace the backwaters of London, then I apologize. "Backwater" becomes a handy word, for I reckon every lane and alley of the metropolis to represent a tiny dirty canal. Down folk come, like the water, forever on the move, be they gentlemen or flatlanders. Such folk keep the streets alive, but they also swirl up an eddy of flotsam—and this flotsam, naturally, is the prostitution of the city.

It can be said that every woman who yields to her passions and indulges in promiscuous intercourse with more than one man is a prostitute. But, of course, the prostitutes I mention are those who make their very living by sale of their bodies to all comers. Some may come from good homes; very often they have gone into service where the master of the house has seduced them, rendered them heavy with child, and then flung them out to fend for themselves. Such circumstances are not uncommon. Others were themselves born bastards, raised in a tradition of whoring and crime. For such Jezebels nothing can be done.

I have it on secret and reliable information that there are no less than sixty-five thousand prostitutes in the metropolis. In ten years that figure will be doubled, and the city will be little more than one vast bordello whose streets no decent folk dare walk. I predict that your famous Haymarket will soon be no more respectable than the Rue Champlain in Quebec.

Where, then, does the fault lie? Well may you ask! And I shall tell you the answer. The fault lies in attitudes of the so-called ruling classes. Great wealth has fallen into the hands of a few, owing to an economy managed entirely by Jewish financiers— a few who feel neither pity nor guilt toward the unhappy plight of those unfortunates they have exploited for almost a century. The ruling or moneyed classes regard with scorn and embarrassment the poor of this country—an ugly reminder of their own ruthless ways. And so they confine the poorer section of the community within the slums of the East End—out of sight, out of mind, so to speak.

Now, since my arrival in this country I have had brought to my attention the notorious "Whitechapel Enigma." It is not for me to remind you of this series of brutally executed murders. Suffice it to say that, whereas the authorities have laid the blame at the door of a mysterious Russian émigré in their attempt to add yet one more ounce of prejudice against the anarchist movement (even to the extent of forging letters from a person calling himself Pollensky), I have formed the opinion that the public have been played double. Grave suspicion must be attached to a certain personage of Royal blood (and you know who I mean). An attempt by the Secret Service to investigate the truth has been scotched.

But the activities of "Jack the Ripper," or call him what you may, have nevertheless served a useful purpose. The scandal has jolted society. Even your ugly old Queen has expressed displeasure. Over the three years since the last murder took place, some effort to improve the lot of prostitutes has been made. It surely seems that only a frequent recurrence of the events of 1888 can ensure that the authorities continue their good work. A constant reminder is needed every few years—otherwise the authorities will slacken off.

It has been suggested that the motive for the various assassinations attributed to me was financial. They say I did what they say I did in order to blackmail. Utter bunk! My behavior was simply calculated to alarm and vex those in authority and position. Never once did I contemplate receiving a cent for my demands. I sought only to tickle up the complacent—and you must own that I tickled them up pretty damn good. . . .

### III

Next day I moved into my room at Mrs. Sleaper's. My headache of the night before had eased somewhat, but I had slept fitfully at the hotel despite the help of a quantity of opium. I was worried for my sight, and dissatisfied with my spectacles. It occurred to me that I should call upon an optician, and Mrs. Sleaper's young daughter Emily recommended James Aitchison, back in Fleet Street.

Mr. Aitchison turned out to be a first-rater, and examined my eyes with care. Short sight—acute in the left eye—and my failure to acquire a suitable pair of spectacles had caused this eye to squint inward toward my nose. He traced back the damage to my youth: too much book work in a bad light, and peering down gun barrels.

Somewhat relieved by Mr. Aitchison's reassurances, I took myself off to a chemist in Parliament Street. Much thought had I put into the question of suitable poisonous substances—antimony, arsenic, even potassium cyanide had I considered. But Nux Vomica won the day. . . .

The young assistant informed me that strychnine was a "scheduled" poison, and asked that I furnish him with my full name and address. I saw no reason to deceive the laddie, and was quite frank with him—explaining that I was attending a course of lectures at St. Thomas' so that he'd see nothing fishy about my request for Nux Vomica. He also took my order for a box of Planter's capsules in American gelatine.

Since I had promised Miss Masters that she would be hearing from me, I returned to my new lodgings and scribbled a note. I decided to call upon her that very afternoon, so I had my letter delivered by an urchin.

I lunched frugally at a small restaurant in the Westminster Bridge Road, and then ventured off toward Hercules Road and Orient Buildings. I had just turned the corner from Lambeth Road when this very handsome lassie crossed the road ahead of me. I think I lifted my hat to her—but, in any event, she half turned and gave me the glad eye. As she was following the same route as myself, it could be that the woman came to the conclusion that I was pursuing her. No doubt she could tell me for a gentleman, in my tall silk hat and dark cape, and I imagine she liked the cut of my jib. I, in turn, could see that she was a harlot, and I reckoned she was drunk by the way she kept lurching about and grinning at me. I decided to make her acquaintance and let Miss Masters wait a spell.

At the doorway of a seedy dwelling to the end of Hercules Road the woman stopped and beckoned to me. Again I raised my hat, and proceeded after her into the dingy hall. We climbed the stairs in silence. On the first landing the woman unlocked a door, and we went in. It was a bedroom hired out for the convenience of the harlot's trade—sordid and unclean, with an unmade bed and unemptied chamber pot.

"Six shillings," she said, removing her coat.

I placed the money on a dresser.

"What's your name, then?" she asked. "Every man's got to have a name."

"Fred."

"Not another one!" she laughed. "The last Fred I knew left me in a proper fix, he did!"

I don't think there was any further conversation for some

time, and I must confess that I forgot all about my rendezvous with Miss Masters that afternoon.

My first encounter with this woman—Matilda Clover (as you must have guessed by now)—was a pleasant experience, for all her buck-toothedness and boozy state. Indeed, I was somewhat piqued when she later insisted that she take her leave.

"Why so?" I asked. It was only four o'clock.

"I've got to fetch Dinky, haven't I?"

"Who?"

"Dinky. Little Dinky's the fix my other Fred left me with."

Customer or genuine paramour, I never ascertained. But Fred's brat had to be fed, and that was that.

"This room," I asked her as she dressed, "do you have it on rent?"

"Yeh. Me and Ellen split the cost."

"Ellen?"

"Elly Donworth—least, her real name's Linnell—we're sort of friends."

"Pardners."

"What's that? Hey, you have got a funny voice! Where do you come from, Fred?"

I gave her a stick of gum. "New York."

"Really? My, you have come a long way for a good time! Haven't you got any girls in New York, then?"

"Plenty. Not as pretty as you, though."

She giggled through her big teeth and the gum.

"Tell me about Miss Donworth," I said. "Can I get to meet her, too?"

"Not if you mind me getting all jealous."

"I'll give you both that 'good time,'" I said. "Deal?"

"Deal, then. Got a bit of paper so I can write down where to find us?"

So she knew how to write? I was truly amazed. . . .

# IV

Much to my annoyance, the capsules I had ordered from the chemist were not available when I returned a couple of days later. American gelatine appeared not to be favored in this country. I insisted that some be obtained for me. Without Number Fives, my tasks might prove very difficult. This time I think the lazy clerk appreciated the urgency, and I left him with a flea in his ear. Might I add that when at last the chemist succeeded in stocking my capsules, they ordered the wrong size! I do not recommend Mr. Priest's shop in Parliament Street.

It came to pass that Miss Clover introduced me to her friend Elly Donworth on the Saturday evening. Miss Donworth, so young that it grieved my heart to think of the vile profession in which fate and circumstances had seen fit to enroll her. At nineteen, she could drink and swear, and rejoiced in regaling our company with her collection of stories. We made a party of it at the York Hotel, Waterloo—a locale where Miss Donworth was in the habit of picking up her clients—and thereafter at the Canterbury Music Hall. The Canterbury transpired to be a poor rival of Gatti's, reaping custom whenever Gatti's, only a few hundred yards away, became full. I was unimpressed by the Canterbury, and said so.

"Not as good as New York, then, dearie?" Miss Clover said.

"Not as good as Chicago," I told her.

"Tell us about Chicago," asked Miss Donworth, and I spun them the sort of yarn they'd appreciate.

Encumbered as I was with both girls, we did no more than drink and chatter that night, and I bade my companions a very good evening shortly after twelve. I had in my mind a plan of action, and now it was simply a question of choosing one or the other of these two ladies to play the important part. Once in my room, I took a heavy dose of cocaine, and lay down to sort the problem out. Before I drifted off into sleep, I had decided: Miss

Elly Donworth it would be—before the wicked world could drag her still further into the slime.

On Sunday I sent to her home address a message for to meet me at half past six in the afternoon on the Tuesday, at the York Hotel. I begged her to come alone, and said that I had certain information of a confidential nature to our mutual advantage. She knew me as "Fred," and that's how I signed off the letter.

I know not if you're acquainted with the York Hotel in Waterloo Road, but the premises enjoy a scarlet reputation. Pimps, procuresses and their fancy men organize the upkeep of the building, subletting rooms to various "wandering beauties of the night" under their command. While the upper rooms present a glossy and comfortable atmosphere, the basement area provides for the less ambitious. You'll not be surprised if I tell you that young Miss Donworth's position was strictly belowstairs.

She was prompt on arrival, and I bought her a glass of wine at the public bar. I believe she was considerably amused by my appearance, for I had affected a pair of bushy theatrical whiskers to cover my own, and I wore no spectacles on this occasion.

"What's with the disguise, Mr. Fred?"

"Hush! I'll tell you later. Right now I want you to drink up and follow me." The less time spent at the York, the better. . . .

Once outside the public house, I entwined my arm in hers and led her under some railway arches, away from street lighting. It was cold and foggy in this place, and the cobbles slippery to the feet, but I required total solitude.

"What's we doing down here?" she asked me more than once, but I implored her to be silent and patient.

The arches contained several nooks and crannies cut into the black brickwork, and into one of these I took her. Positioning her with her back to the wall, my own body blocking the exit, I rested both hands upon her shoulders.

"Well, here's a funny place for it!"

I shook her gently. "No, Elly—for something far more important. Now listen." I could just make out her features in the gloom, but I doubt if she could see my face at all. "Listen," I went on. "You may have wondered why it is that a gentleman such as myself, an American, hides away in this part of London. I expect you've been trying to figure out just who the Hell I am. Well, I'm going to tell you—provided you swear before God never to divulge our secret to a single soul. Do you so swear?"

"Well, I never. . . ."

"Do you so swear!" I took one of her hands and laid it upon her breast.

"Oh, all right. I swear."

"Good girl. Now listen to me . . . I have marked you out as a young lady of intelligence and fortitude, and I feel that you could perform a valuable service for your country. Do you love your country, Elly? Yes, of course you do. Well, you may know that England has many enemies as well as friends. One of England's firmest friends is the United States of America. I am a detective of that country. You're surprised? Of course you are! Now, one of England's greatest enemies is an organization of very evil men who call themselves Fenians. I expect you've heard of them. They like to kill people and blow up houses with dynamite. The Fenians are also the enemies of America. America and England work together to fight the Fenians. That's why I'm in London. I'm in London because we know of a plot to kill your Home Secretary. The Fenians plan to throw a bomb into his carriage and blast him to Glory. D'you understand me, girl?"

I tightened my hold on her shoulders. Her "Yes" was barely audible.

"Now then, Elly, this is what I want *you* to do: I want you to help your country by taking all sorts of very secret messages to various people in your government. That's all you have to do. You will never be in danger—no one will ever hurt you. Understand? Good. I knew you were a brave girl. I think that together we will be able to save the Home Secretary, and when we do I shall tell him, and the police, just what a clever and brave girl you've been. You know, I wouldn't be surprised one bit if your own wonderful Queen Victoria—God bless her—sends for you to visit her at Buckingham Palace so she can thank you personal. What d'you think about that, Elly?" I let her see how excited I was at this fine prospect.

"Yes" was all she could say.

"Now, will you help us, Elly?"

"Yes."

"Fine—fine. You know, Elly, I reckon we've got to drink to that." I drew a small silver pocket flask from under my cape. "I reckon we've got to partake in a real American cocktail to celebrate our new partnership." I unclipped the top of the hip flask. "Here you are, Elly. Genuine cactus juice from America." I handed her the flask and watched closely as she raised it to her lips. "Drink it all, Elly. It's rather bitter, but it's good stuff. Make you feel right dandy." And she took a big swallow. "That's my girl! Now, I'll tell you what I want you to do. . . . I want you to go wait outside the Wellington up the road until I come and fetch you. I won't be long, lassie, so don't be fretting." I moved her out of the alcove. "Now off you go. . . ."

I waited where I was until she disappeared out of the end of the arches, and then slowly walked in that direction. Before venturing out into the streets again, I casually emptied the remainder of my flask into the gutter. She'd gain the Wellington in about two minutes. In four minutes the contents of her stomach would take effect. Accordingly, I would proceed to the Wellington in three minutes' time.

When I reached the Wellington, the effects of the strychnine had already begun and the poor child was lying face down upon the pavement. A man was bending over her, trying to give her comfort, but so massive were Elly's spasms that four other pedestrians were obliged to lend a hand and help him hold her down. Elly was calling out in the most pitiful manner, and my heart was moved with compassion. It is a terrible thing to see an innocent suffer, and I prayed that her torment soon should end.

Somebody had sent for a medical man, and he arrived carrying a black bag. I know not what administrations were made on behalf of little Elly, but soon a carriage came for her—presumably to remove the girl to the hospital. All this I observed from some distance, so you will appreciate that I cannot say what conversation there was. Certainly, Elly was still screaming when they took her away. Wild with emotion and regret, I made my way home. That night I required a considerable quantity of narcotics to help me sleep.

## V

Exasperated with the incompetence of my chemists, I paid Priest's a final visit that Thursday. The dunderheaded assistant must have paid heed to my criticism at last, for I came away this time with a good supply of Planter's Number Fives. I was determined that further operations should not be so crudely executed as in the case of Elly; now that I had the capsules, this could be avoided.

Homicide—any sudden death—appears to fascinate the mind of the Britisher, and I had not long to wait before a report on the inquest into Elly appeared in the *Gazette*. I ascertained the name of the coroner and concluded that it was time to act. I wrote Mr. Percival Wyatt in no uncertain terms—to the effect that I knew that he and his satellites would fail to bring the killer of Elly to justice, and that I would assist them to discover the culprit in return for three hundred thousand pounds sterling. I signed myself off as a Mr. O'Brien, detective, largely to stir the fools into action.

In the face of this document, Coroner Wyatt had little choice other than to steer the 'quest's jury into a verdict of murder by a person as yet unknown.

This was indeed a start—but more was required. Armed as I was now with capsules, I determined to step up my campaign.

# AN UNCOMMON ASSORTMENT OF
# CORRESPONDENCE

## I

Misses Masters and May interested me no more, for they were too familiar with my true identity, and I could not be sure that they had not spoken of me to others.

There remained Miss Clover—to whom, you'll remember, I was known only as "Fred" from New York City. And Miss Clover had been the friend to poor Elly. What better candidate could she be than that?

Once the death of Elly had become common knowledge via the newspapers, I took the opportunity of calling upon Miss Clover at her home address in Lambeth Road. Far from being distressed, Miss Clover appeared to be neither surprised nor unhappy about the lot of her best friend. I saw her in the morning, and she was bleary-eyed from drink taken the night before. She needed a pick-me-up, and at her request I took her down to the Wellington for a slug of gin. Revived, she insisted that we depart immediately for her room in Hercules Road in order to have relations. That, I decided, could not be done: too near the lodgings of May and Masters for my comfort. As an alternative, I suggested that we meet that evening at a music hall of her choosing, and she settled upon the Canterbury. She was becoming brash with drink in the public house, so I took her away and bought her a pair of new boots she admired. I was, you see, quite prepared to humor the lassie, having regard to all the circumstances. We then parted company.

I met her, as arranged, at the Canterbury that evening—around eight o'clock. We drank some good French wine and had a meal of Mr. Corbishly's mincemeats. I'd hoped food might keep the girl sober, but she'd tippled too much over the day and, come ten, she was drunk as an Indian. It was time to leave, and I took her home by cab.

Miss Clover having misplaced her key, we were obliged to sound the bell, and the front door was opened by a female lodger. In the hall I took care to stay in the shadow lest this stranger see my face, and I wished I'd been sporting my theatrical whiskers. As it was, the lodger paid me scant attention, being angered by the condition of Miss Clover, and urging her to hush her tongue in case she woke up the bastard child upstairs.

I found Miss Clover's bedroom to be as squalid as that she used in Hercules Road, and I could scarce arouse myself to oblige the woman her fancies. Having done, she would have me go out to purchase beer. Beer! The drink of navvies and farm-hands. I positively refused. In the end—after considerable argument—she became irate and went herself.

Some time later she returned, with much belching and blundering on the stairway. I guessed that she'd been drinking as she'd walked back with her beer, and her face was blotched and unlovely in the extreme.

"You are unwell," says I.

"I'm thirsty, that's what I am," she shouts.

"Very well." I took the beer from her and removed the cap. "Take this with your beer," I said, handing to her a couple of Number Fives, "it will help you sleep."

"Dr. Graham says I drink too much. . . . I don't drink too much, do I, Fred?"

"Of course not. Your doctor is a fool. Now, just you take those pills; you'll be fine."

She was too intoxicated to question or to argue, and down went the capsules with the beer. Gathering up my coat and hat,

I told her to lie down and rest. This was a mistake, for the moment her head touched the pillow, she began to vomit. I helped her up, and walked her around the room until she had steadied herself. I examined her vomit, but found no trace of the capsules. I then urged upon her to sleep in a sitting position, and put her into a chair. Then I left.

Now, the unfortunate Dr. Graham has been castigated for his diagnosis in respect of his patient Miss Clover. You'll be aware that the doctor insisted she had suffered alcoholic poisoning, and laid all her twitching and trembling at the door of a bottle of brandy. I agree that Dr. Graham is an incompetent moss-head. Having heard evidence as to how Miss Clover departed this earth, plied with cups of tea and doses of soda by her landlady and various other well-wishers, I'll concede that only a person experienced in poisons might suspect strychnine. But Dr. Graham holds himself out to be a qualified medical practitioner, and should have recognized the obvious symptoms. The effects of Nux Vomica cannot be confused with delirium tremens. My advice to you, Cogswell, is to ensure that it be ordered Dr. Graham has his name removed from the register.

## II

Lest I became indolent in my crusade, I searched for a worthy successor to Miss Clover the very next day—indeed, before I was even sure of Miss Clover's fate (although I had very few doubts in that respect).

At the Alhambra concert hall, off Piccadilly, women of the streets have long gathered in search of "gentlemen" customers. It is an establishment frequented by ne'er-do-wells and men-about-town, and therefore attracts the more pricy kind of whore.

To the Alhambra I went that Wednesday evening. I'd dressed myself up quite gay for the occasion, and in no time I'd entered into conversation with a Miss Louisa Harvey. She was petite and fair, no more than twenty-three, and she had a great deal to say for herself. But our chit-chat was general, and she spent much of her time expressing admiration for the hunter watch I was wearing, making it chime and so forth. I told her that I was an American doctor, and that I was working at St. Thomas'. I was prepared to be relatively frank with her. She, on the other hand, was far from frank. I have since learned all the untruths she told me, and I can only say that I'm shocked by the manner this young varmint lied to me. She told me she was a servant —a lie, for she was living and sleeping with a man called Harris up in St. John's Wood. She gave me her address, but the number of the street she deliberately falsified. And her frauds did not rest there, as well you know. . . .

However, the lassie took my fancy, and I waited for her outside the Alhambra. Far from being true to this fellow Harris, she played him false, and willingly accompanied me to a hotel in Berwick Street, where we made love. I understand her man Harris found out about this, and I only hope he gave her a sound thrashing.

While it grieves me sore to tell you what a sucker this girl made out of me, I appreciate that you have heard her version of things, and I feel it only right that I give you mine. Next morning, while she was dressing herself, I observed some spots on her brow. I drew her attention to these pustules, and offered her my services as a doctor. I fully understand a lady's concern with regard to her appearance, and I was truly endeavoring to help this girl. Naturally, the vain little trull didn't want to look unsightly, and she was pleased to accept my offer. I liked Miss Lou—I was prepared to give her my companionship and my money. I never did consider administering poison to her. In any event, we arranged that I should meet with her that same evening on the embankment nigh to Charing Cross. During the day I prepared a simple solution to her problem with pimples.

We met as agreed, and it had been understood that I would simply present her with the pills, perhaps buy her a drink in some nearby tavern, and then be on my way. It is common knowledge now that she had told this Harris fellow about me, and that he was lurking about on the embankment like some kind of spy. I gave Miss Lou the promised pills, bought her a glass of wine and a bunch of flowers, and all the while she and her man were sneaking me up. When she told her tale in court, Miss Lou fiddled her evidence and said that I'd insisted she take some pills so I could see her, and had even examined her hands to make sure she'd swallowed them down. She threw them away without my looking, of course; so much for her brand of gratitude.

I've got a theory about Mr. and "Mrs." Harris, Cogswell—a theory you'd do well to communicate to the police. I reckon they were part of an outfit intent on blackmailing visitors to your city. I reckon they hoped to compromise me—Harris playing the outraged husband—and then take me for every cent I had. Attorney Russell says that I tried to kill this woman with those pills just because I used her name and fictitious death in certain correspondence. Russell's paid to put me down, of course. Anyway, Russell's an old humbugger. . . .

And I don't propose to say a damn thing more about these people, excepting that I hope Lou Harvey dies of the pox.

For a while I decided to abandon the Alhambra, and to concentrate myself on pursuing the death of little Elly now that the inquest had closed. Coroner had my letter from O'Brien; the time had come for an accusation directed at some pillar of respectability. I selected Mr. Frederick Smith, Member of Parliament, of the wealthy and influential firm W. H. Smith & Son in the Strand. It took me some time to compose a suitable allegation, and I eventually did it in this way: To Mr. Smith I offered my services as a counsellor able and willing to protect him from prosecution for the terrible thing he had done to Miss Donworth. I said that two letters had been recovered from her effects, both from a person signing his initials as H.M.B. I forged and enclosed one of these letters, pretending it was a true copy of the original. The letter warned Miss Linnell that Frederick Smith intended to poison her with medicine laced with strychnine, and advised her to have nothing to do with it. The original of this letter, together with a second in similar vein, I told Smith, were in my possession. I suggested that he employ me to save himself and the good name of his family, adding that if he did desire to retain me, he should say so in a notice to be pasted onto the windows of his Strand offices Tuesday next.

I imagined—quite rightly—that Smith would contact the police authorities at Scotland Yard. On the Tuesday morning, the appointed time, I casually passed W. H. Smith's. The notice was there, all right, and I was gratified that I was being taken seriously.

Now, there came into my life at about this time the most pleasing of distractions. Her name was Laura Sabbatini, to whom I was introduced by the resourceful Mr. Aitchison, my optician. I had called upon the good man in order to collect a spare case of spectacles, when into his consultation room came this delightful young lady. She was in her twenties, with a fine brow rising up into luxuriant coppery hair. She was trim of figure, and sweet of manner, and altogether an angel to behold.

She apologized for her sudden entrance.

"Not at all," says I, leaping to my feet.

"Introduce us, James," Miss Sabbatini urged Aitchison, and we were formally made known to one another. I never quite fathomed their relationship. I believe they were second cousins.

Conversation was easy with Miss Sabbatini—or Laura, as she soon allowed me to call her—and I found her readily amused by my anecdotes on America. She, in turn, informed me that she lived with her aged mother in Berkhampstead, her father being dead. It became clear to me that this selfless young woman had waved aside the security of marriage to look after her mother in her widowhood.

"Miss Sabbatini," I said forcefully, "in America we tend to hit the point soon and hard. Will you visit the theater and dine with me tonight?"

She laughed, but didn't decline. She said she'd think about my invitation. I then pretended to take my leave, and sped round the corner to a flower stall. Armed with the biggest bunch of roses you ever did see, I returned and presented them to her.

"Let these influence you in your decision," I said.

Both she and Aitchison were greatly amused, and I knew I'd won the round.

"If you would care to call upon me at seven . . . ?" Laura suggested.

Mrs. Sabbatini was a genteel lady with—judging by the manner of her living—means. She was semi-invalid, however, and relied heavily upon her daughter for the running of the house and servants. She also had a keenness of brain I found disconcerting, and I knew I'd best watch my step.

"And where are you living in London, Dr. Neill?" One of her first questions.

"I'm afraid I'm confined in lodgings at the moment. I've got to be near St. Thomas' Hospital, and I'm not familiar yet with London."

"And what precisely are you doing in London, Dr. Neill?"

"Research. Addison's disease. We're very backward in America, ma'am." Admissions of this kind are very popular with a certain class of Britisher.

"Thomas was trained in this country too, Mama," said sweet Laura, coming to my rescue.

"Also in Edinburgh, ma'am. England has the finest tradition of medicine in the world."

"So we understand," says Mrs. Sabbatini.

I thought of asking how it was a fine English lady like herself had a name like Sabbatini—and whether her husband had been a greaser or a dago. As it was, I confined myself to a small smile.

Laura left the room on some errand.

"My daughter thinks very highly of you, Dr. Neill," said her mother when the door was closed. "But of course she's only just met you, and she is very young."

How offensive can you get?

"My intentions are honorable, ma'am," I said, determined to ignore the insult.

"I'm sure they are. Nevertheless, a young girl has to be protected these days. Besides, you are no longer a young man, Dr. Neill. . . ."

She'd made me at least sixty, the old she-cat; was I to tell her that ten years in an American jail etch a line or two?

"I am thirty-seven, ma'am," says I. "I consider myself to be quite young!"

"Really? In that case, you have been cheated by Mother Nature, Dr. Neill."

"Ten years' ministering to the Sioux under a burning sun will make *any* man old," I told her.

"The Sioux? What are the Sioux, pray?"

"The Sioux, ma'am, are a fierce tribe of Indians—about as fierce as your Afghans out in India."

"And you doctored them?"

"For ten years."

"Then you are a very brave man."

"A physician has a duty to tend the needy, whoever they might be."

"And you are a dedicated man, Dr. Neill. You have been aged by the performance of Christian works. I apologize for what I said."

She was sincere. I'd gambled that this line of talk would win her over.

Laura returned with a cup of chocolate for her mother.

"You have made the acquaintance of a very extraordinary gentleman, m'dear," Mrs. Sabbatini said to her.

Laura blushed with pleasure.

"I knew you'd like him, Mama," says she.

Far be it from me to relate my courting of Laura Sabbatini. The circumstances of my present sad predicament have inflicted upon this gentle dove a wound so terrible I fear it can never heal. Suffice it to say that our love was something quite sublime. My intentions in her respect were always honorable. It has been suggested by certain dirty-minded folk that I pursued her in order to get my hands on her money. That is a base lie, spread about by those who wish to make an end of me. Why, then, did I continue to dose myself with narcotics and pursue my course of criminal conduct? That is a question you may be asking, for it is said that a man in love forsakes bad habits. Well, the answer is not difficult. Drugs were part of my life—and my only salvation from insomnia and the aching in my brain. As for my conduct, I will say this: I had killed twice, not mindlessly, but for good purpose; was I now to abandon all? Was my carefully constructed plan of action to be thrown aside? Were little Elly and Matilda Clover to have died in vain? Never.

Dear Laura and I became as a pair of young lovers during the weeks that followed our first meeting. Theaters, concerts, champagne dinners. Of course, I never took her to my rooms in Lambeth. Our daily excursions would start at her mother's home in Hertfordshire, or else at some convenient hotel in the city. I must have spent a fortune in cabs and carriages. Sometimes Laura would come to London and stay with her friends in Hampstead. Sometimes I'd stop over at her mother's house —when we'd go to church together, walking arm in arm like man and wife. Both Laura and her mother were very religious, you see, and they were overjoyed to discover in me a fine songster. At church, on Sundays, I'd join in with the choir and make the rafters roar. Whenever I stopped with them I insisted that a Bible be placed in my room. Never once did I lay hands upon young Laura. How could I do such a thing to one so fair and tender? How could I ever look into those soft brown eyes again without a feeling of sorrow and shame? Besides, our love was of the heart and soul. There was nothing filthy about it— our love was pure. Only when I made her my own could I bear to give way to passion. You see, I had determined to marry her. And on the 17th November we became engaged. . . .

## III

Having laid the death of little Elly at the feet of Frederick Smith, I decided it was high time I made use of Matilda Clover. Owing to the crass stupidity of Dr. Graham, no inquest into the girl had been conducted, and she'd simply been buried by the parish in Tooting cemetery—rotten and forgotten. No matter, I would excite interest in her cadaver. Eventually the authorities would be forced to take notice.

Mrs. Sleaper, my landlady, was a gossip and a snob, and she followed the antics of the titled as if they formed part of her own family. It was Mrs. Sleaper who made me acquainted with the scandalous facts surrounding the Russell affair. Now, I hold no truck with folks resorting to divorce simply because a husband strays off in the direction of a pretty face once in a while, but in this case my sympathies lay with the Countess Russell. Her husband was a blackguard.

I considered calling upon her to offer my condolences, and I've no doubt that she would have received me graciously. Instead, I decided to help this fine lady in another way—by scaring the living daylights out of her erring husband. I'd furnish the Countess with useful ammunition to be used against him, should she take the notion.

I wrote her at her suite in the Savoy Hotel, and in this fashion: "Dear Your Grace," I begins. "Without playing the nosey-parker, and not wishing to cause you further grief in these hard times, I feel it my bounden duty to acquaint you with certain harrowing facts concerning the Count. Intelligence has brought it to my notice that your husband has been associating with the late Miss Matilda Clover, of 27 Lambeth Road, and that—finding himself under threats from this woman and her criminal intimates—he has poisoned her unto death. Challenge him with these facts, and consult your lawyers!"

I signed this epistle: "A sympathetic friend."

But it was, in my opinion, more important to start a ruckus in the medical profession. I recalled the existence of an eminent physician by the name of William H. Broadbent. He'd been doctoring the nobility and wealthy folk for a number of years, and rumor had it that he'd be made Royal Physician before long. Of course, the fellow was a charlatan—there were no limits to his quackery. It struck me that to stir it up for him would be a pretty smart idea. Everybody likes to watch a big man take a tumble.

Don't expect me to recall the exact wording of the letter (but it's in the hands of Attorney Russell and his minions if you want it). The gist of what I said was this: That I was a member of a detective agency who had in their possession certain evidence that proved without a doubt that the good Broadbent had been hired to assassinate Miss Clover; that Broadbent had carried out his instructions by poisoning Miss Clover with strychnine, and that we were prepared to hand over this incriminating evidence in return for two thousand five hundred pounds sterling —otherwise the matter would be disposed of to the police. I advised Broadbent to put a personal in the *Daily Chronicle* saying that he'd pay. The personal was to be on the front page, any time in the first week of December. I added that I was not humbugging, and that I was in a position to ruin him. I signed off as "M. Malone."

I knew Broadbent would consult the police, and I figured the law officers would suggest he do as the letter demanded, in order to trap the sender. I noticed a reply to Malone in the *Chronicle* of December 4th inviting Malone to call at the doctor's home—and I understand that two detective officers lay in wait for the caller until midday Saturday before Scotland Yard treated the matter as a hoax. Fact is, the police had themselves dragged in the dust over this business by Judge Hawkins; fact is, I wasn't surprised by the authorities' lack of interest in the likes of Matilda Clover—I guess they checked her out and, once they found she was just a trollop resting in a pauper's grave, shelved the matter. Could be that Broadbent told them to throw their hand in. I don't expect *he* wanted publicity of this kind—it was the kind of thing that might have stopped him getting an eyeful of Vicky's paps.

Conscious that I was beginning to run short of funds, I next planned a return trip to Canada. The executors of my father's estate had kept their greedy hands on my money for as long as possible, although I had written and threatened them on several occasions. I reckoned that the sight of me suddenly on the doorstep might jolt these Shylocks into parting with my property. It further occurred to me that I needed some occupation, or "cover," to justify my existence in London in case the authorities came round to me and started asking a lot of damn-fool questions. One night I bumped into Lou Harvey when I was out with Laura—and I darn near died of fright, I can tell you. I pretended I didn't know her, and stalked off pretty smart, but Laura gave me this queer look. Of course, Attorney Russell made out that I'd turned scary at the sight of the Harvey woman because I'd supposed her to be dead, killed off by the pills I'd given her for her pimples. But then Attorney Russell's a professional fact-twister, is he not?

Anyway, it was time to skip out. . . .

A pleasant Yuletide I spent at Berkhampstead. With darling Laura tinkling the ivories. I was in fine voice, and I treated the Sabbatinis and their friends to a fine selection of ballads. I recall the tears in the eyes of her mother whenever I sang "Down in the Valley." I don't think she ever did realize the ditty was virtually composed by the cons of Frankfort Penitentiary in Kentucky, and a firm favorite at Joliet.

> Write me a letter, send it by mail,
> Pack it in the care of Birmingham jail.
> Build me my gallows forty feet high
> So I may watch her as she rides by.

The old witch was near to blubbering by the end of it. . . .

In the New Year I made my will and left all my worldly possessions to Laura. Such was the extent of my love for this woman.

"I've never told you," I said, in the presence of her mother, "but I am a very rich man. If anything befalls me, at least you will be cared for, my sweetness."

I wrote the will myself—you will remember my distrust of lawyers—and gave it her for safekeeping.

"You have called yourself Thomas Cream," said Laura with some surprise.

"My Canadian name—my real name—the name I shall soon be giving to you, my pretty," says I.

We fell into each other's arms.

"You are a very kindly man," says her mother.

And with those words ringing in my ears, I took my leave. For on the morrow—the 6th January, 1892—I was due to depart for Liverpool. I had booked aboard the *Sarnia* for my own home-town of Quebec.

# A SAMPLE CASE OF MEDICINES

## I

The *Sarnia* steamed into Quebec harbor on the 18th, after an uneventful passage. Old memories were revived at the sight of the waterfront, although much had changed. I guessed that the timber boom had come to an end with the gradual decline of sailing ships. I saw nothing of the gangs of timber-stowers, and wondered as to the fate of Wideawake Larrigan and his fellows. Dead and gone—the end of a rare breed of men.

Even the Rue Champlain did little but disappoint. I took a buggy from the quay and up the street. The Strop and Block had been torn down to make way for a smart Frenchie hotel and restaurant. Gone also were the taverns and dosshouses. I felt witness to the death of an era.

I booked in at Blanchard's Hotel and left my baggage. I didn't stop the night there, however, having myself a night on the town instead, in company with a Frenchie lass. Sea voyages put a keen edge on many kinds of appetite.

Next day I telegraphed my father's executors to announce my arrival, and to advise them to quit sitting on their hands. In the hotel foyer I bumped into this fellow, liked the way he sported himself, and got to conversing. His name (as you know) was John Wilson M'Culloch, and he had a room on the same floor as myself. He came from Ottawa, and was a traveling man for a grocery concern. We had dinner together that night, and he told me a bit about himself. I reckoned he might make a good companion on a "whore trail" on account of his easy way. But he turned out to be married, with children, and kind of a prude. It's funny sometimes how you get these laddies, all ready for a smutty story but without the nerve to do anything stronger. I guess they're plumb scared of women, and just a lot of talk.

Just the same, I couldn't help liking the young man, and I took to telling him about my adventures downtown—to remind him of what he was missing. He'd listen to me spellbound, and I think he was basically a dirty dog. I showed him some amazing photographs as well. I don't believe the boy had seen anything like them before, because he turned red as his waistcoat when he looked at them. I should have taken his home address and sent off some copies to his wife, all signed up "Lulu LaZoo" on the reverse. . . .

One morning he complained he was out of sorts, and I took him up to my room to fix him right. It was only a bilious attack, but M'Culloch made out he was going to die, the way he kept on moaning. Later, when he was better, he asked me a lot of questions concerning my business in London. I told him that, as a qualified Canadian doctor, I acted on behalf of various drug companies. It occurred to me that we might be able to help each other. Perhaps I could latch on to his company—Jardine's of Toronto. So we repaired to my room with a bottle, and I showed him my collection of samples. He showed particular interest in my bottle of Nux Vomica capsules—maybe because the container was of that yellow Venetian glass with a fancy stopper. I made out that these were pills to get fallen women out of the family way, and showed him a leather box holding more of my "recipes." Of course, I told him this in jest, just as I went on to show him my theatrical whiskers.

"What in tarnation are those for?" he asks me, googoo-eyed.

"To prevent identification," says I. "When you're burrowing like a mole into a woman, long face-fungus gives them confidence."

As it transpired—from M'Culloch's version of events he gave in evidence—the dunderhead took me seriously. Let me assure you that the only thing he took seriously that night was my collection of Liza Brooks' jewelry—or should I still refer to her as Mrs. Cream?

"They're very fine," he said, ferreting in the tin box in which I stored the articles.

"Sentimental value," I said.

"A lady friend?"

"No—they belonged to a girl who played me double. We got engaged, I had to go to the States, and when I returned she'd given me the go-by and made off with another man."

"I'm sorry, sir."

"Don't be—I've still got her jewels, haven't I?"

M'Culloch looked distressed. "Is that why you abort women?"

"No. Nothing to do with it. I abort women as quickly and as painfully as possible to ensure that they don't ever abuse their bodies again."

"Isn't that a criminal offense?"

"My patients are seldom in a position to go running to the police. They come to me for help, and I help them. And when Tom Cream helps a girl, he fixes her up real good."

How it was that M'Culloch believed what I was saying, I'll never know. Do abortionists advertise themselves in such a fashion and stay in practice?

"All these drugs," M'Culloch went on, pointing at my walnut sample box, "d'you use all of them for abortions?"

I took out four of the bottles and held them up to him. "Morphia, opium, cocaine, and laudanum. These I use for myself. I get these pains in my brain, can't sleep; I need these for myself."

M'Culloch shook his head. "What kind of pains do you get, sir?"

"Across here"—I touched my temples—"and sometimes behind the eyes. Drive a man half distracted, Mr. M'Culloch."

"You ought to see somebody about it, sir."

I laughed. " 'Physician, heal thyself.' . . ."

M'Culloch took his leave after a few days, and we reached no sensible business arrangement after all. However, he did give

me the name of a Mr. Arthur Kingman, of the Harvey Manufacturing Company, who he thought might be interested in my
appointment as a London-based agent. I guess M'Culloch took
my jests too seriously. Fact is, I worried him plenty just before
he left. We were in the hotel sitting room discussing one of the
recent guests, an American gentleman from Buffalo. This
American was spending his money like water, and we reckoned
he wasn't short of cash.

"I could use that man's money," I said to M'Culloch. "Just one
little pill and our friend would be taking a long sleep."

"You'd kill a man for his money?"

"Surely would."

"You're not fooling?"

"Some things I never fool about. One of them's money, young
man."

And M'Culloch made some excuse and quit the room in something of a hurry. When Attorney Russell questioned M'Culloch
in the witness box, M'Culloch made out that I hadn't been
kidding him! Rascally fool. . . .

As a means of approaching this man Kingman, I first placed
an order for five hundred 1/16th-grain strychnine pills, to be
sent along to my hotel. When these arrived, I wrote him offering my services. It turned out that Kingman wasn't too interested in my helping his company, for they rejected my suggestion. This isn't altogether surprising, for the Harvey Manufacturing Company of Saratoga Springs has a reputation for
being slow-witted. If you've got any shares in that company,
Cogswell, my advice is for you to sell them up quickish.

Throughout February I spent my time chasing the executors
of my father's estate, and they finally agreed to advance me a
little over one thousand dollars to tide me over. I informed
Kingman I'd got this money, and urged that he notify his company that I was able now to establish myself back in England
as a first-rate representative. But Kingman, being no more than
a pathetic and timorous underling in the firm, sat on his butt
and did nothing. There were no limits to the lack of initiative
on his part.

I, on the other hand, saw an opportunity to start tongues

a-wagging when I got back to London. I recalled that I'd once been badly treated at the Hotel Metropole—something to do with tipping a waiter—and I worked out a way of taking a jab at them. I caused to be printed several hundred copies of a circular, for distribution among their guests upon my return. I gave the pamphlet a bold heading, guaranteed to stir the readers up: "Ellen Donworth's Death." Then: "To the Guests of the Metropole Hotel. Ladies and gentlemen, I hereby notify you that the person who poisoned Ellen Donworth on the 13th last October is today in the employ of the Metropole Hotel and that your lives are in danger as long as you remain in this Hotel." I signed myself, "Yours respectfully, W. H. Murray," in memory of Frank Murray from Pinkerton's agency. I reckoned I'd be serving out this notice sometime in April, so I dated it for that month. I'd be tickled something dandy to watch the faces of the staff and management of the Metropole as their customers fled the premises in alarm!

But it was time to return anyway, and I booked a saloon berth on the *Britannic,* due to sail from New York on March 23rd.

One final effort to make the Harvey Manufacturing Company see sense—Kingman and I journeyed over to Saratoga Springs, and I saw Oliver Scarman of that organization.

"Thomas Cream, physician, at your disposal, sir," says I, taking in his scruffy office.

"I'm grateful for your interest, Doctor, but our company positively does not require representation in London."

"Your company is not interested in profit, Mr. Scarman?"

"Of course we are! It's just that we have no dealings in London."

"Then it's high time you did, and that's where I'm able to help you."

Scarman frowned and thought for a moment.

"What kind of remuneration were you thinking of, Doctor?" he says at last, with a sly look.

"As a qualified medical practitioner with natural business acumen, I don't think I could accept less than a retainer of one thousand per annum, sir."

"One thousand dollars!"

"Pounds sterling, sir—pounds sterling."

"One thousand pounds! You are off your head, sir!"

"I'm conscious of my worth, sir!"

"You aren't worth five cents, sir. Now get out of my office!"

So much for the Harvey Manufacturing Company. Take my heed, Cogswell, avoid investment in their stock.

Kingman was much embarrassed, and stayed behind to soothe the old buffoon. I later saw him at my hotel apartment. Somehow he'd fixed it so that I'd get a commission on any orders for his company produce I might obtain in London. I hadn't got such an agreement in mind, but it was better than a poke in the eye with a blunt stick, so I consented. I also determined to find a way of teaching that Scarman fellow an awful lesson. . . .

## II

The *Britannic* docked into Liverpool on the first day of April, and I didn't linger. I headed straight for London and Laura Sabbatini.

I took a room at Edwards' Hotel, in Euston Square, before returning to my lodgings in the Lambeth Palace Road. But most of my time I spent at Berkhampstead.

Laura was just as I remembered her—pretty as a picture, shining with good-natured innocence. She was excited about wedding plans, and hopped about like a jack-rabbit, while her mother watched with pride.

I gave Laura some of Liza's brooches and rings, making out that I'd purchased the same during my trip to New York.

"This one's got a name on it," said Laura, examining the back of a silver article. "F. E. Brooks," she read.

"Fenton Ebenezer Brooks," I told her, "the top jewelry store in New York State."

"Oh. Oh, Thomas, it must have been very dear!"

"Nonsense. Anyway, you're entitled to the best, my buttercup."

And I decided to make a gift to her of all of Liza's bits and pieces. I described to the Sabbatinis the success of my mission in the New World. I went into it in some detail, for I was anxious that they understood me to be properly employed.

"I'm afraid I shall be extremely busy," I added.

"You mustn't overwork, Thomas," said Laura. She was always anxious about my health, and she knew I took pills to help me sleep.

I promised to do only the minimum necessary, but warned her not to fret if she didn't hear from me for days on end.

"Will you be traveling, then?" asked her mother.

"Possibly."

Upon my return to 103 Lambeth Palace Road, I was informed by Miss Emily Sleaper, my landlady's daughter, that another medical man had taken a room under that roof. This, of course, was young Walter Harper. Far from being affronted by this state of affairs, I was overjoyed, and looked forward to meeting the young man. There was much we could discuss, and I had one or two theories I wished to put to "a second opinion." But Harper was a hard-working thingumajig, and never about. I gathered that he'd only just qualified, so no doubt he kept up his industry to impress his masters at the institute. No matter, he could wait.

I come now to the demise of Alice Marsh and Emma Shrivell, and don't you suppose that I was endeavoring to steer round this subject. I met up with Miss Marsh at the Canterbury rooms on the Saturday night. I was alone, she was alone, and we just sort of merged together. She was a woman of the streets, twenty-one, and foul of mouth. Never have my ears been subjected to such colorful tirades. Tiny of physique and sharp of features, Alice Marsh's eyes were always on the swivel.

"Where you from, girl?" I asks her.

"Tooting, mister."

And I thought of Miss Donworth's moldering body.

"Where do you live, girl?"

"Stamford Street, mister—with my friend."

"Who's your friend?"

"Emma—Emma Shrivell."

"Is she on the game too?"

"Just started. She's only nineteen, and she keeps coming over all peculiar about it."

"What she needs is a 'gentleman.' "

"What she needs is a d— good ——, mister."

"You mustn't be unkind to her. She's bound to be frightened."

"She's come over from Whitechapel. You've heard what b— well happened to some —— up there a few years back? B— horrible, it was."

"That was a long time ago."

"They never did catch the —— ——, did they!"

"But they found out who it was."

"Did they? I never b— well heard that!"

"His Royal Highness the Duke of Clarence."

"Well, I never. Why didn't they —— well do something about it, then?"

"They were ordered to keep their mouths shut. And it would have been high treason, girl."

"They're —— ——, the lot of them!"

"True. Let me get you another glass. Then we'll repair to your place. All right?"

"If you think you're going to b— well get a good —— out of Emma, you'd better think again, mister." But she gave me her tankard. At the bar I purchased two bottles of beer and a bottle of brandy and a bottle of wine; it was essential that both girls should drink, and I had to cater for Emma Shrivell's unknown tastes.

Stamford Street was unknown to me, and transpired to be one of the more dilapidated streets between Waterloo and Blackfriars Road. The girls both occupied rooms on the second floor, and it was past midnight when I arrived with Miss Marsh.

Her friend Miss Shrivell was already abed and had to be woken by loud bangings on the door. She emerged in her night attire—a dumpy little girl with brown curly hair.

"This 'ere gentleman's brought some drink for us, Em," explained Miss Marsh.

233

Miss Shrivell appeared to be unhappy about joining the party, rubbing her eyes and complaining.

"C'mon, old sleepy-head," says Miss Marsh, and the other at last relented.

We went into Miss Marsh's room. It was spotless clean, much to my astonishment, and the rickety bed was made up. I put down the bottles on a washstand and gathered together some glasses.

"Miss Marsh tells me you're from Whitechapel," I said to Miss Shrivell, uncorking the brandy.

"Whitechapel? No, I'm from Brighton."

"Brighton?"

"Down in Sussex. She's from there, too."

Goddamned little liar, thought I; but I should have guessed by Marsh's accent—it wasn't that hideous rasp common to Londoners of this class.

"So it would be wrong to ask you if you're worried about the Ripper?" I ventured.

"Who's he?"

Such naïveté.

"The gentleman's a doctor," Miss Marsh told her friend. "Says his name is Fred."

"I'm hungry," said Miss Shrivell.

"Have a drink," I said.

"Not till I've had something to eat. Strong drink makes me funny."

"Very sensible."

"I've got a tin of salmon." Miss Marsh began to rummage in her wardrobe, and then waved her hand triumphantly. "Here you are!"

I watched as she unrolled the tin, scraped out the contents onto a saucer, and handed the mess to her friend. Miss Shrivell ate with all the vigor of her tender years.

"Now have a drink," I said when she'd finished.

She took the glass from me.

"And take these," I added, holding out three oval capsules. "They'll help you to sleep."

"What are they?"

"Just medicine. I'm a doctor, you know. . . ."

"Oh, all right." And she washed them down with the brandy.

"I didn't think you'd come up here to let us b— sleep," says Miss Marsh.

"It's late—and I have an early appointment tomorrow," I said.

I offered her three of the same. She studied them suspiciously.

"They're harmless," I assured her.

"So you —— say!"

"They assist a good complexion, too."

"Oh, well . . ." And down they went.

"I'll be in contact," I said, putting on my hat. "You can keep the rest of the drink. I'll call round here pretty soon. We'll have a gay time, we will. Do you like Gatti's?"

"Will you take us to Gatti's, mister?"

The thought bucked up Miss Shrivell no end. Poor lass, I don't suppose she'd had many pleasures in her life. Farmgirl turned pavement whore, subjected to the unloving caresses of filthy men for half a guinea, and for the rest of her days, until she'd be selling wilted flowers outside railway stations, as wrinkled and old as her wares. Better that she'd stuck it out in the dairy. . . .

"Certainly I'll take you there—and to the Alhambra."

"No kidding, mister?"

"You've learned yourself an American expression, bless you! 'No kidding,' as we say. I'll take you other places, too. I'll show you the fashionable cafés and restaurants. You'll be thought of as a duchess—because I'll buy you fancy clothes and hats. Folk will say 'Who in tarnation is that *beautiful* woman?' and they'll be told 'Don't you know? Why, that's Miss Emma Shrivell, the famous actress!' That's what will be said about you, little one."

"And what will they b— well say about *me?*" asked the shrewish Miss Marsh.

"Ah! Of you they'll say this: 'Isn't that the one who should be married to the Duke of Clarence?' "

And thus did I take my leave of two dying women. . . .

235

# III

I am given to understand—from exaggerated evidence—that the two girls commenced their yelling at about half after two, rousing the neighborhood with their ululations. I suppose that would be about right, having regard to the dosage contained in the capsules. Miss Marsh did her hollering in the passageway, clad only in her nightshirt, and was forced to drink an emetic of water and mustard by the landlord. I'll bet two dollars to a steer playing it calm come gelding time that her language was pretty rough. . . .

Miss Shrivell—awakened, no doubt, from dreams of the Alhambra—did her squawking upstairs, writhing about on the floor like a sidewinder and calling upon her already inconvenienced friend.

Police Constable Cumley and an ambulance were called, and Marsh started counting the angels on the way to St. Thomas'. Miss Shrivell died much later, at the hospital. I'm told she suffered much pain. I regret this, and from the bottom of my heart, for she was not a vicious girl. She was a victim of our times—yet another simpleton forced to earn her way upon the streets. She was a victim of British society, of righteous men with ruthless ways. She died as she had lived, unwanted, uncherished, unheeded. Her screams no longer affront the authorities—they are happy that she is gone. I'm sure no one was ever buried in her plain pine coffin with greater speed or relief.

But at least the authorities conducted the inquest into these two women with a grain of expertise. "Death by poison administered by a person unknown." I'd not the faintest notion that Police Constable Cumley had seen me enter the house in Stamford Street with Miss Marsh. I reckon he was on the sneak, lurking in the shadows, obscure and unloved in his blue cape and ridiculous helmet. And I had a strong sense for creepy Peelers, as you might imagine. . . .

As you know, I am not a person without good looks. My brow and profile have been compared with those to be seen on ancient busts of the Roman emperors. Ladies have always found me both attractive and sparkling of manner. My body, well built and upright, has long been remarked upon. Dressed or stripped off, I have presented a formidable sight since early manhood.

Laura, deprived as she was of my company for days on end, naturally wished for some reminder of the man who had selected her for marriage. Portraits are fair enough, provided the artist has the gift and sense to depict the positive features of his subject. I have been painted many times under request, but never has an artist done true justice to me. They tend to paint me with a chin too massive, and with my eyes clinging to my nose. Moreover, never has the intelligent shape of my head— scant of hair and therefore exposed—been embodied with skill.

And so I resorted to the services of a photographer, Mr. William Armstead, of the Westminster Bridge Road, and a personage of some repute. He puffed off portraits of me in some number—one or two of which I found acceptable.

Bill Armstead lived upon his photographic studio with his lady wife; a nice woman she was, although I think she fancied me over and above her husband. (Apart from the slight squeeze when none were about, I did nothing untoward, I assure you. Recollections of Stott still hurt a mite.)

Also acceptable was their friend John Haynes, who lodged with the Armsteads for one pound a week. Haynes and I struck it off dandy. He was a toady, and I was someone prepared to tolerate. In fact, I despised him, and still do. If you consult this laddie, Cogswell, remember what I say, for John Haynes is a twister.

But young Dr. Walt Harper occupied my interest. Who was this fellow? He'd been told by Mrs. Sleaper of my existence under the same roof, yet he chose to ignore me. Never once did he put himself out to make my acquaintance, although I slid a note or two of invitation under the man's door. He seemed set upon shunning me, the little upstart, although he knew not who I was and from whence I had come. I don't know whether Mrs. Sleaper described me to him in unflattering terms. That's as may be, for I recollect a difference with this Jewess at the time concerning the payment of my rent. Perhaps the mean-eyed cat had done me down. . . .

In any event, I was made sore by the doctor's refusal to meet up with me, and I thought I'd pull him down a peg, off his high and mighty perch. Ma Sleaper brought it to my attention that he had a very distinguished father, retired and living it out in the countryside. Trouble a father with regard to his son, and you'll be putting a spiny-joe amid the hound dogs.

It has been suggested that I must have been insane to have followed the course I did. Attorney Russell considered this his ace in the tray, but then Attorney Russell has been exposed as an Irish peat-humper of limited brain and integrity.

First I fished for a bit of information about young Harper, and here I found Miss Emily Sleaper most accommodating. She had made it her business to know everything concerning the young man and his family. She had a habit of tidying up his room whenever the opportunity presented itself, and I reckon she was a snooper. Maybe she hoped he'd take a liking to her and propose marriage. Girls of her kind and class are always on the make, always anxious to better themselves. And there's always some galoot of Harper's means and education ready to fall into their snares.

"Do you happen to know the address of Dr. Harper's father?" I asks of Emily Sleaper. I'd caught her in the laddie's sitting room, flicking about with a feather duster.

"I think he lives in Barnstaple," she said. She suffered from adenoids, and I misunderstood her.

"In Barnstaple—North Devon," she repeated.

That would do; like as not there'd be only one Dr. Harper, F.R.C.S., in that town.

"What you want to know for, Mr. Neill?"

"Doctor Neill, little girl. Please don't be impertinent." I always had the feeling Emily Sleaper disliked me.

"Doctor, then. But what you want to know for?"

I was tempted to order her to continue with her dusting and mind her own business, but a better thought crossed my mind. I'd put her off her Sir Galahad. . . .

"The boy's in bad trouble," I said. "Concerning the death of those two girls."

"What, the ones in Stamford Street?"

"He did them in," I said, adopting her particular brand of slang.

She stared at me with the utmost stupidity.

"He murdered them, Miss Sleaper."

"You're balmy!"

"I wish I was—I sincerely do. But I'm afraid I'm not. Walter Harper killed them, and that's a fact. The police have the proof. Both of the poor wee lassies got letters warning them not to take any stuff from him."

"You *are* mad!" cried Emily Sleaper. She had a nasty look in her eye, and I decided to say no more.

"Just as you please," I said from the doorway. "But you wait and see, my girl!"

Barnstaple in northern Devon. I'd never heard of the place, and never had visited that part of England. I have always found the English countryside depressing in the extreme, with those endless muddy lanes and thicket hedges. Moneyed folk retire to these parts and lord it over the peasants from their great mansions, flogging poachers and riding to hounds with their fat-assed women. The peasants hate them, of course, and I've no doubt that one fine day the tocsin will sound a call to pitchforks. God save the squirearchy when the insurrection begins!

I questioned the Sabbatinis with regard to North Devon that weekend. Laura told me that she liked the countryside, and I did my best to show her the folly of her thoughts.

"There is no freedom for the poor," I said, "and there must be freedom and justice for all."

"You are thinking again of your beloved Indians," says her mother.

"Maybe."

"And what freedom and justice have those wretched natives received from your government, pray?"

"They are well treated, ma'am!"

"Not so, Thomas. You are out of touch. We hear that they are murdered for their land!"

Not being over-familiar with the problem of the American Indian, I was took unawares.

"Do you deny it?"

The old lady was insistent, and I felt not the urge to do battle upon unknown territory.

"Alas—I cannot," and I hangs my head.

"You are a person of both devotion and honesty, Thomas!"

"Vicar asks that you might sing tomorrow," Laura said, changing the subject in her subtle way.

"But of course! Evensong?"

"No, morning service."

I could do no wrong within that household.

And I sought to be effective with regard to Dr. Joseph Harper, of Barnstaple, North Devon.

As "W. H. Murray," I penned the letter so: "Dear Sir, I am writing to inform you that one of my operators has indisputable evidence that your son, W. J. Harper, a medical student at St. Thomas' Hospital"—a deliberate mistake—"poisoned two girls named Alice Marsh and Emma Shrivell on the 12th inst., and that I am willing to give you the said evidence (so that you can suppress it) for the sum of £1500 sterling. The evidence in my hands is strong enough to convict and hang your son, but I shall give it you for £1500 sterling, or sell it to the police for the same amount. The publication of the evidence will ruin you and your family for ever, and you know that as well as I do. To show you that what I am writing is true, I am willing to send you a copy of the evidence against your son, so that when you read it you will need no one to tell you that it will convict your son. Answer my letter at once through the columns of the London *Daily Chronicle* as follows:—'W.H.M.—Will pay you for your services. —Dr. H.' After I see this in the paper I will communicate with you again. As I said before, I am perfectly willing to satisfy you that I have strong evidence against your son by giving you a copy of it before you pay me a penny. If you do not answer it at once I am going to give evidence to the Coroner at once."

So it was, word for word. I made no mistake here, because Mr. Geoghegan furnished me with a copy of that letter and I am looking at it right now.

I see that I dated it the 25th April. In fact I wrote the epistle the day previous.

How is it, then, that the prosecuting forces consider me insane? What can be judged crazy by that letter? No demand was made in earnest—I wrote only to frighten. I deprecate this notion that I must have been off my head.

With the letter I wrote Dr. Harper Sr. I included newspaper cuttings covering not only the demise of Miss Marsh and Miss Shrivell, but also the death of Elly Donworth (an account in *Lloyd's Weekly News*). Perhaps you find this strange, since I was not directly accusing his son of that particular crime. Well, I reasoned it this way: if Harper realized that there'd been a killing previous to that of Marsh and Shrivell with the same *modus operandi*, why then would he not also conclude that his dearest son and heir was responsible for this outrage as well? Of course he would. That's the way I figured it out. . . .

I gather that my letter had an effect akin to jabbing a hornets' nest with a hickory broom, because Dr. Harper Sr. got in all of a frenzy and went war-pathing to the police authorities!

Now, several police officers have sought credit by saying that they were the first to institute some kind of sane investigation into the deaths of these women, and we all know that a policeman will tell any kind of yarn to earn that extra stripe on his sleeve. I think it's right to instruct you what really happened.

Constable Cumley, having seen me at Miss Marsh's house on the night of her death, was looking out for me. He had my description, you see. I don't suppose that he reckoned I'd been connected with the death of Miss Marsh or Miss Shrivell, but he probably thought that if he could find me, I'd pay him handsomely to keep his mouth shut. After all, he'd be able to threaten me by saying he'd report the fact I'd been seen in the company of two loose ladies on the same night they got bumped off.

But it was Police Sergeant M'Intyre who first suspicioned me.

I met M'Intyre through Bill Armstead, and he told me he was

employed by the Criminal Investigation Department at Scotland Yard. I'll own that I didn't believe him, for he was a dapper little fellow with a toothbrush mustache and not much in his head. I think he was related to Mrs. Armstead, but it could be that he was just vain enough to want his portrait taken by Bill. M'Intyre asked me about myself, and I saw no reason to tell him lies. It occurred to me that M'Intyre might have his uses as someone on the inside who'd be able to inform me how inquiries into the death of Clover were getting along.

"What's your interest in this Clover person, Doctor?" he asks me.

"I don't think she died the way they say she did," I said.

"I'm sorry, I don't know anything about her. Who was she? How did she die?"

"Wait and see, Sergeant. It'll all come out in due course." And I left it at that.

In his evidence Constable Cumley deceived the court into believing that he'd caught sight of me again outside the Canterbury on about May 12th, and that I'd been walking up and down, acting peculiar. This is untrue, for I didn't go near the Canterbury on May 12th. He also says he saw me on other occasions that night, eyeing young women. That is also untrue.

You see, I know exactly when it was that the law officers began to show interest in me and commenced to follow me about or have their spies do so. Sergeant M'Intyre it was who gave the game away.

We were having tea at Bill Armstead's house, and suddenly M'Intyre pokes his pipe at me.

"Tell me, Doctor. What exactly is your business in London?"

"Pharmacy. I represent the Harvey Manufacturing Company, New York State."

"I see. Tell me, do you have offices over here?"

"No. I conduct trade from my lodgings."

"I see. Have you been successful—I mean, have you actually sold any of your drugs to anyone?"

"No, sir. Not yet."

"Have you tried?"

"Of course."

"Tell me, then, whom did you try?"

"Well, I haven't actually approached anyone as of yet. But I have several companies in mind."

"I see. Which companies?"

"I have a list—I can't remember their names just like that."

"Not even the name of just one of them?"

"No, sir."

I didn't like this poking into my business, and so I got up and took my leave. M'Intyre said he'd like to talk with me again sometime, and I agreed. I told him I'd be in touch. Beneath his fussy manner, I realized M'Intyre was a snooper. But I did not then appreciate that he was a secret agent.

Back in my rooms, I thought up a way to occupy M'Intyre's mind. If his superiors had set him after me, then I'd give them something to worry about. I worked it all out, and set to my task without delay.

Meanwhile, what M'Intyre and the law officers needed was another "mystery" to solve. The more crowded their books became with unsolved mysteries, the greater the scandal that followed, the wilder the false accusations, and the more scathing the press would be.

On May 17th I took myself out early, insisting that Mrs. Sleaper provide me with my supper shortly after six. I then went straight to the Canterbury and took a chair at a table already occupied by several local ladies in search of custom. Once again I attracted their attention by playing the tune on my watch, and I was soon selected as a companion by a young girl called Violet Beverley. I'm not proposing to deal with this lady in any depth—just let me say that she was around twenty-six, from Brixton village, and of little interest. But she should suit my purpose, and the less I knew about her ways and antecedents, the better.

She had a room over in North Street, by the Kennington Road, and to this establishment we eventually repaired. I had with me my silver hip flask, as well as a case of various pills. At her room we enjoyed carnal experience, and I offered to prepare her an "American Cocktail" by way of reward.

"What's you got in here, then?" she asked of my leather bag while I was mixing her a drink. Her voice was harsh and my brain was in pain, so that the sound of her made me wince.

"Pills."

"Pills. What d'you want with pills, then?"

"I travel for a New York drug house," I said, handing her the cocktail.

She sniffed at the glass and held the contents up under the lamp for scrutiny.

"What's this, then?"

"Back home we call it an Indiana Haymaker," I said. "Try it."

"No, thanks—I've changed my mind."

"Try it!" I insisted. I suppose I was a trifle sharp, but my head was aching fair to busting.

"No, I won't. Why should I? I don't know what it is, do I?"

I think I seized her by the lower jaw and squeezed.

"Just try it."

She became very irate, flinging my hand away, shouting obscenities. I slapped her face hard.

"You b— b—!" And she was at me, clawing like a mountain cat. I hit her once more, causing her nose to bleed, and I wanted to have her throat in my hands.

"Murderer!" she screamed.

Her voice was very powerful, and I had visions of people from the neighboring rooms being aroused and barging their way into the bedroom.

"Shut up," I says, and hurled her to the floor. I pulled a couple of sovereigns out of my pocket and cast them after her. They rolled under the bed, and I reckoned she'd hold her mouth until she retrieved them. My theory was correct, and I was almost out of the door when she re-emerged.

"B— b—!" she yells, and throws the glass of "American Cocktail" at me. I ducked, and the vessel smashed upon the frame, the white liquid running down the woodwork.

I'd bungled—but I could scarcely expect every effort to be rewarded with success. Given the opportunity, I'd seek this

Violet Beverley out again. No woman makes such a damn fool of me. If necessary, I'd eliminate her with something other than poison. But whatever method I did employ, I vowed that her end should be as unpleasant as with the others.

# THE GREAT CONSPIRACY

## I

A great conspiracy had already commenced to be put into operation.

John Haynes is a secret agent in government employ. He pretends to be an unemployed engineer. Of course he's an "unemployed" engineer, for he's never worked as an engineer in his life. The only money he ever earns is placed in an unnamed account at the Bank of England, and his paymaster is the Home Secretary.

I therefore decided to put to John Haynes facts that I knew he would have to report back to the Home Secretary, facts that would show him that I "knew too much."

In order to test his reaction, I let slip an indication of what I knew in the presence of not only John Haynes but also Sergeant M'Intyre and poor unsuspecting Bill Armstead (I don't think old Bill ever did realize what a sucker the other two were making out of him, pretending to be his friends and so forth).

"I'm being followed by day and watched by night," I said.

We were gathered in Armstead's sitting room. M'Intyre's pipe slid from his lips and onto his lap.

"In fact, I've got the notion that this house is under surveillance right now."

They all stared at me stupid, but no one uttered a word.

Words weren't available. Haynes and M'Intyre must have been dumfounded.

But Bill took me to one side in the hallway, just before the party broke up.

"What's this about your being watched, Thomas?"

I patted his hand reassuringly. "Not I, Bill, not I. They are watching upon Walter Harper."

"Who?"

"Dr. Walter Harper—the Lambeth Killer."

"What on earth are you talking about!"

"You'll see, Bill, you'll see."

I just knew he'd inform the others as to what I'd said. . . .

And you know that I *was* being watched, Cogswell—and by nigh on every police officer and agent in London. I could pick them out all the time. They lurked in restaurants, at public houses, upon the tops of omnibuses, outside 103 Lambeth Palace Road. They came in different shapes and sizes, and many wore heavy beards as disguise. I guess most of them were armed—in case I'd make a break for it.

I took care in what I had to eat, and never visited the same restaurant more than once. I knew these men would wish to poison my food and drink, given the chance. I suspect that they interfered with the gas jets in my room, for my nights became times of nightmare and torment. Deadly gases filled the premises, exercising a dreadful influence over the mind, conjuring up illusions of specters and ghouls.

I must be firm and show these people that I was not afraid. I therefore invited John Haynes to dine with me, at the Café de Paris, in Ludgate Hill. I know he didn't wish to accept my invitation, but he had no option, for he had his orders. . . .

"So you believe that you're being followed, Doctor," he says to me.

"All the time."

"Why so?"

"The authorities seek to connect me with the deaths of these women."

"And are you connected?"

247

"Not I. Someone else from Number one hundred and three is involved."

"Who?"

"Walter Harper, a medical student at St. Thomas'. He's well known among a low class of people. He got this girl at Brighton into trouble some time back, you know; he procured an abortion for her. The women in Stamford Street—Marsh and Shrivell—found this out and threatened to expose him."

"So he killed them?"

I nodded.

"How do you know all of this?"

"Sergeant M'Intyre told me."

(This was untrue, but calculated to set one agent at the throat of the other.)

"You should go to the police, then."

Aha! Haynes had betrayed himself; for why should he suggest that I inform the police of what "Sergeant" M'Intyre tells me unless M'Intyre was no policeman? Of course, M'Intyre was no more a sergeant of the constabulary than Haynes was an unemployed engineer.

But I didn't say anything—I just gives John Haynes a canny look.

"How many women do you say this Harper has murdered?" Haynes asked, pouring me another glass. He was trying to make me drunk so that I'd spill the beans.

"Five in all."

"Five!"

"That's my information."

"Who? Do you know their names?"

"Marsh, Shrivell, Ellen Donworth, Miss Matilda Clover—and a girl from St. John's Wood by the name of Lou Harvey." (I threw in the latter's name for good measure.)

"Tell me about them, Doctor."

"Harper killed Clover with strychnine. The authorities think she died of drink. Not so, Mr. Haynes. She died of strychnine poisoning. They should dig her up. Poison will be found."

"Who's this Lou Harvey?"

"Another street wench. Harper gave her something to drink

to fix her. She fell down dead between the Royal and the Oxford
—the music halls." (Quick invention on my part. When Attorney Russell suggests that I told Haynes all of this because I'd
believed she really was dead, he's talking through the back of
his neck.)

"How long have you known all of this, Doctor?"

"For some time. Truth is, I wrote Miss Marsh and Miss Shrivell warning them not to take anything from Walter Harper.
Poor lassies, they didn't heed me. If they'd listened, they
wouldn't be pushing up the grass right now."

"You *must* go to the police," says Haynes. "If *you* don't, then
*I* shall!"

Give John Haynes his due—he was some actor, and playing
his part with gusto. Had I not known him for what he really was,
I reckon I'd have been taken in by the look of surprise and
horror on his face.

Naturally, Haynes reported back to M'Intyre, and I reckon
the authorities started to get red ants in their pants, because the
nextest thing was a desire to question me further.

I received a note at my lodgings from Sergeant M'Intyre,
requesting me to meet him at the Pheasant Public House that
evening at eight o'clock. I figured out that he'd be asking me
to explain a great deal this time, so I prepared myself.

I'd expected him to be alone when we met, but I was not
altogether surprised to find him sitting in the bar with two other
men. These he introduced as Inspectors Harvey and Mulvaney
—false names, I suspect.

"My colleagues and I would like to hear what you've got to
say about all these dead women, Dr. Neill," M'Intyre begins.
"Please regard this interview as official."

Official? Nothing connected with the Secret Service is ever
"official."

"Fire away," says I.

"Perhaps you'd like to start by telling them what you told Mr.
John Haynes the other day."

I repeated what I'd said to that gentleman.

"Have you any idea who these people following you might
be?" the one calling himself Mulvaney asked when I'd finished.

It was a cunning question, and one he knew I dare not answer truthfully.

"None at all," I parried. "But I met with this rip a few nights back—in the Westminster Bridge Road—and she confessed to me that she'd been put out to trail me. She said that I was suspected in connection with the Stamford Street poisoning."

"And what do you know about that affair?"

"Only what I've heard—through local gossip."

"You say you're a commercial traveler, Dr. Neill," the other "inspector" said. "Can you show us anything in support of this?"

"Certainly!" and I delved into my case. I produced several letters and order forms showing my dealings with the G. F. Harvey Manufacturing Company. The two "inspectors" pretended to examine and be satisfied by these documents. Then they left.

"Just a formality," M'Intyre said after a moment.

"Of course."

"This rip you met—any idea who she might be?"

"None."

"Pity."

"I agree."

"And very strange."

"I agree."

"No theories at all?"

"None."

"Pity."

"I agree."

Seeing that he'd get nothing further out of me, M'Intyre gathered up his hat and stick.

"I shall want to see you again," he said.

"Any time. You know where to find me."

"Yes." And off he goes.

M'Intyre and his fellow agents had now to cope with a female investigator they knew nothing about. I had created the impression that some other branch of the government service must be involved without their knowledge. They wouldn't like that at all—it was rivalry.

Four days later M'Intyre tried to contact me again, calling at

103 Lambeth Palace Road. I was feeling a mite poorly—a bad time and dope during the night—and I had Miss Sleaper tell him I was not available. I'd told Miss Sleaper that the house was being watched, and that I was being shadowed on account of my being an American. Miss Sleaper assumed I meant the police were responsible. Miss Sleaper didn't care for the police—they made her "nervy"—so she was pleased to send M'Intyre on his way.

But I knew it was no good just putting M'Intyre off; I'd have to see him sooner or later. But it would be on my terms. I accordingly gave him notice that I'd be prepared to interview him at eight in the evening, and that he'd best bring along with him his notebook and pencil. He came, and I received him while abed. And I made him stand throughout our talk.

"I hope you're feeling better," M'Intyre said, as slippery as can be.

"I think someone has been doctoring my food," I said.

"Who?"

"Young Harper."

"But he's down in Devonshire."

"So you've seen him. . . ."

"Not I. Others have."

"Has he been arrested?"

"Not that I'm aware. Do you think he ought to be?"

I shrugged off his question. "He's skipped out, hasn't he? Don't you find that suspicious?"

"No. It's not Dr. Harper we're interested in, sir."

"So you've tracked down Murray?"

"Who?"

"I only know him as Murray. Possibly *you* know his other names."

"I know nothing about anyone called Murray."

Had he not seen or heard of my letter to Dr. Harper, Sr.?

"But tell me about him," goes on M'Intyre.

"A man calling himself Murray stopped me in the street. He said he was a detective. He wanted to know about young Harper. I wasn't able to help him, of course, since I don't know Harper."

"Just a minute. . . . You claim that Harper's trying to poison you?"

"I do."

"Why should a man you don't even know try to murder you?"

"I didn't say he was trying to murder me. I said he was putting stuff in my food. Don't twist my words, man."

"Very well. But why should he want to doctor your food—this man who is a stranger to you?"

"Why indeed? I am exceeding puzzled."

"So am I, Dr. Neill. Let's go back to this Murray. He asked you about Harper, and you couldn't assist him. What else did Murray say to you?"

I considered that one for a bit. "He showed me a letter addressed to Miss Marsh and Miss Shrivell. This letter warned the girls to be careful of young Harper, else he'd serve them as he'd served Matilda Clover and Lou Harvey."

"We cannot find trace of Miss Lou Harvey. No one by that name has died in London this year."

"You can take it from me that she is dead," I replied.

"Why?"

"It's obvious, isn't it? Young Harper is your man there."

M'Intyre shuffled his feet, and looked around my room. "May I light a pipe?" he asked me.

"I'd rather you didn't."

"Yes—sorry." He picked up a capsule from the corner of the washstand. "What's this, Doctor?"

"One of my pills."

"Yes—but what does it contain?"

"A compound."

"A compound of what?"

"Cocaine and morphia."

"Anything else?"

"Strychnine."

"Isn't that dangerous?"

"That depends upon how you take it."

"You take these pills yourself?"

"I do."

"Why?"

"To ease the aches in my brain."

I thought M'Intyre would wish to question me further with regard to my collection of pills. Strangely, he didn't.

"I can see that you're not very well," he said instead. "I won't trouble you any further, Doctor. You're not thinking of leaving London in the near future, are you?"

"I may. I may have to go back to the States."

"But you haven't made any arrangements in that respect?"

"No."

"So be it. I'll be in touch." And he left me. I guess he was anxious to light up that smelly pipe of his. Anyway, he'd yet another mysterious agent to report upon to Haynes and his superiors. An alarum should commence to find one "Murray— detective."

# MEN OF EVIL WAYS AND MEANS

## I

Owing to the question of time, I'm obliged to keep matters short. On the other hand, it may be that you've become confused by much of what I've had to say, Cogswell, having regard to the evidence given by various witnesses for the Crown. I reckon you've already perused their testimony, and that you've been deceived by it along with the rest. Men of evil ways and means had conspired to make an end of me, and by now the trap had already been sprung.

Next day, by pure chance, I happened to bump into M'Intyre in the Lambeth Palace Road. Or was it just by chance?

"I see that you're up and about," says M'Intyre, with a low-down smile.

"I am, sir, but I am not yet recovered."

"Where are you off to this morning?"

"To purchase tickets."

"You're going away, then?"

"I'm going away today at three o'clock. Will I be arrested if I do?"

"I cannot tell you, Doctor." Obviously, he had no powers to detain me himself. "But if you walk across with me to Scotland Yard I will make inquiries."

Well could I imagine the fellow wishing to lure me into that establishment. "Let's go, then," I replied, as if unconcerned.

We strolled together toward Westminster Bridge. Halfway across the bridge, M'Intyre paused.

"Tell me, Doctor," he said, "do you write with your left hand or with your right?"

"With either, and equally well. Why do you ask?" We began to walk again.

"I just wondered. I was also wondering if I might have a sample of your handwriting."

It was my turn to stop.

"I will not go any further with you," I says to him. "I am suspicious of you, and I believe you're playing me double."

And without waiting for him to reply or comment, I turned and walked back.

I had no real intention of allowing this man to get me into Scotland Yard. I understand that many people who have been enticed into that building have never been seen again. Apart from being a police headquarters, it is also the nerve center of the British Secret Service.

It occurred to me that it was high time I obtained some measure of protection. I was now in the habit of carrying my Bull-dog revolver, but better it was that I wrapped myself within a cloak more subtle.

So I gave a number of confidential instructions to the firm of Waters & Bryan, Solicitors, of East Arbour Street. I ordered that they write Sir Edward Bradford, the Chief Commissioner of Police, to advise him that I was aware of being trailed by the so-called "Sergeant" M'Intyre and other detectives or agents. I added that this was playing havoc with my business in this country. No doubt the commissioner was darned surprised to hear that he had anyone named "Sergeant" M'Intyre in his force! No doubt he started to create a hullabaloo—until he was told to hold his tongue by higher authority. Attorney Russell played it pretty smart later, getting M'Intyre to give his version of events as if he was a genuine Scotland Yard detective!

When I told M'Intyre that I was proposing to quit town at three o'clock, I guess he figured I was going to leave the country. In fact I was only journeying as far as Berkhampstead—to see beloved Laura. She had come to London, having learned of my sickness, and I was due to meet her at Charing Cross. To avoid the possibility of running into M'Intyre again, I now took a cab to that station. Laura was waiting for me in the Ladies' Rest Room.

"I don't think I shall be able to join you and your dear mother," I told her as we embraced.

"Thomas—are you still sick?"

"No, I am much improved, *ma petite*. But I have neglected my work. I dare not spare the time. Please understand."

"I do—but I'm sure it's overwork that has put you to your bed."

"If I promise to return to my bed after . . ."

"Come to Mama's to recuperate, Thomas. Then we will be together. It would be *wunderbar!*"

I said that, *wunderbar* or not, it would be impossible, and she looked forlorn.

"In that case, I insist on coming to your rooms now, Thomas," she said. "I shall tidy up. I'm sure you haven't been looking after yourself, and that your miserly landlady has neglected you!"

She was so positive, so determined, that I had no option but to call a cab and take her to Lambeth Palace Road.

I was anxious lest some detective be in obvious evidence outside Mrs. Sleaper's house, but no one was in sight as the cabbie drew up.

But in the hallway, at the foot of the stairs, stood a man speaking with Miss Sleaper. Tall and entirely clean-shaven, the fellow was unknown to me. I made to go past him, Laura in tow, when Miss Sleaper says to me:

"Dr. Neill, this 'ere gentleman's called to see you."

"Dr. Neill? Thomas Neill?" asked the stranger. His voice was very soft and quiet, and reminded me of someone else.

"Yes?"

"My name's Tunbridge—John Bennett Tunbridge, Inspector, Scotland Yard. I wonder if we might talk somewhere in private?"

It was his manner, gentle yet menacing, that stirred my memory: Sheriff Bram Ames, talking in a foreign accent. . . .

"Yes." What else could I say?

"The lady, sir?"

256

"Miss Sabbatini—my intended."

John Bennett Tunbridge turned to Miss Sleaper. "Perhaps the lady could wait downstairs while the doctor and I have our little chat. Perhaps you could make her a nice cup of tea, miss?"

"No," I said. "No. She can come with us—" And again his manner made me add: "—Inspector."

"Just as you wish, sir. Let us proceed to your quarters, then, sir."

And up we goes.

Once inside my sitting room, John Bennett Tunbridge adopted absolute control. Offering the best chair to Laura, he had me sit in the second most comfortable, while he sat himself down upon a hard upright.

"Are you sure you wouldn't care for some tea, Miss Sabbatini?" he then did ask. He'd caught her unusual name without difficulty, and now pronounced it well.

Laura shook her head. She was plainly bewildered.

"I gather you've been unwell, Dr. Neill?"

"I'm better."

"So pleased to hear it. There are some nasty bugs about this time of year, you know. Best to wrap up warm until the weather's more steady."

He tucked a thumb into his waistcoat pocket, and frowned.

"You know I'm most dreadfully sorry to receive your complaint, Dr. Neill. So, indeed, is Sir Edward—and that's why I'm here."

Relief. I didn't want this particular man for an enemy.

"What's this, Thomas?" asked Laura

John Bennett Tunbridge looked at her with surprise. "Why, hasn't the doctor told you? It's all most embarrassing!"

They both looked to me for my explanation.

"I'm being hounded by the London police, Laura. I wrote the commissioner and begged him to lay easy."

"But why? Why?"

"Because I'm an American. I guess they think something's wrong with my business over here. Not to worry, dear."

"Yes . . . ," says John Bennett Tunbridge, in a kind of a drawl. "But what about your 'business,' Dr. Neill?"

"What about it, Mr. Inspector?"

"Well . . . Let me ask you this: what exactly brought you to England in the first place? And please don't think I'm being just inquisitive!"

I mulled over his question before answering.

"I was in practice in Chicago," I said.

"So I understand."

"I came to England on account of my health. My eyes are poor—I came to consult an oculist. I suffered a long illness in Chicago, sir."

"Ten years long," says John Bennett Tunbridge, as mild as can be.

"Night calls did not agree with me, sir. In consequence, I had to forsake my practice."

"So you represent the Harvey Manufacturing Company, Dr. Neill?"

"Yes. You seem to know a great deal about me."

"Just a bit, Doctor. May I see your sample case?"

I left my chair and took the medicine box from my wardrobe.

"Thank you," said the other. He opened it up, and commenced to examine each of the bottles. "Tell me, what are these pills composed of?" He was looking at the Nux Vomica.

"One-sixteenth grain strychnine," I replied. "Sugar-coated."

"At that rate, this bottle contains quite a large quantity of strychnine. It would be highly dangerous that they should fall into the hands of the public."

"It is not intended to sell them to the public," I said, "but only to chemists and surgeons—who will dispense them in their proper quantities."

"And have you sold any to either chemist or surgeon, Doctor?"

"No. Not yet."

"I see." John Bennett Tunbridge closed the case and came to his feet. "Well, thank you for seeing me, Dr. Neill. I'm most grateful. I trust I haven't used up too much of your valuable time. Good day, sir! Good day, miss!" And he was off.

I think my explanations satisfied Laura, but my mind was all of a buzz following the interview by John Bennett Tunbridge.

Here was a man to be reckoned with—a man who knew too much of my past. "Ten years' illness"—so he was referring to Joliet? What else.

And he didn't waste much time in the days that followed. I understand that he went down to Barnstaple, where he called upon Dr. Harper and son and retrieved the letter of "W. H. Murray."

I had a premonition that the authorities would soon seek to arrest me, and I decided that it was time to skip out. Accordingly, on June 1st, I booked aboard the *Prometheus,* bound for New York. I'd wait awhile in the United States until the ruckus died down a bit. Laura would understand. Anyway, I'd write her, once in America.

I was obliged to haggle with Mrs. Sleaper with regard to my bill, and this had the effect of delaying my departure for Liverpool. For the sake of just two pounds sterling, the barren old faggot impounded some of my possessions, refusing to surrender them until I'd paid. I was damned if I'd pay! But I had to have my belongings. . . .

Trouble was, my continued presence in London gave the authorities the chance they wanted. I reckon they instructed Mrs. Sleaper to hold out and keep me occupied. I'll bet that M'Intyre or John Haynes paid her handsomely to ensure I stayed at Lambeth Palace Road, and threatened the she-cat with a few months' jail should she fail.

Anyway, come the afternoon of the 3rd, I was taking the air in Lambeth Palace Road when up strolls John Bennett Tunbridge with a warrant in his hand.

"I'm afraid you shall have to come along with me, Dr. Neill," he says, as apologetic as a Holy Office friar about to burn a heretic. He read me the warrant, signed by some crooked magistrate called Bridge. I was under arrest for sending a threatening letter to Harper—no more than that!

"You've got the wrong man," I said. "Fire away!"

He showed me the envelope. "This is what you're accused of sending, Doctor."

"That's not my writing," I said.

He extracted the letter from the envelope. "This is the letter," he said. "And this *is* your writing. We have compared it with other specimens of your hand. Now be a good gentleman, sir, and come along with me."

I was charged at Bow Street Court and Police Office, and had John Bennett Tunbridge wire my solicitors. Policemen then searched my clothing and confined me in a tiny cell. John Bennett Tunbridge allowed me to retain my tobacco and chewing gum, and gave me a copy of the evening paper.

"I'm afraid we shall have to search your rooms in Lambeth Palace Road," he says to me. "With or without your permission, sir."

I said nothing. I decided to talk to him no more. Not until I heard from Mr. Waters, my attorney. Why should I assist the law officers? Anything I said to John Bennett Tunbridge would automatically be fed to M'Intyre, John Haynes, and the Secret Service boys.

Come the morning—Saturday—I was brought before the magistrate upon this charge of extortion. I'd discussed the matter with Mr. Waters. I'm not telling you all that I said to him, Cogswell—that's confidential.

"But they've positively identified your writing," Waters said to me before the proceedings began. "This letter to Harper is in your hand!"

Waters was getting windy, and I saw that I'd best calm him down.

"That letter is signed 'W. H. Murray,' " I replied. "It therefore follows that someone of that name wrote it."

"In your hand, Doctor? Come, come."

"Why, indeed!"

A Mr. Bernard Thomas opened the facts of the Crown allega-

*260*

tion to the magistrate, and then asked that the case be adjourned.

"You see," I said to Windy Waters. "They haven't got a scrap of evidence."

"Shh!"

I reckon he was plain scared of this lawyer Thomas. And for good reason: Thomas was hired by the British Treasury, and the Treasury runs the Secret Service in this country.

"Seven days, then," says the magistrate. "The defendant to remain in custody."

"Bail—get me bail!" I hissed at Windy Waters, but he shook his head.

So I was taken from Bow Street to the Holloway jail and became "remanded in custody." I was not a convicted person, and therefore was granted certain privileges—food from outside prison, tobacco, reading and writing materials, and my own suit of clothes. But I had not my essentials for my very existence —I had not my drugs.

Satan himself devised the cruel tortures I suffered. They say that I fell into a coma. Yes, but I was seldom wholly unconscious. My world became nightmary. Voices spoke ill of me from the corners of my cell, faces invaded my dreams to grimace at me, pains tore at my breast and bowels. For hours I'd tramp the small yardage of the dingy room, endeavoring to exhaust myself. When I could no longer stand and flung myself upon my mattress, sleep refused to come, and I'd lie there all of a tremble. And when my eyes at last did close, the frenzy of my dreams began—causing me to call out and wake again, wet with perspiration.

I believe a person from Waters came to consult with me, and that I was incoherent. I know that I begged them for my pills, and I was refused. Of course they'd refuse! They were deliberately torturing me; they wanted me to confess my guilt and betray the others. I knew M'Intyre and John Haynes spied on me. I used to hear them come after dark—I could see their respective eyes looking in on me through the Judas hole in the door. They would whisper to each other. I suppose they think I didn't hear them. But I did—and the things they said would cause a strong man to fall down in a swoon. The prison authorities were in their pay, you know, and the heating in my cell was turned on high. I think they sprinkled my clothes and blankets with pest and vermin, for I had need to scratch myself a great deal, although I never once did find an insect or see a bump upon my skin. One of the most terrible things they did was to trick Laura into the cell next door, where they told her things to make her laugh. One night she laughed long and loud enough to bust herself. I wept that night—my first tears for more than thirty years.


## III


Back on May 5, the grave containing the coffin of Miss Matilda Clover had been opened. Scientist Stevenson was responsible, and he it was who examined her cadaver. Of course, Miss Clover had been interred October last, and it had taken the authorities no less than seven months to engage their senses! Matilda lay under fourteen other coffins, in a veritable nest of the unwanted. But now she was to earn herself a spot of fame. Scientist Stevenson found traces of strychnine in the stomach, the liver, the chest, and the brain—and Dr. Graham was proclaimed a jackass.

John Bennett Tunbridge and his minions had possession of my various letters, and now began to unravel what had fooled the Secret Service for so long.

While John Bennett Tunbridge was piecing things together, busy as a bee, I made a slow recovery in Holloway. I guess the "nameless ones" wished to build me up. It would not do for them to present me to the public bearing the marks of their torture. They wanted me sound of mind and body. Having failed dismally to break me in my cell, they now were anxious to hold me out to the world as little more than a common criminal. They pursued the policy adopted by the detectives in Chicago. I knew that they'd indict me for first-degree murder, stage a trial, fix a verdict, and put me in the pen. I was also confident that, as in the case of Illinois, they'd never contain me in a prison. Fate would set me free.

So when I was taken to Bow Street on the 17th, I was not unduly alarmed.

"What is the nature of this journey?" I asked John Bennett Tunbridge at the station.

"Are you prepared to stand on an identification parade, Doctor?"

"Fire away!"

I was led into a long passage, off the court. A number of men were loitering about. At a sign from John Bennett Tunbridge, some of these men followed us into a room.

"Would you all kindly put your hats on," John Bennett Tunbridge asked of them, at the same time handing me a silk topper. "You too, Doctor, there's a good gentleman."

Hats on, we all waited. I was positioned among all these men. And in came Miss Elizabeth Masters. Since I scarce did recognize her, it's not surprising that she didn't recognize me, and out she went.

Next in was Miss Elizabeth May, and she picks me as her man.

"Would you now all kindly remove your hats?" John Bennett Tunbridge said when Miss May had gone.

With our hats off, Miss Masters was brought back into the room. This time she pointed at me.

Once the parade had been disbanded, I taxed John Bennett Tunbridge.

"Who were those women?"

"Never you mind, sir. But you tell me something, sir. Ever made the acquaintance of a lady named Clover—a Miss Matilda Clover?"

"No. Does she say she knows me?"

"Not exactly, sir. She's finding conversation rather difficult at the moment, sir. But we'd better not talk too much, had we? Otherwise I'll be falling foul of your solicitor, won't I?"

Windy Waters came to see me that evening at Holloway, and —strangely—we were permitted to speak in private, in an interview room.

"You're sure it's safe in here?" I asks of Waters, when the warder had departed.

"Yes, of course it's safe. What d'you mean, 'is it safe'?" He sounded quite cross. He laid his case upon the table and drew out pen and paper. "Dr. Neill, there are a number of questions I must ask you. To be frank, I am greatly troubled by your instructions—or lack of them—and I am stumbling about like a blind man at the moment." He offered me a cigar and lit it before continuing. "First of all, your very name, Doctor. Is it Thomas Neill or Thomas Cream or Neill Cream? The police say you are Thomas Neill. Miss Sabbatini says you sometimes call yourself Cream. Pray, sir, what is your name?"

"Take your pick," I laughs.

"Very well—I shall call you Thomas Neill." Solemnly he wrote that down at the top of his parchment.

"You have heard what happened this morning at Bow Office?" I said as he wrote.

"I have." He didn't look up. "Those two women say that they saw you with Miss Matilda Clover—saw you go into a house in Lambeth Road a few days before she died of poisoning. What have you to say about that?"

"They are liars."

"In a few days' time there is going to be an inquest into the death of this Matilda Clover. You will be required to attend. The prosecution seek to prove you responsible for her death, Doctor. What have you to say about that?"

"They'll be spitting into the wind."

"I hope so." He finished what he was doing and gives me this dog-eyed look. "But I insist that you divulge everything you know to me. Otherwise the position is quite hopeless!"

And so we had a jawing competition for the next hour.

# THE VESTRY HALL FIASCO

## I

I gave Windy Waters a line of talk to keep him happy, and we parted company with a cordial shake of the hand. I could tell that he believed in my innocence, yet he seemed unprepared to accept that Secret Service agents lay at the root of all my troubles. He insisted that only the police were conducting the investigations, and that they were trying to link me onto the demise of Matilda Clover with "circumstantial evidence" and my own handwriting. I told him not to fret so, to keep calm.

"I wish I had your confidence, Dr. Neill" were his final words.

"Hold on to your hat, Mr. Waters," I said. "Just watch their case fall to bits come the 22nd."

For upon that day the inquiry into Miss Clover began—at the ramshackle Vestry Hall in Tooting. Coroner Hicks presided.

Two bogeys from the Treasury came along "to assist" Coroner Hicks—in other words, to ensure that things went hard for me. Top bogey was Charles Gill, one of the lapdogs who attended upon Attorney Russell later, and it was Gill who called the witnesses. Now, British law sure has got some funny ways. First they hold a small inquisition, calling all their witnesses, writing down all the testimony, going through all the motions of a trial—but just in front of some tenth-rate magistrate or coroner. At this 'quest they even had a jury to bark whenever

Coroner Hicks prodded. Then the British have a proper trial—in front of another judge (who knows nothing about the case at all) and yet another jury. Once more the same prosecutors call the same witnesses to recite the same testimony—which by then, of course, they've learned by heart. I can only surmise that this is the reason for the first hearing—to ensure that all their witnesses have got the story straight. I guess you've got copies of witnesses' depositions, or whatever they call them, and I see no need for me to try and recollect everything said by everyone at Vestry Hall.

Morning of the Wednesday, I was taken down to Tooting by two warders. We were early, but Windy Waters was late—hadn't arrived by the time Coroner Hicks, Prosecutor Gill, and the fixed jury had all settled in.

"Is this Thomas Neill?" Hicks asked from his podium.

"At your service," I calls.

"Are you unrepresented?"

"No, sir."

"Mr. John Waters has not yet arrived," John Bennett Tunbridge informed the coroner.

"Are you willing that we begin without your solicitor?" Hicks said to me.

"I am, sir. But may I be provided with pen and paper—to make notes?"

"Certainly. Officer, see to it."

"And may I be assured that whatever notes I make remain with me—and do not get taken off by the police?" I asked.

"What do you say about that, Mr. Gill?" (So Coroner Hicks also bent to the desires of the Treasury.)

"Of course they'll not be taken away by the police. I wouldn't dream of taking such an advantage." That was Gill, as crafty as his calling. He had to say that in front of the press and jurymen.

"In that case, let the prisoner keep his notes. If he doesn't need them, let him tear them up or hand them to his solicitor. No person is an accused in this court until after a formal verdict of the jury. Very well, then, we have much to do—let the proceedings commence. . . ."

I reckon the British were nervous lest knowledge of the poor treatment afforded a citizen of the United States leak out. Windy Waters has told me that any man Jack accused of crime gets this kind of hearing, and that the coroner or magistrate will refuse to commit a case for trial if he is not satisfied the prisoner has a case to answer. Humbug! They laid it on for me because they knew I could burn their fingers.

So Prosecutor Gill commenced to call his case. The first four witnesses dealt with the dying of Matilda Clover, and I was sorry to hear that great had been her torment that chill October night. The girl who had let us in—the one I had taken care not to be seen by too closely in the passage—failed to identify me. Prosecutor Gill appeared vexed, and he turned round to glare upon me when Windy Waters arrived and I told him of her useless testimony. The others were of equal inconsequence. They knew of "Fred," but "Fred" was not I—of course he wasn't, the lamebrained looneys! So much for the first day's hearing. Had the brothers Coon of Illinois been in charge, I'll wager that Prosecutor Gill would find himself fired on the spot!

"Take care," Windy Waters says to me when I expressed my views. "The worst is yet to come."

Next day we reassembled in our various positions, and Scientist Stevenson had read to him by Coroner Hicks what had been said the day previous. Scientist Stevenson spoke as to the autopsy he'd carried out, and he struck me as a man who knew his job. I reckon he and I should have met up sometime; we had much in common.

Next in line was the assistant from Mr. Priest's—my chemist with little business sense—and he told the truth as to my purchase of capsules and Nux Vomica.

What surprise when Prosecutor Gill barked out the name of the witness to follow: "Dr. William Henry Broadbent"! I leaned forward, eager with anticipation. Bold and haughty was this gentleman, looking around the Vestry Hall as if he'd strayed by mistake into a cowshed. In his smooth left hand he carried my letter from "M. Malone." Coroner Hicks had him read it aloud.

"Must I?" protested Broadbent. "Why cannot you just admit the thing?"

"It's part of the evidence, sir," says Prosecutor Gill.

"It's the scribblings of a crank, sir!"

But Broadbent had to read it, nonetheless.

" 'Sir,' " he began and coughed. " 'Sir, Miss Clover, who until a short time ago lived at 27 Lambeth Road, S.E., died at the above address on the 20th October (last month), through being poisoned by strychnine. After her death a search of her effects was made, and evidence was found which showed that you not only gave her the medicine which caused her death . . .' " Broadbent broke off. *"Must* I continue with this rubbish, sir?"

"I'm afraid so, Doctor," says Coroner Hicks.

" '. . . that you not only gave her the medicine which caused her death, but that you had been hired for the purpose of poisoning her. This evidence is in the hands of one of our detectives, who will give the evidence either to you or to the police authorities for the sum of two thousand five hundred pounds sterling. You can have the evidence for £2500, and in that way save yourself from ruin. If the matter is disposed of to the police, it will, of course, be made public by being placed in the papers, and ruin you for ever. You know well enough that an accusation of that sort will ruin you for ever. Now, sir, if you want the evidence for £2500, just put a personal in the *Daily Chronicle,* saying that you will pay Malone £2500 for his services, and I will send a party to settle this matter. If you do not want the evidence, of course, it will be turned over to the police at once and published, and your ruin will surely follow. Think well before you decide on this matter. It is just this—£2500 sterling on the one hand, and ruin, shame, and disgrace on the other. Answer by personal on the first page of the *Daily Chronicle* any time next week. I am not humbugging you. I have evidence strong enough to ruin you for ever.' " Broadbent lowered his hand.

"How is it signed, sir?" asks Prosecutor Gill.

"It is signed 'M. Malone.' "

"And do you know anyone of that name?"

"Of course not! It's some madman!"

"Have you treated anyone by the name of Matilda Clover, sir?"

"Of course not! Never heard of her!"

And the letter was handed to Coroner Hicks, who read it for himself before passing it over to the foreman of the jury.

"Thank you, Dr. Broadbent. Thank you for coming," says Hicks.

Broadbent gave a grunt and stomped out.

Miss Masters and Miss May were called, and told the jury how they first had made my acquaintance, and how they had seen me escort Matilda Clover into the premises used by that woman.

"You cannot be positive as to that identification, can you?" Windy Waters asks of Elizabeth May.

"Oh, yes I can," she replied.

I have already made mention of the fact that poor Laura Sabbatini had been "got at" by the authorities. Well, not only did they succeed in making her desert me, they also induced her to give evidence against me—false testimony calculated to see me a dead man.

"They can't call her!" I calls to Windy Waters when Laura took the stand.

"They can. She's only your intended, not your wife."

Laura took the oath, as nervous as you might expect, and tried to avoid my eyes. Prosecutor Gill examined her gently and with smarm.

"I think you know Dr. Neill as Thomas Neill Cream, Miss Sabbatini?"

"Yes."

"And eventually he proposed to you?"

"Yes."

"Verbally—and by letter?"

"Yes." She choked back a sob. Someone gave her a glass of water.

"And do you have that letter?" Prosecutor Gill handed up the document. "Is that it? Yes. And do you formally produce it? Yes." He turns to Coroner Hicks. "It is in Neill's hand, sir. May the jury compare this letter with the one received by Dr. Broadbent in due course? Thank you." Back to Laura: "Miss Sabbatini, I know all of this is most painful, but please bear with me. Now,

269

I think on the 23rd December of last year the doctor made a will in your favor? Yes. Is this that will?" And up goes the second document. "Does it say 'Thomas Neill Cream, physician, late of the city of Quebec'?"

"It does."

"In his own hand?"

She nodded.

"Yes or no, Miss Sabbatini? We can't record an inclination of the head."

"Yes."

And so my will was produced for the purposes of comparison. But the real corruption on the part of the authorities was yet to come.

"In May of this year," Prosecutor Gill said, "did the doctor ask you to write some letters for him, and did he dictate the contents to you?"

What was the man on about? I hissed at Windy Waters to attract his attention, but he didn't appear to hear me.

"Yes—three letters."

"Have a look at these, Miss Sabbatini. . . ."

I leaned right across to catch a glimpse of what Laura had just been given. One of the warders pulled me back. "Keep still!"

"Are those the letters?"

"Yes. Of course, I didn't know what they meant."

"Did you ask him?"

"I think so. But I don't remember his answer."

"No matter. Now I shall read my copies of these letters. You follow the originals, the ones in your own handwriting. Do you understand? Good."

"Does the first one read: 'To Coroner Wyatt, St. Thomas' Hospital, London. Dear Sir, Will you please give the enclosed letter to the Foreman of the Coroner's jury, at the inquest on Alice Marsh and Emma Shrivell, and oblige, Yours respectfully, Wm. H. Murray'?"

"Yes," says Laura, and sighed.

"And does the so-called 'enclosure,' which the doctor had you write for him, read: 'To the Foreman of the Coroner's Jury in the cases of Alice Marsh and Emma Shrivell. Dear Sir, I beg to inform you that one of my operators has positive proof that Walter Harper, a medical student of St. Thomas' Hospital, and a son of Dr. Harper, of Bear Street, Barnstaple, is responsible for the deaths of Alice Marsh and Emma Shrivell, he having poisoned those girls with strychnine. That proof you can have on paying my bill for services to George Clarke, detective, 20 Cockspur Street, Charing Cross, to whom I will give the proof on his paying my bill.' And is this letter signed, 'Yours respectfully, Wm. H. Murray'?"

"It is."

I called out to Windy Waters, but he waved me into silence as Prosecutor Gill went on:

"Those two letters are dated May 2nd. Now look at the third and final letter—the one dated the 4th. Did Dr. Neill have you write that for him as well?"

"He did."

What had they done to sweet Laura to make her say such things!

" 'To George Clarke, Esq.,' " Prosecutor Gill commenced to read, " '20 Cockspur Street, Charing Cross. Dear Sir, If Mr. Wyatt, Coroner, calls on you in regard to the murders of Alice Marsh and Emma Shrivell, you can tell him that you will give proof positive to him that W. H. Harper, student, of St. Thomas' Hospital, and son of Dr. Harper, Bear Street, Barnstaple, poisoned those girls with strychnine, provided the Coroner will pay you well for your services. Proof of this will be forthcoming. I will write you again in a few days. Yours respectfully, Wm. H. Murray.' Is that the letter, Miss Sabbatini?"

"Yes."

I concluded that they must have subjected Laura to horrible torture in the cellars of Scotland Yard—else they must have drugged her. She now looked pale and anxious, never daring to face me. How could she bear to face me? She had sworn to speak the truth, and she had told a pack of wicked lies. She had abandoned her very soul. . . .

[*At this stage the journal of Thomas Neill collapses into a series of dots and scrawls, and is illegible. We must take it that he was*

271

*overcome by whatever he imagined the truth to be, or—alternatively—knowing the truthfulness of what his fiancee had said at the inquest, he was simply trying to avoid it. V.R.C.]*

## II

They had to adjourn the inquest on account of various witnesses being unavailable. I reckon they needed the time to concoct further evidence. But I was glad of the break, for my health deteriorated rapidly following the testimony of Laura Sabbatini. I spent the weeks loafing in my cell at Holloway, refusing to clip my beard, not caring much whether I lived or died. I believe Windy Waters feared for my sanity. But, far from being insane, I had the good sense to write Laura regarding what she'd done to me. You've got my letters, Cogswell, and you know how I tried to make her go back on her testimony and tell God's truth. I wasn't threatening her like they suggest—I just wanted for her to destroy anything in my hand still in her possession. I realized that old Mrs. Sabbatini must have pushed her daughter into turning against me—she and the Secret Service. Laura had the decency to send me ten pounds sterling when I told her I was short of funds, but she never did write me a single line. I imagine she was instructed not to do so by M'Intyre and John Haynes.

I guess the authorities, having shocked me something nasty by producing dear Laura on their side, next wanted to secure my total collapse by producing Lou Harvey. I'm told that she herself got in touch with Coroner Hicks when she learned of the 'quest reading the newspapers. Horse droppings to that! M'Intyre and company had kept her snuggled up their sleeve for some time, training her to play her part in a manner convincing.

Anyway, come the resumption of the inquest in July, Prosecutor Gill bawls to the court flunkey, and in she comes, looking as pretty as can be.

"He gave me these pills for my spots—at least, he said I had spots," she said.

"But you didn't take them, Mrs. Harris?"

"No. Charlie—that's Mr. Harris—thought it a bit strange for him to be giving me medicines, so I threw them away, didn't I?"

"Did you tell this man where you lived?"

"Yes. Townsend Road. But I gives him the wrong number, didn't I?"

"Why was that?"

"Well, to be quite honest, I found him sort of creepy. What with those cross-eyes of his, and his funny accent. Never stopped stroking me, he did. He was always fidgeting. Never smiled, never laughed. Just talked on and on, putting his fingers on me. I didn't like him, did I?"

"And would you know him again, Mrs. Harris?"

Lou Harvey indicates me. "That's him!"

"Are you sure, Mrs. Harris?"

"Positive."

So the suggestion was that I'd sought to kill this woman. Coroner Hicks and several of the jury were looking at me hard. Windy Waters wasn't helping none, either, sitting there with his head in his hands. From the rear he might have been the Hon. Derek Munn. . . . As for Miss Lou Harvey, was there any need for her to insult me? I could only regret that the pills I gave her had not contained Nux Vomica and that she hadn't taken them.

The prosecution team even dragged into the proceedings, thereby establishing my practice in Chicago, Edward Levy—now living in England. I guess Levy sought to prove my reputation in that city, perhaps even to divulge my spell within Joliet. A vindictive man was Levy. I'd short-changed him, had I not? But his evidence was sorely affected by a sudden announcement by Coroner Hicks. I was so used to surprises by now that I didn't reckon a single thing capable of stirring my interest. But what Coroner Hicks had to say surely did—and it certainly caused some mutterings on the part of the jurymen!

"Gentlemen," said Coroner Hicks gravely, "I am in receipt of a certain communication, addressed to myself at this very hall, and I feel it only proper that I read what this letter has to say." Slowly he extracts a letter from an envelope, scans it a couple of times and then he began to read. " 'Dear Sir,' it says and I suppose that's me, 'Dear Sir, the man that you have in your power—Dr. Neill—is as innocent as you are. Knowing him by sight, I have disguised myself like him, and made the acquaintance of the girls that have been poisoned. *I* gave them the pills to cure them of all their earthly miseries, and they died. . . .' "

"Hell and God damn it!" I shouted, on my feet.

"Quiet!" ordered Coroner Hicks, and hands pulled me down.

"The letter continues: '. . . Miss L. Harris has got more sense than I thought she had, but I shall have her yet. Mr. P. Harvey might also follow Lou Harvey out of this world of care and woe. Lady Russell is quite right about the letter, and so am I. Lord Russell has a hand in the poisoning of Clover. Nellie Donworth must have stayed out all night, or else she would not have been complaining of pains and cold when Annie Clements saw her. If I were you, I would release Dr. T. Neill, or you might get into trouble. His innocence will be declared sooner or later, and when he is free he might sue you for damages.' " Coroner Hicks paused. "Then it is signed, gentlemen. And it is signed, 'Yours respectfully, JUAN POLLEN, alias JACK THE RIPPER' and this person advises: 'Beware all. I warn but once.' Would you like to see it, Mr. Gill?"

Prosecutor Gill took the letter, turned it this and thataway, held it up to the light, rubbed it between his fingers, and looked darn stupid.

"Clearly the work of a crank," he said.

Crank? Had he taken leave of his senses?

"I know who wrote it," I yelled to Windy Waters.

"Quiet, please," came an order.

Windy Waters left his place to come over to where I was sitting.

"I know who sent that letter," I repeated.

"How? Who?"

"First, you must never breathe a word of what I say to anyone."

"Yes, yes. Now who sent it?"

"His name's Larrigan," I said. "Wideawake Larrigan."

# HANGMAN HAWKINS AND OTHERS

## I

I positively refused to furnish Windy Waters with any more information as to the alias of "Juan Pollen—Jack the Ripper," and I consequently left him deeply troubled.

I was aware that Waters must reveal to the authorities everything I told him, even as to the nature of my defense. Now Waters would tell them that I had named this Juan Pollen as one Wideawake Larrigan, and great would be the confusion within the Secret Service. As the call had gone out for the capture of the elusive "Wm. H. Murray," so now would it go out for Wideawake Larrigan. I do feel that Wideawake himself would have been mighty amused by this development of the situation.

Since the letter from "Juan Pollen" was yet another forgery on the part of M'Intyre and John Haynes, those gentlemen would be surprised in the extreme that I (a) accepted the letter as genuine and (b) knew the identity of its author. Explanations would be called for. For my own part, I failed to see how it was the authorities hoped to succeed in having me blamed for the excesses of Jack the Ripper so long after the event. That gentleman had ceased his activities back in '89. Did M'Intyre really believe I could now be named responsible, now in '92? But their motive I was able to fathom. Since the public had come to the conclusion that H.R.H. the Duke of Clarence was "The Ripper," the Secret Service had Royal orders to stifle such dangerous gossip. So the Secret Service must find someone else to blame. Why not, then, some person of foreign blood and far from home? Why not, then, some harmless American doctor?

Naturally, I told Windy Waters nothing of my conclusions.

At the close of Prosecutor Gill's evidence for the Crown, I was invited by Coroner Hicks to speak on my own behalf. Indeed, Coroner Hicks insisted that I be sworn and stand in the witness box, although I made it clear that I was quite unprepared to answer any of his damn-fool questions.

Coroner Hicks summed up to the jury in an angry voice. I think this was because he had failed to get me cross-questioned by Prosecutor Gill. In the event, Coroner Hicks' summary of witness statements was biased, as is expected of magistrates and judges, and he made it daylight clear what verdict he expected from the "twelve honest men." The jury consulted among themselves for twenty minutes and then came back, pretty glum.

"We are all agreed that Matilda Clover died of strychnine poisoning, and that the poison was administered by Thomas Neill with intent to destroy life. We therefore find him guilty of willful murder."

Coroner Hicks picked up his pen with a smile. Prosecutor Gill and John Bennett Tunbridge shook hands. I get this tap on the shoulder from one of my warders.

On the 18th of the month I received two visitors at Holloway. John Bennett Tunbridge came to charge me with murder.

"What, in the Clover case?" I asked him.

"Yes."

"Fire away, Inspector."

He read it out.

"Is anything going to be done in the other cases?" I asked when he'd finished.

"I cannot say at this stage. Would you like to tell me anything about them?"

I shook my head. If I did comment, he'd only dress up my remarks to make them look bad.

My second visitor was Windy Waters. He saw me in my cell, at my request, rather than in the interview room. I figured that there was less chance of our being overheard.

"What happens now?" I asked him.

"You'll be committed for trial from Bow Street."

"All those witnesses *again?*"

"I'm afraid so. Just a formality this time."

You see what I mean about British justice?

So on July 21st I was hauled before Chief Magistrate Bridge, and we went through it all once more. I'll own that I paid scant attention to anything, and at the end of it I was sent for trial at the Central Criminal Court, charged now with the murders of Misses Clover, Donworth, Marsh, and Shrivell, with the attempted murder of Miss Harvey, and with threatening old Dr. Harper. Windy Waters made objection to the number of charges, but he was told to go lose himself.

Waters saw me that night again in prison.

"You will need the services of experienced counsel," he says.

"So now you're telling me that you're not experienced, is that it?"

"No. You don't understand. I am unable to be heard at the Old Bailey."

"Why so? You were in fine voice at the Vestry Hall—when you were awake."

He gave a weak laugh. I didn't see what was so dad-blamed funny.

"Only a barrister has right of audience at that court. I shall have to instruct a barrister, Dr. Neill. I shall have to instruct more than one."

"Go ahead. Just make sure they know their onions. Who's the best in the land?"

"I'm a bit out of touch. It used to be Sir Edward Clarke."

"Get Clarke."

Waters shook his head. "He would not be available. I'll try for Mr. Geoghegan. Yours is a slightly unusual case, if you don't mind me saying so. Geoghegan is an unusual advocate."

"But is he any punkins?"

"He's excellent. A fine orator. Irish, you know."

277

"I don't want no bog-dweller, Waters!" I exclaims in alarm. "Get this fellow Clarke. Tell him I'll pay."

Of course, I didn't get Clarke. I got Geoghegan, together with a parcel of lazy layabouts ready to carry his books and boost his ego. But it was Windy Waters I continued to see during those long summer months, not Geoghegan. After one visit Waters suddenly showed a bit of spunk, for he says to me:

"Dr. Neill—or whatever your confounded name is—I must have your cooperation!"

I was too taken aback to say anything. Waters jumped about like a dervish.

"Here we are trying to defend you on no less than four capital counts," he raged, "and you do nothing to help yourself. In God's name, man, tell me about those letters sent to Broadbent and Harper. Did you send them?"

"Surely not."

"The Crown will say that they are down to you."

"Let the Crown hang itself, sir."

"It is you they are trying to hang, Dr. Cream. If Sir Charles gets those letters admitted, we are done for. Unless, of course, you admit them and can offer some sort of reasonable explanation."

"Who is Sir Charles?"

"Russell. The Attorney-General."

"I thought this was Gill's case."

"It still is. But the Attorney-General will lead for the Prosecution. He tends to in cases as important as this."

My introduction to Attorney Russell.

"What does Geoghegan say?" I asked.

"That if the judge allows those letters to go before the jury, then they will hear about the other deaths as well as Clover's. You will be tried for the murder of Clover first, you see. But if the letters go in, why then the jury will hear of how others have died. Keeping those letters out is your only chance!" He sat down again and passed a hand across his forehead. "Cannot you give me *some* kind of explanation, Dr. Neill?"

So that he might pass it on to M'Intyre, John Haynes, and now this Russell fellow? Not while I was sound of mind I wouldn't!

"So they reckon my case is important?" I asked.

"Quadruple murder trials are not common in this country, Doctor."

"I guess not. What are they saying, then? What do the papers say?"

Waters made a sucking noise and consulted his watch.

"We are not interested in publicity," he said.

"I am."

"Evidently! You don't think it matters that potential jurors can feast their eyes in advance, then?"

"Challenge all but the illiterate if this be so."

Waters began to pack up his papers, casually passing me three cigars.

"Much obliged. They're tough on tobacco in this place."

Waters studied me awhile. His hound-dog look had returned.

"I wish I had your confidence," he said yet again. "Your self-control is admirable. Aren't you in the least bit worried?"

"Nope. I know a bum case when I see one. This man Russell's going to have to be some kind of a wizard to win this one."

Another sigh, and Waters rang the bell for the warder to let him out.


## II


Geoghegan called upon me later in September, a tall gingery man with a soft voice. Only a slight burr in his speech betrayed his origins. I guess he'd been spawned and brought up in Ireland, but, like many of his countrymen, he'd been permitted to make good in Britain, provided he "lost" some of his Irishness. The British salve their conscience this way—set up the less rebellious of the Irish, teach them good manners and English ways, then send them back to the ould country so they can squire it over the peasants.

Well, it was plain that Geoghegan knew how to use a knife and fork. He came along one Sunday morning when other cons were being belted by the prison preacher, and he came with

"I don't think you should make a statement from the dock," he says.

"How's that? Of course I'm not making any statement from the dock. I'm going to give my testimony in the witness box."

He stared at me for a very long time, one side of his mouth twitching.

"Haven't you been told?" he asked at length.

"Told what, sir?"

"In this country an accused person is not permitted to give evidence."

"Baldydash," I said. "I'm going right into that box to tell the jury the true way of things!"

"I'm afraid you're not, Dr. Neill. You are only entitled to make an unsworn statement from the dock—and only then if the judge gives his permission."

"The Devil geld the judge, sir! I've just *got* to give evidence!"

You see, I'd been carefully planning a complete exposure of the British establishment, an unanswerable attack upon the forces of authority who were trying to pull me down and still my voice.

"It's an attempt to shut me up," I said to Geoghegan. "I shall not be silenced, sir!"

"It's nothing of the kind, Dr. Neill. It's simply a rule of law."

Geoghegan and the others were gazing at me with pity, as if I was some kind of an idiot.

"Rule of law, my butt! It's a God-blasted conspiracy! It's this man Russell. It's John Bennett Tunbridge. It's M'Intyre and John Haynes and their satellites. It's Judge Hawkins, too. Hawkins must have been talking to Kellum."

"To whom?"

"Kellum, man. Judge Kellum of Boone County!"

And with that they all upped and left me. . . .


IV


No doubt about it, Cogswell, the reaching claws of the Secret Service had embraced even my own counsellors. I reckon M'Intyre knew I was going to holler my mouth off once the trial began, so he told Attorney Russell, who in turn gave Geoghegan the caution. And so a rule of law is suddenly invented by the British to ensure that I be gagged.

By the time the 17th October came I had resigned myself to the manner of things. I took to long periods of silence. This made those around me pretty jumpy. I reckon they knew I'd something bigger than my arm up my sleeve.

On the morning of my trial I was taken in a police wagon to the Central Criminal Court. We passed the King Lud public house, and I allowed myself the odd recollection.

The "Old Bailey" used to be a lock-up called Newgate. Somebody built the present square building with the same stones, so it still looks like a lock-up. Next door to the court—jammed right onto it—is the new Newgate, and that's where I'm sitting right now. But I guess I'm teaching my grandmother to suck eggs.

My case was afforded the principal court, with a high ceiling and polished wooden paneling. They sat me in the corner of the dock—an area big enough to hold at least a dozen men—and we all waited for Judge Hawkins to come in. Gazing around and about, I took stock of those present. The pews were packed with counsellors—four for the Crown and four for me. The British wear these cloth-and-silk gowns and periwigs, without realizing just how damn-fool they all do look.

Attorney Russell has the aspect of wise old watchmaker. Silver-haired and avuncular, he took his position behind a lectern, surrounded by a bevy of barristers and hangers-on. "Yes, Sir Charles," "No, Sir Charles." Make a man sick to his stomach to behold such crawling. Even Geoghegan was doing his share of bows and scrapes.

But when Judge Hawkins made his entrance, the butt-kissing really started. Now, it is generally known that Hawkins is a man of consummate evil—a relic of the Dark Ages, a monster dressed in stuff and ermine. The passions and loves of this fellow fall neatly into two parts—dogs and horses, and the savage punishment of men who have sinned against the state. I'm no backbiter, but "Hangman" Hawkins is of a metal cast in Hellfire.

"Stand," ordered the warder at my side.

Flunkeys in fancy dress drew back Hawkins' chair, and he

looks straight at me with eyes as hard as glass. He took in my unshaven face and shabby clothing, occasionally running his tongue over those thin lips, flicking it in and out like a lizard.

"Let the prisoner at the bar be seated," and his voice is very high and reedy. I determined to give it to Hawkins at the soonest opportunity.

They swore in my jury, and I pleaded Not Guilty to the charges. Attorney Russell then announces that the Crown shall proceed upon the first indictment, alleging that I murdered Matilda Clover. Attorney Russell remained on his feet, entwining his right hand inside his silk gown. He gave Hawkins a little nod, and commenced to tell the jury all about me and the so-called case against me. A fine picture he painted, too! You heard him, Cogswell, so I'll not repeat all the rubbish he said. He spoke, by my reckoning, for no more than half an hour. How did he expect to present a full case to the jurymen in that kind of time? The jury looked foxed and stupid when he began, and they were still looking the same way when he finished. I don't think Hangman Hawkins listened to a single word—he was writing all the time. I concluded that he was writing out his sum-up in advance.

"The prisoner has the great advantage of the assistance of my learned friend Mr. Geoghegan," Attorney Russell said. "I shall not attempt—I cannot successfully attempt—to anticipate what the defense will be to this charge of willful murder. But one thing at least I may say. Remarkable—might I say, unaccountable—as the circumstances of this strange case might be, one thing at least stands out apparent and distinct. For it is recorded under the hand of the prisoner himself that *if* he was the man who was guilty of the crime laid to his charge, he full well *knew and understood* the nature and quality of his act."

He was urging that I am a sane man. Of course I'm sane—it is others who are mad.

Attorney Russell called Miss May and Miss Masters, and they stuck to their original story. Geoghegan cross-questioned them to no avail, and Hawkins made sure that they were incapable of making any mistake with regard to my identification.

Dr. Broadbent followed—better-tempered than before, on

account of the importance of the occasion. When Attorney Russell finished with him, I expected a tough line of questioning from Geoghegan. Not a bit of it—Geoghegan just let the man go. I scribbled a note and had the boys in blue pass it down to Waters. My message was intended for Geoghegan, but Waters read it through and screwed it up into a little ball.

And the court adjourned for the day.

## V

Now, I had not been provided with either razor or clean wearing apparel since Saturday past. It therefore occurred to me that, with an unkempt red-brown beard and grime-marked clothing, I might not be creating a proper impression upon the minds of the jury. I am a gentleman, sir; the jury should be made to understand that they were trying a gentleman—and not some street ruffian.

Accordingly, on Monday night I summoned the governor of Holloway to my cell. I instructed the warders that this was a matter of extreme urgency, and to ask the governor to attend upon me immediately. Sure enough, Lieutenant-Colonel Milman came darting down like a hare.

"My clothes, man," I says, not rising from my seat and keeping Milman standing. "You must get me a fresh set of clothing."

"I'm afraid that's impossible," replied Milman.

"God damn it, sir, you shall do as I bid. I'm not a convict."

"I'm sorry." And out he goes, leaving me with my prison-besmirched black jacket and pepper-and-salts. I determined that Milman should pay for his stupidity once I was at liberty.

Next day the trial resumed with an account of Matilda Clover's death, and Dr. Graham admitted his mistakes. In dealing with the issue of her death certificate showing Clover's demise as due to drink, Attorney Russell said:

"In giving such a certificate in this way, I suppose you were aware you were guilty of a very grave dereliction of duty?" Russell sounded apologetic.

285

"I'm not aware of it," Graham said, only to be jumped upon by Hangman Hawkins:

"I suppose you knew you were bound to put the *truth* in it!"

The effect of Hawkins' outburst was to shatter Graham's nerve; Mr. Geoghegan got nowhere with him. . . .

Emily Sleaper, well tutored by the authorities, did her best to reveal me as a scoundrel.

"He used to take opium in water, and eat a lump of sugar after," and, "He told me it was young Mr. Harper who'd poisoned the girls in Stamford Street. He said Mr. M'Intyre had told him—or was it Mr. Haynes?" and, "He had this notebook and asked me to burn it," and, "He said that Lord Russell had poisoned the women."

"Did the prisoner appear to be a very inquisitive man?" Attorney Russell asked. "Thrusting himself into persons' affairs with which he had nothing to do?"

"Yes, so far as I could judge."

I listened to the testimony of Scientist Stevenson with relief and interest. In the main, I agree with this gentleman's opinions with regard to strychnine poisoning. But his is only a theoretical knowledge and, given the chance, I could show him things fit to make his hair stand up like an acre of jack pines.

I made a point of showing the jury that I appreciated what Scientist Stevenson had to say, nodding and smiling whenever I could catch their eye. I was in the process of bowing my thanks, as Stevenson was quitting the box, when Attorney Russell's words froze me up.

"Mr. John Wilson M'Culloch," he called, and the echo is taken over by the ushers.

M'Culloch? What in tarnation was M'Culloch doing over here? He was supposed to be in Ottawa. Windy Waters had warned me they'd try to get him over, but I didn't believe him. But here he was, swearing on the Bible, looking as serious and snooty as can be. . . .

M'Culloch must have a remarkable memory, for he ran through near everything that occurred between us at Blanchard's Hotel. And I could see Geoghegan humping and heaving with displeasure while he talked.

"The prisoner showed me these pills. I asked him what they were for. He told me they were to get women out of the family way. He also showed me a pair of divided whiskers. I asked him what they were for. He said he wore them to prevent identification."

But Geoghegan made it a sight worse when he put M'Culloch under cross-questioning.

"Did he spend a great deal of money?" Geoghegan asks him for some peculiar reason.

"Yes—mostly mine."

Attorney Russell seizes upon Geoghegan's fool questions when he examined M'Culloch again.

"You reported your knowledge of Neill to the chief of Quebec police once you knew he'd been arrested for murder in this country?"

"Yes. I was then subpoenaed to come here and give evidence."

"Yes. While at Blanchard's Hotel in Quebec, did you continue to be friendly with him until the end?"

"No," says M'Culloch, staring at me in the dock. "I lost confidence in him. We had a conversation about an American who'd come over there with plenty of money. Cream—as I knew him —said: 'I could give that man a pill and put him to sleep, and then his money would be mine.' I said, 'You wouldn't kill a man for two thousand dollars?' Cream said, 'I ought to have done it.' I shunned Cream after that."

So you see, Cogswell, this was the first time I knew that dim-wit had taken me over-serious.

Attorney Russell continued to summon his witnesses, and I withdrew my mind from the case for the rest of the day. I was thinking about Lou Harvey—whether they'd get her along, as they had at the Vestry Hall and before Magistrate Bridge. Were they going to allow that vixen woman to tell her lies three times over?

At the close of Tuesday's proceedings I saw Geoghegan and Windy Waters in my courthouse cell. The authorities allowed time for discussion before they took me back to Holloway.

"Milman won't allow me my other clothes," I complained.

"I don't think he can. Prison regulations."

I knew the truth to be otherwise—that the refusal was calculated to put me forward as a scruff to the jury, and that my
own counsellors were party to this action.

"The Harvey woman," I said. "Will they be calling her tomorrow?"

Geohegan looked unhappy. "The Attorney-General will seek
to adduce evidence of your alleged attempt to murder her, yes.
He will also seek to prove the other alleged murders—Shrivell,
Marsh, Donworth. I shall try to have that evidence excluded."

"How's that?" I didn't understand the man.

"Because you are only being tried upon the murder of Clover
—not the others, at this stage."

"How's Russell going to prove other cases? Why's he want
to?"

"To show a systematic course of conduct on your part."

"Does it matter if he does?"

"Matter? It will hang you, Dr. Neill."

And with those words of reassurance was I escorted back to
Holloway.


VI


The rubbishy lying double-dealing falsehoods of "Sergeant"
M'Intyre of "Scotland Yard" and John Haynes, "unemployed
engineer," being delivered by those two fixers, Attorney Russell
had the jury leave their benches and the court.

In the box stood a handwriting expert from the British Mu-
seum. This gentleman has a very high regard for his own importance. He judged all letters in my case written by the same man:
me. How the Hell can a man be *that* expert, Cogswell? Truth
is, this pompoid was nothing more than an expert at guesswork.

"My Lord," says Attorney Russell. "The direct evidence in
the Clover case has been concluded. However, I now propose
to call evidence as to the deaths of three other women by
strychnine, and the attempted administration of poison to a
fourth, and to connect these acts with the prisoner."

This was what Geoghegan had talked of last night. Now he came to his feet, only to rat upon me.

"My learned friend Mr. Warburton has addressed himself to this part of the case, and will argue," says he. He'd passed the buck to one of his underlings.

I scarce can be expected to recall all the legalistic jawing that followed. Attorney Russell talked about this "systematic course of conduct" on my part, saying that I was a deliberate murderer of several women, that he could prove I was, and that such proof would dispel any doubts in the mind of the jurymen relating to Matilda Clover. In short, he sought to hang me with a yard of prejudice.

Young Warburton argued to the contrary in a manner most ineffectual, causing Hawkins to raise his hands in gestures of despair and pull long faces.

Of course, Hangman Hawkins had made up his mind before all of this had begun, and he accordingly found in favor of the Prosecution.

"*Does it matter?*" I'd asked Geoghegan.

"*Matter? It will hang you.*"

Back comes the jury, and on goes the trial. I'll trouble you no further with who was called and what they said. I was grieved when Laura appeared and told her tales, dabbing at her eyes with a kerchief. I was too wearied to feel vexation at the mendacity of Lou Harvey. And John Bennett Tunbridge read his version of events from a pocket book, his voice flat and dead. Some people the court called and recalled and recalled again, adding to the over-all confusion. It was thundery weather, Cogswell, and it made it hard for a man to keep his eyes open and his brain a-listening.

"*Matter? It will hang you.*" That's what he'd said. Fine words from your attorney! Did he not realize that I had not been born to hang like a dog? Did none of them understand?

# NO SUBJECT FOR BILLINGTON?

## I

I guess I've expressed my views with regard to lawyers on more than one occasion. I retract nothing—but I'll have the grace to flatter one man in one particular case. You see, Geoghegan spoke up pretty well for me to the jury. I can't say that I was able to figure out everything he said, and I daresay the jury couldn't either. But the gist of what he said was this: Matilda Clover had strychnine in her body when Scientist Stevenson carved her up seven months later—but that was neither proof that the strychnine killed her nor that I had administered the poison. For proof, the Crown relied upon my "letters" and the chain of deaths surrounding that of Miss Clover. Circumstantial evidence. But dare the jury send me to the gallows because they just suspicioned me?

To press his point, Geoghegan told the jury about the first time he'd seen a man sentenced to death. And—blow me down —did not Hawkins turn out to be the man who'd done the honors upon that occasion? I can recollect some of Geoghegan's very words.

"I say between you and the prisoner at the bar, between the Crown and the prisoner, there stands a figure, and that figure is the genius of the law of England."

I guess he meant the figure of Justice. Had he never observed that this figure is blind, is holding a sword, and is a woman? No matter—the words could blind a jury, too.

"It demands that the guilt of the accused shall be brought home to him as clear and as bright as the light of Heaven now streaming into this court." Sunlight was filling the courtroom at that moment, and Geoghegan made use of that advantage.

"Under the protection of that figure, I leave my client, Thomas Neill."

His words nipped my tear ducts, and I buried my head in my hands for the jury to see.

Upon Geoghegan resuming his seat, it was for Attorney Russell to address the jury. He didn't get up at once, looking at Geoghegan instead and moving his lips as if to congratulate my counsellor upon his advocacy.

Then Russell was at his lectern once again, quiet and school-mastery, talking as if he hated everything his "duty" compelled him to say about me. He was fond of reminding the jury of "duty," finishing his speech thus:

"If the course of this evidence has driven into your minds a solemn conviction that this man is guilty, why, then you will discharge your duty conscientiously—you will discharge your duty with fortitude!"

Attorney Russell was less fierce than I'd predicted. But it was the end of the day—maybe he was tired. It was the end of the fourth day—maybe he was plain tired of everything.

And maybe only the words of Geoghegan occupied the minds of my jurymen. Back in my Holloway cell, I pondered the thought. Could be that one or two of the jury had been bedazzled by his line of talk. In that case, the jurymen must disagree —and the trial become a nullity. Lack of proper food and the prospect of Geoghegan's blinking the jury made me light-headed. As you've probably heard, Cogswell, I danced a jig and sang a few songs that night. . . .

## II

But there remained Hangman Henry Hawkins and his sum-up. Hawkins, as I say, has this thin crisp voice. He has a way of enunciating words so as to reveal his own opinions of a particular set of facts.

"The responsibility for the verdict rests not with me," he began that stifling Friday morning. "It is your duty to investigate the facts—with that I have nothing to do. I have to *assist* you, to the best of my ability, in pointing out to you such parts of the evidence as in my judgment bear upon this case."

In other words: Listen carefully, and I shall make it clear to you whether he murdered this girl or no.

Hawkins is a master of insinuation. He openly congratulated Geoghegan upon his efforts—not because he thought Geoghegan was a fine speechifier, but because he wanted the jury to realize Geoghegan had tried to make the best of a bad job. He stressed the value of circumstantial evidence by saying that no crime was susceptible of mathematical proof, and that common sense might lead the jury into thinking Clover's killer could have been none other than the man who wrote the letters—namely, me. He lastly argued that her elimination had been "a diabolical crime by whomsoever committed"—in other words: Someone did it and someone's got to pay for it, and that someone might as well be the prisoner.

"If you are not so convinced," he said, "then the prisoner is entitled to be acquitted." He spoke these words in the manner of a parrot, but changed his tone to add: *"But* if you are satisfied that the prisoner *is* the man who did commit the crime, it is your very *duty* to say so, fearlessly and firmly. Now please decide upon your verdict."

A flunkey swears to hold them in some quiet and convenient place, and the jurymen filed out of court. While they were departing, I stared at Hawkins and Hawkins stared at me. Then he rose, and I was taken below.

They put me in a narrow stone-faced room without a window. A wooden bench ran the length of one wall, upon which both I and my two warders were obliged to sit in a row.

"How long?" I asked the one on my left, a young laddie with pockmarks. I observed that his boots were foul with horse dung, and guessed he walked to work.

"No saying, sir. Can be hours. Isn't that right, Alby?"

The other warder nodded. I don't think he was able to look directly at me.

"Any of your lousy tea?" I asked. "I'm awful dry."

"Not yet, sir," says dung-boots. "In a little while, perhaps."

As it transpired, there was no time for tea. Hawkins had convinced the jury as to their "duty" in a grand fashion, and they returned in ten minutes.

It was five minutes to two o'clock in the afternoon by the clock on the wall, and the Clerk of Arraigns spoke in a room otherwise deathly still.

"Do you find the prisoner guilty or not guilty of the murder of Matilda Clover?"

"Guilty." Very solemn.

I permitted myself a soft chuckle.

The clerk looked up at me, standing now in the center of the massive dock. The fool proceeded to ask me why I should not receive the death sentence. I was about to give him several reasons, when one of the flunkeys standing near the bench calls out:

"Oyez, Oyez, Oyez," or something equally ridiculous. "My Lords the Queen's Justices do strictly charge and command all persons to keep silence while sentence of death is passed on the prisoner at the bar." And he added something to the effect that if anyone did open his mouth, he'd be locked up.

A square of black silk had been placed upon Hawkins' head without my notice, and a chaplain stood at his side.

"Thomas Neill," Hawkins said, awful quiet. "The jury—after having listened with the most patient attention to the evidence which has been offered against you in respect of this most terrible crime, and having paid all attention to the most able arguments and the very eloquent speech which your learned counsel addressed to them on your behalf—have felt it their bounden duty to find you guilty of the crime of willful murder." The reptilian eyes opened wide. "Of a murder so diabolical in its character—fraught with so much cold-blooded cruelty—that one dare hardly trust oneself to speak of the details of your wickedness!"

Hangman Hawkins was in his element, and I gave him the benefit of another chuckle.

"What motive," he went on, "could have actuated you to take the life of that girl away, and with so much torture to that poor creature who could not have offended you, I know not. . . .

"But I do know that your cruelty toward her, and the crime that you have committed, are to my mind of unparalleled atrocity. For the crime of which you have been convicted our law knows but one penalty—the penalty of death. That sentence I must now pronounce upon you, in accordance with my duty."

I took the notion that Hawkins would rather have me boiled alive.

"I would add one word: to beseech you, during the short time that life remains to you—for remember, when you descend the steps from the spot where you now stand, this world will be no more to you—to endeavor to seek your peace with Almighty God. Pray Him to pardon you for your great sin! He *alone* can grant you pardon!

"The crime which you have committed can be expiated only by your death. I proceed, therefore, to pass upon you the dread sentence of the law, which is: that you be taken from hence to the place whence you came, and thence to a lawful place of execution—and that there you be hanged by your neck until you be dead. And that, when you *are* dead, your body be buried within the precincts of that prison within the walls of which you shall have been confined last before the execution of this judgment upon you. And may the Lord have mercy upon your soul!"

"Amen," says the God-botherer beside him.

"You shall never hang me," says I.

And I was led away and down the steps of the dock.

# III

[*Neill was returned to Holloway, and taken from that prison to the precincts of Newgate, where he was placed in the condemned cell. It is not reported that he sang or danced again.*

*Neill's narrative becomes somewhat confusing at this stage; indeed, he has little to say for himself which is either sense or intelligible. The papers contain passages which appear to have been scored out by a frenzied hand. I have tried to decipher these, but I have failed.*

*It seems that Mr. John Waters obtained for his client a respite of seven days in order to obtain affidavits from Canada—sworn by various friends and relatives—to show that Neill was insane. Neill himself disapproved of this attempt to save him, asserting to the end that he was wholly sane. In his own hand, he has this to say:*          V.R.C.]

I'll not bide by Windy Waters' trying to have me locked away in a madhouse. Such establishments are frequently set up by the Secret Service. Well can you imagine the kind of treatment M'Intyre and John Haynes would design for me in such a place! They say that Laura Sabbatini, having been satisfactorily "employed" by the Service, has disappeared. I reckon she's been incarcerated in one of these madhouses—to keep her mouth shut about the lying testimony she gave in court. Others will follow her into similar oblivion, mark me well!

My only salvation lies with His Excellency the American Ambassador. He'll pull me out of this nest of vipers. He'll get me due compensation from the British government, and a written letter of apology from sourpuss Vicky herself, lest I'm much mistaken. . . .

[*Mr. John Waters went ahead with his endeavors to save his client, and obtained several affidavits from Quebec, Montreal, and Ottawa. These were carefully considered by the Home*

295

*Office, but on November 12th Mr. Waters received a letter from the Home Secretary stating, inter alia, that "after the most careful consideration of the affidavits submitted—and of all the circumstances of the case, he has been unable to discover any sufficient grounds to justify him, consistent with his public duty, in advising Her Majesty to interfere with the due course of the law." This letter had to be shown to Neill. According to Mr. Waters, his client took the news very calmly. Neill himself has this to say:* V.R.C.]

You see, they can't say I'm crazy after all! I reckon the Secret Service has been trying to get Whitehall to say that I am insane so that THEY can have me ALIVE. For some reason Whitehall aren't playing the ball game. Why not? I'll tell you: because the Americans at the Embassy are rooting for me. They won't let the Secret Service mistreat one of their own in such a way. So now Home Secretary Lushington has to write and say I'll hang, even though he knows the authorities dare not hang me. The boys at the Embassy will spring me pretty soon now. There'll be no necktie party for Tommy Cream, you wait and see! Mr. Ambassador's a *very* clever man, sir.

[*The next intelligible passage by Neill was written at about the same time as that above, and reads:* V.R.C.]

The warders are quite chatty, and I'm eating that much I guess I'm putting on a bit of weight. Any day now and I'll be out of here. Minding you, we've got a charade to play—the warders and myself. I questioned them regarding "my future." Two of the warders didn't want to discuss things none too much, but the other obliged. Seems the hangman's called Mr. Billington, and the execution "shed" is in the yard outside. I wondered if I could see it by climbing up on the table, but the warders have instructions not to let me do so. Of course they have! Because if I get to have a peep, I'm going to see an empty yard —on account of the fact there isn't going to be any execution.

It's occurred to me that this Billington might be from the Embassy—one of Pinkerton's men in disguise. True or no, I'll be no subject for any Mr. Billington. . . .

God damn it, Cogsby [*This is his mistake.   V.R.C.*], they have commenced visiting a God-botherer upon me! This I shall never endure!

"I've come so that we might pray together," says the fellow, telling the warders to depart.

"Out, child molester, out!" I yelled at him.

"Think of your soul, poor man," he insists.

"Think of your choirboys and shift your butt!" I told him.

"Can I be of no service to you at all?"

"See you in Hades, Vicar. Now, *out!*"

And off he goes, fast as a Buffalo bar-fly. . . .

[*The final sensible passage by Neill was written during the weekend of the 13th and 14th November. I say "sensible" with reservation, for this is clearly the raving of a man in the most piteous frame of mind. I can only assume that Neill, knowing that his execution was set for Monday morning, at last realized there was no escape from the halter. With death so near, so frightful and so inevitable, did reason return to him? Did this reason remind him of the terrible things he had done? Did he become aware of the dreadful suffering he had inflicted upon others? Did that realization cause him to be haunted by those he had slain? And did such hauntings, together with the thought of a place set aside for him hereafter, drive him finally into the shelter of true madness? You be the judge, Professor. V.R.C.*]

Porridge in the morning—bully beef for dinner—stew for tea. Fine food—fit for a man about to swing, Codscup. [*His, not mine.   V.R.C.*] It's gone nine of the darktime, and I'm waiting for the daylight. I've got to wait, you see, because they're hanging me come sun-up.

I've got that scratchy feeling all over again, you know? They're using the BUGS to make my last night hard. But I won't scratch—I refuse absolutely to scratch. My mother always told me never to . . . [*Here it is impossible to read through the crazed scoring on the paper.   V.R.C.*]

I suppose they'll be putting Laura next door pretty soon. Keep her there, laughing and jeering. Maybe they'll get her to put the rope around my neck. Then she'll kiss me, on the lips, and say: "'Bye, dearest, 'bye!"

Time's moving a mite quicker than my hand. I've got to stay very still, you see. Otherwise, the warders will spy me scratching—and that's just what they want! Mustn't disturb the BUGS.

There's a hissing noise just started, coming from the wall under the window. Are they slipping in a serpent or two to scarify me?

Don't mind snakes, so they'll be wasting their time. Bears—it's those big, furry, clawly bears that trouble me. If THEY know that, I'll bet you *all* my considerable fortune that they'll push a BEAR up and out of the pipes.

Half past five in the forenoon, according to the big CLOCK on the wall. They've borrowed the CLOCK from the courthouse, you know? Sneaked it in and up when I was minding things elsewhere. I'm looking at it now. Hell and God damn it, the clock's got a photographic face printed over the dial! I know that face, I do! Well, I'll be a jumper in squid-jigging time! The face is that of BLACK BITCH SAL! She's a-leering something horrid, the old crow. Nice of her to drop by, nonetheless. . . . Wait a spell! The hands a-moved, and it's not Black Bitch! ELLY DONWORTH!

Go away, sweet Elly, go back to your tomb. You can't stay here—you don't want to see me like this, now. Get you gone, girl! GOOD GIRL! That's Tommy's little darling. . . .

"Parson to see you," says a voice, but no one comes. Have they at last understood that I seek no recourse to any religionist?

"Would you like a game of cards? None of your clever poker, though?"

Poker? Yes, I play poker—but I'm no gambling man.

"Never did get to use my derringer," I said.

"Pardon?"

"My over-and-under. Never did get to use it. Forehead and throat, that's the way. Never in the body. Ball's too small."

"Is it some kind of gun?"

"No—you need a Remington for BEAR." Will they try the bears? Spare me from that. . . .

"Would you like a small bottle of beer? You're entitled, you know."

Beer? Never touch it. What lunacy is this?

The clock reads seventeen after six. Daybreak. THEY'LL be coming any moment. I sat my chair like a slab of stone, never to be moved. No sound from next door, however. No sound of Laura.

Keys rattle, and I never did hear the footsteps. Keys rattle and the door flings wide.

I will not look up. I am cocooned within mine own identity. Nothing a milli beyond my skin is for me. Silence—endless silence—only the pish-wish-pish of the window wall.

"Hello, Thomas." Such a voice I have to raise my head. "Hello, Thomas." It was Melvin Solloway, his gown and surplice undone to bare a hairy chest.

"No trouble now, Number 4374," from Preacher/Hangman Rik van Bulger.

"He never was any trouble—not the doc." Chief Warden Passmore.

"I always loved him." Laura. . . .

THOMAS NEILL (CREAM) WROTE NO MORE IN ADDITION TO THE ABOVE.

[*Over the weekend, attendant warders noticed Neill fall into a bemused state—staring about him at objects as inanimate as the cell heating pipes, and answering his keepers' polite inquiries after his well-being with strange comments. At one stage a great trembling shook the condemned man. He was observed to half-rise from his seat, fix the cell door with his eyes, and then fall to the floor with a horrid groan, where he lay and thrashed for several moments. Semi-unconscious, he was placed upon his bed. I understand that Neill's cries and moans did not cease for quite some considerable time. One can only conclude that Neill anticipated his last hours in this peculiar nightmare. V.R.C.*]

## ADDENDUM

# A Commentary on the Neill Case,
# Compiled by Vernon Radcliffe Cogswell, M.D.

*My dear Professor,*
*Having regard to the complexity of our study, I have seen fit
to divide my final observations into four distinct parts. And I
do so as follows:*

*1. Thomas Neill (Cream) was hanged on Tuesday, the 15th
November, 1892.*
*Mr. Billington was the executioner, and gave the condemned
a drop of five feet. Unlike Mr. Berry and Mr. Marwood, Mr.
Billington has always favored the "long drop."*
*Present at the execution were the governor of Holloway and
Newgate prisons, the commissioner of the City of London police, the medical officer of the prisons concerned, and the Reverend Mr. Merrick. Various other minor officials were also in
attendance.*
*Neill appeared indifferent to his end. It has been said that he
thanked those responsible for his well-being during the latter
days for their kindness. I cannot believe that this was really so.*
*It has further been rumored that Neill, just as the trap was
about to be sprung, made a certain observation—that he called
out: "I am 'Jack the . . ." before passing into oblivion.*

300

This I also choose to disbelieve. Neill was executed wearing the standard mask required under Home Office regulations, and I doubt if banter of any kind could have been heard during his last moments. Moreover, we know that Neill was imprisoned at Joliet Penitentiary throughout the year of 1888, and therefore could never have been responsible for the Whitechapel murders. But, as Neill himself has pointed out in his narrative, the search for a suitable culprit for these atrocities will be unending, and it is easy to imagine how so facile a tale came into existence.

Public feeling toward Neill is expressed by the attitude of the crowd assembled outside Newgate at the time of his execution. The sight of the black flag was greeted with wild cheering.

How did Neill in fact meet his end? Fears that he might attempt suicide were, in my opinion, without foundation. Thomas Neill was many things, but not suicidal, and his hopes for a reprieve ran high until the very eve of his execution. And when that awful time did come, Neill suffered neither fits nor hallucinations. He was extremely restless during his last night, certainly—pacing the cell, flinging himself down on his bunk, unable to sleep, and moaning a great deal. And by morning he was exhausted and haggard, and very calm. The prison officials were spared any of his customary outbursts.

Neill ate no breakfast, and allowed Mr. Billington to fetter him without comment or resistance. Neill was hanged wearing the same clothes in which he had been arrested and tried, and his beard was thick and bushy.

Neill died of a broken neck, and it was judged at his inquest —held at Sessions House, Old Bailey—that his execution had been carried out in the most satisfactory manner. His body was buried in quicklime within the yard of Newgate Prison.

2. Upon the trial of Thomas Neill at the Central Criminal Court, I feel duty bound to make the following observations:

There can be little doubt that Neill engaged the innocent services of Miss Laura Sabbatini to write letters to Mr. Wyatt, and to the foreman of the jury in the inquest on Misses Marsh and Shrivell. No one acquainted with the case expresses any *view to the contrary. Why then does Neill deny this had been done? After all, he admits authorship of other correspondence. I can only conclude that Neill convinced himself that he never used Miss Sabbatini in any of his murderous enterprises, that he chose to hold her apart, that he could not bear to realize that he had involved her in the darker side of his existence. I do believe that Neill loved this woman in his own peculiar fashion, and that his very personality became, so to speak, "split" as far as she was concerned.*

*While we dwell upon the subject of Neill's incredible correspondence, let us take a look at the various other recipients. Lord Russell was a natural target, for the Russell divorce case made the major columns of daily newspapers at the time. Neill must have read about the scandal and acted accordingly. Lady Russell was perplexed but in no way injured by Neill's letter to her.*

*Mr. Frederick Smith, a prominent Member of Parliament and head of the firm of W. H. Smith & Son, was a stranger choice. This gentleman's father was upon his deathbed when the letter was written and received, and one may assume that Neill read of that right honorable gentleman's sickness in the newspapers.*

*It is easier to understand Neill's selection of Dr. William Broadbent. That eminent physician was attending a case of typhoid at Marlborough House during the period, and his activities were reported in bulletins throughout each day. However, there was never any question of the doctor being appointed a Queen's Physician.*

*And so we are left with Dr. Harper, the father, of Barnstaple. In his persecution, I think the answer is to be found in Neill's own words. Neill, convinced that he was being ignored and shunned by the son, sought to avenge himself upon the father.*

*Edward Levy was called by the Crown simply to establish that Neill had been in medical practice in Chicago during the early years of the last decade. It so happened that this gentleman was (and still is) a licensed victualer, living in Houndsditch. He had known Neill as Dr. Thomas Cream in America, and was summoned to say so. I imagine that the Attorney-General wanted to paint a background of Neill's medical past for the benefit of the jury, and no more. But Neill speaks of this*

302

*American as a "professional witness," as a man who had once before committed perjury to Neill's benefit. Is Neill speaking the truth? This I very much doubt, although I have been unable to meet Mr. Edward Levy. I understand that the gentleman has since returned to the United States.*

*Miss Louisa Harvey (or "Mrs. Harris"): The prosecution alleged that Neill had attempted to end the life of this lady—that he had given her poisonous pills under a pretext, and that she had the good sense not to take them. Neill insists that this was never the case. According to the evidence, Neill was a man who killed willy-nilly, without thought for either his choice of victim or possible consequences. The Crown asserted that Neill, believing Miss Harvey to be dead by his hand, incorporated her name into his threatening letters. Certainly he did include her name and death in his amazing correspondence; certainly he gave her capsules of an unknown composition, sent her on her way, and never wished to see her again. I believe that he intended to kill her and that he gave her poison. I also believe that he felt outraged and slighted when he discovered that his plans in her instance had gone awry. Neill despised failure of any kind, for he was a determined man. Well might one imagine the fury of this terrible mind when he discovered that he had failed in her case, and that she was alive and well and eager to testify against him. Since Miss Harvey had made a fool of him, Neill's immediate reaction was to brush her aside, to pretend that she had never been selected as one of his victims, because, had she been so chosen, she would have died like the others. Neill, in my view, is most anxious to blur his "incompetence" in her case. I have come to the unhappy conclusion that where Neill says he murdered A, B, or C, he has done so, but where he says he did not murder D, E, or F, one cannot exonerate him from at least a bungled attempt.*

*I opine the above subject to one particular exception—Miss Violet Beverley. She has stated that Neill tried to murder her, and she is not a lady prone to exaggeration. But she does not agree with Neill's version of their meeting, although she does say that he was very cross. She took the view that he was a sick man.*

*Neill's ramblings with regard to the Secret Service are, of course, nonsense. Patrick M'Intyre is a genuine police sergeant in the Criminal Investigation Department of Scotland Yard. He is not, and never has been, a member of any secret government organization. M'Intyre was a personal friend of Mr. William Armstead, the photographer. It was through this gentleman that the sergeant made the acquaintance of Neill. Neill confided in the sergeant his knowledge of the mysterious poisonings, and, horrified, the sergeant reported to his superiors what he'd been told. M'Intyre was neither officially nor directly involved in the subsequent investigation into Neill's activities.*

*Very much the same applies in the case of John Haynes. Mr. Haynes was another friend of Mr. William Armstead. But Mr. Haynes had certain experience as a private detective, or "private inquiry agent," as they are termed. He was widely traveled in his capacity of an engineer, and knew America extremely well. In evidence, Mr. Haynes told the court that he had undertaken commissions on behalf of the British government while abroad, and that he had informed Neill of this fact. Presumably, Neill really believed Haynes to be a government agent, and considered him a useful man to know for this reason. In fact Haynes was never acting for our government during the period in which he knew Neill. His days as a private detective were over. He was merely an "unemployed engineer" endeavoring to find a suitable situation! But this Neill would never accept; in his muddled mind Haynes was an active member of a spy system—and since Sergeant M'Intyre was friendly with Haynes, both men belonged to the same organization.*

*3. What of Neill's antecedents upon the North American continent? Here, Professor, we are ordained to be most mightily confused! As soon as I had in my hands Neill's account of himself, I naturally set about careful inquiries, and I am exceedingly grateful to Mr. John Waters for all his help.*

*Nevertheless, our picture of Neill must remain a sketch of the crudest kind—a portrait blurred by the untruths and exaggerations of the man himself. This much I have been able to verify, from sources on both sides of the Atlantic.*

*Born: Glasgow, 1850, first child to William Cream and Mary Elder. And this family of three emigrated to Quebec between the years 1854 and 1855.*

*Quebec 1855–1870: William Cream prospered in the lumbering trade, and in 1872 he entered son Thomas in M'Gill College. Records of Neill's activities at M'Gill have not yet become available, interest in their pupil having faded upon the removal of his name from the register in 1881. But I have been led to believe that he was an accomplished chemist, a student of no mean ability, who qualified with honors in 1876.*

*1876: A marriage certificate shows that Neill did marry a Miss Flora Elizabeth Brooks of Waterloo.*

*In October of that year Neill registered himself as "Thomas Cream, M.D." at St. Thomas' Hospital, and paid a fee for a course of post-graduate study.*

*1877: A death certificate in the name of Flora Elizabeth Cream, nee Brooks, dated 12th August, shows that this lady died of consumption. Together with this certificate is a claim for one thousand dollars' insurance on the lady's life.*

*1878: Neill certainly qualified at Edinburgh under the auspices of the Royal Colleges of Physicians and Surgeons.*

*He was in practice at London, Ontario, by the month of July. There are no records to disclose his activities during that summer, but I understand that he vacated his surgery and left town after only a few months.*

*1879: Neill was practicing medicine in Chicago.*

*1880: In August, Neill was charged with the murder of Julia Faulkner with "another." Neill was acquitted, and I have yet to be informed as to the fate of "the other." The Chicago police department and the office of the District Attorney have both striven to assist me with interest and perseverance. Unhappily, their records on Neill (or Cream, as they knew him) are slim. They were, at that particular time, more concerned with the demonstrations of "anarchists" within the city.*

*1881: Neill was arrested and charged with the offense of posting "scurrilous cards" to Mr. and Mrs. Joseph Martin.*

*While on bail for the above misdemeanor, Neill fell in with Mrs. Daniel Stott, and the Stott escapade begins. Newspaper* reportage of Neill's trial on an indictment for murder will soon be available. I have consulted the *Chicago Tribune*—an excellent journal—and I have been promised copies of its relevant editions. I have been assured that Neill was arrested in Canada, returned to America, tried in Boone County, and convicted by jury of the murder of Daniel Stott "in the second degree." Mrs. Stott was charged with her husband's murder, but never actually tried. Her whereabouts are unknown.

In November, Neill was incarcerated at the Joliet penitentiary, where he remained until his release in July 1891.

On the 1st October, Neill landed at Liverpool, and he registered himself as "Dr. Neill" at Anderton's Hotel, Fleet Street, a few days later. Neill's diabolical crimes started almost immediately. Having regard to the evidence presented at the coroner's inquest at Tooting, Neill's committal for trial at Bow Street, and the final drama within the Central Criminal Court, I have no doubt that he was in every way responsible for the murders of Clover, Donworth, Marsh, and Shrivell; and, again, I personally entertain no doubt that he also attempted to murder Misses Harvey and Beverley.

4. But what of Neill "the man"?

I visited Neill upon six occasions in all. He was in the condemned cell, but his hopes ran high at the beginning. Only when the Home Secretary had rejected the exercise of Her Majesty's clemency (on the grounds of insanity) did our prisoner advertise the torment of his soul. When I last paid call upon the man, I was bustled out amid florid abuse.

"Get out, Coalscuttle!" Neill urged. "If you want your poxy manuscript in full, don't badger me!"

Those were his words—I remember them well, for it was the last time I laid eyes on him.

I must confess that I withdrew in haste, for Neill roused was a formidable sight! Very tall—nearly six feet, I'd say—he was built like an ox. His neck was thick and his shoulders massive. His hands, however, were exceptionally slim of finger and overall construction, so that his wrists, circular and very hairy, appeared wider than their appendages. Neill's face was of interest. When I observed him, he had grown a heavy beard—red

*and savage like a Viking baresarker. Mr. Armstead's photo-
graphs reveal him shaven but for a heavy mustache. In these
portraits one may trace the great bony jaw, a feature that shows
massive determination, albeit that will be to commit horren-
dous murder. His eyes were of the pale variety, two gimlets set
close to the nose, forever flickering up and down until they
came to rest upon one's own, there to bore with a concentration
I found most disconcerting.*

*His head was bald, and cropped close at the sides. A tall head,
much in the shape of a Minie bullet. Yet I saw no indication of
base brutality in that head. Perspiration lived upon the upper
dome as a cloud brushes the summit of an Alpine peak. I saw
nothing unusual about the skull—indeed, let me say that it was
a fine head. At this stage, I must reveal that I am scientifically
unable to attach any realistic value to the shape of a man's head
so as to judge him criminal or no. Experience has taught me
rather to observe the eyes of such people—to study the eyes and
listen to the tongue.*

*I know that you attach a degree of importance to the move-
ment of patients of this kind. When I saw Neill he was still of
body, although his talk rambled on without pause or change of
tone. His twang of the American accent was pronounced, and
he spoke as in a monologue. Had it not been for the nature of
this man and his chatter, I daresay I'd have put him down for
an incredible bore!*

*But "movement" on his part has been mentioned. In October
last, within the columns of* St. James' Gazette *did there appear
an article on Neill by a man who claimed his acquaintance. He
spoke of Neill as restless, unable to sit alone in public places,
always seeking out the company of others. He said that Neill
was intelligent and worldly, but forever pacing a room, or
moving his limbs "like a dog dreaming." He rolled his eyes, and
seldom laughed or smiled. He carried upon his person photographs of fornication, and spoke much of women he had
known and enjoyed. He drank heavily, chewed gum and tobacco, and took drugs. Only money and poisons and women
were of real interest to him. Our writer ended thus: "In short,
he was a degenerate of filthy desires and practices."*

*Strong words! Perhaps they are justified. . . .*

Neill's verbosity it was that gave him the desire to give evidence on his own behalf at his trial. In Illinois he had been able to do so—and his explanations certainly failed to convince his jury in that part of the world.

As yet in England, an accused man, whatever the crime, is unable to take the oath as a witness on his own behalf. This rule has been criticized for some time, and perhaps it will eventually be changed. Neill might have made an unsworn statement from the dock, with leave from the presiding judge. But I imagine that he wanted the fuller platform, to upbraid and pour scorn upon the prosecuting powers who had brought him to book. Great must have been the fury and indignation of the doctor to discover that his hands were tied by the intricacies of our criminal procedure. Could it be that his London jurymen might have convicted Neill in even shorter a space of time had the prisoner spoken for himself? Well can I imagine the pained look of the Attorney-General, the hopeless despair of Mr. Gerald Geoghegan, and the waspish breathtakes of the learned judge.

May I now come to the question of Neill's mental state?

In England the question of insanity in a criminal is governed by the "McNaghten rules"—the decision of our judges in the House of Lords, given in 1843 following the attempt by a lunatic named McNaghten to assassinate Sir Robert Peel, first minister to our gracious Queen. Stated simply, the "rules" say that no man is to be judged insane unless he can show either (a) he did not know what he was doing at the time, or (b) he did not know that what he was doing was wrong. This is the standard we apply in our courts of criminal jurisdiction, and there can be no exceptions to the rule.

I believe that Neill knew what he was doing was wrong, and that he was compos mentis when he murdered. I cannot accept that his drug addiction rendered him totally irresponsible—narcotics only released the demon within, and we know that he did not require drugs to form the intent to kill. But I do not believe that Neill murdered for money. If financial gain followed, all well and good, but money was never the motive.

*Naturally, I do not accept Neill's own explanation for what he did—that the streets of London required another "Jack the Ripper" for a betterment of the lower orders. This was Neill deliberately trying to mislead me!*

*With the possible exception of Mr. Daniel Stott, whom Neill murdered in order to steal his wife, I believe that Neill killed for the sake of killing. I suggest that the power of poison gave Neill a terrible delight. As a physician, Neill knew that once his victims had taken of his poison they were as good as dead. Once Neill had induced his victims to swallow his mixtures, he invariably retreated. One can imagine the doctor contemplating the agonies of his victims in some secret lair, brooding over their agonizing deaths. For Neill was a sadist—why else use strychnine? Neill was intent upon the mass destruction of his fellow human beings, roaming the vacancies of Lambeth like a creature of the graveyard. He delighted in the excruciating pain he caused, just as he had delighted in slaughter of animals as a child and the torture of his Red Indian guide as a young man. He chose his victims without much thought. Those who challenged and upset him, he would seek to punish with poison. For the rest, he chose women of the streets, simple-minded and without inquiring friends or relations, women who could disappear without much notice. It has been suggested that Neill may have contracted syphilis from a prostitute and now sought to revenge himself upon that kind. This I do not believe—there is no evidence in support of such a theory. Moreover, it is a conjecture commonly adopted to excuse the mass-murderer of women. I understand that the same hypothesis was applied to the killings of "Jack the Ripper."*

*But was Neill "sane"? Legally, yes. But I cannot agree with the recent article in* The Times *which concludes that he was "fully responsible" for his actions. Neill speaks of "pains in his brain." Could it be that this complicated mechanism was damaged? Could it be that the narcotics Neill took added to the over-all malfunction? If so, how can it be said that he was "sane"? I cannot concede that a man behaves in the manner of Neill, killing and torturing throughout his life without either fear or remorse, and be "sane."*

*Neill is now with his God. Whether his God was the Almighty or Satan, we shall never know. But one thing is for certain: until we learn to understand the workings of a mind like Neill's, murderers of his kind will forever be among us.*

*Vernon R. Cogswell*

73 74 75 76 77 10 9 8 7 6 5 4 3 2 1